# ORANGE CRUSHED

## An Ivy League Mystery

## Pamela Thomas-Graham

Author of *A Darker Shade of Crimson*

Simon & Schuster
New York   London   Toronto   Sydney

SIMON & SCHUSTER
Rockefeller Center
1230 Avenue of the Americas
New York, NY 10020

SIMON & SCHUSTER and colophon are registered trademarks
of Simon & Schuster, Inc.

For information regarding special discounts for bulk purchases,
please contact Simon & Schuster Special Sales at
1-800-456-6798 or business@simonandschuster.com

Manufactured in the United States of America

1   3   5   7   9   10   8   6   4   2

Library of Congress Cataloging-in-Publication Data
Thomas-Graham, Pamela.
Orange crushed : an Ivy League mystery / Pamela Thomas-Graham.
p. cm.
1. Chase, Nikki (Fictitious character)—Fiction. 2. African-American women college teachers—Fiction. 3. College teachers—Crimes against—Fiction. 4. Economics teachers—Fiction. 5. Princeton (N.J.)—Fiction. I. Title.

PS3570.H5923O73 2004
813'.54—dc22        2004045365

ISBN 0-684-84528-8

# Acknowledgments

I would like to thank the following people for their unfailing support during the writing of this book: my wonderful team at CNBC, including Debbie Perry, Amy Zelvin, Scott Drake, Bob Meyers, Andy Warren, Lauren Donovan, David Friend, Lilach Asofsky, Ken Wilkey, Steve Fastook, Cheryl Gould, Gladys Nova, Kari Joaquin, Alan Murray, Gloria Borger, Beatrice Meyers, Judy Dobrynski, Carl Killingsworth, and Alfredo Diaz; my talented colleagues at NBC and General Electric; and Bob and Suzanne Wright. For their unerring advice and wisdom, heartfelt thanks go to Jim Cash, Debra Lee, Vernon Jordan, Lloyd Trotter, Art Harper, Ann Fudge, Andrea Jung, Shelley Lazarus, Larry Summers, and Rosabeth Moss Kanter.

I am deeply appreciative of the hard work and counsel provided by Laurie Lotz, Michael Korda, Chuck Adams, Esther Newberg, Pat Mulcahy, Tammy Richards, Elliot Hoffman, Bob Barnett, Tina Brown, Harry Evans, Hilary Rosen, and Laura Josephs. I'm grateful for the friendship of Dauna Williams, Lauren Tyler, Melissa James, Ruth Boyce, Marguerite Donovan, Motoko Huthwaite, Jennifer McGuire, Jay Ward, Andre and Allyson Owens, Margaret Morton, Carla Harris, Deborah Roberts, Al Roker, Judith Riggs, Anne and Andrew Tisch, Pamela and Len Yablon, Stephanie Bell-Rose, Art and Jennifer Mbanefo, Aubria Corbitt and Keith Walton, T.R. and Joanne

Kelly, Kim and Michael Graves, Jan and Bill Lighten, Butch and Roberta Graves, and Ann and Vincent Moore, and all my Jack and Jill sisters and friends from the Boule and the Links.

My deepest thanks go out to my family: Marian and Albert Thomas; Vincent, Barbara, Mary, and Michael Thomas; Richard Graham Sr.; Betty Graham, our dear angel; Richard Graham Jr.; my aunts Azalea, Magnolia, Bessie, Frances, and Julia; and my uncles James and Michael.

But most of all, I thank and am thankful for Lawrence, Gordon, Lindsey, and Harrison. I'm blessed to be able to share my life with you.

For my darling husband, Lawrence Otis Graham

And for Gordon, Harrison, and Lindsey:
brilliance, goodness, and grace

# 1

## 'Dis Side of Paradise

The day ended in ash. But it began in snow.

Snow, and whining.

"Isn't it adorable? You don't see trains like this anymore. It reminds me of when I was a girl. I could've ridden on that little trolley car for hours." The gray-haired woman who had been sitting across the aisle from us could barely contain her excitement. She lovingly patted the side of the silvery metal engine with her white-gloved hand.

"For God's sake," my traveling companion snapped. "It's a New Jersey Transit train car that looks as if it hasn't had a bath since the Fourth of July! If I hear one more person cooing over how cute it is I am going to throw up, I *swear.*"

It was the second Friday in December, and my best friend Jessica Leiberman and I were standing beside the train station in Princeton, having just stepped off "the dinky," the Lilliputian train that ferries passengers back and forth from the Amtrak station in Princeton Junction.

We had just finished the last leg of a seven-hour trek from Cambridge, Massachusetts, that had involved one subway, three trains, two different one-hour delays, and more sugar, fat, and caffeine than were strictly necessary, and we were in no mood for wonder. However, a less cynical and weary traveler would have had to agree with the breathless pronouncements of our fellow passenger. The setting *was* charming: a rustic stone train station that sheltered a two-car train, an amiable conductor, and a handful of rosy-cheeked riders. The dusting of snow covering the slate roof of the station and the surrounding sidewalk looked as if it had been deposited expressly for aesthetic purposes, and the nearby cluster of carolers flanked by a Salvation Army Santa could only have been supplied by Central Casting.

"Merry Christmas!" the effusive woman from the train called to us as she set out across the cobblestone sidewalk.

"We don't all celebrate Christmas, you know!" Jess muttered. As she impatiently stamped her feet, I glanced at her and smiled to myself.

All over Cambridge, people were thanking me for getting her out of town for the weekend.

"Chill out, Jess," I admonished her, taking her by the hand. "Just because he dumped you doesn't give you license to take it out on the rest of us."

"*He* didn't dump *me!*" she blazed. "I dumped *him*."

How could I forget? We'd only rehashed the saga in excruciating detail three times during the train trip. I knew the story. Our fellow passengers knew—and had commented on—the story. The entire eastern seaboard knew the story. I smiled pleasantly without speaking.

"Don't patronize me," she snapped.

"Did I say anything?"

"Just because you're in some kind of Zen state doesn't mean that I have to be, too." Jess turned away, frowning. "I expect you to be on my side, even if he *is* your housemate." Suddenly, her face lit up. "Ricky!" she exclaimed.

Loping toward us across the snow was a tall handsome man in his late twenties with sparkling brown eyes and café au lait skin. In one hand he held a tall paper cup from Wawa's, and in the other, a copy of *The Invisible Man*. An infectious smile spread broadly across his face at the sound of Jess's voice, and every woman within a hundred-foot radius took note appreciatively. I grinned along with them. My little brother has that effect on people.

My name is Veronica Chase—Nikki to my friends, and Professor Chase to my students at Harvard. Ostensibly, I'd come to Princeton to present a paper at a weekend conference at the Woodrow Wilson School of Public and International Affairs on the rise of oligopolies in Eastern Europe. It was just another of the many hoops I was jumping through at age thirty in pursuit of my goal of being the first black woman ever to receive tenure in the Harvard Economics Department. But like Jess, I had left Cambridge on the run—from an acting department chairman who was driving me mad, from the impatient glares of students more caught up in the whirl of holiday parties than in the necessity of turning in term papers on time. And from male troubles of my own.

"What took you so long?" my brother demanded, engulfing me in his embrace. "I was about to send out my posse."

"Hey!" Jess demanded. "I need a hug more than she does right now."

I met Eric's eyes over Jess's shoulder, and we grinned at each other. Despite Jess's penchant for calling him Ricky, I referred to my brother as Eric—pairing us as Nikki and Ricky amused Jess, but it was a bit much for both of us.

"You've lost weight," he said, regarding me critically. "What's up?"

"Not now." I shook my head dismissively.

He looked me over again and then shrugged. "All right, your call. We've got the whole weekend to talk. Let's get going, ladies. Your chariot awaits." He nodded toward an orange metal golf cart, the preferred method of vehicular transportation for jocks around the campus. "It'll be tight, but we should make it."

"I'd rather walk," I replied. "But do you mind hanging on to this?" My gesture was broad enough to encompass my two fairly large suitcases and my high-maintenance companion.

"I've got you covered," he said assuredly. "I'll meet you at the Annex later. What's it gonna be, Jess? Hot fudge at Thomas Sweet's or a martini at Lahiere's?"

"I've have no idea what you're talking about, but I'm up for anything involving alcohol, chocolate, or some combination of the two," she replied emphatically. "Let's go."

"You remember how to get to Woody Woo, right?" he asked as they loaded up.

"Of course! I'll be fine," I replied, suppressing a laugh at the commonly accepted nickname of the Woodrow Wilson School. "I'm going to stop by and say hi to Professor Stokes first."

Finally free, I sauntered slowly beyond Alexander Street and up University Place, propelled along by the bracing winter air and the patrician charms of Princeton. I caught glimpses of the leaded glass windows and stone archways of Pyne and Henry Halls, and their promise of grace and order coaxed me farther up the tree-lined street. The campus hadn't changed at all since the first time we dropped Eric off as a college freshman almost ten years ago. It was still a dream of an Ivy League college: towering elm trees, flagstone walkways, stately Gothic buildings. If you closed your eyes and tried to conjure up the ultimate bucolic college campus, this would be it, particularly at Christmastime. Despite the New Jersey locale, somehow the air was scented with a whiff of the Deep South. Perhaps it was the long wisteria vines that encircled some of the windows, which mimicked the look of the moss hanging from the trees of an antebellum plantation. Or maybe it was the tall Grecian columns on a couple of the campus buildings. Or perhaps it was the perfectly coiffed blond hair and well-mannered demeanor of so many of the students. Whatever the ineffable source of the feeling, it was very real. The lawns were invisible underneath their blanket of snow, but I felt certain that they had been lovingly trimmed to a socially acceptable height.

I was alone with my thoughts for the first time in days, and I wasn't certain that I was happy in their company. I had spent the past three months in a state of professional and personal chaos, and now all I wanted was silence. Silence and distance from the source of the turmoil. Instead, a cacophony of voices rang in my ears—police officers, reporters, Harvard faculty. And my own voice, entwined with his—bitter, angry, and impassioned.

Determinedly, I forced myself to focus on the faces of the passersby. I had wanted a change of scenery, and here it was. Although the scene wasn't really much different from Harvard. A trio of young blond men in varsity jackets passed before me, loudly discussing their squash games as they headed toward Dillon Gym. A lone woman in a plaid miniskirt and a black leather jacket walked by in deep reverie. Two older gentlemen in long wool herringbone coats leaned toward each other, gesticulating broadly with their lit pipes as they climbed the stone stairs toward Blair Arch. Then a young black woman passed me, and I suddenly remembered one thing that was different about Princeton.

At Harvard, in the crush of people in the square and the Yard, no one makes any particular effort to make eye contact with passersby. In most cases, the denizens of Cambridge are either deep in conversation with their companions, or lost in thought. The phenomenon of being surrounded by people and yet utterly unnoticed holds true across lines of age, race, and gender, and it says a lot about what it means to be at Harvard. But at Princeton, the black people always stare.

Not at everyone, of course. Just at the black faces—especially the new black faces. They do it intensely, almost longingly. As if they are hoping to find kinship, or to express solidarity. The first time it happened to me, I felt almost violated by the scrutiny. Now it just saddens me. When the imploring gaze falls on me, I want to stop and embrace the person. My father says it's just another symptom of "WFO"—white folk overload. When living in a small community dominated by blond conservatives, perhaps even the most culturally integrated African-American starts to long for a glimpse of brown skin and dark hair. Whatever the reason, in my experience the black students of Princeton tend to have the look of people living in occupied territory—wary, lonely, and deeply tired.

Which was what was so striking about the young black woman who passed me that afternoon. She was none of those things. I watched her, expecting The Look in return, and instead received a cool appraisal that told me instantly that my hair wasn't quite right, my boots were a bit scuffed, and my overall appearance was of absolutely no threat to her. In the moment that it took me to suppress the urge to whip out a compact and freshen my lipstick, she was gone.

Perhaps things were changing here, after all.

By now I had reached the heart of the campus and was surrounded by Gothic buildings. Straight ahead of me was McCosh Hall—then my destination: Dickinson Hall, a three-story off-white limestone structure with oversize leaded-glass windows. The building housed Princeton's Program in African-American Studies, and I was planning to make a call on Professor Earl Stokes, the country's leading scholar on urban economics and rumored to be an impending addition to Harvard's Afro-American Studies Department. In addition to being a leading light in Princeton's Economics Department, he was also the head of the university's tiny Program in African-American Studies.

Certain circles on the campuses of both Harvard and Princeton were currently in turmoil over the news that Earl might be leaving Princeton to come to Cambridge. He had been born and raised in Princeton, and his departure would be quite a blow to the university's claims regarding the diversity of its faculty. The Stokes family had been a fixture in the town of Princeton for three generations. Earl was a best-selling author as well as a highly respected scholar. His last book, *Color Counts,* had sat atop the *New York Times* best-seller list for almost six months, and he made frequent appearances to discuss economics and race on the talk-show circuit and at the White House. Intense and righteous, he had the air of a minister and accepted the reverence that resulted from it with quiet pride. I had met him when Eric ran into some trouble as a Princeton senior and needed to be bailed out, and we'd kept in close touch through the years. He had become a mentor and a role model for me, and had quietly lent a hand from time to time when I needed help understanding the high-stakes game of academic politics. So I was thrilled to hear that he might be coming to Harvard.

Thrilled, but a bit bemused. Because I had heard that he wouldn't be coming to lead Afro-Am, which was what one would expect for a man of his stature. The rumor was that he would join as just another member of the department, which was being reinvented by another star black professor, Percy Hubbard. And we all knew that "Butch" Hubbard could be trouble.

Butch Hubbard was in many ways the mirror image of Earl. Where Earl was unflappable, Butch was mercurial. Where Earl tended to base his painstakingly accurate arguments on months of tedious research, Butch was just as happy to share his opinions based on nothing more than how he happened to view the world that particular morning. And while it caused Earl great physical discomfort to ask for funding for even his most cherished research studies, Butch Hubbard was the type who'd cheerfully hit you up for money for some new program at Afro-Am if you happened to be stopped at a red light on the sidewalk next to him on Mass Ave. If you had cash, you had his interest. Expensive national surveys, original works by black artists to outfit his office, and high-priced African theme parties aboard yachts were all academic funding opportunities for the rich and famous.

Hubbard was always on. Always selling. In fact, my brother used to jokingly refer to Hubbard as "Sportin' Life" because he was so much like the charming rogue in *Porgy and Bess*. It was a fitting moniker for a man who perfectly blended an Oxford degree with ghetto-fabulous style. He was someone who not only loved to play people, but did it effortlessly. I worried that Earl didn't quite know what he would be signing up for if he decided to join Butch Hubbard's team, but I trusted that he was smart enough to do his due diligence before he made the move. Besides, I wanted Earl in Cambridge. So I was keeping my mouth shut about Butch.

I entered Dickinson Hall and went down a narrow flight of stairs. A cramped, extremely damp hallway with stained wooden doors lining both sides surrounded me. The faint hiss of steam grew louder as I walked down the hallway, and I shed my scarf as the temperature began to rise. I felt like I was paying a call to the boiler room. But this was where Princeton had chosen to house Earl Stokes's office. It seemed disrespectful to a man of his stature. Butch Hubbard, his Harvard counterpart, had one of the best offices on campus in Cambridge.

Earl's door was ajar when I reached his office. Even though he had his back to me, I knew it was he. The unfashionably long Afro, the tattered sleeve on his brown tweed sport coat. The chatter of NPR on the radio. This was definitely Earl Stokes's office.

"Nikki Chase?" A rich baritone voice boomed as two brown eyes peered into the mirror above the desk and a wooden swivel chair spun around. His embrace engulfed me in the scents of wool and 1970s-era Pierre Cardin aftershave. I inhaled deeply and felt a surge of contentment.

"What are you doing down here?" he exclaimed.

"I came down for a couple of days for a conference at Woody Woo, and of course I had to stop by. Do you have a minute?"

"For you? Of course!" he said with a broad smile. "Sit down."

"Whew! I see why you're building a new building for African-American Studies. It's like a furnace down here!" I declared as I tossed my jacket over the back of my chair. "How's the construction going?"

"Pretty well," Earl replied. "But it's a lot of work." He gestured to a large stack of blueprints on the floor in a corner. "Between fighting with the university trustees over whether this is an 'appropriate use of funds' and arguing with the Princeton building authority over zoning variances, it's a wonder there's time to teach. But when we get this thing built, it'll be a showplace for the department. *Almost* as good as what y'all have up north at Harvard." He grinned wryly.

I sensed my opening and jumped to the topic I really wanted to discuss. "So is it true?" I asked eagerly.

Earl leaned in close as his large brown eyes widened for dramatic effect. "You mean the job offer?"

"Of course that's what I mean! Tell me the whole story. How did it happen?"

He smiled again. "How did it happen?" He paused for dramatic effect and leaned back in his chair. "Well, it was damn near overnight. I'd been working for over a year researching how the economic successes of different American ethnic groups shaped certain American cities. We issued the final report a month ago, and it got covered in *Fortune* and several academic journals. And then I get a call from President

Townsend asking me to come up and give him a hand. We know each other because we served on that Presidential commission on urban development, you know."

It took me a moment to note the real news in what he had just said. "Did you say *Townsend* called you?" I asked sharply. "Don't you mean Butch Hubbard?"

A shadow passed over his face, and I leaned forward. "Don't you mean Butch?" I repeated.

Earl shifted in his chair. "No, I don't. He had very little to do with it."

I stared at him. "How is that possible?" It was completely unheard of that a department chair would have an appointment forced on him. That wasn't the way things were done in Cambridge.

"You know Hubbard was a real favorite of former President Barrett," Earl said, leaning forward again.

"Sure." Harvard's recently departed president, Leo Barrett, had given Butch Hubbard free rein and significant funding to revive the Afro-American Studies Department. At the time, everyone had assumed that his commitment to the department stemmed from their personal friendship. They were cut from the same cloth, both relatively young, debonair raconteurs who loved being at the nexus of academia and pop culture. As it turned out, President Barrett had a much closer affinity for Afro-American Studies than anyone knew. But that was another story.

"So what are you saying?" I asked. "That President Townsend isn't such a big fan of Hubbard's?"

"He's trying to restrain some of the excesses that were allowed to flourish during Barrett's presidency. Do you have any idea how much money has been spent on the Afro-Am Department since Hubbard took it over?"

I certainly had some idea, having attended a few of the lavish parties organized by Hubbard to mark new appointments, anniversaries, and the like. A couple of years ago, he had established an annual spring gala during which he took over one of the Houses for the weekend and flew in the glitterati from New York and points south. The champagne was always first-rate, the quality of the dancing a bit less so. It had never crossed my mind to ask who was paying for it all.

"But what is Townsend expecting that you'd be doing?" I knew the answer before the question passed my lips. Earl would be the new president's spy.

"I'd be specializing in urban economics. Much of the same work that I have been doing here. I'd use my *Color* book, and some other texts." His tone was light, but our eyes met, and I heeded his tacit warning not to pry further. This was varsity-level faculty politics, and I'd be better off staying away from it.

"Speaking of which, how would you like to be the guest lecturer for my course on Monday?" Earl continued. "I'd like to get you in front of my students, especially the women. They need to see someone like you."

"Are you kidding?" I feigned being taken aback, but I was flattered. "I wish I could, but I'm only staying for the weekend."

"Come on, Nikki. Harvard can spare you for one extra day. This class is cross-registered with Afro-Am and Economics, and it meets on Monday morning. I've got some really interesting students in the class."

I shook my head, laughing.

"We're doing *Color Counts*. You've read the book. We'll do the class together. It would be fun. You're a role model for these kids. And I'll have you home by Monday evening, I swear. You can meet some of my students and colleagues at the Afro-Am anniversary party tonight, for starters." He turned and rapidly shuffled through a stack of folders on his credenza. "Here, take the syllabus." He passed me a manila folder with some loose papers inside. "You'll see it'll take you no time to prepare."

I hesitated for a moment, reflecting on how good it felt to be in his company, and how liberating it was to be away from Cambridge. I would normally have had two sections of Intro Economics to teach on Monday—but with the end of the term approaching, I had already given the students notice that they should take that time to work on their term papers. This was a no-brainer.

"Deal," I replied.

We playfully exchanged a high five, and then I tucked the folder into my backpack. "You realize that Irvin is going to *kill* me for this."

"How is that going, anyway? He still exacting punishment?"

Carl Irvin was the acting chairman of the Economics Department at Harvard, and had been on a personal vendetta against me ever since I helped put his best friend, the former head of the department, behind bars.

"That's putting it mildly. I'm presenting a paper at the ABA convention in January in New York, and he's tormenting me with revisions."

Earl leaned forward conspiratorially. "You can't say a word about this. But Townsend has found a replacement to lead the department. Someone who might be helpful to you."

"Are you sure?" This was *major* good news, if it was true. I had gone from racing along the fast track to tenure to dangling on the precipice of termination since my adventures earlier that fall. Somehow, contributing to the downfall of the president of the university *and* the head of my department had left me persona non grata among the powers at Harvard. And with word trickling back that I'd been involved in some trouble at Yale just before Thanksgiving, I could feel even my few remaining allies starting to distance themselves from me. Not that I blamed them.

"I spoke to Townsend about you, by the way."

"Thank you for doing that."

"I was happy to. Relax, Nikki," he said. I guess he could tell that I had stopped breathing. "He likes you."

"Not possible."

"Of course it's possible! You're a brilliant young scholar who happens to be black and female, and you almost single-handedly exposed a serious embezzlement scheme that was costing the university millions of dollars. Why shouldn't he like you?"

"Not to mention the fact that my discovery helped clear the way for him to gain the presidency."

Earl shrugged. "That certainly doesn't hurt your case. The point is, he knows exactly who you are, and he thinks well of you. Just remember my advice."

"Get back to work and stay out of trouble. I hear you."

"Do you?" he said dryly. "Because I've got a friend in New Haven who says your name was all over town a couple of weeks ago. He sent me an envelope full of articles from the *Register* and the *Yale Daily News*. At least two of them were on the front page."

The implicit criticism from him stung. "That wasn't planned!" I retorted, defensively. "I went there to comfort a very old friend, and it just got out of control."

Earl nodded, a bit skeptically. "That's what I told Townsend, Nikki. But you'd better keep your head down from now on. You're at a critical point in your career, and you've got to deliver. You don't want to have a reputation as a magnet for trouble. Your job is to teach and get published—not to find dead bodies."

"What, do you think I'm seeking this stuff out? Listen, by Monday night I'll be back in Cambridge, and in the unlikely event of murder or mayhem, I will run in the opposite direction."

Somehow, I didn't get the impression that he believed me. It was high time to get this conversation onto a different track.

"So how would Eula feel about leaving Princeton?" I asked. Earl's wife was apparently painfully shy, so shy that I had never met her in all the years that I had known Earl. Eric said that she kept a very low profile on campus, seemingly content to tend house at their modest colonial off Witherspoon Street.

Earl frowned slightly and sat back in his chair. "She's not happy that I'm seriously considering it."

I shook my head sympathetically. "That's too bad. Is it that she has a lot of friends here in town?"

"Yes, that, and she doesn't think that she'd like Harvard."

That was no surprise, given what I had heard. Eula Stokes would be signing up for a lot if she agreed to move to Cambridge. It was going to be nearly impossible for her to be a homebody up there. Faculty spouses had a serious and well-defined role to play in the social scene, and bucking that trend would diminish Earl's stature.

"Would it help if I talked to her? You know, give her some idea about what Cambridge is really like? There's a lot more going on up there than there is here. She won't be bored, and there are more black folks there than she may realize."

"Perhaps it would help if she heard that from someone other than me. I think she's coming around, anyway. After last week, I think she's convinced herself that I'll have a heart attack if I stay here any longer." Earl snorted at my quizzical expression. "It has nothing to do with my health. It's the idiot cops in this town. They pulled me over again last Saturday two blocks from my house. I've lived here my entire life, and some twenty-year-old white boy asks me to prove that I'm the owner of the vehicle I'm driving."

"Get out of here."

"That's exactly what I'm thinking of doing. The sight of a black man behind the wheel of a Mercedes obviously offends some deeply held beliefs in this town. I'd be happy to oblige them by getting the hell outta here."

I wanted to say that Princeton wasn't the only community where the cops had a hard time grasping the concept of black people driving luxury cars. But he didn't need me to tell him that.

"So wouldn't you miss it here, Earl? After all these years?"

His words were striking then, and haunting later.

"Nikki, believe me. I am already gone."

# 2
# The Dismal Science

"The slope of the Lorenz curve has flattened significantly in the Prague metropolitan area, indicating a sharp increase in competitiveness. Currently, the Gini coefficient is 0.50, down from 0.78 only a year earlier. And as they say, once the Gini is out of the bottle, it's impossible to put him back in."

Fifty faces looked solemnly back at me, unmoved by my feeble attempt at humor.

*I could kill Carl Irvin for sending me to this conference.* I was standing at the lectern in a small classroom at the Woodrow Wilson School, feeling the awful prickling sensation at the back of my neck that signaled that I was losing my audience. I had never felt entirely comfortable at Woody Woo, given the barren plaza outside and the Cold War decor inside. And now I was in the process of making a fool of myself. Some days economics really *was* the dismal science.

I'd been tagged to be the third in a series of five lectures on the opening afternoon of the "Eastern Europe at the Crossroads" conference. My diabolical acting department chairman had insisted that I attend the conference, even though the subject matter was not exactly on point with my area of expertise, which was multinational business economics.

He had bullied me into preparing a review of the changing market structure in the Czech Republic just for this event, and it had taken a solid five weeks of effort to come up with what felt like startlingly obvious insights. I was convinced that it was just part of his continuing campaign to punish me for exposing fraud in the Harvard Economics Department, and so far, I was indeed suffering. Normally I loved attending conferences, as there was usually at least one great presentation, a couple of serious flirting opportunities, and plenty of good dish about who was doing what to whom. But this was not my crowd, not my subject, and definitely not my idea of a good time.

"Hasn't the Gini coefficient been totally discredited as a measure of market concentration?" The querulous voice rose from the last row of the classroom, accompanied by frowns all around the room. The speaker was pale, goateed, and clearly spoiling for a fight. "Really, Professor Chase, your analysis is based on a fundamentally flawed metric."

I know the rules of academic life as well as anyone. Solidify your own reputation as a brilliant scholar by frequently and loudly criticizing the work of your peers. I didn't take the comment personally. But I stood a little straighter. Maybe this was going to be fun, after all. *Bring it on, Goatee.*

"Certainly, in Western economies, the concentration ratio provides a more accurate gauge of structural power than the Gini coefficient," I replied. "However, I believe that in a market as dynamic as Prague, it is critical to assess all firms, not just the largest ones. Calculating a four-firm or even a twelve-firm concentration ratio doesn't give a complete picture under current conditions. The concentration ratio also doesn't make clear the influence of the newly privatized government monopolies, which still dominate certain sectors."

Mr. Goatee, reacting more to my tone of voice than the content of my reply, slumped back in his chair. I felt the energy level in the room go up a notch and looked expectantly into the audience.

"Is the Herfindahl index relevant in these markets?" an Indian woman asked from the front row.

"Absolutely. The issue is the lack of detailed information in some market sectors. As you know, the Herfindahl calculates the sum of the squares of the sizes of a firm in a market, and it requires granular detail on market share, which is still somewhat difficult to obtain, even now." Good question, I thought. *But come on. Ask me a tough one.* I scanned the room, and paused for a moment on a man in the third row. As our eyes met, his expression seemed to express amused sympathy. That, and a decided appreciation for the height of the heels on my black suede boots and the brevity of my plaid wool skirt. I took the bait and cold-called him. "You seem to have a question, Mr . . ." I nodded in his direction.

"Mr. Lopez. Carlos Lopez." He had a great smile and knew exactly how to use it. "This may be a bit off point, Professor. But I'd be interested in your views on this week's EC decision to block another merger."

My eyes lit up. Now we were talking.

"Well, rather than share my views, let's debate it. You all know that the European Commission has to rule on all mergers or acquisitions between companies with significant revenue in Europe, even if neither of the two companies are European. Three times in a twelve-month period, the EC vetoed a significant merger between two non-European companies. And they've made it clear that they intend to delay a number of pending deals. Should the commission have that kind of power?"

"Absolutely not!" called out a blond woman in the back of the room. "Why should some regulator in Brussels have the right to interfere in a business decision between two American companies?"

"On the contrary," Mr. Lopez responded. "Who is going to protect the interests of the European Union nations if not the EC? National borders have no relevance in economic terms anymore. What two U.S.–based companies decide to do can have a direct impact on the health of the economy and the quality of life in Europe."

"But if American regulators approve a merger, who is the EC to try to overturn that ruling?" the blonde shot back.

"Better yet, what is the proper forum for resolving the situation if American and European regulators disagree?" I interjected.

With that, we were off on a heated debate that lasted the remainder of my time slot and then some. My eyes met Mr. Lopez's again as the discussion was ending, and I signaled my thanks, but declined the implicit invitation in his expression. One of the well-established perks of an academic conference is the opportunity to flirt shamelessly. But after the autumn I had just had, flirting with handsome dark-eyed men fell into the category of high-risk behavior. Like I'd told Earl—from now on, I was keeping away from trouble, in all its various forms.

However, by seven that evening, Mr. Lopez's black hair and eyes seemed deliciously tempting and rare. Eric, Jess, and I were at the Annex Bar on Nassau Street, drowning in a sea of blondes. The dimly lit room was illuminated only by the glow of a display of bottles and glasses behind the bar and the high-wattage, Doublemint smiles of the assembled crowd. It was a scene that replicated my Michigan childhood memories of Grosse Pointe or Bloomfield Hills—circa 1975. *Go Tigers.*

Meanwhile, Jess was pleasantly drunk and had become obsessed with understanding the intricacies of the Princeton eating clubs. "So, let me get this straight. When you were an undergrad here, Ivy, Cottage, and Tiger were all-male, and Tower and Cap & Gown were coed?"

"That's right," Eric replied. "They were always the most exclusive clubs—the selective ones—the ones that require bicker if you want to get in. The other eight clubs—Campus, Terrace, Charter, Dial Lodge, Colonial, Elm, Cloister, and Quadrangle—were open, and you got in through a lottery."

"So are these like fraternities?"

"No. You don't live there. It's just where you eat your meals."

"It's like the finals clubs at Harvard, Jess," I interjected, a bit impatiently. "And the secret societies at Yale. And the fraternities at Dartmouth. Every one of the Ivy League schools has some mechanism to keep the white males feeling safe and in control."

"Come on, Nikki," Eric said sharply. "You know the eating clubs are not just for white people."

This was a sore spot between us and had been since his junior year in college. I stifled the urge to resume the argument that we had been having for years on this point. Eric had been a member of Tower Club, over my strong protests about his supporting a social system explicitly designed to exclude women and blacks.

Jess, completely oblivious to the edge in our voices, continued on. "Nikki, did you realize that three of the clubs were all-male up until just a couple years ago?"

"Yes, I did. Did you, Eric?"

"Can I get another Corona over here, please?" His expression pleaded with me not to start up on him again.

"Come on, Eric. You're a proud Tower alumnus. Tell us what it's like to be on the inside," I baited. As much as I admired the beauty of the campus and envied the intimacy that came from small classes and a small student body, the clubbiness of Princeton was a perpetual irritant to me. Eating clubs, house parties, cane spree, class uniforms—they all seemed carefully calculated to preserve barriers between the boarding school establishment and the rest of the campus community.

"The eating clubs are no different from Harvard's finals clubs or Yale's secret societies," Eric responded defensively. He waved at a tall blond man wearing a swim-team coach jacket and another man wearing a sweatshirt that read "PDS." They both returned a double thumbs-up sign. I swallowed hard to prevent gagging.

"Eric, only a few dozen people join those elitist groups at Harvard and Yale," I protested. "Here, the whole social life is built around these clubs and 'The Street.' The Street being Prospect, where all of the clubs are located.

"Another one for you?" our waiter interjected, gesturing toward my empty wineglass.

"Yes," Eric said emphatically. "And hurry."

"Your brother said this used to be a bowling alley," Jess said, apropos of nothing. "So," she said, turning to Eric. "Has she told you what's bothering her yet?"

"Jess," I shot her a warning glance. "Don't."

"No, we haven't spoken about it yet," Eric replied. "Judging from her expression, I think it may take another glass of cabernet. Maybe two."

"Why are you bringing this up?" I snapped at Jess.

"Because you'll feel better if you talk about it, honey, that's why. Talk to your brother. I'll be right back," she announced, rising a bit unsteadily to her feet.

Eric looked grave as he watched Jess weave her way through the crowd. "This is about Dante, isn't it?"

I nodded silently.

"Did he hurt you? Do I need to go up to Cambridge and bust him up?"

"No, you don't," I said hurriedly. He was looking at me with the same expression he used to wear when he was six and I was ten and he'd insist on defending my honor over some playground slight even though he was half my size at the time. "I'm all right, Bun." He smiled at the old endearment as I fumbled in my purse for a cigarette and lighter.

"That's your third one in the last hour." He frowned at the pack of Marlboro Lights in my hand.

"Eric, get off of it, okay?"

"Jess is right. Better to talk about it than to suck down a pack a day."

"Look, I've been on a diet, I haven't had a French fry in over six weeks, there is no hope of my *ever* having a boyfriend again, and I'm too broke to go shopping. Something's got to give here." I defiantly took a deep drag on my cigarette as he regarded me reproachfully.

"It's not that big a deal," I continued, exhaling. "For a few weeks this fall, Dante and I were getting close. But we had a fight." I stopped Eric with a gesture before he could interrupt me. "Not just *a* fight. *The* fight. And now whatever it was that we were doing is over, and that's that."

"Doesn't look like it to me," he retorted, eyebrow raised.

I shook my head adamantly. "I can't discuss this, Eric. I am talked out. Really and truly talked *out.*" I read the concerned expression in his eyes and softened my tone. "Look, you know what I went through the last time. I was crazy for him and he dumped me. With no explanation.

Just because he showed up unexpectedly in Cambridge this fall does *not* mean that I am going there again. Simple. I'm through with him."

He read my obstinate expression and wisely retreated. "So how was Earl when you saw him?"

"He's good. I'm a bit surprised, but he seems serious about possibly leaving town. I don't get it."

"Neither do I. He's really popular here."

"Plus he grew up here. He has real roots in this town. And his wife evidently doesn't want to move."

Eric shook his head in bemusement. "Princeton treats him like a king. After all, how many professors get to be in two departments? His classes are always oversubscribed, and the U-Store is constantly advertising his books and putting them in the front window."

"The only negative thing that he said was that the cops have treated him pretty badly. He seemed really angry about that."

Eric stood up abruptly from the bar and signaled me to move to a table away from the hubbub around the barstools. A group of student-aged patrons had just entered the basement barroom, and a few others were making their way down the steep staircase. "There's something you should know," he whispered as we carried our drinks over to a small table near the corner.

"What?" I hissed back.

"Earl is working on a new book."

"You couldn't have told me that at the bar?" I asked, speaking more loudly. "That doesn't sound like a state secret."

"Look, this is a small town—and everybody knows everybody," Eric replied. "And some people in this town are not going to like this book."

I nodded in anticipation, and Eric leaned closer. "I heard that it's some kind of exposé. Something about the police, and local leaders, maybe the university. But something that will embarrass people here."

"Where did you hear that?"

"A friend told me. It's all over Afro-Am."

"I still don't get why you're whispering. People write embarrassing books all the time."

"Look, Nikki, this is not a city like New Haven or Cambridge. There aren't thousands of faculty members and multiple campuses. This is a tiny college in a tiny rich town. No law school, no medical school, and no business school. Just one campus—and everybody knows everybody's business. And cares a lot about what other people think."

"Yes, I suppose that here in Peyton Place, people have time to worry about things like that. I don't know how you can stand it here, Eric." I winced as another group of students entered the bar and gave the bartender a thumbs-up.

"I'm not like you, Nikki. I like small towns. I could ask you how you can stand to be in a place as big and impersonal as Harvard."

"I know, I know—I never met even half of the people in my college class, and you knew two-thirds of your classmates by their first names."

"It's true, Nikki. I like being in a place where I really know people and they know me. Here, I can keep up with my students very easily."

"I just can't make myself love a school that was so inhospitable to blacks." Princeton's biggest claim to fame was Woodrow Wilson, who presided over the university before becoming president. In both positions, he supported segregation vehemently. In my mind, the fact that his name was placed on Princeton's Woodrow Wilson School of Public and International Affairs didn't change the fact that he was one of the reasons that Princeton embraced the very undiplomatic policy of refusing admission to blacks even seventy-five years after Harvard, Yale, Brown, and the other Ivy League colleges began admitting their first African-Americans.

"Look, Harvard had a Jewish quota just like everybody else," Eric said. "None of these schools has a pristine history. Let's just leave that stuff in the past."

"Okay, okay, truce!" I cried. "Here comes Jess."

"Hey, guys! Look what I found." Jess was on the arm of a tall Nordic-looking man in a Princeton sweatshirt. "Ernst says that there's a great new club just down the street from here. So I'll see you later tonight, okay?"

I started to corral Jess and pry her out of Ernst's possessive grasp. His expression was expectant, but I knew that she was so on the rebound that all he was in for was a long evening of stories about her broken heart and her perfect ex-boyfriend, Ted.

*Wait a minute,* I thought. Better him than me.

I met Jess's eyes. "You sober enough to be left alone with your new friend?"

"Yes, girl. I haven't had *that* much to drink tonight. Right, Ricky?"

"She had a couple of Cosmopolitans before you got here, Nikki," Eric confirmed. "I wouldn't let her drive, but she'll be okay on foot."

I met Eric's eyes, and then nodded in Ernst's direction. "You know everyone in this town. You know him?"

The two men smiled at each other. "Yeah, I can vouch for my man Ernst," Eric replied. "He's a straight-up guy."

"Then have fun, kids!" I said brightly, waving at Jess. I turned to Eric. "We've got to get going, anyway. This party's in an hour."

We set out down Nassau Street for Eric's dorm room in Holder Hall. In addition to being a graduate student in the Program in African-American Studies, he was a resident adviser in an undergraduate dormitory, and Jess and I were planning to crash in his living room during our visit. "So who do you think will be at the Afro-Am anniversary party?" I asked.

"Oh, the usual suspects. Plus, I heard that Butch Hubbard is coming down. I think I saw him in town earlier today."

"That man must be a genius. How is he getting all these people into his department at Harvard?"

Eric shook his head. "I don't get it. He snatched up Charlie Rumson from Cornell, and Shirley Betts-Caldwell from Columbia. And I hear he's working on Leroy Harris at Stanford. He's everywhere."

"He must be paying an incredible amount in salaries. There's no way that the Harvard name alone would do it. I just don't get where the money is coming from. He's spending millions on that department, and I can't believe Harvard is footing the whole bill."

Eric laughed. "All I know is, people say he's been flying into Mercer County Airport on a private plane. And you know he's always on TV—

doing his spot on *Today in America*. I saw him riding around Princeton in a stretch limo once. Sportin' Life is livin' large."

"I didn't know he had a gig on *Today in America*!"

Eric nodded. "Oh, yeah. Started this fall. Brother man has a column in the *Times*, a long-term contract with PBS, and a morning talk-show slot."

"What does a Harvard professor talk about on *Today in America*?"

"Anything that is vaguely black," he answered. "Black literature, black music, black heroes, Black History Month, black politics, black slang, black business, you name it. That guy can put a 'black spin' on anything, and sell it to anybody," Eric added. "He has a piece in the *New Yorker* this week on why blacks love to dance. Can you imagine? I'll never forget that PBS special he did on black people's affinity for fried chicken."

I wasn't sure if I was more appalled or jealous.

"He has his shtick down pat," Eric continued. "Just enough urban grittiness to titillate the suburban whites, but then he has that Harvard bow tie and suspenders that make them feel like he's safely Ivy League. He makes them think he's teaching them something important about black culture. I'm sure he's figured out a way to use Earl up in Cambridge."

Based on what I had just heard from Earl, Hubbard's party days might be coming to an end. I wondered if his finely tuned antennae had picked up on that. Probably not, or he wouldn't be in town now for a black-tie party celebrating Earl's Program in African-American Studies. Still, I wondered. *Who's zoomin' who?*

If Butch Hubbard really was in town, this promised to be one hell of a party.

# 3
## Scenes from a Marriage

"**I feel like I'm getting dressed** for my own funeral." Earl Stokes groaned slightly as he straightened up from lacing his dress shoes. "Don't believe what anyone tells you, Nikki. Getting old sucks."

"You are *not* old, Earl. You look wonderful."

I was sitting at the well-worn wooden table in the kitchen of Earl Stokes's house on Witherspoon Street. In the midst of getting dressed for the Afro-Am soiree, Eric and I had gotten a call from Earl asking us to come by so that we could all walk over to the party together. Eric had declined the invitation, since he was still dithering over which bow tie and cummerbund to wear. Unbeknownst to me until Earl called, Eric had a date for this party. He was in a frenzy over his attire, which was very out of character for him. Unlike our older brother, Jason, who is as dapper as they come, Eric was usually the classic Princeton preppy, with the big decision of the day being whether to pair a blue or a white cotton shirt with his khakis and brown leather loafers. For once, it was the men in my life who were fussing over their clothes. I had packed the only floor-length evening gown that I owned, and was just happy to be able to sit down and breathe at the same time. The only good thing about a breakup so painful that it takes your appetite away is that all your thin clothes fit.

"I don't see why they have to have this party, anyway," Earl groused. "It's not like most of these people are wishing us well."

"What are you talking about? People love you here."

"Some do. But there are a whole lot who would be happy to see me go." He elaborated further in response to my quizzical expression. "Like the people who don't like the fact that I'm tenured in two departments."

"Are you getting it from the Afro-Am people or the Economics Department?"

"A little of both. The Afro-Am folks want to know whose side I'm on. For the most part, the people in Economics couldn't care less about Afro-Am, but there are a couple of big honchos in the department, like the chairman, who've been upset ever since I won the MacArthur Foundation prize." He kneeled and used his reflection in the door of the stove to adjust his tie. "It's minor-league jealousy, but sometimes it's tiring." A melancholy look washed over his face, just briefly, like a passing cloud. I felt sorry that something was bothering him on a night that should have been a celebration. Maybe that was why he had wanted company on his walk to the party.

"Eula, don't you want to come in and say hello?"

At first I didn't know who Earl was talking to. I hadn't heard a sound, but suddenly the door between the kitchen and the dining room swung open, and a tall, dark-skinned, heavy-set woman emerged from the adjacent room.

"I had no idea you were *entertaining,*" she said as she leaned against the door frame. She crossed her arms against her ample chest and regarded me critically. "I don't believe we've met, young lady. I'm his wife."

I rose quickly to my feet, a bit taken aback. Although I'd heard a lot about her, in all the time that I had known Earl, I had never met his wife. And this wasn't quite what I was expecting.

"Eula, honey, I'm not *entertaining,*" Earl said soothingly. "This is Nikki Chase. You remember Eric Chase, who stayed with us that time when he was an undergrad? This is his sister. You've heard me talk about her."

The woman's arms immediately relaxed, and her mouth loosened into a smile. "Oh my goodness, child," she said, taking my hand. An embarrassed expression washed across her face. To my surprise, her hands felt like softened butter. So delicate for such a large woman. "I'm sorry. I know we've never met, but I've heard so much about you from Earl."

"It's all right, Mrs. Stokes," I replied. "This is a big night for you. I shouldn't be here so early. I'm sure you need some time to get ready."

"Oh, but I am ready, child."

I feigned a pleasant look to hide my surprise. This was a black-tie event, and she was wearing a housedress. A faded, floral, very large and loose housedress.

"You look wonderful, Eula," Earl said. He actually seemed sincere. "Let me just get the studs for this shirt, and then I'll be ready."

"All right. I have to keep packing while you do that. Come on up with me, child. We can talk while we wait."

I followed her up a narrow flight of stairs to the second floor, all the while staring at the back of her garment. Could she really be planning to wear that to a black-tie party? There had to be a way for me to gently suggest that she change her clothes. It would be an awful night for both of them if she didn't.

Eula's heavy footsteps led us into a small bedroom at the end of a dimly lit, carpeted hallway. An open suitcase lay on one of the two twin beds in the room, unfolded clothing piled next to it. I noted the framed copies of prayers and psalms decorating the walls and smiled wryly in recognition—my favorite aunt had similar tastes in bedroom decor.

"I feel terrible about going away this weekend, with everything going on," she said, beginning to fold a faded pink sweater at the top of the pile of clothes. "But I promised my mother in Brooklyn that I'd spend Saturday and Sunday with her, since it's her birthday. At least now I'll know who was with him."

A strange choice of words, I thought.

"Hair gel, comb, curlers, brush," she whispered aloud as she rummaged through a drawer. "Toothpaste—right." She headed for the beige-and-pink bathroom adjacent to their bedroom just as Earl came up the stairs.

Earl paused at the door as his wife started pulling toiletries and vials off the bathroom shelves and tossing them in a makeup case that matched the luggage in the bedroom. "Eula, are you paying attention to what you're taking?"

"Course I am," I heard her say.

"Hey, those are my special pills," Earl interrupted while trying to catch a vial flying toward the makeup case.

I picked the vial up after it hit the floor. "Stokes, Eula D.," I read. They were not Earl's pills.

"Look, you're the only one around here takin' sleeping pills. I'm not gonna be *accidentally* walkin outta here with *your* pills. Ya hear?" As I watched Eula standing there, it dawned on me that she looked at least ten or fifteen years older than her husband. Perhaps it was the difference in their attire, but nearly a generation seemed to separate them. Eula put her hands on her hips and stared impatiently at her husband.

"Thanks a lot for going there and puttin' my business in the street, Eula." Earl smiled sheepishly at me.

"Listen," Eula retorted. "Your business is *all over* the street. What goes around, *comes* around."

I wondered if this was the beginning of a fight or just a friendly ribbing between husband and wife. Either way, I was starting to wish that Eric had come with me. It was too odd to be witnessing this solo.

"Pills, alcohol, and Lord knows what else," Eula added sharply. "Not the smartest combination of tension busters, mister. What you need to do is slow down and praise God for the bounty you've been given. You wouldn't need all these tension relievers if you just visited with the Lord now and then. We got *four* good colored churches all right here on Witherspoon, so you got no excuse."

"Yes, Eula," Earl responded, surprisingly calm in the face of this sudden onslaught. "We should really be going."

A chill wind swirled around us as we stepped onto the front porch of their modest house.

"Smells like snow," Eula pronounced, peering at the sky from the top of the porch stairs. I heard the scrape of a window closing as we set off down the street. If I hadn't known better, I would have sworn that the noise came from the second story of their house.

"Please let me know if there is anything I can do to help you if you decide to move up to Cambridge," I said to Eula, desperate to break the silence that seemed to descend on us the moment we left their front yard.

"Thank you, child. But I don't think that we'll be doin' that. Can you imagine the thought? Movin' so far, at this age! Where would I get my hair done up there?" Earl's eyes met mine over Eula's head, and he smiled a bit wearily.

I tucked my arm into Eula's as we walked up Witherspoon toward Nassau Street. "If you do come, I'll take you to the hair salon I go to in Harvard Square," I said comfortingly.

As we crossed Nassau Street, I watched an orange suburban transit bus pause briefly at Princeton's front gates and then pull noisily away, leaving a dismissive cloud of gray exhaust fumes in its wake. Students escaping to New York City for Friday-night adventures, I thought. Part of me wished I was getting out of Dodge, too. Eula was continuing to scold Earl over the very idea that they might consider leaving Princeton, and I felt completely unsure about whether it was appropriate for me to comment one way or the other.

Just then a sound pierced the cold night air. A clear and lyrical tenor, singing the opening notes of "O Holy Night." Soon a rich chorus of male voices joined the soloist.

"That must be coming from the Holder archway," Earl said softly. "The a cappella groups on campus do a number of free concerts during the holiday season."

We walked more slowly as the singing continued, the ancient hymn swirling around us in the darkness. Ultimately, we paused quietly to listen to the final strains. I marveled at how silent this campus could be, unlike Harvard's. For a moment, it seemed as if the carol was descending on the hushed campus from heaven itself, a small bauble to mark the season.

"I guess there are a few things I'd miss here," Earl remarked quietly, as we resumed walking down the path that led between Nassau and Stanhope Halls.

Eula made a sound suspiciously like a grunt. "More than a few, I would think," she retorted. The magic moment was definitely over.

I glanced over the wide green quadrangle beside us, momentarily distracted by the upside-down cannon buried in its center. No wonder Earl wanted an escort to this party. His wife was ready to take his head off about this potential move.

Eula clutched her pocketbook as we continued along the flagstone path. "I'm just glad that tonight will be a chance for President Stern to meet some of the good black church folks he doesn't even know live in this town. He's yet to fellowship with us, you know."

We came to a stop at a crosswalk that ran in front of two identical windowless, white marble Greek buildings. They had weathered marble steps that stretched from one end to the other, four sets of tall white Ionic columns, and imposing sets of brown double doors.

"Oh, here we go again." Earl sighed, exasperated.

"What's the problem?" I asked while watching Earl look from one building to the other.

"I don't know which one we're going to," he answered. "One of these is Whig Hall and the other is Clio."

Eula shrugged her shoulders. "Don't look at me."

The door on the nearer building swung open. Eric's head emerged through the opening, and a burst of music swirled out after him. "Hey, there you are!" he called excitedly. "I've been looking all over for you! You just missed Fleming's speech about you, Professor. Come on!"

As we climbed the wide staircase toward the entrance, we could hear the strains of a swing band and an exuberant tenor, along with chattering voices and laughter. The party was clearly already in full swing.

"I can't believe that man couldn't wait until I arrived," Earl said angrily. "He can't resist trying to make me look bad."

"I can't say that I blame him for startin' on time. I told you we were gonna be late."

"Eula! Please!" Earl said sharply.

She lowered her voice. "Livin' on colored folks' time, same as always," she muttered under her breath.

"Professor and Mrs. Stokes!" Eric was beaming at us, completely oblivious to Eula's cranky running commentary. A beautiful, thin black woman stood beside him. "I want you all to meet my date, Kayla French."

It took me thirty seconds. But then I realized why Kayla French looked so familiar. I had passed her on campus earlier today. She was the black woman who had given me the dismissive stare when I walked by her. The first black person on this campus who had ever been unfriendly to me.

"Kayla is a freshman here at Princeton," Eric was saying to Earl. "She's very interested in the Economics Department. She's thinking of selecting that as her major."

"The professor and I have met," Kayla interjected. "I'm taking his course on race and economics, remember?"

"If I may?" A diminutive older man abruptly interrupted our conversation as the music died down momentarily. He gave Earl a hearty handshake and shook his head profusely with an approving smile. "Professor, I can't tell you how much interest you've brought to the college with your writings and your course work. This anniversary is a fine occasion."

In an almost deferential tone, Earl answered, "Why, thank you, Mr. Wolf. Thank you. Thank you very much. That's very kind of you."

The orange-and-black bow tie around Mr. Wolf's neck moved up and down as he swallowed. "I've purchased two copies of your last book for our collection, and I must say that you are to be congratulated. It is quite interesting."

I stepped back to give them some room to speak, but stopped abruptly as I took in the elderly man's attire. Black corduroys with orange embroidery at the cuffs, black wingtips with orange and black shoelaces, orange and gold cufflinks at his wrist, tiger lapel pin on his jacket, black-framed glasses speckled with orange paw prints. From head to toe, the man was a walking collection of Princeton paraphernalia.

I caught Eric's eye and whispered a question. "Who is that? The manager of the university store?"

"No," Eric laughed softly. "That's Jeb Wolf, the Official Overseer of Princetoniana."

"What?" I hissed.

"The Official Overseer of Princetoniana."

I searched Eric's eyes for a hint of sarcasm. "You're joking, right?"

"No, I'm not," he whispered. "Every twelve years, the president and Board of Trustees appoint a prominent alumnus to serve as full-time Overseer of Princetoniana. It's a prestigious job."

I knew that I should stop gossiping and properly greet Kayla. But this was too rich. I pulled Eric far enough away that we could speak in normal tones. "Besides wearing a horrendous wardrobe," I began, "what exactly does this Overseer do?"

"Generally speaking, he preserves our history. He maintains an archive on all alumni, keeps track of important events and anniversaries in the school's history. He also keeps all the yearbooks and documents produced by Princeton, and maintains copies of any materials that reflect on Princeton's history or its image. It's also his duty to challenge any negative attacks on the college's reputation. He basically guards our image and our place in history."

*Wow*, I thought. *You are totally drinking the Kool-Aid.*

I noticed that Kayla French had followed us, and now she rolled her eyes at me. "This Overseer also directs letter-writing campaigns. My mother just got something from him asking her to write the *Post* to protest some story they just wrote about President Stern."

"I know you think it sounds strange, Nikki," Eric said defensively, "but once you've been around here a while, you start to realize how important it is to have somebody who knows the history and all the facts about the school. That way, you don't have a lot of outsiders getting the wrong information or wrong impression about Princeton."

"Isn't that what the Public Relations Department is for?" I asked, incredulous.

"No," Eric replied. "The PR people only deal with outsiders. The

Overseer is more for us. He helps those on the inside—the students, parents, faculty, alumni, and staff—better understand the school's history and image, and our own role of contributing to it. He's class of 1958, third generation, so he's really one of us."

There was absolutely no point in objecting to this, so I just nodded.

"Yes, Professor," I heard Jeb Wolf remark to Earl. "I'm eager to hear about this new book project you are researching. It sounds intriguing."

"Well, Mr. Wolf, I can't say much right now, but it will examine a fascinating period of Princeton's history and how the school interacted with the black community economically and socially."

I'd never heard Earl address anyone at Princeton as "Mr." until now.

Wolf offered Earl a blank expression in return for his last comment. "As I said, we're eager to learn more about the book. It sounds intriguing."

The little man gave Earl a congratulatory pat and then shuffled off, looking considerably older than a class of 1958 alumnus should look.

I turned back to Eric, intending to introduce myself properly to Kayla. The two of them were chatting with another young couple, so I took the opportunity to give her the once-over. She was easily among the best-dressed women in the room. While most of the women were dressed in modest mid-calf satin dresses and looked like escaped midwestern bridesmaids, she wore a black minidress studded with bugle beads and sleek black alligator-skin pumps that looked suspiciously like a pair of thousand-dollar Jimmy Choos that I'd seen recently in the window at the Copley Square Neiman Marcus. It was an incredibly expensive ensemble for a college student. I took in the Judith Leiber purse, the embroidered shawl, and the earrings that appeared to be genuine diamond studs. Every hair in her sleek chignon was in place, and her makeup seemed professionally applied. She looked as if she were on her way to a far more important party after this one. There was some serious money and serious planning behind that ensemble. I knew it wasn't really fair to Eric, but I couldn't help wondering.

What was a girl like *that* doing with my brother?

Just as I was about to speak to her, a middle-aged man with silver hair stepped to the podium and began to quiet the crowd. "Good evening, everyone," he began. "For those of you who don't know me, I'm John Stern."

I wouldn't have known the face, but I recognized the name. He was the president of Princeton. A striking forty-something redhead stood beside him, a black mink coat slung over her shoulders and a glass of champagne in her hand. "You've already heard from Hayden Fleming about what Earl Stokes has meant to the Economics Department. Now I want to give a moment of recognition to the woman who has helped fund so many of the activities of the Program in African-American Studies—a woman whose roots at Princeton go deeper than anyone we know: Board of Trustees member Alexandra Van Patton Fleming."

"Thank you, John," the woman said as she handed her fur to the university president in a smooth gesture. "We're all moving from one holiday party to another tonight, but I want to thank you for joining me and John in paying tribute to Earl—he is an absolute pillar of Old Nassau. He is the backbone not just of Afro-Am, but also of our esteemed Economics department. Everyone in this room and in these two departments knows that Professor Stokes's credentials and contributions are unparalleled. Rhodes Scholar, Phi Beta Kappa, MacArthur Fellow, best-selling author, renowned commentator, journal editor, and Presidential adviser. Earl is a true example of Princeton in the nation's service."

The room broke into loud applause.

"As our nation's esteemed president remarked recently to the Fed chairman," continued Alexandra, "the MacArthur Prize people knew what they were doing when they called Earl Stokes 'America's Newest Economic Genius.' Here's to you, Earl."

The room laughed and applauded again.

Earl bowed graciously. "Thank you, Zanda. Thank you," he called out.

"Why was she leaning so hard on that economics angle?" I whispered to Eric.

"I don't know. I heard that she wants to shake up the Economics Department. There's some bad blood there."

Kayla snorted softly. "Bad blood? That's putting it mildly."

"Who is she, again?" I asked. "Faculty?" I watched as Earl embraced the attractive redhead.

"No," Eric explained. "Alexandra Van Patton Fleming is old Princeton. She sits on the board, and her father was president here about twenty-five years ago, and her grandfather was provost before that."

I saw Eula watching her husband clink champagne glasses with Alexandra. She kept a safe distance, but never took her eyes off of him.

"Did you say her last name is Fleming? Is that any relation to the head of the Economics Department? Isn't his name Hayden Fleming?"

Kayla interrupted. "Yeah, there's a relationship. He's her ex-husband."

*Oh, my.* And I thought Harvard faculty politics were incestuous.

Even my brother couldn't resist dishing about this. "She and Hayden Fleming were married for about five years, and they split up a couple of years ago. They don't get along at all."

"Well, it seems like she's a bit late if she's trying to use Earl as a wedge against her husband," I commented. "If he really is going to Harvard, what's the point?"

"Maybe she thinks she can get him to change his mind and stay here. Earl would be the natural one next in line to take Hayden's place as head of the Econ Department. And I'll bet she can be very persuasive."

After a parting buss on the cheek from Alexandra, Earl returned to his wife's side with a broad smile on his face. "She is always so gracious to me," he mused.

"Yeah," sniffed Eula. "I wonder why."

As the music started up again, my eyes fell on a heavy-set student who was traipsing around the edge of the room with a notepad and pencil in his hand.

"You seem to have a reporter on your tail," I said softly to Earl, nodding in the student's direction.

"Don't pay any attention to him," Earl said, waving at someone across the room. "That's just Bo Merriweather. Editor of the *National Prospect*. BMOC."

I looked at him quizzically.

"Big-Mouthed, Opportunistic Conservative," Earl elaborated. "He's been after me ever since I gave him an F in my Harlem Renaissance class. He says that the F kept him from doing his junior year at the London School of Economics."

"I imagine that an F would keep you out of lots of places. How did he manage to fail a class?" I hadn't given out more than a couple of F's in five years of teaching at Harvard. Students usually had to try to actually fail a class.

"Well, Bo basically argued against everything the course addressed."

"What does that mean?"

Eula broke in as a waiter offered us a plate of hors d'oeuvres. "It means that boy spent the whole semester arguin' that there was no Harlem Renaissance because there was *no* culture, *no* intellect, and *no* historical significance to be found in—"

"In *Harlem?*" I interrupted, incredulous.

"No," answered Earl. "In *any* black community here *or* in Africa."

"You must be talking about Bo Merriweather," Eric rejoined the conversation. "We just saw him trying to get an interview with Sportin' Life."

"Who?" asked Eula.

"Oh." Eric smiled. "I mean with Butch Hubbard."

"Oh, is he here?" Earl was suddenly distracted. "I need to speak with him."

Eula smiled. "Now, him I like. You know Pastor Smalls had him speak at Beulah just two years ago. He raised the roof!"

I was still on Bo Merriweather. "Why would someone be dumb enough to 'dis black people in front of the head of the Afro-Am Department?"

Eula was so agitated she could barely get the words out. "I'm telling you, the conservatives at Princeton are like no other conservatives on this planet! They come from that southern tradition, and they just get all up in your face. Just a few years ago, they invited the Grand Dragon of the KKK to speak on campus. Yes!" she said, reading my expression of skepticism. "Yes, they did! Pastor Smalls and all of us did everything we could to stop it. And when a group tried to start a fraternity on campus in 1983, the initiation required the pledges to urinate on the front door of the Third World Center, where the minority students socialize. And the Dean of Student Activities wouldn't even criticize them for it. Lord have mercy."

"I remember when *all* that stuff happened," Eric interjected. "But I think Princeton has changed a lot in the past few years."

"Humph," said Eula. I couldn't argue with her on that one.

"Harvard has the *Salient*," Eric prodded me. "It's no surprise that we have a conservative campus paper, too."

"Pastor Smalls says that Bo Merriweather is like gasoline thrown on a fire," Eula continued. "That boy brags that when his older brother was a high school junior back in South Carolina, he stabbed a teacher for making goo-goo eyes at him. And they say he's got a gun in his dorm room closet. Lord, I know he's crazy. And you see these pictures on the wall here? Southern war heroes, every one of 'em. And believe me, they weren't fightin' for *us*."

I wanted to tell her that if she moved to Cambridge, she would only see portraits of abolitionists and Democrats on the walls. But unfortunately, that wasn't the case, even at my beloved Harvard.

"Hey, Stokes, about time you showed up!" A heavy-set jocular black man in his early fifties laid a thick arm around Earl. He was almost a foot shorter than Earl, so the embrace landed somewhere near Earl's waist.

"That's Lloyd Eastman," Eula whispered to me. "He's Earl's number two in Afro-Am."

"You just missed hearing Fleming explain how proud the Economics Department is to share you with us lowly Afro-Am types," Eastman declared.

"I could kill that man for embarrassing me like that," Earl said quietly. I had never seen him so angry.

"Come on, man," Lloyd Eastman said. "Everybody here knows what his problem is."

"What's his problem?" asked Eric, sotto voce.

"Oh, Earl thinks that Hayden Fleming is threatened by him." To my

37

annoyance, Eula actually raised her voice, as if she were hoping that Earl would hear her. "But I don't think he's all that bad. He keeps trying to get Earl to give up some of his responsibilities, and I don't blame him. That man and I agree on one thing, and that's that my husband is trying to do too much. Two departments, won't let Lloyd here help him with anything, he's got his too-active social life, plus publishing the journal. And now this book. It's too much. I think Fleming realizes that all this is going to kill Earl."

"What he realizes," Earl said firmly, "is that I'm making him look bad. His big fear is that Stern might make me chair of *both* departments. He can't wait to get me out of here. I should stay on, just to spite him."

"Now *that's* what you should be doin'. Stayin' right here, where people respect you." Eula's face brightened until she saw Earl's expression.

"You got to cut the man some slack, Earl," Eastman said lightly. "He did just make a contribution to Beulah Baptist Church in your name."

"Two hundred measly dollars," Earl retorted. "But, Nikki, you should meet our great chairman. He's someone you should know."

I nodded and excused myself. I had never intended to monopolize so much of Earl's time that evening. But I felt Eula clinging to me, even now as I stepped away. She was clearly horribly ill at ease in this environment, and I tried to chalk her needling of Earl and her loud complaints about the school that paid her husband's salary up to nervousness. If Earl had been with her this long, there had to be something in her that was better than what I had seen so far.

I paused beside one of the many mahogany bars that lined the sides of the room and idly surveyed the crowd. Ropes of pearls, diamond earrings, and splashes of red taffeta in a sea of black tuxedos and black evening dresses. Evergreen wreaths and sprigs of mistletoe dangling from every doorway, and increasingly drunken smiles on almost every face. Christmas carols and jazz standards wafting through the air. All the elements of the perfect swanky holiday party. Then I saw a man's dark head bend toward a petite blond woman's, and I inhaled sharply.

*Stop it,* I commanded myself. *It's not him.*

It wasn't Dante Rosario. I closed my eyes tightly and exhaled. I'd managed to go a whole hour without thinking about him, amid the idle chatter of these Princetonians. I'd fought off the thought of him, even though the rich timbre in the voices of the male choir singing on the quadrangle had almost undone me. But one glimpse of someone who looked vaguely like him, and I was practically immobile with anger and desire.

"You look like a sister who *needs* to exhale," said a deep voice, close in my ear. My eyes flew open, and I took in a sight quite different from the scene around me. A tall black man with dreadlocks and a serious expression looked down at me from about eight inches over my head. "I beg your pardon?" I said sharply.

"I know. Cliché, right? That waiting-to-exhale thing. But, girl, you gave me the opening, and I had to take it," replied Mr. Dreadlocks.

His eyes were roaming all over me. I took a step back and regarded him critically. Brooding eyes, strong cheekbones, and flawless dark brown skin. A kente-cloth cummerbund and bow tie complemented an extremely well-fitting tuxedo. I could stand a few minutes of that, no problem. "If you say anything about my getting my groove back, this conversation is over, understand?"

He laughed, and I found myself liking that. There was nothing of Dante in him, and I liked that even more. "Right, right," he said. "If I keep this rap up, you're gonna make me pull a disappearing act."

"You're a day late and a dollar short, Mr.—"

"Yusef. Just call me Yusef. And you are?"

As I was about to reply, a shadow passed over his face, and his smile was replaced by a disdainful smirk. "Are you one of the many worshippers at the shrine of Stokes?"

I glanced behind me and realized that Earl had walked by with Zanda Fleming. They seemed deep in conversation. "If you mean, am I here to show my support of Professor Stokes, then the answer is yes."

"So you really buy into this assimilationist, heal-the-cities bullshit that he writes? You look too smart for that."

I looked at my companion more closely and realized that he was so wired that he was practically bouncing on the soles of his feet.

"If you believe that, then why are you here?" I asked sharply.

"Oh, I'm not one of the faithful. I'm here because I was paid to show up." He said it defiantly, as if he was hoping someone would overhear.

Now I was plain confused. "Are you one of the waiters?"

"No, sister." His sardonic smile returned. "Not yet, anyway. I've gotta jump. But I'll see you around."

I watched him walk off into the crowd, completely mystified about what had just happened. I turned to find Eric and Kayla a few feet away from me.

"I see you met Earl's son," Eric remarked.

I turned to look back into the crowd, where the dreadlocked head had just disappeared from view. Then I looked at Eric. Then back into the crowd.

I'd known Earl Stokes for eight years, and he'd never mentioned that he had a son.

Never.

# Permanent Fatal Errors

"**T**here isn't a man anywhere on this planet who wants to sleep with me! I cannot *believe* this!"

"Jess, he was being a gentleman. You should be grateful."

Saturday morning found me warming up my laptop computer, which I had squeezed into the last remaining inch of clear space on Eric's ancient wooden dorm room desk. I hadn't checked e-mails since I left Cambridge early the prior morning, and I had two hundred and forty-two unread messages in my in-box. A half-filled coffee cup beside me, my finger poised on the delete key, I was ready to start the day's work. But Jess was still rehashing the night before.

"I looked good, didn't I?" Jess said plaintively.

"You looked fabulous, honey," I said soothingly. "You're going to feel a lot better after you take a shower and have some coffee. Trust me." I was secretly delighted that Ernst had turned out to be as trustworthy as Eric had said he would. The last thing Jess needed was some guy preying on her when she was drunk and on the rebound.

"I guess I talked too much about Ted," she muttered.

"Yeah, guys hate to hear about how great their predecessors were. Performance anxiety and all that," I said mildly, shooing her toward the shower. I was certain that she and Ted would reunite about ten minutes after she returned to Cambridge. In the meantime, I just had to keep her from doing something stupid with one of these Princeton preppies.

"I'll make a fresh pot of coffee, okay?" I called after her, smiling to myself. It was fun having my best friend from college around first thing in the morning again. Living alone had its rewards, but that was the one thing that I missed about college dormitory life—the feeling that all of your best friends were under one roof, just a room or a hallway away.

After a quick stretch to work out the remaining kinks in my neck from a night on Eric's loveseat, I hunkered down over my computer. Unfortunately, my most recent e-mail message was from Carl Irvin.

*"Haven't heard from you,"* was all the missive said. No salutation, no "Hope you had a nice trip." He was letting me know that he wanted the latest version of the paper I was presenting at the upcoming annual ABA conference in New York City. Never mind that I hadn't had a chance to work on it because I was too busy getting ready for yesterday's conference presentation. Never mind that in less than an hour, I was supposed to be back at Woody Woo listening to a day's worth of presentations on topics of marginal interest to me. When Carl Irvin wanted something, my world ground to a halt. I really hoped that Earl was right when he said that a new department head was going to be named any day. Then the next time Irvin sent me off on some ridiculous errand like this Eastern European conference, I could say "Research *this*."

I tapped furiously on my keyboard, longing for the good old days before Irvin figured out how to use e-mail, when it was only his irritating phone messages that I had to respond to. "New draft in the works," I replied. "You'll have by Monday morning. Conference going great, my presentation yesterday well received." Resisting the urge to sign the message with an expletive, I hit the send button and went to make more java on Eric's decrepit Mr. Coffee machine.

By the time I returned, there was a menacing-looking error message waiting for me. "Undeliverable message," read the heading. The text read "Your message to <u>carlirwin@harvard.edu</u> was undeliverable due to permanent fatal errors."

"Great," I muttered. "I'd like to inflict a permanent fatal error on *him.*"

I shut down my computer to check the connection to the modem and then restarted it. The laptop obediently buzzed and whirred back to life, but when I tried to get back into my e-mails, my cursor froze in place like a stubborn mule.

I glanced at my watch, fighting a rising tide of panic. I had thirty minutes until the morning session of my conference started at Woody Woo, and I had to get a response back to Irvin before I left. And I really didn't want to call him. Heaven forbid he was in his office on a Saturday morning, I'd have to actually speak with him, and I was trying to do as little of that as possible at the moment. That was the one beauty of e-mail—it was a lot easier to be civil when I didn't have to hear his arrogant, condescending tone on the other end of the line.

"Come on," I muttered, as I tried all the usual tricks. I hit escape. I hit control-alt-delete all at once. I hit enter, shift, even typed the words *please help me* on the keyboard. No luck.

Clearly, it was time to call Matthew.

Matthew worked at the computer help desk at Harvard, and I considered him an indispensable part of my life. He'd talked me through severed modem connections, software bugs, dead batteries, and a couple of very messy breakups in the three years that he'd been working at Harvard. His voice was soothing and authoritative, with the merest hint of a midwestern twang. In my imagination, he was thirty-something, tall and slim, with a goatee and really interesting eyeglasses. I had a bit of a crush on him, if the truth be told. Of course, I'd never met him. Ours was a telephone kinship, borne over the airwaves—which had proved far more durable than my terrestrial romantic relationships.

"Matthew!" I wailed after dutifully waiting on hold until he became free. "My cursor is frozen, my e-mails are coming back with fatal errors, and I have to leave here in twenty minutes!"

"Okay, let's take a look," he murmured in my ear. "Let's do a wait for guest, and see what's going on."

"Wait for guest" meant that he could take control of the cursor from his computer, while I could still see it moving on my screen. It felt very much like letting someone else take the steering wheel on a car that you've been driving. I'm a card-carrying feminist, but I confess that it felt heavenly to temporarily surrender control to him.

"So where are you?" he asked, as I watched the now-animated cursor moving slowly across the screen of my laptop.

"Princeton," I replied dreamily.

"Snowing down there?"

"Yes, at least it was when I woke up this morning. Just flurries. It's pretty. Makes you feel like the holidays are coming. Is it cold in Cambridge?"

"Yes. It's a wool sweater day," he replied a bit distractedly. The cursor traced a path across my toolbar.

"Really? What color is yours?" I inquired lazily. "Your wool sweater, I mean."

"Orange," he replied.

*Orange sweater,* I thought. Juicy.

"Wow! You have a ton of e-mails here. You must not have checked in at all yesterday." He paused for a moment. "Yes, I see what the problem is here. You just misspelled Irvin's name. Rushing?"

"With 242 e-mails and a half hour to read them, you bet I was rushing. Is that really all it was?"

"That's all it was. The cursor was frozen because you didn't give the computer enough time to reboot. I've told you a million times: you have to count to twenty before you start pounding on the keyboard, kiddo. Okay, you're driving again." The cursor stopped moving for a moment, and then I took it back over with my mouse. "I see you have a message from your boyfriend."

"Where?"

"It's about a third of the way down from the top. You okay?" he prodded, when I didn't reply.

"I'm fine, he's not my boyfriend, and thank you for the quick fix."

"Whatever you say, Nikki." He laughed easily. "Stay out of the cold down there, all right? Those short skirts you wear don't go with snow."

"Matthew, we've never met," I chided, laughing. "You have no idea what kind of skirts I wear."

"Believe me, I can tell, Nikki. You are definitely the short skirt type."

I smiled as I ran my hand over the hemline grazing my thigh. Maybe extraterrestrial relationships really *were* the way to go.

The phone rang almost immediately after I hung up. I picked up the receiver, expecting to hear Matthew's voice reminding me of something I should do with my recalcitrant laptop. Instead, I heard Eric's voice.

"Turn on the television," he commanded.

"Are you all right?" I asked sharply.

"Yeah, I'm at Kayla's. Just turn on the television, Nikki."

I flicked on the ancient Sony, and a male voice emerged even before the picture. *"Once again, our top story this morning,"* I heard. *"An overnight fire on the Princeton campus destroyed the shell of a new building that was to house the university's Center for African-American Studies. Authorities are on the scene. We'll have more on this breaking story throughout the day, and on our newscast live at five."*

"Poor Earl," I murmured into the phone. "What a lousy break." I wondered how this would affect his decision about leaving Princeton. It would be harder for him to leave with the symbol of his department having just gone up in smoke. I could see the headlines now: TIGER, TIGER, BURNING BRIGHT.

"Can you believe it happened the same night as the anniversary party?" Eric asked urgently. "It's like someone was trying to make a statement or something." He sounded rattled, and I instinctively tried to soothe him.

"Come on, Eric, I'm sure this was an accident. Probably some teenagers messing around with matches after a keg party. No one is going to bother burning down a building that wasn't even half-finished."

"Whatever the case," Eric interjected, "we should try Professor Stokes and see if we can do something to help out."

"Okay, I'll call him and call you right back," I said. But before I could dial Earl's number, the phone was already ringing again.

"Hey," I answered eagerly, fully expecting to find Earl or Eric on the other end of the line. But it wasn't. Instead, a clipped female voice demanded to speak to me.

"This is Nikki Chase," I replied, glancing at my watch. I was supposed to be out the door ten minutes ago, but this conference was going to have to wait until I could talk to Earl. "Who is this?" The officiousness of the voice made me think that it was the conference registrar, already hunting me down because I was late for the session at Woody Woo.

"This is Detective Maureen Kelly from the Borough of Princeton Police Department, Miss Chase. I need to ask you some questions. Would it be convenient for you to come down to the station this morning?"

"Honestly, no, it wouldn't," I replied, without thinking. "I'm late for a conference, and I have a phone call that I have to make. What is this about?"

When I remembered the conversation later, the pause before her answer seemed to last an eternity. "Well, Miss Chase, Professor Earl Stokes seems to be missing. No one has seen him since he left a party you both attended last night. We're looking for some help tracking him down."

"**Short stack** with chips, side bacon, one percent, and a large squeeze. Double over easy, two silver dollars, two sausage and one ham, small squeeze, and a special—hold the cream. And where's my chocolate cow with an everything? Welcome to P.J.'s. Okay, honey, what'll it be?"

My brother looked up at the twenty-something waitress who'd just fired off three orders to the cook and now stood over our table next to the counter with an impatient pencil and order pad. Her blond ponytail stuck out of the back of a red bandanna on her head.

It was Eric who had argued that the best way to gain information about Earl's whereabouts was to get out of the dorm and into a place with lots of locals. Princeton was a very small town, and it wasn't possible to disappear without someone noticing. I'd just returned from the police station, where I'd had to recount everything that I'd seen at the party last night. The cops were still trying to find Eula—I'd told them that she was supposed to be leaving to visit relatives in Brooklyn after the party. Earl's secretary had been the one to call the police after he didn't show up for a breakfast meeting with President Stern that morning.

"So what did the cops say? Do they think that something bad has happened to Professor Stokes? Do they think his being gone has something to do with this fire?" Eric was peppering me with questions, having placed our breakfast order: chocolate chip pancakes for himself and blueberry ones for Jess and me. I pointed to my empty coffee cup as the waitress finished scribbling on her order pad.

I shook my head. "I really can't tell what they think. They told me that they usually don't consider someone to be 'missing' until they've been gone for at least twenty-four hours. But Earl is a big deal in this town, so I think they're covering their bases just in case." I was fighting a rising sense of dread about Earl's disappearance. I didn't want to be pessimistic in front of Eric, but Earl would never miss a meeting with the president of the university unless something was seriously wrong. And as dismissive as I had been about Eric's theory that this fire was someone sending a message, I had a sick feeling in my stomach about the timing of the blaze and Earl's disappearance.

"This place is really hopping," Jess remarked as she looked around the crowded diner. New patrons were pouring in at the door while others stood out on the wide sidewalk. "Is this a big student hangout?"

Eric shrugged. "Not on weekdays, but it is on Saturday and Sunday mornings. Otherwise, everybody eats at the clubs. And the freshmen and sophomores eat in Commons."

"Commons? Wow, you must be older than you look." Our waitress had reappeared over Eric's shoulder, holding a pot of coffee.

Eric laughed. "How true."

Jess looked up at the waitress. "What did you mean by that?"

"Sorry, honey, but nobody refers to the dining halls as 'Commons' anymore. That stopped back in 1984 or '85. Now they're residential colleges."

"I know, I'm still calling them Madison and Upper Cloister," Eric said ruefully.

The waitress smiled and trotted off to pour coffee for two cops who had just sat down at the crowded counter. *Police officers are just like raccoons*, I thought idly. *Where there's one, there's always two.*

"What's Madison and Upper Cloister?" Jess asked gamely. I knew that she was chattering to take my mind off Earl. She knew me well enough to know that I was really worried about him. I listened to her talk to Eric with half an ear while I simultaneously tried to catch snippets of conversation from the adjoining tables. This was a small town, I told myself again. Someone had to have seen him.

"When I was an undergraduate, one of our dining hall choices was Madison Hall— it was the biggest, and it fronted on Nassau Street." Eric was off on another Princeton history lesson. "Then there was Upper Cloister and Lower Cloister, which were next to Holder Courtyard. Holder Courtyard is where lots of the sophomores lived. And then there was Upper Eagle, which was where the WASPs ate." He stopped abruptly. "Are you all right, Nikki?"

"Yeah, yeah," I muttered, a bit impatient. I wanted information about Earl. Not more Princeton trivia.

"So everybody starts off eating in Commons, and then as upper-classmen, they join these eating clubs?" Jess said, sipping her coffee.

"Most do. Unless you're black, keep kosher, or are too poor to join a club. Then you would . . . uh, then you would . . ."

Jess looked at Eric expectantly. "Then you would what?"

He looked down at the chocolate chip pancakes that had just been placed before him. "Wow, I'm trying to remember. I guess then you'd . . ."

"Then you'd eat at the student center, join a co-op at 2 Dickinson, or cook for yourself in a campus kitchen like *I* did, Little Rich Boy." The waitress in the red bandanna rolled her eyes and slid a third hot plate onto the table in front of me.

Eric suddenly looked a bit embarrassed. "That's right, and the kosher dining hall was called Kosher Stevenson, where my roommate Ariel ate. I really should have remembered that—and 2 Dickinson and the student center in Chancellor Green Hall."

Jess looked up from her blueberry pancakes and stared at the waitress, who now had her hands on her hips.

"So, did you go to Princeton or something?" Eric asked.

"Or *something?* I know this apron and this job might suggest otherwise, but not only *did* I go to Princeton, I *do* go there *now,* Little Rich Boy."

Emboldened by Eric's wry smile, the waitress continued. "And let me guess. You were in Ivy? No, you've got a decent body—maybe Cottage. I took two years off after junior year—back when I used to date one of those Cottage buffoons. But now that I'm back, I'm a little rusty at placing you club types."

"Pick it up," a voice shouted from the counter. "Martha—double over easy, with a chocolate cow and a twist. Pick it up!"

"That's me. Gotta go." The waitress was off.

"Did you see him leave the party last night?" I turned to Eric.

"Nikki, I told you. Kayla and I left right after you did." I was cursing myself for having left the party early. After my close encounter with Earl's son, I'd decided that I'd had enough for one day and headed for Eric's dorm. I'd slept so deeply after the long day of traveling that I hadn't even heard Jess come in.

"What I don't get is why they can't reach Eula." I mused.

"I think that makes perfect sense. They're probably together," Eric said calmly. Despite his earlier agitation, he now seemed completely unfazed. "Maybe she convinced him to go with her to visit her mother."

I shook my head. "If that were true, he would have called to tell President Stern not to expect him."

"Oh, boy, here we go again," Jess declared. "She's getting that look in her eyes."

"No, I'm not!" I protested.

"Ricky, don't you agree?" Jess teased lightly. "She's got that Nancy

Drew expression on her face." Jess leaned toward me. "Honey, don't start jumping to conclusions. Wait until you hear more, okay? You're going to have enough trouble explaining to idiot Irvin why you aren't at Woody Woo right now."

I nodded distractedly. It wasn't *my* trouble that I was worried about at that moment. It was Earl's.

I looked up to see two uniformed cops approaching our table. One was talking into what looked like a walkie-talkie, while the other one looked right at me. I realized that they were the two who had been eating at the counter just moments before.

Looking back on the moment, I sometimes fantasize that the cops swerve in the aisle and go to another table. Or that they sit down and announce that they have found him and that he is safe. But that happens only in the fantasy. What really happened is that the lead cop said soberly, "Nikki Chase?"

And I knew it right then. Before he pulled up a chair from an adjoining table, before his partner looked at me gravely and with the utmost concern. Before he quietly told me in a voice both deep and sorrowful, I knew it.

Earl Stokes was dead.

# 5
## Post Mortem

In an era of twenty-four-hour cable news outlets with an insatiable need for new material, it took no time at all for the word of Earl's death to go out over the airwaves. But there was surprisingly little information provided, other than the most basic facts. Even so, by five o'clock that evening Eric, Jess, and I were still huddled around the ancient Sony television in Eric's room in Holder Hall. Even though there didn't seem to be any new information, we couldn't stop obsessively hunting for new tidbits.

*"In a major development today, the body of Princeton professor Earl Stokes was found at a construction site on the Ivy League campus. The professor, aged fifty-one, was best known for his best-selling book* Color Counts. *The professor's charred remains were discovered at midday today when police crews surveyed the burning remnants of the future home of the university's Program in African-American Studies—"*

"That's exactly what they said an hour ago, and an hour before that. Are they really just going to keep repeating the same thing over and over?" Jess sighed, exasperated.

"Are you all right, Nikki?" Eric was looking at me with a worried expression.

I shook my head and looked back at him. "No. Definitely not. I am not all right."

*"More on this breaking story after the sports report,"* I heard the talking head say. "The local news is doing the story after sports," I said sharply. "Can you believe it? *After* the *sports,* they're going to tell us more about what—what happened to Earl."

When I first heard the news, I went numb. An hour later, the tears came. Now I felt ferociously, savagely angry. "Give me that remote," I ordered curtly.

"Honey, what can I do to help?" Jess asked softly. "Do you want an Advil—or a cigarette?"

"No!" I shouted. "I want the damn remote!"

Jess mutely handed it to me, and I madly flipped channels, looking for coverage. The president's office had issued a statement naming Lloyd Eastman as the acting chair of Princeton's Program in African-American Studies, and one of the cable networks was promising an exclusive interview with Eastman later that night. A different network kept flashing the photograph from Earl's last book jacket, which was at least five years out of date.

"He hated that picture, you know," I snapped. "I should call them and tell them that he hated that picture and that he looked nothing like that, and that if they are such a damn great news organization, they should get a freaking up-to-date picture of the deceased."

"Go back to the local channel, Nikki," Jess implored. "They'll get back to the story."

"Right. After the sports. Like I'm going to wait until after they announce some freaking hockey score—"

"Wait!" Eric called out "Go back two channels. It's Sportin' Life!"

Sure enough, it was Butch Hubbard on the screen. A petite redhead was interviewing him on one of the cable outlets.

"—so it must be absolutely devastating to see such a close friend die this way? Someone with so much promise and such a bright future?" the redhead chirped.

A close-up of Hubbard filled the screen. As always, he cut a striking figure in a dark suit and red Harvard bow tie. His sad expression seemed to fill the TV set. "And that is exactly the point that I'm trying to make, Lacey. You hit it right on the head when you said 'promise.' As I've pointed out so many times before, our nation has so few black intellectuals who are able to give direction to the young blacks who are looking toward the future. And this promise"—Hubbard gestured broadly with an outstretched forefinger—"this promise—this promise that this young black teacher had was so great. He was just making a mark."

Lacey, the redheaded anchorwoman, nodded with an air of concern and empathy. "And as you so astutely pointed out, Professor Hubbard, this is not just Princeton's loss. It's also Harvard's loss. I understand that you were taking him under your tutelage and were about to bring him to Cambridge to help him develop even further. Isn't that right, Professor?"

"Lacey, you are so right. So right *indeed*." Hubbard leaned dramatically toward the camera to emphasize his point. "Lacey, what I saw in this young man was a promise that I just knew had to be encouraged. Had to be fed and nourished in order to develop. I had convinced the Harvard fellows and president that we should bring this young teacher on board. In Cambridge, we could take care of him and teach him so he could blossom."

"Young teacher?" I snarled. "Fed and nourished? Help him develop? Earl Stokes was a tenured professor in two departments, and a best-selling author. What's he talking about?"

"So, if you're just tuning in," Lacey noted with a businesslike demeanor, "it's just been reported that African-American Studies professor Earl Stokes of Princeton University was found dead today. We are told by our special guest, Professor Percy Hubbard, that Stokes, a best-selling author, was just finishing a controversial book about the school and town of Princeton."

The camera opened to a wide angle, and Hubbard shifted his torso to face more of the camera. He was gripping something in his left hand.

"Oh, my Lord. Is that a handkerchief he just wiped across his eyes? I don't believe it!" Jess exclaimed.

The camera closed in tightly as Hubbard looked tearfully into the lens. "What I want to offer to all of you who are watching, to the scholars, to the Princeton University community, to Earl's beloved wife, Eula, to the students who studied under him, to the young black children and to the American public who never had an opportunity to know this great developing black thinker, is a message that I hope none of us will ever forget."

Hubbard then reached into his pocket and pulled out a white sheet of paper. He unfolded it while also pulling out his wire-framed bifocals. "I want to offer this short poem that I've dedicated to Earl Stokes's memory. I wrote it earlier today after I learned of his untimely death."

The camera pulled back to a wide shot to reveal a dark-skinned man wearing a bright dashiki and sitting in front of two small African hand drums.

"I call this poem 'Tomorrow's Black Child,'" Hubbard continued while looking down at the sheet of paper in his hand. He began to read softly as the drummer performed quietly in the background.

| | |
|---|---|
| Like the rain in Zimbabwe | *drumbeat, drumbeat* |
| Like the rain on Harlem's autumn leaves | *drumbeat, drumbeat* |
| There is a soft sound in the streets. | |
| A soft sound in the shadows. | |
| | |
| Like the drums of our past | *drumbeat, drumbeat* |
| Like the drums of our future, | *drumbeat, drumbeat* |
| There is a soft cry in the streets | |
| A soft cry in the shadows. | |
| | |
| Like the wind in our jungle | |
| Like the wind in our alleyways, | |
| There is a soft step in the streets | |
| A soft step in our shadows. | |
| It's the sound of Tomorrow's Black Child | *drumbeat, drumbeat* |

Tomorrow's Black Child
Just waiting to grow, to learn, to bloom
Tomorrow's Black Child.                    *drumbeat, drumbeat*

The spotlight on the drummer faded to darkness as the musician lifted his hands off the instrument and the camera moved back to a close-up of Hubbard. He quietly removed his glasses, folded the white paper, and returned it to the breast pocket of his jacket.

"Wow! Was that ever powerful?" The perky anchorwoman touched her chest. She seemed mesmerized. "So powerful and heartfelt." Hubbard stared down sadly into his lap.

I clapped a hand over my mouth. I was definitely about to throw up.

"Professor, I want to thank you for that very moving tribute. So moving. I also understand you've got an announcement to make. If you'll share it with our viewers."

Hubbard's big, sad eyes brightened as he looked up at the camera. "I'm happy to announce that I've created a special scholarship program in the name of my friend Earl Stokes. I'm looking for a corporate sponsor to guarantee its longevity, but I'm personally contributing $50,000 of my own money to launch this program, which is designed to identify and reward young black inner-city high school students who have turned their lives around." Hubbard paused.

"I'm calling it the Earl Stokes Memorial Tomorrow's Black Child Fund," he added, gazing into the camera's eye. "And I will personally oversee the fund's administration through my office at Harvard. Even though I am also running the school's renowned Afro-American Studies Department, I want to personally take on this important project, too."

"And how fitting," added the anchorwoman. "How very fitting a tribute to your friend."

The newscast shifted to another story, and Eric, Jess, and I stared at each other for a moment. Eric asked the obvious question before anyone else could get the words out. "How the hell did he have all of that ready to go when we all just learned that Professor Stokes was dead six hours ago?"

None of us had an answer for that. "Did you notice that he wasn't in the same studio as the interviewer?" Jess said.

"That's right," I nodded slowly. "The caption under him said that he was in Princeton. He's still down here. He hasn't gone back to Cambridge yet."

It was clear that thanks to Butch Hubbard, the media coverage of Earl's death had the potential to spin completely out of control. "I'm going to try Eula again," I said, reaching for the phone. I'd called Earl's house five times in the last four hours, but each time there had been no answer.

"Grace and peace," a male voice said.

With the telephone receiver at my ear, I paused and looked back at the number displayed in my organizer. "Oh, I'm sorry. I'm trying to reach the Stokes residence."

The deep male voice rumbled, "Grace and peace. How can I help you?"

"Well, I'd like to speak to Eula Stokes. Is she there?"

"Who is calling?"

I was reluctant to offer my identity, given the somewhat odd behavior of the speaker on the other end of the line. I still wasn't sure that I had the right number. "I'm a family friend."

"Then you should leave your name. I'm Reverend Creflo Smalls, the family pastor."

I had remembered Eula mentioning Pastor Smalls the day before. "Oh, Pastor Smalls. My brother has attended your church several times."

There was a long silence. "I see."

"Yes, he lived with Earl and Eula for a while."

"Are you white?" the pastor asked.

"I beg your pardon?"

"You sound white."

"No!" I answered, dumbfounded. "I'm a good friend of Earl's, and I've just seen the news. I need to speak with Eula."

"Hmm. Are you one of the *special friends* Sister Eula has told me about?"

Special friends? What was he talking about? "I suppose that I am," I answered tentatively. *Just put her on the phone.*

"Well if that is the case, you needn't be calling Sister Eula," the pastor responded emphatically. "In fact, I should say that now that Brother Earl is gone, all of you can give Sister Eula some peace. All of you vixens have picked her dry with your calls and your visits. Don't think she didn't know the temptation and the deeds that all of you lured Brother Earl into. Drinking and running around. He let all of you cause this God-fearing woman enough pain—so let her be."

Then the phone went dead.

I stared at the receiver, flabbergasted.

Butch Hubbard was in the spotlight, milking Earl's death for his own greater glory. And a bizarrely hostile minister was monitoring Eula's contact with the outside world. I didn't know what Lloyd Eastman, acting chairman, might be planning for his television appearance later that night. But the way things were going, it was risky to count on anyone properly representing Earl's memory, now that the media circus had come to town.

Earl Stokes had worked too hard to have his legacy defined by a showman and someone who was quite possibly a charlatan, both with their own agendas. It definitely wasn't what Carl Irvin would have wanted me spending my time on. But it was increasingly clear that it was going to be up to me to do what Earl would have wanted done.

# 6

## The Lady and the Tiger

The chimes from the university chapel tolled eight o'clock as I walked hurriedly along the shadowy paths of Prospect Gardens, an oasis of pine trees and manicured flowerbeds in the center of Princeton's campus. The heels of the only pair of pumps that I'd brought with me from Cambridge were sinking deep into the slushy mix of snow and sand that covered the flagstone walkway, but the fragrant early-winter air, redolent of evergreens and pinecones, was some compensation for the icy trip. On a night like this, it was almost possible for me to love this campus, decked out for Christmas like an upscale small town, where even the curmudgeonly local policeman would soon don a Santa costume to bring toys to the few underprivileged children Princeton could scare up.

Out of the gloom, the Italianate contours of Prospect House gradually came into view, the path forward now lit by a stately row of lamps that mimicked old-fashioned gaslights. Even though I was late, I slowed my pace a bit to prolong the magnificence of the walk. I'd forgotten how beautiful it was, but in the clear sapphire air, one could see Princeton's faculty club for the former mansion that it was. The building's oversized doors and arched windows were bedecked with diminutive white

Christmas lights and elegant wreaths with formal red bows. Warm golden light spilled out from both stories of the house onto the snow below. It could have been a grand mansion in Tuscany on Christmas Eve. The only thing missing was a uniformed butler at the entrance proffering an aperitif.

After my bizarre conversation with Pastor Smalls, I'd impulsively called Alexandra Van Patton Fleming and asked her if she would meet me somewhere that evening. Eric and Jess had done the best they could, but I'd felt that I had to talk to someone who had really known Earl. Someone who was feeling the loss as deeply as I was. And someone who could help me ensure that the grandstanding of Reverend Smalls and Butch Hubbard wouldn't mar Earl's legacy. To my surprise, she immediately offered to meet me for dinner, since she had canceled all of her plans for the night when she heard of Earl's death. She had suggested that we rendezvous at Prospect and eat in the faculty dining room. It would be completely empty on a Saturday night during the holiday season, she'd declared. That sounded great to me.

"Nikki Chase?"

I turned to find Zanda Fleming striding toward me, her trademark black mink coat resting elegantly on her shoulders. The light from Prospect illuminated her, revealing vibrant red hair, a blur of diamonds, a short forest-green wool dress, and tall black leather boots. At a discreet distance behind her, a black Mercedes purred quietly while a uniformed chauffeur emphatically closed the passenger door. Suddenly, I was grateful that Jess had loaned me her black crushed velvet jacket and skirt. It was all I could do not to curtsey before Zanda. Instead, I involuntarily reached up and smoothed down my windswept hair.

"Miss Fleming, thank you so much for agreeing to see me. I really appreciate your taking the time." *Stop gushing,* I reminded myself sharply. Being in close proximity to haute couture always has that effect on me.

"Call me Zanda," she said. Turning slightly toward her car, she called over her shoulder. "Freddy, I'll be back at ten o'clock."

The chauffeur nodded smartly and returned to the driver's side of the car. *Does one really need a full-length mink coat to walk a couple of steps from a car to the front door?* I wondered idly. Having never had a mink or a driver, I wasn't in a position to know.

"So how long have you been at Harvard?" Zanda asked as we crossed the threshold and headed for the coat check.

"Four years at the college, then a brief hiatus on Wall Street, an MBA from the B-School, and now almost four years in the Economics Department."

"Yes, I remember Earl telling me about you. And I just read something about you, too. Something about your solving a murder, I think?"

I waved my hand dismissively. "Minor, unpleasant episode."

She smiled wryly. "So this minister—this Pastor Smalls—really called Earl a womanizer."

"Technically, he called *me* a vixen and said that Earl drank and ran around. You get the gist."

She shook her head. "I can't imagine where he got that from. I told my partner what you said, and neither one of us could believe it. Hello, Harold," Zanda said. She turned her back toward the elderly coat check attendant and allowed him to tenderly remove her mink. "We'll be upstairs for a couple of hours."

"Yes, Miss Fleming," Harold replied deftly. He lovingly hung the coat on a padded hanger. Then he accepted my black wool jacket with an expression that could only be described as pitying.

"This is lovely," I commented, as we climbed a broad staircase. I almost felt that I was complimenting her on her own home.

Zanda nodded as if she had designed the space herself. "Having once lived here, I have mixed feelings when I visit—but I do think they did a much better job with the Christmas decorations this year."

It dawned on me that since Prospect had originally been used as the primary residence of each Princeton president, she had no doubt lived there as a child when her father was president in the late 1950s. No wonder her mink was treated like a member of the family here.

"It's a pity that they moved the president's residence off-campus after the riots in the sixties," Zanda mused as we walked down a wide hallway lined with crystal sconces. "It was a lovely touch to have a family living here. Now it's just another public space." She paused to straighten a copy of the *Princeton Alumni Weekly* that was askew on an end table.

A public space with enough oversize crystal chandeliers to furnish an entire development of suburban McMansions, I thought, but who's counting?

We were soon ushered to a prime table for two, right next to a broad set of windows in the faculty dining room. The windows overlooked a footpath, and below us a steady stream of students and faculty flowed by, their scarves whipping along in the wind. The dining room was decked out, literally, with boughs of holly. The tables, discreetly placed apart from one another to ensure privacy, were covered with crisp white linens whose starch content matched the cuffs in the sleeves of the waiters' immaculate shirts. All white men past the age of fifty or so, the waiters looked as comfortable in the room as the furniture and the timeless holiday decor, lending the scene as traditional an aspect as one can find north of the Mason-Dixon line these days. Part of me sank right into the comfort of the well-upholstered chair the waiter pulled out for me with old-fashioned courtesy. Another part of me wondered if there was a single white face behind the facade, in the kitchen, or in the bowels of the building where the linens were sorted and the dirty dishes washed. My reverie was interrupted by Zanda's breezy greetings to the captain and the waiters. She spoke to them as if they were family retainers, which in a sense, they were.

"So, tell me, why did you call me?" I looked up to find Zanda regarding me with an amused smile.

"Well, as I said on the phone, I'm concerned about what Butch Hubbard and this minister may do to Earl's reputation if someone doesn't get out there and start talking about his real legacy. Did you see Butch Hubbard on television tonight?"

She shook her head. "Other than 'NET and 'NJN, I can't say that I watch much television."

A waiter in black tie approached with a silver tray bearing a single glass of white wine. "Your usual white burgundy, Miss Fleming. And what may I get you, miss?" he inquired.

I hesitated. White burgundy was my absolute favorite, but well above my budget.

"This is all on me, of course, Nikki," Zanda said, accepting her glass. "I for one intend to get very drunk tonight, and I certainly hope that you'll join me."

"Then I would love to have a glass of the same thing," I told the waiter.

"In that case, just bring the bottle, will you, Jeffrey?" Zanda ordered.

"Thank you," I said, turning to her. "This is very nice of you." Despite the somber occasion, I had to admit that so far, it was fun hanging with the queen.

She waved the gratitude away with the back of her hand. "Mind if I start?"

"Please, go ahead. We were talking about what Hubbard did on television tonight," I resumed. "He basically said that he was sponsoring Earl's transfer to Harvard, and laid claim to him as if Earl were Butch's invention. It was all about how clever and generous Butch is, and nothing about Earl and what his life was about."

"Why do you care so much?" Zanda leaned toward me. "What does it matter if Hubbard gets a little free publicity at this point? What's the harm?"

A wave of disappointment washed over me. Suddenly, I felt exhausted. I'd been wrong to think that Zanda Fleming would be a natural ally for me. Despite her effusive words at the African-American Studies party the night before, she obviously had no interest in how Earl would be remembered. I looked down at the table, horrified to find tears prickling at my eyelids. *No crying in public,* I admonished myself. Especially not now.

Suddenly I felt the warmth of her hand on my arm.

"I'm serious," she said softly. "I'd like to know why this is so important to you."

The sudden intimacy of her gesture was disarming. I looked up to find her staring at me intently. "Earl was one of the kindest men I knew," I said simply. "My brother Eric got into a jam when he was an undergraduate here. Some kid accused him of cheating on a test, and it turned into a racial thing. We found out that this kid had falsely accused some other black students of violations of the honor code, and it got really messy for a while. For some reason, Earl decided to help Eric out, to the point where he had Eric living in his house for a little while to give him a quiet place to study. I was at Harvard doing graduate course work, so my parents asked me to come down and thank him in person for what he did for our family. And ever since, Earl has just been there for me. If I needed advice, or a recommendation, he would do it. No questions asked. I have no idea why, actually. I mean, the irony is that in some ways I didn't even know him all that well."

"Excuse me, madame." The waiter was back. "Would you care to order now?"

"Green salad to start, and then the Dover sole. With the beurre blanc, Jeffrey—you know how I like it done."

*Atkins diet,* I thought. Or maybe the South Beach. No surprise.

Zanda smiled apologetically. "I haven't even given you time to look at the menu."

"Don't worry—I've got the gist of it. I'll have a green salad, too, and the grilled tuna. Medium rare." As the waiter departed, I glanced over with a conspiratorial grin. "I'm trusting you on the fish thing. Usually these Ivy League places can't be trusted to do anything other than prime rib or a hamburger. But you've clearly eaten here before."

She smiled back, surprised. "Yes, well, that's true. I've worked long and hard with them on how one prepares seafood properly. We'll see how they do tonight." She took a sip of wine. "What did you mean when you said you didn't know Earl well? I thought you were his protégée."

"I guess I was." It felt odd acknowledging that status. "But it's becoming clear to me that I really only knew him professionally. Like I knew he was married, but I just met his wife for the first time yesterday. And I had no idea that he had a son."

A shadow passed over her face. "Yes, Yusef."

"What's that all about? Why didn't Earl ever talk about him?"

"Typical father-son issues, I think. Yusef is their only child, and he has this sense that he has to prove something to the world. That he's more than Earl's son. It's ironic that they're in the same profession."

"What?"

"Yes, Yusef is a professor of African-American studies. At the University of Chicago."

"How come I've never heard of him?" I asked, incredulously.

"He uses a different last name. Jones. It's all part of their rift."

"Wow," I said slowly. "I had no idea."

"Earl's life was . . . complicated," Zanda said.

"In what way?"

"Well, take his wife. It was a real problem for him that she was never around to support him socially. She hates almost everything about Princeton, and she has always refused to attend a lot of the functions that he needed to be seen at."

"Well, it doesn't seem to have hurt him," I replied. "Look at how successful he was."

She smiled slightly. "I'll take a bit of the credit for that. I walked him around a fair amount in the early days." She laughed aloud at the expression on my face. "Oh, I know what you're thinking. What's a white lady socialite doing escorting a black Afro-Am professor around town?"

"It's not the typical arrangement," I murmured. "Unless you're trying to stick it to your ex-husband."

"You've been doing your homework!" Zanda exclaimed.

"I'm sorry—I shouldn't have said that. I'm just wiped out—I haven't slept—" I stammered.

"No, no, no apologies." Zanda leaned back in her chair and took another sip of wine. Then she smiled appreciatively at me. "I like people who take the time to figure out who they're dealing with." For the first time, I felt that I had her full attention. "No, I wasn't doing it to stick it to Hayden. That was just a nice added benefit. No, I did it because Earl was fabulous company. I met him at a cocktail party, and he had me in stitches dishing about the people there. He was so much fun that I considered it a favor to me, not vice versa. My partner hates to go out, so it worked well for all of us."

There it was again. That awkward phrase, *my partner*. I thought she'd meant her business partner. Now I wasn't so sure.

Zanda sighed, and I looked up to see her dabbing at her eyes. "I can't believe I'm getting all weepy. Sorry. I'm no good with death."

I shook my head in sympathy. "Well, who is?"

"Christ, it just reminds me of—" She stopped abruptly and cleared her throat.

"Have you lost someone recently?" I asked softly.

"No. *No.* Not recently at all. I keep thinking about a miscarriage that I had a few years ago. I hadn't thought about it in months until tonight." She looked up with a wry smile. "And I have no idea why I am telling *you* this."

"It's a tough night," I said quietly. We both drank silently. At that moment, I was truly grateful for the plush, tradition-laden surroundings, cocooning us, however falsely, from the harshness of life outside the large oak doors of Prospect House.

It was after the waiters had cleared the salad plates that I played my best card with Zanda. "You see, the real problem is that if Eula and Yusef won't get out there and talk about what Earl accomplished in his life, then Butch Hubbard will make it look like Earl was just a second-string player in his academic field. He'll make it look like Earl was just about to hit the major leagues by moving to Harvard, but that he never made it. And Princeton will have lost its last bit of cachet in this field of study."

Zanda inhaled sharply, and I followed her gaze to the footpath below. I wasn't sure at first, but as a figure approached along the path, I realized that it was him. Butch Hubbard was still in town, making his way very hurriedly across the Princeton campus. He was wearing a long camel-hair coat and a plaid Burberry scarf. His hands were buried deep in his pockets, and I could see streaks of silver in his curly black hair as he crossed before us. Because of the way the shadows fell, I hadn't noticed

until he was right in front of us that he had a companion. Lloyd Eastman was barreling along beside him, gesticulating broadly. Perhaps the
most curious part was that they were walking against the flow of traffic.
Most of the pedestrians below, throughout our entire meal, had been
students heading toward Prospect Street, presumably to have a late dinner or catch a party at one of the eating clubs. Hubbard and Eastman
were going deeper into the campus. Butch clearly wasn't heading home
just yet.

"Why is he still here?" I muttered under my breath.

Zanda's eyes began to glimmer as she watched the pair disappear
from view. "I don't know. But you may be right, Nikki. It's probably
time that we found out."


**Midnight found me** standing alone beside the pile of burned rubble
that was to have been the new Princeton Center for African-American
Studies. Police tape encircled the site, but to my surprise, it was not attracting any curious bystanders. Quite the contrary. Perhaps it was due
to the cold, but no one was stopping at all. Behind the rubble, a halogen
glow illuminated the E-Quad, Princeton's engineering campus. A trail of
sneaker prints in the snow led off in that direction, and as I watched, a
trio of bespectacled boys followed it, presumably off to a late-night review session in one of the classrooms there. Across the street, music
pumped out of the partially opened windows of Charter Club, an oversize Georgian house, and Cloister, which Eric always said was more low-
key than the other eating clubs. That night, it was holding its own on the
decibel level. Life was continuing with gusto all over campus. And I was
too tired to object.

A hollow numbness had settled over me on the walk from Prospect
House. I stood motionless for a period that felt simultaneously like
several hours and mere seconds, breathing in the stench of burned wet
wood and staring at the ashes, and the police tape, and the end of
Earl's life.

I couldn't remember the last thing that he'd said to me. The lack of a tangible memory of his final words had become a kind of dull repetitive ache in my chest over the course of the past couple of hours. I kept mentally circling back to this particular pain and probing it, the way I used to run my tongue over a sore tooth when I was a child. As if by feeling that tiny grief over and over, I could put off the larger one that was waiting to engulf me. I knew it was irrational to keep focusing on that one thing. But I couldn't stop trying to remember. There had been so many things that he had said that I would never forget: "Turn your thoughts into actions," and "Keep it real," and most of all, "Stay strong." His death had come too fast and it was too final and I wasn't ready and I wanted so badly to just have one more chance to see him. To thank him for everything he had done for me. To ask him for some final words of wisdom. To hear him say that as he was dying he wasn't lonely or afraid. I felt the hot rush of tears coming and resolutely blinked them away. Earl would have hated the maudlin sight of me sobbing at the scene of his death. The least that I owed him was dry eyes and some dignity.

A year—even six months—before, I'd had no real conception of death. Up until three months before Earl's passing, I had been to a total of three funerals in my entire life: those of two grandparents and a high school classmate who had taken a wrong turn off an overpass on the Jeffries Freeway four months before our graduation. At all three, the grief I felt was shamefully perfunctory. The two grandparents had died when I was too young to have really known them, and the classmate was an acquaintance, not a friend. So having not known the deceased particularly well, I felt a mixture of pity for those who had loved them and a selfish relief that I was just an observer of the mourning. I thought that I had decades before anyone I loved dearly would die.

But suddenly, in the short span between autumn and winter, three people had died around me. And each time, I had known the deceased better and better. It felt like death was advancing on me, circling closer, successively striking at someone more dear. My Harvard MBA and two years on Wall Street had trained me to wheedle, cajole, persuade, and bully my way into getting what I wanted from life. They had in no way prepared me for the irrevocability of death. At different points in my life, I have been convinced that there are only two kinds of people in the world. At one point, I thought it was blacks and whites; then I thought it was men and women; later I became convinced that it was Democrats and Republicans. But now I know that there really are only two kinds of people in the world: those who have experienced a permanent personal loss, and those who haven't.

Which brought me back to Earl.

Why on earth had he decided to come here at such a late hour of the night? I pondered the thought as I slowly walked the perimeter of the construction site. The light gleamed off something metal wedged into the soil, and idly, I picked it up: a gold cufflink with a tiger's head. What was Earl thinking as he stood here? I wondered as I slipped the bauble into my coat pocket. Was he bursting with pride after an evening of praise for his department, and dreaming about an even brighter future at Princeton? Or was he saying goodbye to this place, and making plans for a new life at Harvard? *Why didn't you bring someone with you? Why didn't you ask me? Why didn't I stay at that stupid party?*

"I beg your pardon, miss?"

I looked up to find a young blond policeman standing before me.

"I didn't say anything," I said, startled.

"I heard you say, 'Why didn't I stay?' " He glanced around briefly. "Who were you speaking with?"

"I'm sorry," I said wearily. "I was just talking to myself. I'm sorry."

"It's late. You should probably head home, miss," the officer said.

*Yes,* I thought. If home were closer, I would most certainly head there.

Instead, I headed for Eric's room. Not to sleep—there was no chance of that, given how I was feeling. But as I walked, I remembered that there was one thing left for me to do that day.

I booted up my computer and again faced my e-mail box. By now, there were 347 unread messages. At that moment, I was interested in only one of them.

Matthew had said that there was e-mail from him, somewhere in this mess of reminders about meetings, student inquiries, and nagging one-line missives from Carl Irvin. There had been no interaction between us for exactly two weeks. But now, somewhere in here, there was a message from Dante Rosario. And at that moment, I wanted nothing more than to receive it.

It was well buried, but I found it—just below a notice from Amazon.com about a new biography of John Maynard Keynes. It had come in on Friday, just after I'd left Cambridge. I double-clicked, and stopped breathing.

This is what the message said:

> To: Crimson Future Committee Members
> From: D. Rosario
>
> Just a reminder: the next meeting of the Crimson Future Committee will take place on Wednesday, December 12th at 10:00 a.m. in the Faculty Club, Room 10. President Townsend will brief the group on his vision for the future work of the committee.
>
> RSVP regrets only to Angela at 5-5456.

I read the words, and then I heard the sound, as clearly as if it had been whispered in my ear. *Wpht,* it went. Like the sound of a candle being extinguished.

It was the sound of my idiotic hope of reconciling with Dante Rosario being snuffed out.

After a long pause, I turned to e-mail number 346 and began to read.

# 7

## Never Too Early

"**B**eautiful lady, how can I help you?"

The singsong voice interrupted my reverie as I stared at the breakfast selections in the glass case at Panera Bread on Nassau Street at 6:00 A.M. on Sunday. I had decided to hit the street after four hours of restless sleep on the loveseat in Eric's dorm. I'd left Jess tangled in a pile of blankets on the sofa. Eric was AWOL again, presumably at Kayla's. Since he wasn't using his bed anyway, I wasn't clear on why we had to sleep on the living room furniture, but whatever. I'd left his room in a fugue state, feeling half dead and hoping that coffee would resurrect me. At the sound of the voice, I looked up and refocused my gaze, and a brilliant smile came into view. It belonged to a lithe young black man behind the counter.

"I'm sorry, what?" I said, distractedly.

"I said, 'Beautiful lady, how can I help you?' " the counterman said, more loudly this time. I suppressed a smile as he grinned at me. There was no question that I was at least ten years older than him—*way* too old for him to bother with me. The fact that he was doing it anyway, and at that hour of the morning, made me immediately fond of him. After all, it's never too early to flirt. And for that matter, never too late.

"Well, what do you recommend?" I said, meeting his eyes and

71

returning the grin. "I've got it narrowed down to either a pumpkin muffin or a blueberry one."

A conspiratorial smile flickered across his face. "Try the blueberry." He lowered his voice. "That pumpkin one has been in there since Thanksgiving."

"Sold. That and a large coffee with milk. Are you Ghanaian?" I asked as he retrieved the muffin and put it in a white paper bag. His voice and features marked him as an African, and now I was trying to place his country of origin. "My college roommate was born in Accra."

"No," he said. "Côte d'Ivoire. The Ivory Coast."

"Okay, so I was close."

"Yes, you were. I'm Jide," he said, pronouncing it "Gee-day."

"Nice to meet you, Jide. I'm Nikki," I replied. "Oh, and don't forget this," I reminded him, gesturing to the newspaper tucked under my arm. I had taken a copy of the *Trentonian* from a large stack at the front of the store.

"The paper is full of stories about that professor man who died," he commented as I passed him a five-dollar bill. "He was just in here a couple of nights ago. It's too bad. He was a nice man."

"Yes, he was," I responded automatically. It took almost thirty seconds before what he had said sank in. "Did you say he was here two nights ago? You mean Friday night?"

Jide leaned against the counter and nodded after a brief pause. "Yes. It was Friday. I work the overnights, and I remember he was here. All dressed up and talking about some party he had just been at."

"Was he alone?"

He nodded. "He said he had spent the night at a party full of beautiful women, and yet here he was, all by himself."

My heart turned over, thinking about it. Earl must have stopped in for a snack or a cup of coffee on his way to the construction site. I wondered if this was a regular stop for him.

"Was he in here often?" I asked, setting my breakfast back on the counter.

"Sure, he came in all the time."

"Did he say anything else that night?" I asked casually, not wanting to overplay my hand. "About where he was going after he left here?"

"I'm sorry, miss lady," said Jide, flashing his wide smile again. "All we talked about was football, you know, what you Americans call soccer." He hustled behind the counter to get a coffee for a tall, thin man who'd come in quietly after me. "It's almost time for the World Cup Trials, and all Africans, even the expatriates, are watching."

I hadn't known Earl Stokes to be a fan of soccer. Apparently, there were many things I hadn't known about him.

I thanked Jide for his help and settled in at a small, Formica-topped corner table with my coffee, muffin, and the *Trentonian,* whose lead story featured an unflattering head shot of Earl superimposed on a grainy rendition of the charred building site. The article, by staff reporter Beatrice Maxwell, described Earl Stokes's death as "a tragic accident," quoting several unnamed police sources who speculated that Earl may have been paying an early-morning visit to the site and accidentally set off the blaze that killed him. How and why this might have happened was glossed over in favor of more cursory summaries of the highlights of Earl's career. At least there were no additional quotes or commentaries from Butch Hubbard; apparently Beatrice Maxwell and the *Trentonian* lacked access to those at the top of the media food chain.

One quote toward the bottom of the article almost made me gag on my muffin. It was from Bo Merriweather, editor of the conservative campus newspaper the *National Prospect:* "Despite the tragedy of Professor Stokes's death, it must be pointed out that Princeton has no compelling need for a Program in African-American Studies, let alone an expensive new building to house it. A profound misappropriation of funds has now been derailed."

I remembered Eula Stokes's observation at the party that the conservatives at Princeton are like no others on the planet, and I heard myself emit a strangled laugh. Jide looked my way, a quizzical expression on his face.

The irony was that the one thing Earl had in common with Bo Merriweather was what I'd call an essentially conservative nature: but whereas Merriweather was a reactionary, Earl was simply a stand-up guy who believed in old-fashioned virtues such as loyalty. In his habits he was methodical and meticulous, and I found it hard to conjecture a scenario in which he'd accidentally start a fire, even in the wee hours after a party at which I'd seen him drink only a single glass of champagne. The construction of the Center for African-American Studies was to be the culmination of all that he'd accomplished at Princeton: how could he possibly put that in jeopardy?

But that left only one other scenario, and I wasn't ready to go there yet. Because if this wasn't an accident, then I'd be back in the middle of a maelstrom. And I was going to need a lot more than coffee, a muffin, and a cute counterman to steel me for that.


"When you comin' home, child?" Rafe Griffin asked when he heard my voice on the phone. I'd found a quiet corner in the spacious lobby of the Nassau Inn and dialed Cambridge on my cell phone so that I wouldn't disturb Jess in Eric's dorm room. I was curled up in a plush crimson armchair, my back to the wall and no one else in sight save the lone hotel receptionist.

"Maggie's missing you," Rafe said. "And so am I. She's planning this Christmas party, and I sure wish you were here. 'Cause it's turning into a full-time job helping this woman out with this thing!" He laughed heartily. "This whole weekend, she had me scrubbin' pots and ironin' linens and diggin' out ornaments. I mean, when am I supposed to do my Christmas shoppin'?" A Sergeant Detective on the Harvard police force, Raphael Griffin is a fifty-something blend of old-school West Indian charm and hard-nosed common sense. In the four months since we'd met in September, he'd started a romance with my landlady, Maggie Dailey. And he'd become my sounding board and friend. If anyone would know whether Earl's death seemed suspicious, it was Rafe.

I laughed sympathetically. Having been through it many times, I knew what an ordeal party preparations were when Maggie was involved. That was certainly one reason to stay in Princeton a little longer. "I'm sorry to call you so early in the morning. And I miss you all, too. But I won't be back for a little while. At least a few days. They haven't set the date for the funeral yet, but I'm sure it will be here, and I need to stay for that. And there are some things that I may need to look into."

Rafe was suddenly serious. "I don't know if I like the sound of that."

"Well, I have kind of a bad feeling about what's going on down here. I need you to tell me what you think about this." Rafe was silent as I filled him in on the things I had seen in the past twenty-four hours. The basics of Earl Stokes's death had already been all over the news in Cambridge, spiced with local speculation regarding the "poaching" from Princeton. According to *The Boston Globe,* President Townsend would only confirm that he had talked with the widely admired Professor Stokes, and that the discussion had been ongoing at the time of his untimely death and was obviously confidential in nature.

By the time I had detailed Butch Hubbard's grandstanding and his nocturnal walk around the campus; Bo Merriweather's diatribes; and Pastor Creflo Smalls's insinuating attitude toward Eula Stokes's late husband, not to mention his longstanding enmity toward Bo Merriweather and his conservative cronies, Rafe had heard enough.

"Child, get back here on the next thing smokin'," he said, gently but firmly. "You got courses to teach, and other fish to fry. Leave this mess to the locals."

"But Rafe—could it be murder? The papers and everyone are saying that it was an accident, but with everything going on down here, don't you think it could be something more?"

There was a pregnant pause, after which he replied, "Haven't I taught you anythin' ?"

"I know—the chances of it being a crime are almost nil. And even if it is, I should leave it to the professionals. But if someone did this deliberately, I can't just walk away from it, Rafe. You know that."

"What I know is that if someone did this deliberately, they are watchin' you right now. If they're smart enough to kill a Princeton professor, they are sure smart enough to know that you're the type who'll start messing around in this. You better think about that."

"I know how to take care of myself, Rafe."

"You know the wisest thing my daddy ever said to me? Don't confuse having been lucky with bein' smart."

"Touché!" I laughed wryly. "My amateur status in the field of detection has never been in question. But seriously, Rafe—what if this was murder? I mean, there are plenty of people around here who seem to have a motive. Don't you think I could help in some way?"

"You know, you sound like you're *hopin'* that it was murder, child." Rafe's voice was suddenly gentle. "Now, why would that be?"

The question stopped me cold. And it slowly dawned on me that he was right. I *was* hoping that Earl's death was deliberate. Because a murder investigation would give me something to do with all the helpless, restless sadness inside of me.

"He was such a good man, Rafe," I said softly. "It's just not right that he's gone. It's so hard for black people to make it in this world, there are so few role models and people to look up to, and now another one is gone. It's just not right."

"You need to come home, Nikki," he said quietly. "When can you get yourself here?"

The warmth of his concern was like a physical presence, flowing through the phone line and wrapping me in a tight embrace. We stayed that way, in silent companionship, for a long moment. Then I reluctantly broke the spell.

"I told you—I can't come back for a few days. I really do have to stay and see this through. So what do you think I should do while I'm here?"

"Child, you're gonna do what you're gonna do no matter what I say. Just be careful. You're down there by yourself, and I'm not gonna be able to help you if you stir something up."

"Look, it's like you said. There's probably nothing to it, anyway. I mean, the cops haven't called me since they told me about Earl's death, and no one around here seems to think it was anything but an accident. You tell Maggie that I miss her. And I that I'll be home in time for that party of hers."

I hung up with Rafe's last words of advice echoing in my ear. "Just remember, Nikki. A cat's only got nine lives, and you've used up a couple of yours, now, already."

# 8
## The Amen Corner

It's hard to find a neighborhood in Princeton that you can honestly call the other side of the tracks, but the lower Witherspoon area just four blocks north of campus probably qualifies as the next best thing, in that it is everything that the rest of the affluent, white, austere town is not. While lacking in glamour and high-end retail, the area felt warm, safe, and genuine to me—populated with the kind of folks I grew up with.

Creflo Smalls's ministry was housed on a small unnamed alleyway off Witherspoon in a small white clapboard building, which from a distance wouldn't have been out of place in a sleepy southern town. But when you drew near, it was clear you had entered the realm of a man who knew how to unite spirituality and commerce. In the shadow of the steeple, the large parking lot was full of late-model cars and SUVs. Two long white charter buses with "Beulah Baptist Praises the Lord" written on the side were parked at the back. An awkwardly proportioned concrete addition at the back of the church expanded the size of the building by at least a third.

It was Sunday morning, and as I'd planned to go to church somewhere in Princeton anyway, I'd decided to combine worship with a little detective work by visiting Reverend Smalls's parish. I felt certain that I'd be forgiven for mixing the two if it did turn out that something hadn't been right between the minister and Earl Stokes.

A smiling woman in a white suit and a white hat with a veil shook my hand warmly on the porch and gestured me onward, into the church. I stepped past small clusters of elderly women, also in hats, who were murmuring happily about how well the Christmas wreath sale had gone the prior day. Once fully inside, I could see that there were announcements on the bulletin board in the entry foyer for a bingo night, a say-no-to-drugs support group, a church-sponsored bus trip to Atlantic City for seniors, and a voter registration drive. It made the Episcopalian church I attend back in Cambridge look positively slothful by comparison.

I followed the general flow of traffic down the hall, stopping to read a couple of the announcements to the congregation posted on the walls. At the entrance to the sanctuary, I passed two large plastic palm trees in shiny gold planters. A deep-pile carpet led me through large wooden double doors toward the pews. Both the carpet and the pew cushions were a shade of red so bright that I had to blink a couple of times to stay focused on the altar straight ahead. Just before the altar were several ornate wooden chairs; the one in the middle was substantially larger than the rest, and embossed in large gold letters were the words "Dr. Creflo Smalls." Hanging from the ceiling were various brightly colored felt banners, reading "Give," "Tithe," and "Offering."

That morning there was already barely a seat to be had in the rows packed predominantly with well-groomed children and middle-aged and elderly black women in broad-brimmed hats. To my surprise, Eula Stokes was prominent among them in the front row. She was dressed in a black wool suit that was much more flattering and dignified than the housedress she had worn to Earl's party at Princeton. From my vantage point twelve rows behind her, it actually looked as though she was beaming up at Reverend Smalls in a manner that could only be called adoring. She certainly didn't look like a woman in the first stages of mourning for the loss of her husband.

"Excuse me, ma'am," a high-pitched voice said. I turned to find a handsome little boy, who appeared to be about five years old, standing in the aisle beside me. A young woman who must have been his mother smiled at me and then looked down at him. "What do you say, Tyrone?" she asked firmly.

"I did say it!" Tyrone protested adamantly. "I said, 'Excuse me, ma'am.'"

I smiled at his mother. "He did say it," I said. "He was very polite. Here, please, let me slide down."

I moved farther into the pew, and Tyrone and his mother sat down on the aisle. It was a couple of minutes before 11:00 A.M., and there wasn't an empty seat anywhere in the church. We were seated so closely that it was impossible not to make eye contact with the other parishioners. In each face, I saw friendliness and welcome. Perhaps my skepticism about Smalls and his church was misplaced. These people reminded me of the ones I'd seen every childhood summer when I visited my grandmother down South. Good-hearted church folk, who were what my father called the salt of the earth.

Promptly at 11:00, a full-throated gospel choir filled the Beulah Baptist Church to the rafters with beautifully modulated harmonies. I watched Eula's face as they sang, and saw her close her eyes tightly as the chorus swelled. It was impossible to know what she was thinking.

The service progressed through hymns, scripture readings, and two rounds of offerings—one for the foreign missionaries and one for the Beulah general fund. Visitors were welcomed with singing and handshakes, and urged to stay for refreshments after the service. I had the feeling that even in December, they'd be serving really delicious sweet iced tea, like my grandmother used to make.

About an hour into the service, Reverend Creflo Smalls left his center chair and mounted the pulpit to begin his sermon. He put on his glasses and looked out at us.

"Praise the Lord, brothers and sisters!"

"Yes," some members responded.

"I said *praise* the Lord," he repeated.

"Yes," came the response, a little louder this time.

"Now, brothers and sisters, I *know* you can do better than that," he exhorted. "So let me say it again. *Praise!*"

"*Yes!*" came the response, and this time, I could feel a current run through the room. The congregation was engaged now, and it was as if an engine was starting to hum.

"Now this morning, brothers and sisters, we have to go deep. I say, we have to go *deep* inside and find all the—all the *greed,* and all the *self-ishness,* all the *meanness* in our hearts, all the greed and all the selfishness and all the meanness in our minds, and we have to push it out!"

A woman in the row in front of me called out, "Yes!"

"That's right, my sister. We'll not have greed in our *minds,* not have greed in our *hearts.* We are *opening* up our hearts."

"Opening up our hearts," came the response.

"And we are *opening* up our minds," Smalls declared.

"Amen," someone shouted.

"These are dark times," the reverend called out. "*Dark* times. Evil is loose in the world, and our spirits feel oppressed, they feel downtrodden, they feel—they feel *dis*pirited. In times like these, we want to close down, to hold back, to take back. But I say, no! I say we must *open* our hearts."

The congregation was abuzz now, with amens and responses, hands beginning to be outstretched. Despite my proper high-church upbringing, I found myself wanting to join in. That's how good a speaker he was. These *were* dark times. And I did need some light. I closed my eyes and listened to the ancient rhythms of the sermon.

"Do you want to be free?" he challenged.

"Yes!" the congregation responded.

"Are you ready to be free?" he demanded.

"Yes!" came the response. I found myself whispering it under my breath. *Yes.*

"To be free, we must be open," the reverend declared.

"*Open,*" came the response from a man with a baritone voice. "Yes, open."

"Then open up your hearts, my brothers and sisters. Yes, we are opening up our hearts. Opening up our minds. And people, we are opening up our pockets. Giving everything we have."

My eyes flew open. Several people had stood and were beginning to sway with their hands outstretched. Reverend Smalls was bathed in sweat, his red and gold robe swaying in time with his congregation. The organ began to play a hymn as he cried out, "That's right, my people. Opening our hearts, our minds, and our pockets. Giving everything we have."

Several men in dark suits began to move through the sanctuary with wicker baskets outstretched. I saw several women reach for their purses and begin to put bills in the baskets. Others began to clap in time as the minister reached a crescendo. "Open hearts!" he exhorted. "Open minds! Open pockets, holding nothing back."

By my estimate, the collection must have totaled thousands of dollars in cash that morning. I saw people putting several $20 bills in the baskets. And I wondered, heaven forgive me, exactly where all that cash was going.

At the conclusion of the service, Reverend Smalls headed for the back of the church to greet the congregation as they exited, and when I finally made it to the head of the line, I extended a hand to greet him.

"Grace and peace, sister," he said, smiling unctuously. "This must be your first visit to Beulah. I don't recall seeing you here before."

"Good morning, Reverend," I said. "This is my first visit. I'm Professor Nikki Chase. We spoke on the phone yesterday. Earl Stokes was one of my academic mentors."

The reverend's eyes narrowed slightly, then strayed over my shoulder to the woman after me in line; clearly, he was ready to move on.

But I wasn't ready to be moved. "I'm just glad to see Mrs. Stokes out and about so soon after her husband's death. She seems to be taking refuge in the welcoming arms of the church."

"Praise Jesus for the spirit of Sister Stokes," he said sharply. "Leave her alone. She is sick in her soul that her husband is no longer here to sing God's praises with us. Who are you to question her?"

"I'm just a friend of Earl's, concerned that his memory be preserved the right way, and that justice be served," I said softly. "I just wanted to talk with Mrs. Stokes yesterday. To express my sympathy."

"She's had enough of Earl's *friends*." He spit out the words as though they were curses, and waved me away with an extended arm. "Sister Stokes doesn't need to hear from her husband's former associates right now. This is my church, and under its roof I will not tolerate anyone stirring up more demons for this woman to cope with. I'd kill for her, as I would for any of my flock. Now good day, sister."

I could feel the woman in line behind me bristling at his harsh tone, and I knew that my visit to Beulah Baptist today would yield no answers. As far as Creflo Smalls was concerned, I was either a vixen or one step away from being in cahoots with the likes of Bo Merriweather: neither was a welcome prospect. And as far as I was concerned, he was either an overly protective but sincere minister. Or a truly bad man who was taking money from good people who were trying to do the right thing. I turned sharply on my best black go-to-church heels and headed out into the blessedly crisp winter sun. It was shining down on all God's children—but it shed no light on what was really going on at the Beulah Baptist Church.

"At the end of the second quarter, Pittsburgh is still scoreless," the announcer intoned.

"You're gonna owe me big, Ricky," Jess teased. "I told you, you'll never get rich backing the Steelers, babe."

"Oh, this from the woman who picked the Oilers over the Pats last weekend. Gimme a break," Eric retorted.

"Pats, Oilers, as long as they have nice butts, who cares?" I declared.

"Oh, man," Eric groaned. "Give him the ball and let him run! You're losing anyway—let the rookie have the ball!"

"Halftime," Jess announced. "Got to pack." She uncurled herself from the battered loveseat pillow.

It was Sunday afternoon, and back in Eric's room, we were on our second football game and our second six-pack of Heinekens. I'd lost count of how many jars of honey-roasted peanuts and bags of Pirate's Booty littered the floor.

"No!" I protested. "You can't leave. Not yet." I felt my spirits flagging as Jess retrieved her chic leather suitcase from Eric's closet. Meanwhile, Eric was conspicuously silent. I guess I could understand that. We'd pretty much taken over my brother's living room for the weekend, and despite his warm hospitality, I knew he wouldn't mind reclaiming his digs. Even though he seemed to have suddenly taken up residence with Kayla, anyway. Until the first game started that afternoon, I hadn't seen him in his room for more than half an hour since we arrived.

"You're deserting me," I pouted. "Leaving me alone to cope with the forces of right-wing conservatism, hustling preachers, and mediocre preppy fashion."

"Hey," Eric protested. "I'm taking that personally!"

Jess looked at me with her large brown eyes and laughed. "I'll miss you big-time on that long ride home, girl. Seven hours, and no one to talk to." A fourth-year resident in obstetrics and gynecology at Massachusetts General Hospital, Jess had to be back by tomorrow morning to make her rounds.

"I'd join you in a New York minute if I could," I told her. "You know that."

"You know how I know it's time for me to go home?" said Jess as she packed up her toiletries from a shelf in the bathroom. "Because this football game is getting me seriously randy. I mean, that quarterback's muscles are really *talking* to me. How pathetic is that?" For the journey back to Cambridge, she was dressed in a dark burgundy knitted minidress and short black suede ankle boots and, for the record, did not look pathetic at all.

I collapsed back onto Eric's couch, which was upholstered in a rec-room plaid that had gone out of fashion twenty years before. "I hear you, darlin'. I just have to face it," I said with a sigh. "This football game is as close as I am getting to a man for the foreseeable future."

"Well," she said brightly, "look at it this way. We won't have that awkward dilemma about what gifts to get our boyfriends for the holidays this year!"

"Man, talk about a silk purse from a sow's ear . . . only you could come up with that one." I reached for a pack of cigarettes. "The difference is that you'll be back with Ted before I get back to Cambridge, and I'll be out there on my own."

Jess shook her head adamantly.

"Fifty bucks," Eric interjected. "Fifty says you're back with Ted by next weekend. Ernst said that you wouldn't shut up about him."

"You're on," Jess laughed. "And I'll put some money down on Nikki and Dante. I'm thinking that they're under the mistletoe by Christmas Eve."

"Are you kidding?" I exclaimed. "We haven't *spoken* for two weeks."

"I didn't say you'd be talking to each other." She smiled mischievously. "I just said you'd be under the mistletoe."

"Give me a little credit, will you? I am not *that* weak."

"Yeah, right. When are you coming back to Cambridge?" she called over her shoulder as she headed back to the closet.

"I'll be down here until the funeral on Wednesday," I replied, "plus there's Earl's class tomorrow. I promised him I'd teach it with him, so I'll do it solo in his memory. The funny thing is that he gave me the folder that was supposed to contain the syllabus when I saw him in his office Friday, but when I opened it, it was full of some other papers instead."

Jess looked up at me from the front door of Eric's room, where she had positioned her suitcase. "So do you really think the fire that killed Earl was an accident?"

"I don't know," I admitted reluctantly. "I talked to Rafe, and he thinks that I'm just looking for trouble. I went to Smalls's church today, and to be honest, I think he could be straight up. It's hard to know. Then there's Bo Merriweather, but the guy is like a cartoon character—it's hard to imagine him actually committing murder. He was skulking around that party like Dick Tracy."

"You think he could be hiding in plain sight?" Jess suggested. "The guy could be crazy like a fox."

"Yeah, I guess it's possible."

"Didn't you say that Earl was working on a book, too, a kind of exposé about this place?"

"That's the rumor."

"The people at the top wouldn't exactly welcome that either, right?" Jess continued. "They find someone to set up the fire and make it look like Earl did it. That way, they get rid of a building, the future of a whole course of study, and a major player who's about to run off to the competition. The threat to the established order is eliminated, at least for the time being."

Sometimes Jess amazes me. She can spin out observations that are spot-on and straighten the crease in her skintight Earl Jeans simultaneously.

Jess threw on her DKNY boiled-wool coat and engulfed me in its wide, soft sleeves. "I'll call you tonight to tell you how many candy bars I ate in order to endure this trip without you, girl. Keep the faith, but watch your back. If these people who set up Earl start seeing you as a player, too, you'll be in what my Jewish grandmother used to call deep shit."

I hugged her back. "Somehow, that doesn't sound Yiddish to me."

My best friend grinned widely. "It's English for the kind of trouble that you can't get out of on your own."

Eric scooped up her suitcase, and they left me alone. Which meant that if I did get into trouble from there on in, I was going to need some new friends.

# The Color of Money

**S**unday dinner was a slice of pepperoni and mushroom pizza, and my companions for the evening were the ghost of Earl Stokes and the specter of Carl Irvin. Though I'd read Earl's best seller *Color Counts* with great admiration when it was first published three years earlier, I wasn't entirely confident that I could fill the author's shoes without some serious last-minute preparations, especially without the syllabus Earl had meant to pass along. When I'd opened the folder that he'd given me, which was supposed to contain his course materials, I'd found instead a sheaf of papers that seemed to have something to do with the construction of the new Center for African-American Studies. So now I had a little over twelve hours to create a lesson plan worthy of Earl. This was in addition to my day job, which required me to spend some time on my AEA paper that evening, too.

I cleared the small tabletop that served as my brother Eric's dining area and lined up not just Eric's dog-eared, notes-in-the-margins copy of *Color Counts* but also the latest draft of the paper I was to present next month at the annual American Economics Association conference in New York City. I had promised my acting department chairman a new version by the next morning, and I had no desire to leave myself open to more e-mail sniping by failing to deliver as promised.

Lining up two icy Diet Cokes for further sustenance, I went first to Earl's widely heralded analysis of the economic infrastructure of America's most forlorn and abandoned urban neighborhoods in the last thirty years. Using my hometown of Detroit along with Philadelphia, Baltimore, and Chicago as his touchstones, he examined how street culture had evolved to echo structurally—if not stylistically—the classic American capitalist hierarchy. Instead of CEOs, you had not only drug kingpins providing capital no bank would supply, but also entrepreneurs of all stripes—barbershop owners, restaurant operators, clothing designers, hip-hop record producers, former athletes—channeling black dollars back into the surrounding neighborhoods with unprecedented success in the late 1980s and well into the '90s.

Though politicians of both parties who advocated government-sponsored "empowerment zones" had embraced Earl's theories, his research suggested that most black business people preferred to go it alone, eschewing the red tape and political kickbacks that such support inevitably entailed. By carving out viable economic enterprises independently, these entrepreneurs avoided the traps into which so many "poverty pimps" fell in the 1960s, when individuals enriched themselves like corrupt third-world potentates, with very little "trickle-down" effect in areas hard hit by the loss of manufacturing jobs to nonunion areas of the South from which their own ancestors had migrated forty years earlier. In every way, color does indeed count, Earl argued, because though green will always be the main color in America, race, politics, and money are inextricably woven into the social fabric.

As I read, and reread, and made copious notes to augment the ones Eric had already scrawled on the margins of the book at his first reading, I knew that this was Earl's real legacy: his low-key but persuasive presentation of facts and data, and the manner in which he marshaled his arguments to connect potentially dry economics with the hard facts of people's lives and means. This was economics that mattered in the most visceral way. I understood now how Earl Stokes could have made enemies in this town. In his own way Earl Stokes had been a true subversive, the kind who seems to fit into any social situation, yet always keeps his eye on his own agenda. Had he gone too far, I wondered idly, chumming it up with the likes of Zanda Fleming? The tensions at the party had been palpable: between Earl and Eula Stokes, Bo Merriweather, and even Earl's son, Yusef. Had Earl made concessions in order to raise the necessary funds for the center? Had he compromised his principles with the wrong people, and been forced to pay the ultimate price?

*Snap out of it,* I admonished myself. Earl's death had been a terrible accident. Inventing a sensational murder investigation inside my head might be a welcome distraction, but that didn't make it a reality. And I had work to do.

I polished off my first soda and scribbled additional notes to alter the paper that I had just presented at the Woodrow Wilson School. For the first time, I realized that there were parallels between the economies of emerging nations in Eastern Europe in the wake of the Cold War's collapse and the neighborhoods in Earl's book. Weren't they emerging economies, too, finally developing self-sufficiency after years on the collective dole? Maybe this trip had a hidden purpose Carl Irvin never could have foreseen; maybe somewhere Earl Stokes was still looking after me, despite the lost syllabus, his hostile widow, and her questionable spiritual protector. I might actually be able to publish this paper somewhere now, by creating a juxtaposition that illuminated both areas of inquiry.

By the time I'd finished revising my AEA paper, it was 2:00 A.M., and I felt as drawn as an undergrad who'd been up all night cramming for a final. The next morning was showtime. I laid my head down on Eric's couch and slept more soundly than I had in weeks. All I could remember when I awakened was a dream about Rafe Griffin's pecan pie, soft, oozing with nuts and cane sugar, topped with whipped cream as white and fluffy as a cloudbank.

**When the phone rang** at the crack of dawn on Monday morning, at first I thought I was still dreaming.

Pamela Thomas-Graham

"Hello?" I croaked. I assumed it was Jess, ready to give me the down and dirty on her trip back to Cambridge the night before.

"Nik," a male voice said softly. It was Dante Rosario. Two weeks too late. I was upright and wide awake in a nanosecond. "Rafe told me that one of your friends died."

"Yes," I replied, my tone as brisk as I could manage at that hour. "A dear friend. A professor here."

"I'm sorry." He paused. "Anything I can do for you? Would it help if I came down?"

"No, that would definitely not help."

"You sure? I'm pretty good in a crisis."

"Really? I've never found that to be the case." I don't think that I fully realized how angry and hurt I was until that moment. "My experience is that you show up when it suits you, and move on when you get bored."

"Is that so?" The hint of amusement in his voice incensed me.

"It would certainly explain why I haven't heard your voice in two weeks."

"Nik, *you* said you wanted space—"

"And *that's* the one time in the ten years that we've known each other that you actually do what I ask?" I heard the shrillness in my own voice, and paused to regroup. "I am totally fine, and I definitely do not need your help, Rosario."

"It's becoming really clear to me what you need, lady," he said, and this time the whisper of laughter in his tone was even more unmistakable. "The problem is, I can't deliver it through the phone."

"Oh, cut it out," I snapped. I'd been heartsick for two weeks, and he was obviously completely unscarred and oblivious. "My brother is here. And the professor's son has been just fantastic. Believe me, I'm getting *everything* I need."

The length of the pause before he responded was truly gratifying. I'd actually managed to score a direct hit. "My mistake, then," he said coldly. The temperature had dropped at least 70 degrees between us in the blink of an eye. "I'll see you, Nikki."

I hung up the phone and stared pensively at the ceiling. I hadn't succumbed to the sound of his voice. I had even declared that I was moving on to another man. So why was it that even though I had won the round, it felt like losing? I swung my feet off the bed and headed for the shower, where presumably no one could hear me scream.

By 8:00 A.M. I was on my way to Fisher Hall. As I approached the Economics Department's office on the main floor of the limestone and red brick structure, I saw the back of a man's head where a secretary would usually sit in the foyer that fronted a series of offices along a hallway lined with portraits of what looked to be Princetonian elders going back generations. Even in a modern building such as this, Princeton was nothing if not tradition-bound.

"I'm Professor Veronica Chase from Harvard," I announced hurriedly, "and I'm going to be teaching Professor Stokes's class at nine-thirty this morning. I need a syllabus, and quickly. The file Earl left me didn't contain the material he intended it to."

When the man's head turned to face me, I saw that he was in fact among the better-looking temp secretaries that I had seen in my day: dark blond hair graying at the temples, strong angular features, and piercing hazel eyes. He had the intelligent aura of a first-rate foreign correspondent, and I guessed that he was in his late forties. His manner was distinctly not subservient.

"Is that so?" he said coolly, looking me up and down with undisguised amusement. "I didn't see any authorization for a guest lecturer."

"Earl authorized it," I said, equally coolly. "I was to teach the class with him, and in his memory I plan to go it alone. Now can you please supply me with that syllabus? I'm in a bit of a hurry." With only an hour and a half to spare before class, I needed to look over the paperwork to make sure my notions gibed with Earl's official plan.

"I would have been the one to authorize any changes in the schedule," said the man, rising from his chair. He was well over six feet tall. "I'm Hayden Fleming, head of the Economics Department." He extended his hand, and I shook it quickly, hoping to mask my embarrassment.

"Nikki Chase," I stammered. "I didn't realize—"

"Obviously not," he said, grinning confidently.

"I didn't meet you at Earl's party," I said, eager to supply an explanation of sorts.

"I tend to avoid forums for potentially dramatic encounters with my ex-wife." His voice was low and steady. "I stayed long enough to pay my respects, but that party was not a place I would choose to linger."

I remembered my brother Eric's observation at the party that Zanda Fleming might have been pressuring Earl to stay at Princeton not only to ensure that a prestigious scholar stayed in place, but also to keep the heat on her ex-husband. Earl would have been the next in line for Fleming's roost in Economics. With another best seller or two, not to mention the successful construction of the Center for African-American Studies, Earl would have been a shoo-in.

"I've seen some of your articles in the *Journal of Modern Economics*," Hayden Fleming continued. "You've done some nice work, Ms. Chase." He frowned slightly. "But you have no authorization to teach Earl's class. I had planned to do it myself, just to get the students through the term. They've had enough to deal with, losing Earl—we all have."

Before I had a chance to respond to his unexpected compliment, we were interrupted by the arrival of a tall, redheaded woman with crisp, no-nonsense carriage.

"This is my secretary, Mary Caruthers," said Hayden Fleming. He paused and then looked straight at me. "Mary, see if you can locate another copy of the syllabus for Earl's course. Professor Chase needs it immediately." Then he disappeared into his office a few steps away.

Taking his instruction to his secretary as implicit approval of my plan to teach Earl's class, I huddled quickly with Mary Caruthers, the kind of woman who probably could have run a department single-handedly if she'd been born forty years later. We ascended the stairs to the main floor.

"Follow me to the copy room," she said conspiratorially. "I'll unearth the syllabus. Anything to get away from the boss—he's been in a foul mood all morning. Bright and early, at seven-thirty or so, I heard him yelling on the phone at someone to beat the band." She glanced at me. "So you're going to teach Professor Stokes's class. That's nice. We are all going to miss him. He was so much fun to talk to. A lovely man."

True to my impression of her, Mary was blindingly efficient. In short order, with syllabus in hand, I was headed down the hall to the room where Earl's class was to convene an hour later. Supplied by Mary with a large cup of burned-tasting coffee and a rather stale jelly doughnut, I settled in for quick review. Thirty minutes or so of steady progress was interrupted by the arrival of a young woman in her early twenties in an oversize man's tweed coat. Her blond ponytail trailed out from the back of her black knit watch cap like the tail of an animal. Something about her was familiar, but I couldn't place her.

She approached the long wooden table where I was working and said bluntly, "I haven't seen you since you were laying into a pile of blueberry pancakes."

P.J.'s coffee shop—she'd been our waitress there. I remembered the sharp blue eyes and the casually insouciant manner, hardly typical of a diner waitress. "You're a student here?" I asked, recalling somewhere in the depths of my sleep-deprived mind that she'd told us as much as she teased my brother about the eating clubs on campus.

She extended her hand. "Martha Waterstone—please call me Marti." After hesitating, she asked me: "Wasn't it in P.J.'s that you got the news—about Professor Stokes? I saw the cops approach your table."

"It was. I'm Nikki Chase," I said. "Earl was one of my mentors, and he had asked me to teach this class with him today. I still can't believe he's gone." I smiled at her. "That was my brother Eric, a graduate student here, that you were calling Little Rich Boy."

She reddened. "On weekends it gets so hectic in the restaurant, I go into overdrive. My waitress mode becomes very useful in keeping my mother off my back. She doesn't approve of my working at P.J.'s."

"Why not?" I asked. "Lots of students work part-time while they're in school."

"I dropped out of Princeton after sophomore year and bummed

around Asia and Australia for eighteen months," she explained, taking off her overcoat and folding it over the back of a chair by the window. "My family was horrified." She paused, as if contemplating whether or not to disclose a particularly close-held secret. "I'm a fifth-generation Princetonian. My great-great grandfather was the first Waterstone to go here."

"That's a lot to live up to," I said, noting her dewy skin and prominent cheekbones, as well as her baggy cargo pants and black combat boots. If you were a modeling scout looking for a more raffish variation of the classic blond WASP, Marti Waterstone would fit the bill to perfection. She struck me as the kind of girl who'd buy a cherry-red convertible with part of her inheritance sooner than a tan Volvo, or even a BMW coupe with discreetly tinted windows.

"This town seems to be full of old, old families—maybe even more so than in New England," I continued. "But why the waitress gig? Surely you can't need the money."

"Oh, but I do," she said, reddening an even deeper shade. "Once I quit school, I was cut off by my family. Now that I'm back, my father agreed to foot the bill for the tuition—over my mother's vocal objections—but it's up to me to pay room, board, and books."

"When you're making a small fortune on Wall Street as a trader in the family firm, you can look back at your stint at P.J.'s as a lesson in market economics, micro version," I said lightly.

"My family's in real estate," Marti told me, not visibly offended. "I'm thinking law school, something public-interest-oriented. That's one of the reasons I enrolled in Earl's class: I've read *Color Counts* three times."

"Great," I said, with genuine relief. "Then I'll count on you to talk a lot, and help make everyone forget that I'm a poor substitute for the man himself."

"All you have to do is keep Earl's ideas in the air—he follows the book pretty closely—and watch out for the war of words," Marti warned me.

In short order I understood her point; the second student to arrive was none other than Bo Merriweather, so meticulously groomed that he could have gone directly from class to the set of *The McLaughlin Group*. He seated himself in the front row, center, and took out a sheaf of papers, which he shuffled and rearranged conspicuously.

As he busied himself self-importantly, the rest of the class filed in gradually. They were an eclectic assortment of approximately twenty students, including my brother's girlfriend, Kayla French. She was turned out as precisely as Bo Merriweather—though at the other end of the style spectrum—in a short black knitted jumper and a leopard-skin blouse. She was the only woman in the room wearing heels, and looked more like a buyer for the modern designer department at Saks than a college student. As she sat down directly behind Bo Merriweather, I saw at a glance that this was going to be a challenging assignment, and a very long morning.

What ensued in the next ten minutes was more like a match of the World Wrestling Federation than the rarefied intellectual discussion that these kids' parents were paying good money for.

"Let's begin today with a moment of silence in memory of Earl Stokes," I said soberly.

The vast majority of the students obediently looked down at their laps. The women closed their eyes. But I noted that Bo Merriweather stared defiantly at the front of the room. That should have been enough of a warning to me about how the morning would progress. But it quickly became more obvious.

As I declared the moment of silence to be over, Bo raised his hand. "May I ask a question before we start?" he asked loudly.

I nodded, and he continued. "What exactly qualifies you to teach this course to us, given that you aren't even a member of the Princeton faculty?"

Audible gasps and groans issued from several of Bo's classmates. But having taught at Harvard for four years, I was surprised by absolutely nothing anymore. Marti Waterstone shot Bo a look of utter contempt as I held up my hand to quiet the class. "That's a perfectly legitimate question, Mr. Merriweather. So let me break it down for you. Harvard College, Harvard Business School, two years on Wall Street, and currently teaching in Harvard's Economics Department. Any questions?" I shot him a look that said, *Bring it.*

Kayla French's eyes met mine, and she grinned. Bo exhaled noisily and then shook his head. "Great," I concluded. "No more questions. Now let's talk about *Color Counts.* What's the central premise?"

Kayla raised her hand. "The central premise is that race has a measurable effect on the economic prospects of African-Americans, but that it can be overcome when black people band together in entrepreneurial ventures in their own communities."

"Which is a profoundly flawed premise," Bo Merriweather interjected. "In the American capitalist system, there is no viable correlation between race and economic achievement or the lack of it. In fact, affirmative action and other fraudulently based entitlement programs have done nothing but hold black people back from merit-based achievement in the economic as well as the political arena."

Cries came up from all sides of the classroom at this. "You are totally misrepresenting Professor Stokes's book," a blond woman in the third row called out. Simultaneously, a slender black man declared, "Are you saying that any black person who achieves something *hasn't* done it based on merit?"

"I've had enough!" stated a redhead in the last row. "Professor Chase, you should eject him from this class." The student rose and pointed at Bo. "It's totally clear that this guy enrolled in this class as a spoiler. He has no interest whatsoever in the contents of *Color Counts.* It is disrespectful to Professor Stokes's memory to allow him to trash the book and keep us all from learning from it. I don't know why Professor Stokes put up with it when he was here."

Silence descended in the room, and twenty faces looked at me expectantly.

I leaned against the large wooden desk at the front of the room and crossed my legs. "How many of you want to make a difference in the world once you get out of college?"

The question was met with puzzled frowns and an incipient grin from Marti.

"Because if you want to make a difference in the world, you had better learn right now that this is what you're up against," I continued. It was clear to all that by "this," I meant Bo. "I could ask him to leave. But the truth of the matter is that you *are* learning by having him here. You could sit around agreeing with each other, but that won't get you very far. If you can successfully counter what he's saying, *then* you're ready to take on the world."

There was smiling and nodding from most quarters. "Now, Mr. Merriweather. You were saying something about merit, affirmative action, and economic progress. Give it to us again, this time in English, and let's get to it."

What ensued was a passionate, articulate debate about affirmative action, government economic development programs, the issue of stigma, and the nature of a meritocracy. As the class hit its groove, I could almost feel Earl over my shoulder, encouraging me to make them think, to help them articulate their beliefs, to arm them for the rest of their lives with data and logic about what it meant to be black in America. That was how *I* was going to try to make a difference in the world.

At the conclusion I was still on overdrive, and decided to tackle Bo Merriweather head-on as he reconnoitered with an overweight young woman in a houndstooth jacket, a mirror image of himself. I was coming to the conclusion that he was a harmless blowhard—a classic schoolyard bully who turned tail at the first sign of opposition—but I wanted to get close enough to him to confirm that hypothesis. "May I speak with you a moment?" I asked innocently.

He looked over at me suspiciously. "I'm on my way to American Government, advanced seminar, where we'll get some real history and theory, not this tangential, misguided excuse for economics."

"That's exactly what I want to address," I said, in what I hoped was a smooth segue. "I may not agree with everything you say, but I admire the forthright way in which you present yourself."

"Is that so?" Clearly, he was not convinced.

"I know some people over at Morgan that you might want to talk with as you approach graduation," I told him, referring to one of Wall Street's top investment banking firms.

"Look, Professor Chase, I see what you're trying to do," he said with a condescending sneer. "You did your best today under difficult circumstances, because let's face it—*Color Counts* is a crock. Earl Stokes was coasting on its best-sellerdom, snowing the pseudo-liberals who have friends in high places, both here and at Harvard. If he'd left for Harvard, a lot of people around here would have said 'good riddance.' He was dangerous to America, and even more pernicious to this school and its history."

It was all I could do not to laugh at his braying tone. The hyperbole was coming so fast and furious that it was impossible to take it seriously. Unaware of my amusement, he continued, unrelenting. "I hate to speak ill of the dead, but Princeton is better off without Earl Stokes, and the tell-all he was writing for his own continued advancement and glorification."

Something in his tone set my radar humming. The rhetoric was absolutely poisonous. And why would Bo Merriweather know or care about this book that Earl was supposedly writing? "You seem to feel *very* strongly about all this," I said soberly. "It's almost as if you're taking it personally."

He smiled a Cheshire cat smile. "Oh, but I do. I take the end of that building project as a personal victory. I mean, what's next? The Department of Irish-American Studies—in a pub, maybe? And what about a mini-Tara, for southern students like me? This is one country, Professor Chase, and we can't stand tall and united as leaders of the free world economy with splinter groups staking claims right, left, and center."

Bo's female friend touched his arm, and he turned away from me. "I've got to go. I've got class."

*Not hardly,* I thought as he retreated from view. I had a terrible image of this hateful kid as a successful Republican politician in a few years. All he needed to do was tone it down a little, smile more frequently, and he'd be the darling of the ultraconservative set. All the more reason for me to keep an eye on him. Because I wasn't sure what it was—but there was something personal at stake for him in Earl's book. I was sure of it.

I decided to head back to Hayden Fleming's office to ask Mary Caruthers for access to a phone in a quiet office. I was hoping to call Cambridge and leave a message for my boss. But to my dismay, Carl Irvin was in.

"I see an e-mailed document here from you, Professor Chase," he said, "but what I don't see is a teacher addressing the needs of her students. Your absence on campus today is completely unprofessional."

I explained my need to stay at Princeton until Wednesday to attend Earl's funeral: surely he had seen the coverage of the fire in the Boston papers. I also detailed my substitute teaching stint that morning, and the positive manner in which the paper I had presented at the Woodrow Wilson School had been received. Most importantly, I reminded him that my students had already been told to take the day to work on their term papers: they wouldn't have required my presence, anyway. Temporarily appeased, Irvin signed off after extracting a promise from me to check in with him once I'd returned to Cambridge.

Carl Irvin's icy tone alternated with Bo Merriweather's juvenile taunts in a noxious tape loop in my brain as I descended the steps of Dickinson Hall to Earl's former office. I was hoping to speak with his secretary about the details of his funeral arrangements. It truly seemed like an eternity had passed since I'd seen Earl in his overheated warren of an office in this very spot on Friday afternoon. At a small desk outside his office, a young black woman with gold hoop earrings and three-tone fingernails was checking herself out in a handheld compact. The desk had been empty when I came by the day that Earl died—I guess she'd been out that afternoon.

"You need something?" she asked breezily, taking in my boots and neat wool dress.

"Are you Professor Stokes's assistant?" I'd spoken to Earl's secretary on the phone several times through the years, but had never met her. The voice I remembered from the phone did not match this persona. Somehow, this wasn't the image that I thought Earl would want as his face to the Princeton Economics Department.

"No, I'm a temp," the girl said, warming slightly. "I guess Cheryl took the week off—the shock of the boss dyin' and all . . . " She looked me in the eye. "She's pretty messed up about it."

After getting the funeral arrangements and leaving a message for Cheryl to call me as soon as she returned, I decided to hit the Starbuck's on Nassau Street for a cup of strong coffee. The swill that the Economics Department had provided that morning had left me craving quality caffeine. Anticipating the wonderful aroma of a good cup of joe, I hurriedly pushed though the doorway of the main entrance to Dickinson Hall and found myself practically in the arms of Earl's son, Yusef. Hastily, I took a step back and regarded all six feet, four inches of him. He was wearing a conical fur hat atop his dreadlocks that accentuated his height and regal bearing.

"Well, well, it's the party girl," he said, smiling down at me.

"It's Nikki," I stammered, suddenly self-conscious. Maybe it was because I'd just thrown him in Dante's face. But I was suddenly very aware of how handsome he was. "Party girl would definitely be an overstatement."

"Shoot, I'm sorry to hear *that,*" he replied.

"I'm sorry to hear about your father," I said soberly.

In an instant, the flirtatious grin was gone, replaced by a frown. "Yeah. Thank you."

"I was just at his office getting the arrangements for the funeral. Please let me know if your family needs any help with anything."

He snorted. "I doubt that. My mother will be pulling together some three-hour service at Beulah that will have Earl spinning in his grave."

I looked at him, surprised. "The secretary downstairs just told me that the service will be held at the chapel on campus here. Not at your mother's church."

A hurt look passed swiftly over his face and then disappeared. "Well. Shows how much I know. I guess I'd best check in with that secretary myself."

He started to turn away, and I blurted out the first thing that came to mind just to keep him talking to me. "I was just teaching Earl's undergraduate class—or at least, trying to, after the shouting died down. It's a tough crowd; one of them was hell-bent on refuting every last one of his ideas."

"That was Earl," Yusuf replied. "Letting his feet be put to the fire, time after time."

I looked up at him, surprised by his tone. "There's dignity in that."

He laughed, with what I perceived to be a bitter edge. "There's also a futility, and a downright foolishness." He looked at me soberly. "Earl and I agreed on absolutely nothing. I told him he was wasting his time at a place like this, beating his head against a wall of traditions and attitudes as thick as a truckload of oak planks. People around here were never going to treat him right. Just look at where his office was." He gestured back toward Dickinson. "In the basement—in the bowels of the building."

"So I noticed," I told him. "And now the new building that was going to be his legacy is gone."

"Yeah, in that *accidental* fire." Yusef laughed bitterly. "Like we're supposed to believe that."

"You think it was deliberate?"

"Of course it was! That's the whole point. These people aren't going to let black folks get a brand-spanking-new building. That was *never* going to happen. I told him that."

"Well, the cops seem to think it was an accident."

"Right, because you know the upholders of the law in this town investigate the death of black men to the nth degree."

"If you believe that, then what are you going to do about it?" I demanded.

He looked startled, as if it was the first time that he had considered that question.

"I mean, if you really believe that—that your father's death was not an accident, and that race may have had something to do with it—don't you *have* to do something about it?" I goaded.

I felt him really seeing me for the first time. "You're really not a party girl, are you?"

"No, I'm really not," I replied.

"Well, sister, you gave me a challenge. We'll see what I can do with it." He pulled a somewhat tattered piece of paper from his pocket. "In the meantime, I want you to come to my lecture tomorrow."

I unfolded the paper and read that he would be speaking on campus the next day at three. The topic was "The Endangered Black Man: From Lynching to Welfare Widower."

"I set this up before he died so that I'd have something to do while I was in town for that party of his. I was going to cancel it. But I have some things to say."

"I'll be there," I said. "I wouldn't miss it."

I watched him as he disappeared into Dickinson Hall. Then I looked up into the brilliant winter blue sky. "I'm on the case, Earl," I murmured. "If there is something here to find, I just recruited us another pair of arms and legs to help dig it out."

# 10

## A Good Witch

I was beginning to see Eric's well-worn dorm room as a safe haven. It was full of battered furniture and the benign remains of generations of undergraduate lives: of late-night cramming, whispered confidences, friendships formed, then undone by career moves and personal realignments and the settling in that comes with maturity, assuming one's proper place in the world, especially as a graduate of one of the country's most prestigious universities. Sometimes I teased Eric about his status as a graduate student: all he'd ever done was go to school. Was he really ready to become an academic—to enter the tumultuous world of faculty politics and the demands of academic research? To never quite have enough money or enough time, and to face the prospect of moving to the hinterlands just to find work? I wasn't sure myself sometimes if I could tough it out, and I was a lot more hardheaded than my little brother.

My ruminations were cut short when I saw a phone message that Eric had inserted under the rim of my desktop: the Princeton police had called. I was wanted immediately for further questioning.

I grabbed my backpack and hurried down to the lobby of Holder Hall, passing a gaggle of students in the smoking lounge, and two girls in low-slung jeans huddling over a survey of English literature that could have been used as a doorstop. How could these highly intelligent, but otherwise typical kids coexist here with the likes of Bo Merriweather, who had the aura of a battle-toughened, middle-aged man?

The Borough of Princeton police station is on Monument Drive, a relatively quiet commercial block at the end of Nassau Street. Flanked by a couple of retail stores, the building blends in perfectly with its bucolic suburban surroundings.

Given the stories I'd heard from Earl about his treatment by the local cops—the frequent road stops for nothing but the crime of driving while black—I wasn't sure what to expect as I entered the station. I was ushered into a starkly appointed interrogation room, where a Latina woman gave me the requisite watery cup of coffee. Facing me across the scarred wooden table was the young blond cop I'd run into at the site of the fire, and a short, stocky woman with her hair pulled back in a bushy, ginger-colored ponytail flecked with gray. She was dressed in a dark blue blazer and badly tailored black slacks and looked nothing like the female investigators on television, with their tight, cleavage-enhancing sweaters and swaggering couture leather coats.

I'd had more dealings with cops in the past three months than in my prior thirty years, but this was the first one I'd encountered who was female, which intrigued me. I knew from bitter experience at Harvard and on Wall Street that just because she was a woman didn't mean that she was automatically my ally. Quite the contrary. So I wondered: *Are you a good witch or a bad witch?*

"I'm Lieutenant Maureen Kelly," she said, extending her hand. "Thanks for coming in. This is my associate, Officer Carl Bellock, who's working with the Fire Department to investigate the origin of the blaze that killed Professor Stokes." The inflections in her voice had a South Jersey tinge: Wildwood, maybe, or one of the other shore towns? With her no-nonsense demeanor, dowdy style, and intelligent eyes, Maureen Kelly could have been a defrocked nun who'd decided to take a more direct approach to tracking down the sinners of the world.

I sat down in a straight-backed chair that was no doubt designed to make the sitter feel as though she had been sent to detention for the day. It was so uncomfortable that you'd want to tell your story straight, then get out of there as quickly as possible.

"You attended the party where Professor Stokes was last seen, in the company of him and his wife," she began. "What, exactly, was the nature of your relationship with him?"

I wondered what Eula Stokes had already told them, given her overly suspicious nature, fueled by Creflo Smalls's righteous indignation on her behalf.

"Earl—Professor Stokes—was my mentor, and a friend to both me and my brother, a graduate student at Princeton. We both admired him greatly; we saw him as a friend, too, almost as a father, an avuncular figure." I paused to consider my words carefully; I wanted to dispel any notions that I had ever been romantically involved with Earl. Not only that—I was unsure of the angle of this questioning, and of the nature of the overall investigation. "There aren't many role models for aspiring African-American academics, especially in my area, economics," I continued, trying to present myself as the picture of professionalism and composure.

"Did Professor Stokes seem at all disturbed the evening of the party?" Lieutenant Kelly asked. "How would you describe his state of mind at the time?"

"The celebration was in his honor," I said slowly. "He was—well, I guess you could say he was reflective. He'd been approached by Harvard, and I think he was assessing what Princeton meant to him, who his friends really were." I paused and looked over at her associate, who sat as stiffly as a Marine recruit. "When you get to be famous, as Earl was, it becomes harder to figure out who's with you, and who may just be jealous."

"An interesting point," conceded the lieutenant, nodding.

"Professor Stokes's family has been in Princeton for three generations, so this was a big decision for him, obviously," I continued.

"We know the family," said Maureen Kelly in a flat, noncommittal tone.

I wondered if that included Eula, or even Yusef: what business might they have had with the police prior to Earl's death?

"May I ask the current status of the investigation?" I straightened in my chair. "Because what I've told you is exactly what I told the other officers after Earl dropped out of sight, that is, before we knew he was dead."

"I am not at liberty to divulge details," said Lieutenant Kelly, smiling slightly.

Finally the silent, stoic Carl Bellock joined in. "Professor Chase, did you observe Earl Stokes taking any medication that evening, before the party started—anything that might have impaired his judgment later?"

I felt myself start to simmer internally, like a pot on the burner whose flame has been turned from medium to high. They knew nothing. This was the same shuck that had appeared in the *Trentonian* last week: the fire may have been an accident, but it was Earl's doing, somehow. Had Eula told them that she, and perhaps Earl, had both been taking pills?

As paranoid as Eula may have been about Earl's wrongdoing—real or imagined—I couldn't believe she would have given such personal information to the police. She fancied herself not just a born-again Christian but also a race woman; and with his record as an activist in this town, her protector Creflo Smalls had to be well known to the local constabulary, and hardly eager to get to know them any better than he may have already. It just didn't make sense.

I looked over at Officer Bellock coolly before responding. "I didn't observe Earl doing anything of the sort before the party. While there, I saw him drink one glass of champagne, period." After a short pause I added: "Earl could handle the spotlight without that kind of help."

"You weren't in his company the entire evening, though, were you?" Maureen Kelly pointed out.

"That would have been impossible," I replied evenly, "given that he was the guest of honor, and had to circulate among a large group of people."

"Professor Chase, it has come to our attention that you have, shall we say, involved yourself in previous police investigations in other cities in a way that is beyond the call of duty for a university instructor." Lieu-tenant Kelly smiled, to make sure that it seemed as if she were bestow-ing a compliment. "I am assuming that if you come across any information regarding Professor Stokes's death, even after you leave the area, you'll be in touch with us," she continued.

I felt myself slump down in my chair a bit, viscerally relieved that the interview seemed to be drawing to a close.

"I'll do whatever I can to see that Earl's name is cleared of any suspi-cion," I said, looking directly at both of them.

"Thanks again for stopping in to see us, Professor Chase," said Lieu-tenant Kelly as she showed me to the door. "You can rest assured that we're doing everything we can to look into the circumstances sur-rounding Professor Stokes's death. He was a man of stature in this com-munity."

Too bad you didn't know that while he was still alive, I thought to myself as I listened to the heels of my boots hit the floor of the corridor and echo down its length.


My brother had decided that it was high time I got to know his girl-friend Kayla better, and so we had a date that evening for me to give her the once-over. Dinner was set for seven-thirty at the Honey Pot, a cozy bistro with flowering plants in the windows, checkered tablecloths, and first-rate nouveau American cuisine. It was sophisticated but unpreten-tious, a perfect place for students to feel grown-up without busting their budgets.

I arrived about five minutes early and ordered myself a glass of chardonnay from Sonoma County. The Honey Pot is the sort of place that identifies the origins of even the potatoes on the menu, so I felt confident that this wine would be the real thing. As I waited for my companions, I wondered what the evening would be like. I'd been through this drill many times with Eric, since he considered me the advance guard of the family. If his girlfriend met with my approval, then she could be introduced to our middle brother, Jason. The ultimate honor was dinner with our parents, and very few women ever made that cut. We children had all been told not to bring anyone home unless he or she was the right sort of person. And we all knew what that sort was: well educated, churchgoing, ambitious, polished, and hardworking. No conservatives. And no one who wasn't black.

Of course that raised an obvious question about what I had been doing throughout the autumn in the company of Dante Rosario. Being both Italian and politically conservative, he was the very definition of a man who could never be brought home to my family. I am quite certain that this was part of his allure for me. That, and his truly extraordinary brown eyes.

I just hoped that things would be different for Eric this time. Unfortunately, his affairs of the heart usually ended the same way. He'd fall really hard for some girl and then she'd break his heart. I always wanted to track them down later and strangle them with my bare hands for taking advantage of his good nature. He was the kindest, most sincere man, and he treated women with a respect that bordered on reverence. Which undoubtedly made him too nice to be taken seriously by the twenty-somethings who floated through Princeton. I kept telling him that New York City, a short bus ride away, was filled with black women looking for a handsome, good-hearted black man. But his love of Princeton kept him in town most weekends, certain that the love of his life was just one date away. At heart, we were both hopeless romantics. And we had the scars to prove it.

Promptly at seven-thirty, Kayla and Eric arrived hand in hand, the very picture of young Princetonians on their way up in the world. Beautifully turned out in a cashmere V-neck sweater, a thin black pencil skirt, and patent leather boots, Kayla was indisputably gorgeous. I wondered what it must feel like to be an unqualified beauty. Most days, I think I look pretty good—but only when compared to other college professors. I can hold my own in a room full of academics. This girl could hold her own on a fashion runway. I watched them as she waited quietly for Eric to choose appetizers for the three of us. Clearly he took his role as a man attached to a woman of Kayla's potential star power with great seriousness—the way he'd approached things all his life. Our Long Island oysters arrived, to be followed by Maryland crab cakes, greens from Marin County, and vegetables from the Carolinas. You needed a road map of the interstate highway system to get around this meal.

"I really appreciated your participation in class today," I told Kayla. The candles on our table, no doubt handmade in a tiny village in Maine with extra-long winters, cast a butter-colored glow on the single diamond in the pendant around her swanlike neck. Her carriage was that of a highly self-confident ballerina: no wonder my brother was enchanted.

"I hadn't expected to have to take so much time dealing with Bo Merriweather," I continued.

My brother groaned at the mention of his name. "That guy turns up everywhere, like a bad penny. I just read the latest edition of that newspaper that he puts out, the *National Prospect*. The cover story claims that people from the local community—namely, Reverend Creflo Smalls—set the fire to discredit Earl."

"You have to be kidding me," I exclaimed. "Why would Reverend Smalls want to discredit Earl?"

"Isn't that the point? None of it makes any sense. He's just trying to set us against each other—the old divide-and-conquer strategy," Kayla observed. "That guy's so out there, sometimes I hear myself saying things I'm not even sure I believe, just to stand up to him and his outrageous accusations." Eric glowed proudly by her side.

"How much of his act is just glorified street theater?" I asked. "If no one paid attention to Bo Merriweather, he'd wither, like a vampire in the sunlight."

"That's part of the problem Professor Stokes faced." Kayla sighed. "If he ignored him in class, Bo would ratchet up the outrage level even higher, just to get additional attention—like a little kid. One week he actually said that the legacy of slavery in this country is exaggerated by African-American academics looking for bigger grants. Reparations were even thrown in as another example of what Bo calls black-on-black: black people blackmailing the white establishment."

"Kayla told me that after class one day even Earl, as patient and gentlemanly as he was, almost came to blows with Bo," Eric interjected as he polished off his last crab cake.

"Earl told him he was a social misfit, out of touch with the times and with his peer group," Kayla related. "They were so loud that I heard the whole thing from the hallway just outside the classroom door. Bo let Earl know that he wasn't alone in his opinions. He said he had people behind him, in positions of power at the school. He even told Earl that he'd better tone down his rhetoric—as though Earl Stokes were Stokeley Carmichael, born again," Kayla said with derision. "Or he might find his enterprise in trouble. I think Bo meant the new building—the symbol of African-American Studies' future ambitions."

"Did he actually mention the building?" I said, intrigued.

"He said Earl's *enterprise*," Kayla reiterated.

"Could mean a book, or even a course of study," Eric added.

"I wonder if the Princeton cops know about that conversation," I said, and described my visit to the station earlier that day.

"My sister is channeling Nancy Drew," my brother explained. He filled Kayla in on my role in solving the murders of Amanda Fox, the wife of one of my best friends at Yale; and of Rosezella Fisher, a dean of students at Harvard who'd come up the hard way.

Kayla smiled as he went on and on. "Your brother is very proud of you, Nikki," she said. "I guess you know he refers to you as the Master of Time and Space."

I laughed. "I know. If only it were true." I smiled at Eric fondly. "I'm proud of him, too."

"So do you think that I should mention this conversation with Merriweather to the police?" Kayla asked.

"Absolutely. It can't hurt." I gave her Lieutenant Kelly's name, and she promised to call the next day.

As we greedily devoured a cobbler made from Georgia peaches for dessert, Lloyd Eastman, the acting chair of the Program in African-American Studies, walked past our table in animated discussion with Zanda Fleming. I was reminded again of what a small campus Princeton was—apparently, there were only a handful of places where one could get a decent meal.

The diminutive Eastman was at least four inches shorter than his companion, but the volume of his voice more than made up for the height difference. I heard him declare, "If you ask me, we haven't been tough enough in our standards. If we want to be a full department, we have to be more selective in who we admit into the program."

"What do you suppose that's all about?" I asked, nodding in their direction.

"He's probably lobbying to ensure that he goes from being acting chairman to actual chairman of the department," Eric said wryly. "She'll have a lot of say in who gets named as Earl's replacement. Brother man isn't wasting any time."

"Do you think they'll go with him, or with someone from the outside?" I asked coyly. I really wanted to know if Butch Hubbard might have his sights on Princeton. I remembered seeing Eastman and Hubbard walking together the night after Earl died. Maybe he'd been sussing out the competition. Earl had been certain that Butch's carefree days at Harvard would be drawing to a close under the new regime. What better soft landing than to move to Princeton now that Earl was gone? I hadn't been able to catch Zanda's eye as she passed our table, so I had no idea what she was thinking. But I sure hoped that she was pumping Eastman for information about Hubbard.

"If I had to bet my own money, I'd bet they go with an outsider," Eric speculated.

"What's Eastman's reputation?" I asked, sipping my espresso. "I don't recall reading much about him or his work."

Eric shook his head. "I can't see him getting this job. He doesn't really publish. He's not considered much of a scholar. But he's actually a great lecturer. Have you ever heard him speak, Kayla?"

She shook her head. "Not yet. But I've heard the same thing. I just think it's a shame that Princeton would have to hire an outsider for a big role like that. It doesn't give the junior faculty here much hope if they do that every time." She gave Eric an affectionate gaze that signaled her unfailing loyalty to this particular potential junior faculty member. To my relief, she seemed sincerely fond of my brother.

After dinner, Kayla excused herself to go to the library for some last-minute cramming. Eric and I headed in the direction of Lahiere's for an after-dinner drink. Our boots scratched noisily on the nearly deserted streets, now covered in a downy layer of fluffy, newly fallen snowflakes.

"So what do you think?" he asked eagerly.

"I think I need to get into Earl's office," I mused.

"*What?*" he exclaimed.

"Oh, I'm sorry. You meant what did I think about Kayla."

"Yes! Stop goofing around. What do you think?"

"She's lovely, Eric. And she seems very smart. *Very* smart. Is she nice to you?"

He smiled broadly. "Yes, she is."

I slapped his arm playfully. "I'm not talking about that kind of nice. I mean, does she seem like a good person?"

He regarded me seriously for a moment. "I hope so. I think so. I mean, I hope so."

"That's not a ringing endorsement, Bun," I said, lighting up a cigarette. "That's all that matters in the end, you know."

"Did you mean it when you said that you need to get into Earl's office?" he asked, abruptly changing the subject.

"Yeah, I did. Why? Can you help with that?"

It turned out that he could. We made a detour to a late-night pizzeria just off campus, where the people who clean and scrub and buff Princeton's hallowed halls were known to take breaks from late-night maintenance. Larnell Davis was right where Eric had figured he would be: between a slice of pepperoni and a slice with sausage and green peppers. Dressed in baggy cargo pants, an Avirex bomber jacket, and a black watch cap, Larnell could have passed for one of Princeton's less preppy students, if not for his mocha-colored skin and watchful, streetwise eyes. Hip-hop style had united a whole generation in a way no political machinations ever could have managed.

"Wassup?" he said to Eric, grinning. "Who's the fox?"

"That would be my sister, the professor," Eric replied, laughing. "She needs your help, my brother."

I explained my connection to Earl, and my need to gain access to his office.

Larnell raised his eyebrows as he sipped from a large container of Gatorade. "This is a decent job, you know? Pay isn't great, but it supplements what I get from my DJ gigs. I don't want to blow it."

He said he'd think about lending me an extra passkey only after I promised to be in and out by seven the next morning, well before any of the secretarial staff had made an appearance. Eric's offer of a pair of tickets to a Nets game sealed the deal.

Holding the key tightly in my hand, I felt an elation that I hadn't experienced in a long time. Perhaps there was nothing suspicious related to Earl's death. At least if I could get into his office alone, I could convince myself of that. "I owe you, big-time," I told my brother as we reentered the winter wonderland.

"I'll get my reward in heaven," he said over his shoulder, trekking down the slippery walkway. "Isn't that what Grandma always told us?"

I had to hope he'd get it sooner than that, but I had cause to worry.

On our way back to Holder Hall, much later that evening, I saw a couple deep in conversation in the front window of the Acropolis, a New York-style Greek coffee shop that stays open until 1:00 A.M. to accommodate students looking for a late-night caffeine fix. Eric had consumed sufficient alcohol at that point to dim his peripheral vision, and so thankfully, he didn't notice. But I did.

Lit up like a tableau in a department-store window were the unmistakably manicured dreadlocks of Yusef Jones and the smoothly coiffed, ever-graceful head of my brother's girlfriend, Kayla.

# 11

## The Real Deal

I made good on my promise to Larnell Davis: at a few minutes before seven o'clock Tuesday morning, I had completed my mission and was ravenous for breakfast. I'd entered Dickinson Hall under cover of darkness, almost tripping on the poorly lit, narrow stairs that descended to Earl's office. I shed my wool coat immediately, as steam heat permeated the empty halls, giving the basement of the building the same barometric pressure as a small Caribbean island.

My hands were shaking as I inserted the key in the lock of the old wooden door with the frosted glass panel in the front. Some Nancy Drew I was. I don't recall her ever showing the slightest sign of nerves. I wasn't sure what was making me more nervous: that there might be something to discover in here. Or that there might be nothing at all.

The scent of Earl's signature Pierre Cardin aftershave lingered in the book-lined office, sending me instantly back to my last meeting here with Earl. "Steady," I heard myself whisper into the silence as tears pricked my eyes. I rooted around in the drawers of the oversize wooden desk, but it yielded very little: the misplaced syllabus for Earl's course; a slew of the expected Economics Department memos from Hayden Fleming, all highly officious in tone; and a cache of toiletries and medical incidentals.

As far as I could tell, none of the pills were stronger than basic pain relievers for headaches, stomach pain, and indigestion, all byproducts of the high-stress life that Earl's wife had chided him about.

I paused for just a moment to look at the photos on the top of Earl's desk. There were precious few. One of him with Eula on the porch of their house. One of a much younger Earl wearing a mortarboard and accepting a diploma from a beaming white-haired man. And one of him with Yusef. I hadn't even noticed it on my prior visits to his office, because it was tucked away in a corner. I could see the resemblance between them in this photo much more clearly than I had in real life, perhaps because in this photo they both wore radiant smiles. They had the same nose. The same strong eyebrows. And the same proud set to their mouths.

Nestled into the same corner with the photo of Yusef was a framed poem by Langston Hughes.

### Luck

*Sometimes a crumb falls*
*From the table of joy*
*Sometimes a bone is flung*
*To some people*
*Love is given,*
*To others*
*Only Heaven.*

That was what I needed more than anything right now, I thought. *Luck*.

Neither the desk nor the adjacent shelves contained the manuscript for Earl's purported tell-all, although two chapters of what looked to be a sequel to *Color Counts* lay on the bottom rung or a storage unit near the side door. I slipped the pages into my backpack, just in case.

I had been in Earl's office for almost ten minutes before I realized that someone else had evidently been there before me. The tall stainless steel filing cabinet to the right of Earl's desk, obviously the place where he would have stored files that needed to be easily accessible, had been broken into. I could see that the small locks next to the handles on the doors had been mutilated with a screwdriver, or maybe an ice pick. The scratches and dents looked fresh, with light flakes of paint ready to fall from the dented metal. That didn't look like the work of Lieutenant Kelly and her men. Too obvious. Inside, the clearly labeled files were in a state of disarray, as though the thief had been in a hurry, or piqued at not finding what he or she had been looking for.

At the bottom of one upended file was a letter from Earl to the Princeton president, recommending that the number two in African-American Studies, Lloyd Eastman, take over Earl's role leading the program and the construction of the new building, should Earl indeed leave Princeton to pursue what he termed "other opportunities."

I stopped my search abruptly and thought for a moment. Something was nagging at me. At first I couldn't place the feeling. Then I realized that there was a key detail missing in my mental inventory of what had been here when I last saw Earl the prior Friday. The reference to the new building in the letter jogged my memory. There had been a pile of rolled-up blueprints and architectural renderings on the floor in the corner of his office. And now they were gone. Every one of them. Vanished—up in smoke, perhaps, like the building itself.

The clock at the top of Earl's desk said 6:45 A.M. Time to vamoose before the secretarial or janitorial staff made an early appearance. I placed the files back in a state of random chaos and slipped out the door, locking it behind me.

I had just reached the top of the stairs when I reared back, like a rider whose mount has been startled. Before me stood Hayden Fleming, larger than life, or at least larger than your average departmental chairman.

"Professor Fleming!" I exclaimed, feigning delight.

"Pinch-hitting again, Professor Chase?" he asked with a wry smile. "I don't think Earl had any classes scheduled for today." Surprisingly, he made no reference to the hour, nor did he ask how I'd managed to gain entry to the building.

"I was just checking to make sure Earl hadn't left me anything else to work on," I replied, hoping that a hint of potential collaboration would suffice.

"I was working on something with Earl, too," said Fleming, lending me his arm as I ascended the last of the stairs. "A departmental overview."

I said nothing about the obvious fact that we were both far too early to gain access to the office from the temp, who wasn't due until 8:30. What possible plausible excuse could Fleming have for being here? His office was in Fisher Hall, the headquarters of the Economics Department, which by my estimate was about an eight-minute walk from Dickinson Hall.

"You know, Ms. Chase . . . ," he said slowly, scrutinizing me closely.

"Please call me Nikki," I insisted.

"Since we last met, I've been thinking." He looked over at me and smiled, demonstrating a row of pearly whites that could have qualified for a toothpaste commercial. "You'd be a tremendous addition to the Princeton faculty."

You could have knocked me over with a proverbial feather: courtesy from Hayden Fleming, let alone a job offer, was the last thing I expected in the halls of Dickinson at 6:55 A.M.

"Why, is your quota of African-Americans off now that Earl's no longer with you?"

I regretted my tart tone the minute the words passed my lips. "I'm sorry. I guess I'm just, well—I'm surprised." I was also annoyed. He had offered me his arm as we climbed the stairs, and now I found his hand on my shoulder. Perhaps it was some kind of instinctive tribal loyalty to Zanda Fleming—but I didn't like being this up close and personal with Hayden Fleming.

He smiled again, and withdrew his hand from me. "I understand your perspective. It's true that I'm keenly aware of the lack of black faculty members in my department. I was concerned about it well before

Earl's tragic—" He paused. "Accident. Now it's an even more pressing issue. And we have not a single women on the staff in Economics."

"Really?" I pretended to be surprised, though Earl had mentioned it to me a number of times. *How convenient for you, then, to be able to check both of those boxes with someone like me, so that you can get back to your real work.*

I put my coat back on and pulled my wool beret from my shoulder bag. "Professor Fleming, I am enormously flattered by this overture," I told him in as sincere a voice as I could manage. "But this isn't a time for me to make major changes in my life, and that's what leaving Harvard would be right now. I'm just not ready."

"I understand," he said, putting his arm around my shoulders as we approached the front door of the building. I steeled myself not to recoil from him. I'd already insulted him sufficiently for one morning.

"I suppose it was inappropriate of me to bring it up, given Earl's funeral tomorrow," he continued smoothly. "You're still in a state of shock, as we all are."

"Truer words were never spoken," I told him. "I guess I'll see you at the service tomorrow."

"That's a helluva way to send a guy packing," Hayden Fleming replied, cocking his head playfully to one side.

It was a good thing it was winter, and that my burgundy wool coat was strong and thick—the better to hide the fact that Hayden Fleming was literally making my skin crawl. I wanted to advise him to save the blond charm offensive for someone who'd appreciate it.

But he had already disappeared back into Dickinson Hall. At least I'd beaten him to Earl's office. Or had I?

Desperate for my morning shot of caffeine, I crossed the postcard-pretty campus, where the morning's icicles dripped from the eaves and copper gutters of several of the buildings. As I headed for Nassau Street, I rehashed the scene I had witnessed in the window of the Acropolis coffee shop last night. I could still see Kayla and Yusef now, like players in a movie that kept running over and over in my mind.

In truth, they made a handsome pair. It was clear from the way

119

they'd been speaking—each head bent in the direction of the other—that they were on intimate terms of some sort. My breath quickened, and I walked even faster as I contemplated the implications of this for my brother. And, to a lesser extent, for me.

I was disappointed, I had to admit it. I'd thrown his name at Dante Rosario to get a reaction, but my declaration of attraction to Yusef Jones wasn't a complete falsehood. He was tall and strong and witty and sexy, and I had been looking forward to sparring with him. At the very least. So how had Kayla French beaten me to the punch on him?

They had both been at Earl's party, but Kayla had remained by Eric's side for most of the evening, as far as I could recall. What possible link did they have, other than the fact that Yusef's father had been Kayla's teacher? True, Yusef was a professor of economics, Kayla's field of study: was the get-together professional in nature? Given that it was after midnight when I saw them, I could only view that option as unlikely, especially given that Kayla had lied. She had told me and Eric that she was going to study at the library after we'd left the Honey Pot.

My encounter with Hayden Fleming had been equally unsettling, from its early-morning surprise element to Fleming's creepy presumptuousness about his own appeal. Why, in truth, would he want to replace Earl with me as the department's token black professor? I had only published articles in a handful of academic journals. My first book was at least a year off. And though my reputation as a teacher was very strong, I knew that because of my involvement in two investigations that fall, I was also viewed now as unpredictable, a wild card—basically, as a potential thorn in the side of any department chairman. I couldn't believe that hiring me would be seen as a feather in Hayden Fleming's cap.

I could only conclude, at least without having consumed a single cup of coffee, that my worth to Fleming was as a Harvard professor; that an act of reverse poaching would satisfy some highly competitive urge to even the score. But as far as I knew, Earl had not even made a final decision at the time of his death. What factors was he weighing as he stood there at the building site, contemplating the future of a department he'd worked so hard to establish, but which would open a new base of operation with someone else, potentially, at the helm?

And who would that someone else be? With Earl out of the picture, Lloyd Eastman was in at Afro-Am, and Hayden Fleming was secure at Economics. Earl was the real deal, hence threatening to someone like Fleming. So why would Fleming search for a report in Earl's office at six-thirty in the morning, when he presumed he'd go undetected? Was there more to it than academic rivalry?

By the time I got to Nassau Street, I'd acquired a world-class migraine. Mere coffee would not suffice. I decided to pay a call on my new friend Jide. He took my breakfast order with infectious high spirits: his team had beaten Senegal last night in the World Cup trials in Dakar. "It is wonderful to see you, as always," he greeted me.

Even failed Nancy Drews need infusions of enthusiasm to keep going. "And you, too, Jide," I said with genuine conviction. "How's life treating you?"

The woman behind me in line glared, annoyed that I was engaging the counterman while she anxiously awaited her own caffeine fix.

"If you don't mind," she interrupted. "One medium coffee, with milk and two sugars."

Jide filled her order while continuing his conversation with me, smiling all the while. "The sun shines brightly the day after the Ivory Coast is triumphant in Dakar," he laughed, gesturing toward the window, where thick, top-heavy gray clouds filled the pane and suggested yet another snowstorm on the horizon.

"I hope it doesn't snow tomorrow for Professor Stokes's funeral," I said.

Jide looked over thoughtfully as he piled large-size cups into a dispenser. "I will say a prayer for his spirit as he travels to the next world. He was a good man, but he had troubles. Maybe now he has found peace." He put my bagel and coffee onto a dark green plastic tray and placed it gently on the edge of the counter for me.

"What kind of troubles?" I asked, trying to sound casual. I took the tray and handed Jide a five-dollar bill.

He hesitated, and looked around the room. It was still early, and there were only a handful of customers in evidence. "I don't want to speak ill of the recently departed."

I wondered if my headache would ever go away, at this rate. "We can't hurt Professor Stokes now, Jide."

"I think his problems were with women," Jide confided in a low voice. My heart sank in my chest like an anchor in the ocean's depths. There it was again—that hint that Earl was a cheater. Would I have to reassess everything I'd heard from Eula Stokes and Creflo Smalls? And was Yusef Jones just a chip off the old block?

"I remember one time I saw the professor man, it was late—two A.M., maybe," Jide told me. "He was arguing with some blond woman I'd never seen before." He paused. "There'd been others: black, white, blond, hair the color of fire. The professor man had a taste for every sort of woman, like a man who wants to sample not just one kind of ice cream, but all the flavors in the case."

I still wasn't convinced. This wasn't the Earl I knew. "Well, you know he was a professor. Who's to say that those women weren't people he worked with or taught? Or just people he liked to flirt with?" Hair the color of fire. That had to be Zanda Fleming.

Jide shrugged, as if to say, *Believe what you will, I'm telling you what I saw.*

The coffee on my tray smelled delicious, but I wondered now how I'd keep it down.

"You said that he was arguing with one of them. Did you hear what they were arguing about?" I asked, unsure that I even wanted an answer to my question.

"No," he said as he took a bagel order from a student in a plaid hunter's jacket. "It was quiet in the store at the hour, but they were speaking in low voices about private things—that I could tell." As he turned to the next customer, I could tell that he could no longer ignore his work.

I nodded appreciatively for his willingness to talk to me for so long. "Thank you, Jide."

I took my tray over to the table by the window and quietly sipped my coffee. The feminist in me was furious about the possibility that Earl would have disrespected his wife and his wedding vows so publicly that a counterman knew about it. But the race woman in me wanted to explain his behavior away as the result of stress and scrutiny and a need to prove his worth to himself.

Now more than ever, I really did need to know if Earl was the real deal.

# 12
## Old School

**Y**ou know you have a relationship problem when you start a conversation with a man hoping to hear one four-letter word and end it muttering a completely different one under your breath. The latter word was at the top of my mind Tuesday morning at ten-thirty, as I relived for the nth time my phone conversation the prior day with Dante. After my breakfast stop, with its disturbing revelations about Earl, I found myself completely out of sorts—hopped up on caffeine and stir-crazy. What I needed was exercise, but I hadn't packed any gym clothes because I hadn't planned to be staying in Princeton this long. I quickly broke down and went to the U-Store for a pair of running shoes, borrowed some sweats and a windbreaker from Eric, and went for a run across the campus. The paths had been cleared of the prior day's dusting of snow, and the brisk air was just what I needed to clear out the cobwebs and help me think clearly about my situation.

I was fascinated by the varsity league politics of the Princeton Economics Department. I had thought things were challenging in Cambridge, but clearly learning to play games was the price of the ticket to success everywhere. What on earth had Hayden Fleming been thinking, blurting out a job offer to me at six-thirty that morning? The more I thought about it, the more amateurish it seemed. And the more oafish his clumsy pawing of me seemed, as well. This was a wealthy, sophisticated man—arrogant, but not a boor. His behavior just didn't ring true. Which meant that I must have really startled him, and this was his way of distracting me. *Employment, sex, offer her anything to keep her mind off of*—what?

Also, though I hadn't noticed them before, there were posters for Yusef Jones's lecture that afternoon taped to the kiosks all over campus. Which reminded me again of how little I understood about him. I had gone onto the Internet after my encounter with him the prior day and done a search to see where he taught and what other information I could glean. It turned out that Yusef Jones was quite well known in certain circles. He taught African-American Studies at the University of Chicago, and was on the cusp of breaking through in the popular press. Just like his father had. The articles that he had written showed him to be the sort of black intellectual with an unerring instinct for provocative material, whose topics were often ripped, literally, from the most recent headlines. From what I could tell, Yusef actually made Butch Hubbard—with his clubby bowties and cropped hair—look old-school by comparison. From what I could tell, Yusef was the type who'd be welcomed into the posse of a rapper whose latest CD had just gone platinum, whereas Butch would remain at a safe distance, analyzing the lyrics for some upscale white magazine with a fascination for gun-toting pop stars.

I rarely doubted my decision to pursue the academic life. But on a day like this, with my crazy demanding boss and my decision to buy a pair of sneakers causing me to have to forgo meals out for a week, I found myself fondly recalling my prior life in the business world. Despite the backstabbing competition from colleagues at my own and other investment banks, at least then I was getting paid enough to buy whatever I wanted. It was a rough-and-tumble environment, but it made no claims to be otherwise. It was always just about the Benjamins.

My father had always told me that I had more drive than my brothers; that I was most like my grandfather, the owner of a string of dry-cleaning stores in downtown Detroit, and one of the leaders of the black business community in the 1920s and '30s. Though the Depression almost knocked him out, he came back slowly, enabling my father to attend college and become a CPA. Each generation of the family needed someone with a head for business. In my generation, it seemed to be me. Now here I was, broke and living in the land of theory, not practice. I wondered if my grandfather would be disappointed in me.

I checked my watch. Twelve-thirty P.M. Yusef's "Endangered Black Male" lecture was scheduled for Alexander Hall at three. I wanted a nap before I had to face a crowd that would no doubt include Eric and his girlfriend, Kayla. It would require all the self-control I could muster not to react to the sight of them together, not to flinch if I saw them so much as holding hands.

Back in Eric's room I found a message from Jess on the machine. She'd already called yesterday to say that she'd gotten home safely, and to let me vent about my conversation with Dante. Now she was back at the hospital, and wanting to fill me in on some cute new intern. And no, she swore, she was not back with Ted.

A quick check of my e-mail yielded nothing but hectoring missives from Carl Irvin, and reminders from Matthew to clean and defragment my hard drive. I lay down on Eric's couch and fell into a sleep so deep that when I woke up to the jangling telephone, I couldn't remember why I was back in a dorm room, so many years after leaving undergraduate life behind.

I picked up the telephone and heard my brother's voice. "Nikki, I can't make it to Yusef's lecture this afternoon."

My heart skipped a beat. "Is there something wrong?"

"I'm just under the weather." He sniffled. "And I don't want to miss Earl's funeral tomorrow. I'm at Kayla's, and I'm just going to hang out here the rest of the day, okay?"

"What time is it?" I mumbled, reaching for the alarm clock on the table next to the sofa.

"Two-thirty," my brother laughed. "Sleepyhead."

"I was up very early this morning," I defended myself. "Not that you'd know, since you never seem to be here anymore. You know I'm not trying to chase you out of your own room, right?"

"Of course I know that! By the way, Larnell will want his keys back, pronto. You can find him over at Dickinson. The other folks on the cleaning crew are pretty sharp. They don't miss much. They know more about what goes on around here than most department chairmen."

"I don't doubt it," I told him.

"So I won't be at the lecture, but Kayla will."

"Got it," I said, pulling myself off the sofa in one jerky motion. "Hey, you know you can come home, right?"

"It's not a problem, Nikki. Not a problem at all."

After a quick shower, I approached the mammoth Alexander Hall just as snowflakes began to moisten the wool of my beret. Despite the fact that several inches of snow were predicted to fall by later in the day, a group of about thirty-five protestors had assembled in front of the building with bullhorns, sandwich boards, and other regalia more often associated with striking unionists. Typical of Bo Merriweather and company, I mused, to co-opt the opposition in the art of protest. How ironic: demonstrations such as this one were now prevalent on the right, when not so many years ago they would have been the nearly exclusive province of the anti-Vietnam War and civil rights movements. In America the exercise of free speech, like economics, is open to anyone with the nerve to come to the party. I saw no visible police presence, a noticeable difference from the era of left-wing demonstrations.

A nearly all-white crowd of students was making their way uncomfortably past the gauntlet of Bo Merriweather's troops into the large lecture hall. I spotted a large black woman in a broad-brimmed, fur-trimmed hat, and realized that it was Eula Stokes. With a sigh of relief I took note that she seemed to be unaccompanied. I was in no mood for Pastor Creflo Smalls.

"You commit the crime, you do the time!" Merriweather shouted into the bullhorn with his fist in the air, as if he'd been studying tapes of Jesse Jackson protests. "Black men put themselves in prison when they steal from, and kill, their own people."

A large white woman in a down parka marched by with a sandwich board that read: "My ancestors never enslaved a living soul. Live free now! Support human life in all forms." She was flanked by three older women waving small American flags; it was as if we were all attending a snowier version of an Independence Day rally. Given their average age, it was clear that Bo had recruited a sizable contingent of off-campus activists to swell his own ranks. I saw no more than a dozen student-age protestors. Like many other rabble-rousers, Bo seemed to have no qualms about employing ringers.

"Go back to your Pat Robertson videos!" yelled a student in a cowboy hat as he made his way into the hall.

As I hustled my way through the crowd, I almost ran into a small man dwarfed by a large black overcoat, and sporting a long orange scarf that reached well past his knees. It was when I looked down and saw the black-and-orange shoelaces in his wingtip shoes that I recognized Jeb Wolf, the Official Overseer of Princetoniana. He stared through his black glasses speckled with orange paw prints, as though he knew me but couldn't quite remember why.

"Nikki Chase," I said. "I saw you at Earl Stokes's party. I was a friend of his."

He looked genuinely pained by the reference to Earl. "I'm so sorry about what happened."

Unwilling to make further small talk, I hurried past a group of Princeton students in a self-conscious clump at the back of the assemblage and finally entered the low-lit, dry, well-heated interior, which felt like a former chapel in the Gothic style converted to a lecture hall. Despite the fact that the lecture wasn't scheduled to begin for another ten minutes, the auditorium was almost full. Kayla was down front, so I sat in the next-to-last row. Besides Eula Stokes, I recognized a number of other parishioners from Beulah Baptist in the audience.

To my surprise Larnell Davis was directly behind Eula; the townies had banded together, perhaps out of a self-protective instinct. In fact, white students and a smattering of professors from other departments made up the majority of the crowd. Besides Kayla French, two other students from Earl's class had shown up: the African and the dread-locked young man who'd called for the removal of Bo Merriweather. I wondered if he'd have occasion to do the same this afternoon. Next to Kayla sat Marti Waterstone, wearing her signature watch cap, though the hall was quite toasty in temperature.

At precisely 3:05 Lloyd Eastman made his way to the podium, installed on what had once been the altar of the chapel.

"Brothers and sisters, students and fellow faculty members," he began, spreading his arms as if to embrace a real congregation. "The Princeton Program in African-American Studies is pleased to present today a distinguished speaker, currently holding the W. E. B. DuBois Chair in African-American Studies at the University of Chicago—at the tender age of thirty-six!" There were appreciative snickers from faculty present.

"We would like to dedicate this lecture, 'The Endangered Black Male,' the third in the Eustace R. Miller Memorial Series, to the memory of our esteemed friend and colleague Earl Stokes, so tragically taken from us at the height of his powers. Our brother's spirit lives with us still. The future home of this department may lie in ruins, but we will rise from the ashes, like the phoenix of mythology."

"Amen!" said Eula Stokes, as though she were in attendance at Beulah Baptist. A murmur of affirmation rippled through the first two rows of students. I remembered that Eric had said that Lloyd Eastman was known for his speaking skills, and I wondered how long this introduction might be. He was obviously enjoying himself, and clearly auditioning for the department chairmanship.

"Earl always told us to stay strong, ladies and gentlemen, and that's what we will do. Stay strong, stay with it, and rise, rise, rise. Earl may be gone, but he has left a legacy—his son, Yusef. A fine man and a scholar in his own right. And now," continued Eastman, "please welcome Professor Yusef Jones. His second book, with the same title as this lecture, will be published next year by Columbia University Press."

Yusef strode to the podium like a man born to the spotlight. He wore a brightly embroidered, almost floor-length dashiki over baggy black pants, and his dreadlocks formed a leonine halo around his chiseled face. He seemed to rise, literally, in stature as he spoke, towering above the microphone stand.

"Thank you, Brother Eastman," he began. "Or should I say Acting Chairman Eastman—"

I felt myself flinch at the reference; how quickly Lloyd Eastman had stepped into Earl's shoes.

"Brothers, sisters, townspeople, students, fellow teachers—welcome, and thank you for coming out in this gathering storm." He paused and smiled widely and graciously as his eyes swept the room, like a king acknowledging his subjects. "That is in fact what I want to address today—the storm that is coming, as surely as night follows day, if we continue to ignore the fact that more black males between the ages of fifteen and thirty-four are incarcerated in this country than are enrolled in college, or any kind of technical training."

Yusef paused and stared out at the audience, expressionless. His head pivoted slowly, surveying the crowd. His eyes narrowed, and his forehead furrowed. He almost seemed to be looking for someone in particular. Then he suddenly pointed his finger at a young black man in the audience. "You there!" he shouted at the unsuspecting young man. "Too black, too strong. And you! Too black, too strong," he repeated again in an angry voice, pointing to another young black man. "And you. And you. And you!" he shouted forcefully as he pointed out black male faces in the various rows. The audience was silent, almost frozen. "All of you, and I do say all of you, are in trouble," he shouted, as he pointed out the black men in the room with a wagging finger and sweeping hand. "Every single one of you is gonna get it. Every single one of you brown-skinned men is gonna get it!"

The audience sat in uncomfortable silence.

"Yeah, I know it. I know you're thinking that you go to Princeton, or you live in Princeton, or you work at Princeton, or you're too smart, educated, rich, or hardworking to get into trouble." He smiled sarcastically at the crowd. "Yeah, I know what you're thinking. 'Who the hell is he comin' up in here telling me that I—a well-dressed Princeton student—am gonna be in trouble? What does some dreadlock-headed dashiki-wearin' Negro know about upwardly mobile black people like me?"

A few in the audience laughed uncomfortably.

"That is what you're thinking!" Yusef continued triumphantly. "But I'll tell you why I'm right about all you black men in here. I'll tell you why you're all in trouble—why you're all endangered. Because one day you'll get arrested for a crime you didn't commit. Or not hired for a job you deserved. Or not get paid what you're worth—and then you'll explode. And prove yourself to be the uncontrollable animal that they think you are anyway."

I was amazed and frankly impressed that he would give such a speech at a school like this. And I wondered if this audience was going to go along for the ride.

"How can you black men get in trouble? Just by being yourselves. Let me tell you what I mean." Yusef stepped away from the lectern and pointed to two black men in the third row. "You two stand up."

The two boys—one dressed in a yellow Izod pullover, the other with a red baseball cap—stood up. They smiled comfortably and looked around at their friends—most of them white.

"Now, you in the yellow shirt," Yusef said. The student nodded. "You're gonna get arrested someday," Yusef declared.

The student laughed and shook his head in denial.

Yusef smiled sarcastically. "Now, I didn't say you're gonna commit a crime. I'm saying that some white girl just like the one you're sitting next to right now is gonna one day pick you out of a lineup because you look just like the suspicious man who just snatched her purse on a dark parking lot."

Yusef pointed to the student next to him. "And your friend there, with that baseball cap on his head. After he graduates from medical school and moves to some fancy white town, he's gonna get stopped in his BMW by some jealous renegade cop who says he ran a red light."

The boy in the red cap crossed his arms defiantly.

"And when he starts to argue with the cop," Yusef shouted at the crowd, "he'll get hit upside the head and find a bag of crack suddenly planted under the front seat of his car. Whoops! There goes his medical license and his livelihood!" Yusef looked around the lecture hall. "So how's that Princeton degree gonna save your black behind then?" He returned to the podium, and took a deep breath. "My brothers and sisters, the problem of the incarceration of the black male is not an academic problem for you. It's not a theoretical issue for you to debate in some classroom. If you think your Princeton credentials are going to immunize you from this problem, then you are wrong. Dead wrong. Too many of us are sittin' in our ivory towers, shaking our heads over the plight of those poor 'black youths' we keep reading about in the newspaper. Thinking it's a pity, but I have to study for my finals so I can get my A-plus average and get on with my bourgeoisie life."

"Shame!" shouted Eula Stokes.

"That's right, sister, and I know I don't even need to tell you all," he continued, "America has the highest rate of incarceration of any major nation except Russia!" The audience slowly began to nod, and Yusef's face began to glow as if backlit.

"You need to care about this, you black folks of privilege. Especially you privileged black *men*—because this ain't no case study. This is your life. If there ain't no justice for poor black men, there ain't no justice for you, either." When he leaned forward to speak into the microphone, his rich baritone vibrated through the sound system to the upper reaches of the hall: Yusef Jones was preaching to the choir in more ways than one. And so he did, for the next hour and fifteen minutes, reeling out statistic after statistic to support his argument that America's failure to provide gainful employment or decent schooling for an entire generation of young men had forced them de facto into drug dealing or other avenues of illegal gain. It is the revenge of young black men, Yusef Jones thundered, that suburban teenagers in malls across the country are wearing baggy pants with no belts, aping prison styles, to the horror of their parents.

He was a riveting speaker, and so thirty minutes passed before I noticed it. But there it was: a hand gesture that Yusef made repeatedly to emphasize his points. He'd circle his forearm tightly, arm bent at the elbow, hand in a fist, thumb extended. The movement was odd enough to be distinctive—and I was certain that I'd seen it before.

"We have to reclaim our cultural icons," he was saying, "before we find Pepsi trying to sell beverages with an image of Malcolm or Martin."

"*Marti,*" I breathed. The man sitting next to me looked at me strangely, and I smiled reassuringly so he wouldn't think I was crazy. Marti Waterstone, the bohemian rich kid who was a waitress at the pancake shop, was the other person who frequently made that exact gesture. I'd seen her do it in Earl's class. So how had she and Yusef Jones come to share the same mannerism? The odds that they'd happened upon it independently seemed slight. If he lived in Chicago and was so estranged from his father, how was it that Yusef was so intimately connected to the women of Princeton? I could still see him in the coffeeshop window, leaning toward Kayla French.

Eula Stokes interrupted Yusef's speech more than five times to shout affirmations and encouragements; there was no further sign of Bo Merriweather and his cohorts for the rest of the proceedings. Yet at the end of the lecture Eula exited the hall and headed down the snow-covered walkway having made no attempt, it seemed, to see Yusef privately. As my grandmother would have put it, the Stokes family was a caution. Maybe it was a blessing Earl had never confided much about them over the years.

I was surprised that Eula was unaccompanied by a girlfriend or a family member. Or her faithful minister. But she seemed to be alone, and the opportunity was too perfect to pass up.

"Mrs. Stokes," I called out as she nearly collided with a leatherjacketed man in high boots. Instantly I dropped my eyes after meeting his; obviously Officer Carl Bellock of the Princeton police was working undercover. I could only wonder if his presence could help explain the quick dispersal of Merriweather and company.

"Mrs. Stokes," I said again. "What a wonderful speech! You must be so proud of your son."

She had been walking quickly, as if to avoid me, but like any good mother, she couldn't resist hearing praise for her child.

"He's such a powerful speaker," I chattered on, matching her pace. "I had no idea that you and Earl had a son, and such a talented one. I was really moved by those statistics, weren't you? Has Yusef always been such a powerful speaker?"

I saw the conflicting emotions wash over her face, the desire to get rid of me openly warring with the chance to brag on her son to an appreciative audience. Maternal pride won out. "Well, yes, he's always been a fine speaker. Raised that way, learned it in the church. He could have been a preacher, but he chose the teachin' life—had to compete with his father, you know."

"Sons can be like that." I nodded empathetically, thinking about my brother Eric's utter lack of interest in anything that even remotely resembled a spreadsheet.

"Child, you'll catch a death of cold, out in this weather with no hat," Eula admonished me. I whipped my beret out of my shoulder bag and put it on.

"No question about it, your son is a gifted speaker," I said. "Can I help you get home, Mrs. Stokes? These sidewalks are getting very slippery."

Eula looked over at me, her large brown eyes scanning me from head to toe. "Well, yes, I suppose some company would be good right now. I told my friends I wanted some peace this afternoon, but now I don't know."

I took her arm and we set off down Witherspoon.

"I heard you were at Beulah on Sunday," she commented.

"Yes, I was hoping to see you. To ask if there was anything I could do to help you. I mean, with the holiday coming and everything, this is such a difficult time, I thought that I could at least keep you company. But you had so many folks around you, I decided to wait." I paused for a moment. "I hope Reverend Smalls conveyed that I asked about you."

"Oh, yes, he did. I guess I got no worries now," she said abruptly.

"Not about moving to Cambridge, that is. No need to find a new doctor, or someone to do my hair the way I like it, or a church that'll have and hold me."

Silently I noted her choice of words—the way she was asking a church to perform a husband's duties.

The houses on Witherspoon Street were well kept but modest, more befitting a civil servant than the recipient of a MacArthur Award like Earl Stokes. I suspected that the more worldly and sophisticated Yusef Jones lived in more fashionable surroundings; I pictured black leather and a plethora of chrome, not to mention original African art adorning every tabletop.

The most striking thing about the first floor of Eula and Earl's three-story house was the relative scarcity of books. Aside from a double-width bookcase flanking the fireplace in the living room, which was filled with popular novels such as *Roots,* self-help titles, and volumes addressing spiritual empowerment, there was no evidence whatsoever that a man of Earl Stokes's intellectual prowess had ever lived here.

I busied myself in the kitchen preparing Eula's tea while she collapsed into a well-worn wing chair in the living room.

"Child, you got a sweet side, especially for a Harvard girl," she called through the arched doorway.

I smiled. "My momma thanks you. She raised me right." I ran water from the tap into a tea kettle and then nonchalantly asked, "So do you think Princeton will name Lloyd Eastman the permanent new chair of the African-American Studies program? He seems to be a very good speaker."

"Yeah, he makes a good speech. But it takes a lot more than that to run the program. We wanted it to attain full department status when that building got done. And that takes money and support from the president himself," Eula retorted. "You need someone with some standin' to get all that done. Nobody knows who Lloyd Eastman is."

"So who do you think they will give the program to?" I asked innocently.

"I know who I *wish* they'd name," she replied. "Butch Hubbard.

That's the kind of quality person we need here to straighten these folks out."

"Isn't Eastman tough enough to do that?"

Eula waved her hand dismissively. "He's trying too hard to keep the white folks happy. That man will never make waves. Now, Butch would tell them about themselves!"

"But why would Butch Hubbard leave Harvard?" I probed.

"*New president,* child. No tellin' what things are gonna be like up there now. That's what I kept tellin' Earl."

The teakettle whistled, and I poured hot water over mint tea bags in two cups; one said "The Lord Protects and Heals," and the other featured a ceramic terrier on the side.

"Oh, you found my favorite mug." Eula beamed as I entered the room and set the cups down on the coffee table. "I always wanted a dog, but Earl was set against it. Might keep him up nights whining, he said, and he needed to get up fresh for the next day." She looked over at me. "Geniuses can be very selfish people to live with, you know."

"Sometimes I think I should find myself a nice carpenter to settle down with."

"Had me one," said Eula, perking up in her chair. "My first husband was a house builder and a God-fearing man. He was heavy, though, and had diabetes. I met Earl in church just six months after James passed."

I was quickly discovering that Eula Stokes was a woman of parts.

"Earl was lonely, too, when I first met him," she continued.

Earl Stokes had never struck me as a man in need of company, but I said nothing.

"You know, child, those teaching folks live in books, in a world apart. Sometimes a man like Earl needed some earthy comforts."

*Apparently so,* I thought.

"Speaking of books, Eula," I said as casually as possible while sipping my tea. "Would it be okay if I had a look around Earl's study? There's a book he meant to lend me for a paper I'm working on, and I never got it from him. Would that be all right?"

She waved the back of her broad hand in my general direction. "Go on, child, go on. Earl's world—that's what I call his study—is on the second floor. I need to keep my feet up here and rest a spell longer."

"I appreciate it, Eula," I said as I slipped out and ascended the staircase in the center hall. Earl's study was directly to the left at the top, easily visible for the rows of books so tall and sloppily stacked that they nearly cascaded out the doorway.

Unlike the rest of the house, everything about the room spelled out Earl's interests: whole rows of sociological and economic tracts on American cities; Daniel Patrick Moynihan's once reviled analysis of the welfare system; books by Jane Jacobs, John Kenneth Galbraith, and Paul Johnson as well as the crème de la crème of the African-American intelligentsia.

Aside from an orange and black Princeton pennant hanging from the old-fashioned reading lamp on the desk, there was little of the school itself in evidence: obviously Earl had tried to keep his teaching and administrative paraphernalia in his office. This was intellectual home base, and hence no place for memos from the likes of Lloyd Eastman and Hayden Fleming.

It was when I pulled opened the middle drawer of the desk, hoping to find a section of the purported exposé of Princeton, that I hit investigative pay dirt—Earl's electronic organizer. Even more luck—it was the same type I once had, a Palm Pilot, so I actually knew how it worked.

I slipped it into my shoulder bag and descended the stairs. Eula Stokes was sound asleep in her comfortable wing chair.

After pulling the front curtains shut, I settled onto the couch opposite her. When she woke, she might want someone to talk to. In the meantime, I had Earl's Palm Pilot to occupy me. As I retrieved it from my bag, I smiled in her direction, and mouthed a silent sincere prayer: *Rest well, Sister Stokes.*

# 13
## White Out

The snow had been falling all day Tuesday, and when I looked out of the window of Eric's dorm room that evening, the Princeton campus presented a postcard-perfect vista of a dignified, historic center of higher learning on a small-town grid. The snow coating the spire of the chapel gave the building the aura of a gingerbread confection ready to be decorated for the Christmas season.

In fact the whole atmosphere on campus seemed lighter, giddy with anticipation of the holiday break and reunions with friends and family. Despite my utter lack of enthusiasm for meetings or consultations with Carl Irvin, I was missing Jess and Rafe and Maggie something fierce. Although it was not something to be openly acknowledged, I was missing Dante, too. It felt as though I'd been in Princeton for weeks, not days; I was more than ready to go home.

But that was for tomorrow, after we all got through the funeral. In anticipation of departure, I pulled out my suitcase and threw in anything I knew I wouldn't wear again while I was here, including the party finery from the African-American Studies gala. Three-inch heels were not exactly the proper footwear for snow-lined paths in any event. By the time I'd packed most of the bag, taken a shower, and changed into heavier wool slacks, an Irish knit sweater, and boots, I was up for an out-ing—but where? Eric was cramming for finals with Kayla, so I was on my own. I decided to hit the Alchemist and Barrister pub on Wither-spoon Street for a cheeseburger and fries, some comfort food on a night when I could use some.

Part of my restlessness was the result of my initial review of Earl's electronic organizer earlier that day. I'd been disappointed with what I'd found so far. Not that I really knew what I was looking for, anyway. His Palm Pilot gave me access to his calendar and his address book, but the volume of entries was so voluminous that it had yielded very little in terms of useful information so far. If I ever needed to call the Commerce Secretary, I now had both his private work line and his home phone number. But that was about it in terms of actionable data. I decided to have another go at it later that night. But in the meantime, I was too restive to sit still— despite the frigid temperature, I needed a walk.

The chimes from the university chapel were tolling seven when I set out across the campus toward the village of Princeton proper. Snow crunched merrily underfoot, even on paths that had been recently swept. The campus looked even more magical than it had from Eric's window, with Christmas lights twinkling from the rafters, doors, and windows of high Victorian, Georgian, and neo-Gothic exteriors. Though students hurried to and from the eating clubs, the library, and the dormitories in an end-of-the-semester flurry, the snow hushed all that it enveloped, calming me even as I mentally rehearsed what I would tell Carl Irvin about my progress on my AEA presentation once I got back to Cambridge. I could only postpone that conversation for one more day.

Lost in thought, I almost walked right into a tall blond woman in a long fur coat and a colorful silk Nepalese hat with fur trim that framed her classic cheekbones; Marti Waterstone was out of grunge, hence barely recognizable.

"Marti, I'm so sorry!" I exclaimed. "Mentally, I was back in Cam-bridge."

She laughed. "Didn't I see you leaving Professor Jones's lecture this afternoon?"

I nodded, remembering their shared distinctive hand gesture. "He's a brilliant speaker," I said lightly.

"He's also *very* hot. Don't you think?" I nodded wryly. Yes, I did think so. Apparently, lots of women did. "I saw the demonstration on the five o'clock news tonight," she continued. "Bo Merriweather really knows how to get those cameras rolling, doesn't he?"

"He likes the spotlight almost as much as Yusef. If he were just a little smarter, he'd be dangerous."

"Maybe he already is," she said cryptically.

I caught the hint, but chose to let it go by. I wasn't feeling particularly Miss Marple at that moment. "I almost didn't recognize you, looking like a runway model lost in a Doctor Zhivago fantasy," I teased her instead. "Where are you off to?"

"The annual Christmas party at Ivy. Why don't you come along?"

From what I recalled of my brother Eric's detailed delineation of the eating clubs—as hierarchical as the bloodlines in the Hapsburg monarchy—Ivy Club was at the pinnacle of Princeton exclusivity. Of course Marti Waterstone was a member.

"I'm hardly dressed for the occasion," I said, waving my arm down the front of my coat to point out my wool pants and boots.

"It's snowing," Marti continued, undaunted. "I kind of doubt that the spaghetti-strap crowd will be there in droves. It's not like most of these kids know how to dress, anyway." She pulled aside the front panel of her fur coat to reveal a floor-length velveteen skirt and a simple cream-colored silk blouse. "I'm wearing Sunday best, nothing more elaborate."

I could only imagine what would constitute something more elaborate to Marti; perhaps one of those dramatic dresses by that new Japanese designer, where the gorgeous fabric has been purposefully shot full of holes. Perfect for a rebel with a substantial budget.

"Besides," she said, "you'd be hard pressed to look anything less than pulled together, Professor Chase. I bet you're one of those people who look perfectly composed the minute you step out of the shower in the morning."

Now she had me laughing, and walking with her down the path lined with crisply manicured, snow-crusted bushes. What the heck—it was nearly Christmas, and some spiked eggnog and eavesdropping among the Princeton upper crust had to beat a solitary dinner at a fancifully named pub. What were the holidays for, but mixing and mingling?

The scene at Ivy made even my dinner with Zanda Fleming at Prospect House look bush league in comparison. It would take an American version of the Merchant-Ivory team, preferably from the South, to do justice to the nearly surreal sense of tradition, entitlement, and old money—lots of it—that suffused the very air these revelers breathed.

Though I saw no spaghetti straps in evidence, there were indeed a few bare shoulders on display, despite the wintry weather outside. Marti quickly dismissed them as "Bryn Mawr or Wellesley girls down for the evening." Two statuesque blondes—are there no short pedigreed WASPS?—had positioned themselves in the corner of the room in black velvet cocktail dresses with cowl necks that bled into the sleeves. The club, housed in a nineteenth-century dark brick building, was modeled on counterparts in London, and the long, narrow rooms had the dimensions of an urban townhouse. The more crowded the room became, the higher the voices rose—the better for me to cruise, like an anthropologist observing the rituals of a wholly foreign tribe.

As we entered, our coats had been taken by two black maids in crisp white aprons. Involuntarily I cringed; one of them closely resembled the faithful retainer played by Butterfly McQueen in *Gone With the Wind*. Other than the older black male waiters angling their way through the crowd bearing trays of shrimp and hot hors d'oeuvres, I was the only black person in the room. From the coat-check attendant to the bathroom matron to the elderly gentleman who reset the balls on the pool table in the parlor, I was the only black in the building who wasn't working that night. Marti Waterstone seemed to regard the situation with amusement.

"Don't worry, I promise no one will ask you to do the dishes," she giggled, taking me by the arm as though she were my tour guide.

"This is a far cry from P.J.'s," I shot back, tucking my backpack into a dark corner of the vestibule. No need to draw attention to the fact that I was woefully underdressed.

Marty grinned. "I've never been trained in classic French service, like these guys. I wouldn't cut it at Ivy."

Despite the fact that almost every woman in the room, including Marti, sported strings of real pearls—no freshwater substitutes here—I spied a small contingent in a far corner turned out in a near-uniform of Ralph Lauren-style equestrian, with well-tailored riding jackets and full woolen skirts. If I stayed in that vicinity, I would fit in fairly easily, except for the color of my skin. And my hair texture. And my political beliefs.

"Nothing doing," said Marti, dragging me to the opposite corner, where the bar had been set up. "We're heading for action central, not the horsey set."

Glasses of champagne in hand—the eggnog looked so rich that I'd have to work out exhaustively for a week to trade the calories—we made our way to the center of the room, only to be waylaid by none other than Hayden Fleming, resplendent in a crisp white shirt and a well-tailored wool sport coat.

"Professor Chase, Miss Waterstone," he said, nodding in our direction.

"Happy holidays, Professor Fleming," said Marti in a somewhat frosty tone, as though she were greeting a distant relative she'd rather encounter at weddings and funerals only.

Ever so subtly I saw Hayden Fleming looking me up and down, no doubt noting my comparatively rustic mode of dress. "Marti corralled me out on the footpath," I said, laughing in what I hoped was a devil-may-care manner. Bantering with Hayden Fleming wasn't high on my list for the evening. I couldn't imagine anything less relaxing than warding off his overtures, professional or otherwise.

Taking off in Marti's wake, I walked toward a large evergreen in the corner, ablaze with tiny white lights and draped with strings of popcorn and dangling candy canes. I saw her being greeted by a tiny woman with porcelain skin like that of a doll, dressed in a long plaid skirt with a train and a ruffle-fronted blouse, her curly black hair held in place by the sort of black velvet headband once favored by Hillary Clinton.

"This is my former roommate from Miss Porter's, Bitsy Dupree," explained Marti. "Bitsy, Professor Nikki Chase from Harvard."

"I didn't know you were a Miss Porter's girl," I teased Marti.

"She wasn't, much," said Bitsy, giggling. "She got kicked out and had to do a year at—what was that place called—Taft? But we had to let her back in, because she's a Waterstone, which is like being a Pyne at Princeton."

"No, sweetheart," Marti interrupted with an uncharacteristically serious tone. "It's like being a *Waterstone* at Princeton."

Bitsy laughed confidently. "Oops. Hit a nerve."

"Oh, please," said Marti with a pained smile. "What are you drinking, Bitsy? Bourbon? Maybe you've already had one too many."

"Ladies, it's a pleasure to welcome you," interrupted Jeb Wolf, who had turned in his orange and black accessories in favor of a green bow tie festooned with small red wreaths. "Did you realize that this is the hundred and seventy-fifth Christmas party sponsored by Ivy?"

"The mind boggles," Marti commented.

"It's a divine party, Mr. Wolf," Bitsy enthused. She grabbed the arm of a tall blond man in a tuxedo at her side. "Have you met my fiancé, Charles Butterworth? We dated while he was at Hotchkiss. In fact, we just booked the Princeton chapel for our wedding, a month after graduation. Charles will be heading off for Wall Street, and I'll be starting my internship at *Town & Country*."

Marti looked daggers in my direction, and we hightailed it back to the bar for fortification. Two glasses apiece later, we'd overheard enough about the Andover crew team, a student-teacher sex scandal at Groton, and the size of the Chapin School's endowment to last a lifetime.

I excused myself and stepped into the ladies' room, which was full of blondes furiously applying lipstick in the cloudy mirrors above the sink. As I entered one of the stalls, I was greeted by the sight of floating lettuce leaves in the toilet bowl, a sure sign of bulimia, curse of the rich young white girl. Some days, I was actually proud not to be a size 2. If that was what it took, the price was way too high.

As the crowd at the mirror dispersed through the doorway, I decided to refresh my own lipstick. That was when I heard it—a soft gasping sound emitted from one of the other bathroom stalls. Someone was crying, I thought. Perhaps another high-strung former debutante was having a rough night.

Then the door swung open, and to my surprise, there was Zanda Fleming. A high-strung former debutante *was* apparently having a rough night.

"Zanda? Are you all right?" I said quietly.

A look of surprise and embarrassment crossed her face, followed by a wry smile. "Hi," she said wearily. "I—I hate parties sometimes."

"Can I help?"

She shook her head. "Man troubles. No one can help with that."

I remembered seeing Hayden Fleming earlier in the evening, and I wondered if he was the source of the trouble. As much as I'd recoiled from him, I had to concede that he could be the kind that might take some time to get out of your system.

"Well, it may not help, but at least you should know you're not alone," I said consolingly. "I'm in a complete mess over someone, and the only salvation is that he's three hundred miles away right now."

"Why do we do it?" she asked rhetorically, as she pulled a sleek sterling silver compact from her evening bag.

"Because it's better than the alternative?" I shrugged.

"I'm not so sure about that," she replied, crisply snapping the compact shut. "Lesbians are very chic right now, you know." She smiled wickedly.

"So, I saw you having dinner with Lloyd Eastman," I began.

"Yes." She sighed dismissively. "I don't know why John insisted on naming him the acting chairman of the program. There is absolutely no chance that we'll be naming him the permanent chair, and it's just messy to have to manage that. Of course, the board members will all spend time with him, anyway, along with the real candidates for department chair. We can't let this drag on too long." I was itching to ask her more, but a flock of debs noisily entered the lounge, and when I turned back to Zanda, she was gone.

I mused on her question about the things we do for men as I looked for Marti in the crowd near the bar. I'd encountered only one eligible male the entire evening, a waiter bearing a strong resemblance to Sidney Poitier in his heyday. He served me a piece of toast with a dollop of caviar on the top, with the line, "What's a nice colored girl like you doing in a place like this?"

"Slumming," I'd told him with a wink.

As Marti and I took our coats from the white-gloved attendants, we could still hear her friend Bitsy Dupree regaling Jeb Wolf with tales of purported misbehavior at her coming-out party in New Orleans, where she was a sixth-generation debutante from a family of lawyers and state senators.

"Obviously Bitsy's the result of generations of inbreeding," said Marti, without a hint of irony.

I laughed, partially to cover up my own confusion. Had Earl been part of an underground network here? How else would he have gathered information about old money families, and secret histories known only to a select coterie? Had his indecision about leaving a place his own family had called home for three generations been fueled by knowledge he could no longer keep to himself?

As I pulled my coat on, I looked around for my backpack.

"You haven't seen my bag, have you?" I asked Marti as she pulled on a pair of black leather gloves.

"Where'd you leave it? Maybe in the ladies'?"

Ten minutes of fruitless searching turned up nothing. The pleasant buzz that I'd been enjoying had entirely dissipated as I'd realized what a truly stupid thing I had done. I hadn't left a bag unattended anywhere, ever, since I'd moved to New York. It had become a reflex to always know where my wallet was. I'd let this Gatsbyesque setting throw me off my game, with potentially disastrous results. I was pretty sure that

Earl's Palm Pilot had been in that backpack. I honestly couldn't remember whether I had taken it out earlier that day.

"Dammit!" I muttered. "I can't believe this!"

"Wow—what did you have in there, anyway?" Marty was looking at me with a concerned expression.

"Oh, the usual—all my credit cards, ID, cash—all that stuff that's a serious pain in the ass to replace."

"You better report it, then," she said briskly. "It'll probably turn up when they clean up later tonight. But if it doesn't, you're going to need to have reported it stolen in case someone starts using your credit cards." She tucked her arm in mine. "The Princeton cops are just down the street. I'll walk with you."

The frosty air was a tonic, its clarity rendering the frost-covered plantings in Prospect Gardens in sharp outline, like elements in a moonlit still life. We walked down Prospect Street past the other eating clubs—Colonial, Quadrangle, and Tower—and were about to go by Campus Club, all glittering with bright lights and holiday finery, when we heard footsteps on the path behind us. Marti snorted as a blond student in a baseball cap and a long striped scarf hanging practically to the snowy ground hustled past us, seemingly in a hurry.

"That's Holden Caulfield's younger brother," Marti told me. "You can tell by the scarf, and the befuddled, soulful expression."

"He must be lost around here," I said, thinking back to the social scene at Ivy.

Marti stopped dead in her track and looked over at me. "So is everyone else, Nikki. That's the dirty little secret of a place like this. It's all a masquerade, with the right clothes and accent and social connections helping you gain access to the club." Marti didn't sound the least bit tipsy. "Me?" she continued. "I'm with Groucho Marx in spirit—if the club is willing to take me, why would I want to join?"

I envied her insouciance. I was still furious with myself.

Soon the Princeton police station loomed before us at the end of Nassau Street, its cinderblock walls starting to look all too familiar. The officer on night duty was none other than Maureen Kelly.

147

"Doing some late-night sleuthing, Professor Chase?" she asked as Marti and I approached.

"Not exactly. I'm pretty sure my backpack just got stolen," I said sharply.

"At Ivy, of all places," Marti added.

Maureen Kelly looked over at her. "Wouldn't be the first time."

She led us down a hallway lined with "Wanted" posters, and we entered a spartan room dominated by a single wooden table. After declining cups of sludgy, late-night coffee, we slumped down into the chairs on either side.

Maureen Kelly gave Marti another look. "You're a student? Don't you get hassled by the animal rights people? They're active on campus, if the number of permits filed for demonstrations is any indication."

"Mind if I smoke?" asked Marti as she pulled out a pack of unfiltered Camels.

"Go right ahead," said Maureen Kelly, who seemed to be enjoying Marti's performance as a rich bohemian. I shook my head as she proffered the pack to me.

"I don't give a damn about the animal people," Marti declared, blowing circles of smoke into the air above the table. "They're as crazy as Bo Merriweather and his crew. Fanatics are fanatics, no matter what the ideology."

"I'm worried about my bag being stolen," I said slowly, "I think there might have been something important in it."

"How could some pickpocket at Ivy know what was in your purse?" asked Kelly as she sipped muddy coffee from a Styrofoam cup.

"He couldn't," I posited, "unless he was paying close attention." For reasons I couldn't quite articulate, I was loath to say more in front of Marti, a fact Maureen Kelly seemed to absorb as if by osmosis.

"Come with me," she said, motioning Marti to the door. "I want you to fill out a report, too. You're a material witness."

Before she'd returned I'd made up my mind to share some information: maybe Rafe was right, and someone was watching what I was up to. Or maybe it was purely coincidence that my bag had gone missing.

Either way, my gut was telling me that it was time to enlarge my posse.

Maureen Kelly sat down on a chair opposite mine and put her elbows down deliberately on top of the table. "All right, Professor—let's get down to it."

"Look, I don't know if my bag was stolen. But it's possible that someone thought that the keys to Earl's office were in there. I was in his office yesterday morning—very early."

"Looking for?" she prompted me.

I shrugged. "Just looking."

"Find anything?"

"His files had already been rifled by the time I got there. Maybe they found what I was looking for—a manuscript. Supposedly it's an exposé, with plenty in it to rile people not only at the school, but all over town."

"Where are the keys to his office now?" she asked me.

"In my brother's dorm room. They weren't in my bag, but Earl's Palm Pilot may have been. I found it earlier today, and I can't remember whether or not I took it out."

"You've been a busy woman." Maureen Kelly looked at me with annoyance writ large on her face. "Look, Professor Chase, we talked about this before." She leaned back in her chair. "You have to leave the investigating to us. We're not all about pulling black people over on the roads, you know. Some of us are just trying to do our jobs."

I said nothing.

"You know some other things, don't you?" she said, leaning across the table.

I sensed an opening and played it cool. "I have a different level of access than you do. So yes, I know some things."

"This isn't a game, you know, Professor," she replied sharply.

"Nobody knows that better than me," I snapped back. "But I don't even know if this was a crime, whether it was an accident, or what. I just know that things don't seem right around here."

"Okay, then let me give you something to think about, Professor. We found an accelerant at the site."

I felt my heart beat hard against my rib cage, like a bird fluttering against the bars of a cage. "You mean, you found evidence that it was arson?"

She shrugged. "Looks like it."

"My bag was stolen tonight," I concluded soberly.

"Yep," she replied crisply. "Your bag was stolen tonight." She rose from her chair. "I'll get one of the officers to walk you girls home tonight. You let me know when you're going to be leaving town, all right?" As she led me down the hall, the rubber soles of her sensible shoes squeaked on the linoleum floor tiles.

"This is a small town, Professor. It's pretty hard to keep a secret here," she said as she ushered me out the door.

I think we were all counting on that.

# 14

## The Good Life

I awoke the morning of Earl's funeral feeling both melancholy and annoyed. The sky was slate gray, and the sound of small ice pellets pinging on the windowpanes made me certain that freezing rain was the forecast for the day. It was the kind of morning that makes one think of hot tea, buttered toast, and the futility of life in general.

How could it be that so many good people were dead and so many bad ones still alive? I brooded while in the shower. It was a question that my brothers and I had debated many times growing up in the late 1960s and early '70s. Medgar Evers and Martin Luther King Jr. were gone in their primes, and Byron de la Beckwith and James Earl Ray had lived into their eighties, surrounded by their grandchildren. Both of my parents were political junkies and had a penchant for working on quixotic, losing political campaigns. We kids had all inherited that gene, and as a result had spent almost every election night of our lives moping and debating why so many smart and decent people kept losing elections to dim-witted, manipulative ones. It hardly seemed worth it to try to be good—to live a good life—when it appeared that the bad guys were winning at every turn. The good guys were apparently all being either knocked around by life or killed.

My sensible mother ultimately gave me the answer that satisfied my frustrations. "You have to live the life that makes you certain you did right," she'd said quietly, after our lamentations had run their course. "At your funeral, do you want to be remembered for winning some election or getting some big job? Or for having done what's right, the best way you knew how?"

I wondered if Earl would be satisfied with how he'd be remembered today. He'd been wildly successful by any measure. And I wanted to believe more than anything that he'd lived a good life. I'd been fretting over what Jide had said about Earl's interest in a wide variety of women, none of whom were his wife. As a feminist, I considered disrespecting women to be a felony. Learning that he might have been cheating on his wife with not one, but several women had shaken the foundation of my adoration for Earl. But I didn't want to spend the day of his funeral in a disapproving snit. He deserved better than that. No matter what he'd done that had been less than noble, the rest of us were the poorer for the loss of him. That was the simple truth, and it hurt, like an ache that lingers long after you've applied the hot compress, or the Tiger Balm, or taken the prescribed number of aspirin. Earl Stokes had spent his entire adult life examining the impact of race and class on the texture of our lives, yet he never succumbed to cynicism, despair, or easy grandstanding, and for this reason he would be my hero always.

As I brewed a pot of coffee, I thought about what the funeral might be like. Would whoever had set that fire be present? In my very limited experience with murder, I had discovered that the culprit often turned up at the funeral. Which meant that I needed to keep a clear head, even as I was mourning Earl.

Sipping the watery discharge from Eric's Mr. Coffee, I started to get dressed. I'd left out my go-to-church clothes the previous day: a demure navy wool suit with a slim knee-length skirt and a cropped, fitted jacket. It was warm, stylishly cut, and unassuming, perfect for a funeral on a winter's day. Underneath all this sobriety was a blazing red silk blouse. I'd worn a pair of gold earrings the night before that I planned to wear again, but somehow they weren't on the table in the living room where I'd left them. Maybe Eric had passed through and put them on his dresser for safekeeping, I thought. For the first time since I'd arrived at Princeton, I went into his bedroom.

It was typical Eric—neat as a pin. On top of his chest of drawers, I spied a glint of gold and thought that perhaps I had discovered what I was looking for.

It turned out that I had. But it wasn't my earring.

Lying on top of a pile of loose coins and receipts was a gold cufflink with a tiger's head and some sort of crest. It looked somewhat familiar, and it took me a minute before I placed it.

Then I realized: it was identical to the one that I had found on the ground at the site of the new Center for African-American Studies the night after Earl died. I stared at it, dumbfounded, then picked it up and turned it over in my hand. It was definitely the same design as the one I had found. Of course, it could be a complete coincidence. It was clearly Princeton issue, and there must be hundreds of these in use all over campus. But if that were true, there should be two of them on this dresser. And there was only one.

*Eric, why is there only one?*

The jangle of the telephone nearly made me jump out of my skin.

"Hey, it's me." My brother's voice rang cheerily in my ear. "Look, Kayla and I decided to go out for breakfast, so we'll just meet you at the church, Okay? Like at about ten-fifteen."

I agreed and hung up abruptly. My brother and Kayla—inseparable, it seemed. I had a very bad feeling, and it had a lot to do with her.

The two of them greeted me an hour later on the just-shoveled walkway leading up to the entrance to Waterstone Chapel. Somewhat self-consciously, I embraced them both. Kayla was on Eric's arm, every bit the attentive helpmate. My brother looked like he'd been up half the night: deep, dark pouches beneath his lively eyes gave him the appearance of a graduate student with an overdue thesis. I needed to talk to him about that cufflink. But this clearly wasn't the time.

I made a mental note to ask Marti which of her many illustrious ancestors had endowed this chapel. My question was answered once we'd stepped through the ornately carved wooden doors into the vestibule, where a discreet brass plague read, "Built in memory of his wife, Lucille, by Bertram Waterstone, Class of 1910."

Wordlessly we gravitated to the left side of the central aisle, in a row behind Lloyd Eastman and three students I recognized from Earl's class. The chancel at the front of the church was devoid of the usual floral arrangements; the funeral announcement in the paper had asked that in lieu of flowers, donations should be made to Beulah Baptist Church. Eula Stokes, resplendent in yet another purple broad-brimmed hat, was sitting in the front row of the church, accompanied by Pastor Creflo Smalls and a group of eight or ten women who appeared to be congregants from Beulah Baptist. I figured that they'd be disappointed in this service, which was bound to be High Church; there'd be no gospel music and testifying in the aisles of Waterstone Chapel.

I was wrong about that, or at least part of it. No doubt in a conces-sion to Eula Stokes, Princeton had imported one of the soloists from Beulah Baptist, and a contingent from their choir. Solemnly I watched Hayden Fleming, Jeb Wolf, and President Stern and his wife seat themselves on the right side of the chapel to the strains of "Amazing Grace."

"Is there a black person in America who can leave this world to any other but that song?" I heard Kayla say in a stage whisper to my brother, who shot her a silencing look.

The service was conducted by a tall, silver-haired priest, a perfect exemplar of Episcopalian dignity, whose sonorous voice echoed into the farthest reaches of the neo-Gothic interior. The chapel had been designed in the mode of Notre Dame, though in scaled-down propor-tions more appropriate to a Protestant denomination that eschews the more melodramatic iconography of Catholicism. There were marble baptismal founts in the chanceries off the main altar, but fewer statues of the Blessed Virgin, and a less gruesomely rendered crucifix than might be found in a Catholic house of worship. Still, flying buttresses supported a high, beautifully painted dome in the ceiling, from which legions of cherubs awash in fluffy white clouds beckoned to the lost souls below. It was an oddly exuberant, almost whimsical tableau, with its suggestion of joy in the afterlife.

When I was six, as my mother tells it, I asked my grandmother if she would still make my favorite sweet potato pie once she joined the angels. To which she replied without missing a beat, "Baby girl, you don't need sweet potatoes up in heaven. You got God's love to sustain you, morning, noon, and in the evening time, too."

I found this too abstract for consolation.

And what consolation did we have now that Earl was gone? President Stern led the tributes, calling Earl "not just a nationally recognized scholar, and a third-generation resident of the town of Princeton, but a true leader, whose students warmed to his support, yet respected the rigors of his classroom."

Hayden Fleming was next, citing Earl's collegial spirit, and his versatility in chairing two departments simultaneously. The latter comment caused my brother's eyebrows to arch upward. Fleming was followed by Lloyd Eastman, who spoke of the many years that he had known Earl—how they had met as young graduate students at Princeton and worked together almost their entire adult lives building the Program for African-American Studies at Princeton. I felt tears pricking at my eyelids as he spoke of Earl as the older brother he never had. "Many of you were lucky enough to have known him for a few years," Eastman said simply. "But I had him in my life for over twenty years. And he made me the man I am today."

Then Zanda Fleming rose to speak, having been diplomatically spaced apart from her ex-husband. Her voice choked up as she began: "I am proud to have called Earl Stokes a friend, as well as an esteemed colleague, someone whose commitment to the study of our country's economics as well as the history of its African peoples was complete and profound."

The finale in the stream of eulogies was an Academy-worthy performance in grandstanding, in the guise of remembering Earl Stokes. When Butch Hubbard took the lectern and grasped it like his own personal pulpit, I realized at a glance why he was still in town: as long as he had a captive audience, Sportin' Life would oblige with a performance.

"Brother Stokes," he thundered, like Adam Clayton Powell in his heyday, "you are with the spirits of the ancestors now, and will guide us from the world beyond the one we cling to, full of petty preoccupations, foolish diversions, and insignificant altercations."

"Help me, Jesus," I heard my brother say under his breath.

"You will be the light in the continuing darkness, a beacon in the storm that engulfs so many of our inner-city communities," he bellowed, his voice rising and falling like a backwoods preacher's. No matter what else you wanted to say about Butch Hubbard, you couldn't deny that he knew how to put on a show. Still, if he started to recite pseudo-African poetry, I knew I wouldn't be able to keep my peace. Luckily he spared us by moving on to one of the more pastoral psalms, then to poems by Langston Hughes and Countee Cullen. If he had ended there, I knew it would have been fine with Earl.

"Brothers and sisters, Earl Stokes was a mentor, a teacher, a father and a husband, and an economic theorist of national renown," Butch Hubbard continued. "But most of all, he was a proud black man."

"Amen, brother!" exulted Eula Stokes from the front row.

"All praise Brother Stokes!" chimed in two of the Beulah Baptist congregants, in unison.

At the end of Butch Hubbard's exhortation, it dawned on me: Yusef Jones was nowhere to be seen. A son missing a father's funeral—that was deep, no matter what their differences had been.

This ceremony had been the perfect embodiment of the divided nature of Earl's life. There was pomp, and there was official recognition, a black gospel choir and an adoring throng of students. But where was the heart of Earl?

Just as I formed the thought, a single strain of music pierced the silence in the chapel. It was a jazz saxophone, wailing mournfully to the tune of "St. Louis Blues." The sax man was joined by a trumpeter. Together they stood shoulder to shoulder and played out the song. That, I thought, was the music Earl would have wanted to escort him home. I wondered who had arranged for the one element in the service that he really would have appreciated.

Afterward, Eula Stokes and Creflo Smalls positioned themselves outside the front door of the chapel to greet exiting mourners, like the parents of the bride in a wedding receiving line. I embraced Eula, and shook the hand of Pastor Smalls warily.

"Thank you for coming, Professor Chase," said Creflo Smalls, as though the ceremony had been entirely his doing.

In a way, it had, we learned as we huddled on the walkway next to the churchgoers from Beulah Baptist, a veritable Greek chorus of gossip, opinion, and commentary.

"The Lord can't accept a man's soul from a place like this," said a dark-skinned man in a wool fedora. "Should've had the service at Beulah."

"Earl wasn't a regular at Sunday services," chimed in a large woman wrapped in zebra-skin fake fur. "Sister Stokes and Pastor Smalls let them have it here, long as the choir came. It was a compromise."

"Ain't no compromise in the afterlife," scoffed a woman in a stylish red turban. "You're saved, or you're not."

"Easy for you to say, Sister Watkins," retorted the woman in zebra skin. "You drove your husband out—now who's the one who's damned?"

"My people, my people," I heard Kayla say to my brother with a sigh.

"Sisters, maintain your dignity," scolded the man in the fedora, "'specially in this place, where you got white folks all around."

As if on cue Jeb Wolf walked by, accompanied by Zanda Fleming, who waved to us as she climbed into a waiting limo, like a movie star acknowledging the hoi polloi. In their wake scurried a small blonde woman, barely five feet in stature, whom I'd seen earlier in the chapel looking mournfully at the casket from the second row.

"Who's that?" I asked my brother as we watched the woman steer clear of both the impromptu receiving line and the Greek chorus and hurry down the walkway as though someone were pursuing her.

"I think that was his secretary, Cheryl," he said, peering after her.

"Now there's an unholy alliance if ever there was one," Eric muttered under his breath.

Hayden Fleming and Butch Hubbard were deep in conversation.

Indeed: now that Butch Hubbard no longer had to deal with Earl's imminent arrival at Harvard, would he consider decamping himself? Hayden Fleming was perfectly capable of greasing the wheels with the Princeton Powers that Be. Stranger things had happened in the annals of internecine war games between Ivys.

"How come I don't feel comforted by that service?" Eric said.

"With that cast of characters?" said Kayla. "They had all the warmth of the guy who introduces the President at the State of the Union address."

"All show, no go," my brother chimed in. "I wonder where Yusef was?"

There was a marked silence in which I tried determinedly not to look at Kayla.

Finally she said, "Maybe he just needed some time to mourn alone. Everyone has their own way of dealing, you know."

Eric shrugged his shoulders. "All I know is, I feel like I've been run over by a truck. And I miss Earl already."

We all said "Amen" to that, and headed our separate ways. Kayla said that she had a World Civilization class at noon, and my brother had a graduate seminar presentation on Zora Neale Hurston and traditions in African-American folklore at 12:30.

And I had an intercept to execute. I had noticed that while most of the crowd had dissipated, headed to Earl's interment at Princeton Cemetery, Lloyd Eastman had pulled on his coat and now seemed headed in a different direction.

"Professor Eastman," I called out as I walked rapidly behind him. "Do you have a moment?"

It had occurred to me that Lloyd Eastman was the precise mirror image of Earl: short and barrel-chested, fair-skinned and loud-voiced, with the demeanor of a high-school wrestling coach. Perhaps that was why they had worked together successfully for so long. From what I could tell, Earl had provided the intellectual horsepower needed to lead the program and attract national recognition and funding. And Eastman had supplied the enthusiasm and loyalty required to hold it all together. Eastman paused and turned to wait for me to catch up to him, nodding a greeting at a couple of men who walked past first.

"Of course, Professor Chase," he said, looking a bit startled. "I'm on my way back to Dickinson. I would be at the cemetery, but I have a class to teach in about an hour."

"I understand. I'll walk with you." I fell into step beside him as we emerged from the chapel and into the frozen landscape. Mercifully, it had stopped raining, but the flagstone walkway was a sheet of ice.

"If I may?" he said gallantly, offering me his arm.

"Thank you," I said, and slipped my hand into the crook of his elbow. "These heels are not exactly cut out for this weather."

"I still can't believe that this has happened," Eastman said as we set out across campus.

"I know. I have to leave for Cambridge this afternoon, and part of me wants to stay, because it will seem even less real after I'm away from Princeton."

I felt a throbbing sensation underneath my fingers, and realized that his arm was trembling. "Your eulogy was just wonderful, Professor Eastman. This must be very difficult for you," I said gently.

"Yes," he said simply. "I worked with Earl for over twenty years. He was my partner building this department in the face of some real opposition. I honestly don't know what we'll do now that he's gone."

We had reached Dickinson Hall, and he ushered me into a small but surprisingly immaculate office in the basement, near Earl's old office. He shut the door and motioned for me to sit down on a well-worn leather armchair across from his desk.

"So do you think that there is any chance that the building will still be built? Or is that impossible?" I asked.

He sighed heavily. "I'll tell you straight, Professor Chase—" he began.

"Please call me Nikki," I interrupted.

"All right. Straight up, Nikki, I don't know that it would have been completed, even if he were alive."

"Why do you say that?" I asked, startled.

"Had you seen how ambitious a project this was?" From the bottom drawer of an oversize wood desk that seemed to take up half the room, he pulled a roll of architectural blueprints and rolled them out on top. It looked like the stack of plans that I had seen scattered on the floor in Earl's office when I went to visit him the day I arrived in Princeton. I guess Eastman had taken them for safekeeping. "Come, look at this."

I leaned over his shoulder and peered at the papers. Close scrutiny revealed that the new Center for African-American Studies was to have been a real showpiece—a bold, dramatic building that would have staked a claim for the importance of the program at Princeton in no uncertain terms. There were three separate wings pictured, with a dining area and a specialized library in addition to class and lecture rooms and staff offices. Materials were listed primarily as glass, burnished African woods, and slate from Vermont. Nothing I had seen at the ruined site had prepared me for the scope and ambition of what I saw before me now.

"This was going to be a magnificent building," I breathed.

"Yes." He nodded slowly, and a smile played across his lips. "World class. Nothing like it anywhere else. Not even at Harvard."

"How many square feet was the Center going to be?" I asked, looking again at the blueprints.

"Just over 200,000." I could hear the pride in his voice as he spoke the number.

"How were you going to pay for this? It couldn't have been budgeted strictly to African-American Studies," I mused aloud. "Your program is far too small to fund something like this."

Eastman smiled cryptically. "There was more than one source of funding, believe me. We could never cover this out of our budget."

"Is that why you said that it might not have happened?"

"Let's just say that there were many people who wanted to see any capital expenditures on this campus go to other projects. We were fighting for our lives to keep the construction moving forward. And now this."

"So if this building never gets built, where will the funding that was earmarked for this go?"

The professor shrugged his shoulders. "You'd have to ask the president that." Before I could respond, he glanced around furtively, as if he suspected that someone was eavesdropping. Then he continued speaking, at a lower volume. "I know for a fact that there are other departments and programs that have already lined up with new funding requests, now that the Center has been destroyed. Can you believe that crap? It hasn't even been a week."

"Would that student, Bo Merriweather, be in that crowd?" I asked.

He snorted derisively. "You better believe it. He and his *National Prospect*. He has big plans for that rag."

"He was a problem for Earl, wasn't he?" I asked soberly.

Eastman nodded. "It was almost as if it was personal between the two of them. The way they would go after each other, I told Earl to be careful that the kid didn't bait him into doing something foolish." He glanced discreetly at his watch, and I took the cue to leave.

"I'm keeping you from your work," I said quickly, gathering my coat and bag. "Thank you for showing me those plans. Earl had talked about the building, but I had no idea that it was going to be so grand."

He walked me to the door. "I'll be interested to see if the president has the will to go forward with this project now. It would mean the world to us if he would."

I nodded and began to climb the stairs outside his office, accompanied by images of flames licking the sides of the building, rising higher and higher in an infernal spiral, like the paintings of hell my grandmother had shown me in a book her pastor gave her.

"There's places besides heaven, baby girl," she'd cautioned, "and they're not places you need to know real well."

Though I knew my grandmother was a woman of surpassing wisdom, I also knew, even then, that I had to see both sides of the picture for myself before I could tell which end was up.

# 15

## A Friend of My Youth

"That's right, ladies and gentlemen. I AM EATING FIRE. What's that you say? Yes, little boy, it's real fire. But it's perfectly safe. In fact, watch carefully so that you can try this at home, when your mommy is away."

The crowd laughed appreciatively at the wiry young man twirling a stick with flames at both ends on the small plaza in front of Wharburton's Bakery. Even in mid-December on a 15-degree afternoon, Harvard Square was filled with street performers displaying varying degrees of malice toward their audiences. I'd passed a guitarist in front of Café Algiers who was insulting anyone who didn't make a contribution to the tin cup on the sidewalk in front of him, and a sax player who called out random compliments to the passersby. I had two tickets to a production of *Antigone* at the Loeb Theater in my new backpack, and the fuel from a Charlie's Kitchen double cheeseburger in my veins. It was great to be home.

I walked down Brattle Street toward Mass Ave, dodging piles of snow and ice patches and soaking in the peculiar charms of the Square at holiday time. The Brattle Street Florist Shop was overflowing with fragrant pine boughs, and Wordsworth's front windows held copies of *The*

*Christmas Alphabet* and a history of the song "White Christmas." Cardullo's white sidewalk sign urged shoppers to come in and sample the Belgian chocolates and Italian panetone. One homeless man hawked copies of the street newspaper *Spare Change* in front of Urban Outfitters, and a second one stopped me at Nini's Corner to remind me that the holidays were coming and to kindly inquire if I could spare some coins. I could and did, even though my social worker mother always says that it's better to refer such people to the nearest social services office. The banners with the off-kilter gold lighted stars and undecipherable swirls were making their annual appearance high above Mass Ave. The kiosks at the entrance to the Yard proclaimed that three days hence Winter Weekend would commence, with the annual Lowell House Waltz competing for space with a film festival at Dunster House. Not a manicured bow or preppy white Christmas light in sight. We definitely weren't in Princeton anymore.

But I still couldn't get Earl out of my mind. On the Amtrak ride north from New York City, lulled by the rocking motion of the train and the buzzing of my fellow passengers, I'd replayed his funeral over and over. Was Yusef Jones's absence tied in any way to Kayla's presence? And was her demeanor toward my brother connected in turn to the fact that Earl's only son did not make it to his father's send-off? Was Eula Stokes's relationship with Pastor Creflo Smalls already deepening in the wake of Earl's death? Why, indeed, had Eula agreed to have the service on the Princeton campus? Did Pastor Smalls have his own reasons for wanting to placate Princeton officials? And how had Butch Hubbard inserted himself onto the roster of speakers?

I swore I'd seen Detective Maureen Kelly at the back of the church, too. The casket had been closed, no doubt due to the damage to the body from the fire; hence there had been no official opportunity for friends, colleagues, or family members to walk singly up the aisle and be observed by the entire congregation. Yet the petite blond woman had gone up to the casket, anyway, as if in desperate need of a chance to say goodbye, even in highly constricted circumstances. Was she one of the many women Jide had seen in Earl's company at Panera? Most puzzling of all were the building plans I'd seen surreptitiously. There had to be another financial force behind this project. Could Zanda Fleming have been in love with Earl, or just bent on doing further damage to her ex-husband, somehow, in her quest to support Afro-Am at the expense of Economics? Who else would have had the access, and the influence, to come up with the millions needed to erect a building of this sophistication and architectural ambition?

And most troubling of all, what was my brother's cufflink doing at the site of a murder? I'd ended up running for my train and hadn't had a chance to talk with him at all after the funeral. But I knew I was going to have to deal with that at some point soon.

It seemed to me that the answers to at least some of my questions lay in a better understanding of what Earl had really been intending to do before he died. Stay at Princeton, or come up here? So I'd decided to pay a call on Harvard's Afro-Am Department. I had a feeling that someone over there would know what Butch Hubbard had been up to in recent weeks.

I made my way across the snow-covered Yard, dodging clusters of students on their way to an early dinner. The buildings surrounding the Yard are a symphony in red brick, neo-Georgian splendor, low-slung and companionable. Contrary to myth and legend, the ivy is mostly gone (bad for the integrity of the bricks); yet in the pink dusk of a winter day, it still felt timeless, as though Yankee squires still held forth rather than nuclear physicists and Nobel Prize-winning poets.

The Afro-Am Department is housed in the Barker Center, the building that was once the Freshman Union. The stately red brick Georgian building held innumerable undergraduate memories for me—the terror of my very first meal at Harvard, the illicit thrill of drinking coffee for the first time, the incomprehensible lure that the pinball machines in the basement had held for my first real boyfriend, the cheap Spanish champagne we'd smuggled in to drink a toast on the last evening of our freshman year. The building's renovation was unmistakably handsome, and it had become a wonderful setting for a number of departments in the humanities, including Afro-Am. But every time I saw it, a small part of me felt the loss of who I was at eighteen.

I walked quickly up the shallow stone steps and into the warm maroon and green decor of the Barker Center. Afro-Am's headquarters were on the second floor, up a double-height flight of stairs. The splendid setting was an undeniable testament to Butch Hubbard's political clout and powers of persuasion. These were magnificent quarters—when I was an undergraduate, the Afro-Am Department had been housed in a small white clapboard house on Kirkland Street. Bolstered by Butch Hubbard's ability to attract the best and the brightest in the field, Afro-Am at Harvard had grown to ten full-time faculty positions, five teaching assistantships, and over twenty-five course offerings per term. It was the largest, most comprehensive African-American curriculum in the country, the envy of even the most prestigious black colleges, who'd lost star professors steadily to Sportin' Life, with his access to a national, and international, arena. It would have taken years—or a truly immense war chest of money—for Princeton to catch up, even with Earl's new building up and running.

A bronze bust of W. E. B. DuBois stood watch over the entrance to the suite of offices that held Harvard's "dream team" of African-American scholars—the "talented tenth," for sure, if ever there was such a thing. I pulled open one of the glass double doors and entered, in search of someone who was not quite so well known. Yet.

"You tell that son of a bitch that it was Janice Borden who did the primary research for that book, and it's Janice Borden who should get the credit for it!"

I stood in the hallway by an opened office door, waiting for a break in the action.

"No dice."

I was only hearing one side of this phone conversation. But it didn't seem to be going particularly well.

"That's right." The female voice started up again, this time with a fist slam on the desk. "You just let them know that they'll get the final chapters when I've got a redrawn contract that gives me top billing. He screwed me out of it the last time, but he's not here to do it again."

A pause ensued. I hadn't intended to eavesdrop. Really. But this didn't seem to be the kind of conversation that one walked in on in the middle of.

"No, I'm not being a bad sport about it," came a low sarcastic whisper. "I'm a good sport. A bad sport would say, 'Give me the whole advance and sole credit since he's not around anymore.' Here's what a good sport sounds like: They're not getting the final chapters until I know I'm getting top billing. And if I don't get it, I'm going with somebody who will give me what I want. Goodbye!"

Taking the sound of a receiver being slammed down as a sign that the conversation had ended, I knocked.

"What!" commanded the voice.

"Janice Borden," I said smoothly. "It's been way too long."

A heavy-set black woman with henna highlights in her short brown hair regarded me severely from behind a massive ebony desk. Then, slowly, a Cheshire cat smile spread across her face.

"Nikki Chase! Why, it has been a while. How long were you standing there?"

"Not long," I said sweetly. "I hope I'm not interrupting anything."

She smiled even wider, as her hands straightened the knot on the Hermes scarf flung casually over her rust-colored cashmere twin set. "Of course not! I was just having a little dispute with my auto mechanic. They think we don't know a muffler from a carburetor. You know how they try to play us. Like a sister doesn't know her way around an automobile." She sighed, and gestured for me to sit in a high-backed wicker chair whose like I hadn't seen since Huey Newton posed in one in a famous photograph. Adorned with large green plants and wall hangings hand-embroidered by subsistence farmers in Zimbabwe, Janice's office was exquisitely calibrated to be both homey and intimidating. "So, girl, I'm reading about you everywhere."

The expression of faux concern on her face was so well executed that

I almost fell for it. With Janice, the blade goes in so smoothly that it takes several minutes to feel the pain.

"You're quite the hero," she continued. "But it must be hard to convince those Econ folks to take you seriously, now that you're a crime fighter."

My eyes glanced up to a wall full of framed diplomas—the Westlake School, Harvard College, and Harvard Business School. Almost identical to my own educational background. Therein lay the problem. Janice had been a year ahead of me in college, and for some reason she had viewed me as a rival since the day we met. I hadn't even realized it until a man I was dating told me that she had filled his ears with stories about how I had been her protégée in college, and had turned on her when we both got to business school. Both parts of this story were patently untrue. What was true was that we had both grown up as certifiable members of the black upper middle class—she in Los Angeles and me in Detroit—and now we were both successful black women at Harvard. We should have been close friends and allies—but apparently Janice felt that the place was too small for the two of us. And she would be thrilled to see me gone. It was sad, but true: the old-school HNIC phenomenon (that would be Head Nigger in Charge) was very much alive and well in our generation.

"I'm supposed to be going to St. Kitts for the holidays with my mother and grandmother," Janice informed me. "But if I don't get some of these students on their way home to Grosse Point or Larchmont, I won't be seeing a beach or a palm tree anytime soon."

Okay, so perhaps I was jealous of her and wouldn't mind seeing her gone, either. Because quite frankly, Janice Borden seemed to have it all. She was on a fast track to getting tenure in Afro-Am, and unlike me, she had a stellar relationship with her department chair. In fact, it had been rumored that the proximity of Janice's office to Chairman Hubbard's at the Barker Center had led to other intimacies, as well. The rumors were fueled by the fact that Sportin' Life's wife had gained a great deal of weight since the birth of their third daughter.

"So what's up, Nikki?"

"I'm sure you've heard about Earl Stokes. I just got back from Princeton today."

She closed her eyes and shook her head dramatically. "That's been the only thing on my mind the past few days. The only thing. And it's just killing me that I had to miss the funeral."

"He was my mentor, so I know how you feel."

Her eyebrows arched. "Was he *really*? He was my mentor, too. That's how I got this job. He and his wife were just so kind to me, and I'll never have another friend like him."

"Yes, I met him through my brother when my brother was an undergrad there, and Earl was always there for me." I forced myself to sit back in the chair. Were we now actually arguing over who was grieving for Earl more?

Janice smiled and rubbed the arms of her sweater. "Well, girl, I can tell you he was solid. They did not want to hire me here. I had the grades and the journal articles in all the best history journals and African-American history conferences. But you know how they are when they are looking at us."

I nodded with understanding.

"If you're white, you can come from Ohio State," she said, sinking into an almost sister-girl ghetto inflection. "But if you look like us, you'd better be double Ivy League."

I laughed. That was something we could agree on, at least.

"I remember how I met Earl when I was researching my dissertation." Janice got up and pulled a thick binder off a shelf above her desk. "I even dedicated it to him."

"Wow!" I said, while looking at the heavy tome. "The History of Entrepeneurship in Nineteenth-Century Black American Communities."

Janice shook her head. "It was what gave him the idea for his book *Color Counts*."

"Really?" I said dryly. I was certain that every friend, colleague, neighbor, and associate of Earl's had tried to claim some kind of credit or inspiration for contributing to his wildly successful book. Why not Janice?

"Yeah," she continued. "Sometimes it annoyed me that I got barely a mention in his acknowledgments. But who the hell was I to complain? He got me a job at this school and has been fighting for me ever since. That's how I got published so fast. Speaking of Princeton, take a look at this." She reached for a bright-orange-colored magazine that looked strangely familiar.

"I got this piece of crap in my mailbox this morning. The newest issue of the *National Prospect*. The biggest load of junk you ever saw. I don't know why Princeton puts up with this."

"First Amendment, remember? I was the guest lecturer in Earl's Afro-Am class," I added. "And believe it or not, the editor in chief of this rag is in the class."

"Of course he's in it. Probably to keep tabs on Earl. I heard that these kids were obsessed with Earl. Everything he wrote, said, or did."

"For what purpose?" I asked, flipping through the glossy magazine.

"In the short term, so they could mock him in the magazine for the pleasure of their readers every other week."

"And the long term?"

Janice stood up for effect. "So they could get enough support from alumni and students to get rid of any department, professor, or program that was supportive of blacks, Jews, women, gays, or any other minorities that might oppose their conservative agenda. They're rotten people."

A memory of my conversation with Lloyd Eastman flickered through my mind. If the building isn't completed, he'd said, the funds earmarked for it will go somewhere else. I looked at the cover of the magazine. It featured a garish cartoon of a heavy-set black woman with a rolling pin in her hand, a bandanna over her hair, and large red lips. She had a wide torn hoop skirt, and she seemed to be trampling over the American flag and a frightened tiger. The headline above the cartoon read, THIS ISSUE—"AUTHOR" TONI MORRISON TRAMPLES OVER OUR AMER-ICAN AND PRINCETON TRADITIONS. Next to this Aunt Jemima-like cartoon ran a laundry list of other articles:

WAA, WAA, WAA! FEMALE CO-EDS WHINE
ABOUT SEXISM AT THE NUDE OLYMPICS

PROSPECT'S OUT LIST: THE GAY NINETIES
ARRIVE AT NASSAU HALL

HOW JEWISH MONEY RUINED THE
UNIVERSITY OF PENNSYLVANIA

WHO'S JIVIN' WHO? FIRST IN A SERIES ON
"SCHOLAR" EARL STOKES AND HIS ILK

I laid the magazine down. "Why do I feel like I need to wash my hands?"

"I'll bet those knuckleheads were dancing in the streets when they heard about Earl. The paper here said it was a tragic accident. But somebody told me that it may not have been an accident."

I knew her well enough to know that Janice was baiting me. But it suited my purposes to play along. "Yeah, the papers here are just aping the *Trentonian*. But I did hear that the police are looking into arson."

Janice's large brown eyes narrowed. But I noted that she didn't look surprised. Just watchful. "And what are you looking into, Nikki?"

I gave her a guileless smile in response. "What do you mean?"

She leaned forward in her chair. "Look, you and I both know that there aren't many of us." If you included Nell Poindexter, a biographer of Ralph Ellison in the English Department, there were three of "us" at Harvard: black women professors under forty within the Faculty of Arts and Sciences. Over forty constituted an even smaller club. The faculties of the professional schools were a little better—but not much. "We have to stick together for survival," Janice continued.

I had never harbored a single doubt regarding Janice Borden's survival skills.

"You can't keep playing detective and keeping the wolves at bay at the same time," she declared flatly. "Carl Irvin isn't your only problem around here. What happened to Earl was a real tragedy, Nikki, but it's not your burden to take on. You've got enough of those—we all do."

"Earl never trusted the police in Princeton," I said. "I think it was one of the reasons he was planning to leave."

"He wasn't leaving!" Janice snorted. Her tone was definitive. "I know everyone was saying that he was coming here, but he wasn't. That man wasn't leaving Princeton for anything. He and Butch would never have been able to work together. Girl, can you imagine that pissing contest?"

"If that's true, then why was Butch down in Princeton so much? He was one of the key speakers at Earl's funeral today. They must have been close."

"I doubt that," Janice said skeptically. "It's just that Butch regards himself as a spokesman for black academia, because he's got access to money, and to the political movers and shakers. And I'm sure he respected Earl."

Maybe Earl had more access to money than people realized, I thought as Zanda Fleming flashed again through my mind. Sometimes it's the quiet ones who surprise you.

Seemingly deep in thought, Janice paused: "I know Butch thought highly of Earl's writing, particularly *Color Counts*, because he told me to read it after I published an article in a French magazine on the business of hip-hop. In terms of African-American economic empowerment, Earl's work was the touchstone."

Exactly. It was widely known at Harvard that Butch Hubbard had also helped Janice place a piece in the *New Yorker* about the historical role of playing the dozens, and its influence on the development of rap. Though Janice writes in a mix of European-influenced academic jargon and street lingo, with specific musical references mixed liberally throughout, her academic arena isn't far from Earl's own. Would she indeed have been happy if he'd made his way to Cambridge? Or would he have cramped her style and her ability to move up through the ranks? And if Earl's way of doing things had been a corrective within the department to Sportin' Life's high-profile, big-spending ways, Janice Borden might have found herself with every reason to wish that Earl Stokes had never left the hallowed halls of Princeton.

It was 6:30 P.M. by then, and despite my cheeseburger on the go earlier that afternoon, I found that I was hungry again. So perhaps I was experiencing low blood sugar. But the thought crossed my mind that Janice Borden—or Butch Hubbard, more likely—could easily have benefited from the death of Earl Stokes. It seemed that just about every person who crossed my path had an agenda that intersected in some way with Earl's, giving a whole new meaning to the phrase "six degrees of separation."

I took my leave of Janice and made my way across the Yard, this time noting the plethora of holidays that were actually being celebrated in Cambridge. Menorahs, Christmas trees, and Kwanzaa candles were visible in the windows of the dorms. "Happy Winter Solstice," read one hand-lettered sign. I thought about Jess and her annoyance that at Princeton only one of the aforementioned holidays seemed to be on anyone's mind.

I had to stop suspecting every person who crossed my path of foul play, and get on with my life. What I really needed was to deal with my boss, Carl Irvin, and plan not just next semester's classes, but my movements for the fast-upcoming holidays. My mother had been pressuring me and my brothers to come home to Detroit this year, and if I didn't make travel plans shortly, I'd be hard pressed to get a plane ticket, let alone a decent fare.

Abruptly, out of the darkness came the flickering of light: a veritable field of small, white handheld candles illuminated the front steps of Memorial Church. Wasn't it too early in the evening for carols from the Krocks? However, no songs rang out in the cold night air; instead, I heard shouts of "A living wage today!" Cafeteria workers, custodians, and office personnel, among others, paraded in front of the church in orderly lines, hoisting placards that read, I CAN'T FEED MY FAMILY ON $7.50 AN HOUR and THIS IS CAMBRIDGE, NOT MANILA. When I heard someone call my name, I turned on my heels in surprise.

It was Percy Walker, the building superintendent at Littauer Center, which houses the Economics Department. He was still dressed in his green Buildings and Grounds overalls. Since he makes a supervisor's salary, his attendance at the rally was a real show of support for his crew in the building. It didn't hurt that all the Buildings and Grounds workers, no matter what the level, were members of the same union.

Percy embraced me. He has always reminded me of my grandfather; over the years we've become good friends. And as my brother Eric has also learned at Princeton, it is always good policy to have friends in the Buildings Department.

"Are you here to support our action?" Percy asked.

"To tell you the truth, I just got off a train from Princeton," I told him. Now that I was practically engulfed by the crowd, I could see that the union members had been joined by a significant number of students, as well as at least one faculty member: Hal Wasserstein from Sociology, an unregenerate lefty who could be counted on to show up at every campus demonstration.

"Nikki, join us," yelled Hal, who was wearing a sandwich board emblazoned with the message, A JUST WAGE FOR A GOOD DAY'S WORK—THE RIGHT OF EVERY WORKING MAN OR WOMAN.

Who could argue with such a sensible-sounding proposition? As usual at a place like Harvard, the problem was perception: alumni donors and groups like the Ford Foundation were eager to endow new buildings, or chairs in academic departments, that would bear their respective names and trumpet their magnanimous gestures. But who wanted to give money to raise the wages of cafeteria workers? That had to come out of the general fund. And as tuition and other costs had escalated to a yearly sum of nearly $45,000 per student, administrators sensitive to the pleas of less-than-wealthy parents tried to hold the line by freezing the wages of those least able to fight back, or complain publicly.

A tightly argued editorial in the *Crimson* had turned the tide of campus opinion, so it seemed, by detailing the costs of living in the greater Boston metropolitan area, down to the price of a spaghetti dinner for a family of four, not to mention transit and housing costs. This was juxtaposed with a monthly breakdown of expenditures in the president's household, including a floral bill that equaled a Buildings employee's monthly rent and utilities. As incendiary journalism in the time-honored tradition, the piece had worked wonders for the turnout: at least two hundred people milled about the Yard, now joined by a contingent of twenty or so led by none other than Butch Hubbard.

He nearly swept by us—then stopped abruptly. "Brother Walker!" he said exuberantly, high-fiving a beaming Percy. "Sister Chase!" he continued, clearly caught up in the crowd's high spirits. "I'm so glad that you could join us on behalf of the most righteous cause on campus!"

"Wouldn't miss it!" I said brightly.

Like a political candidate preparing to address his adoring supporters, Butch Hubbard pushed his way through the crowd and leapt dramatically on top of an overturned milk crate, succeeding Keisha Adams, a receptionist at Alumni Relations who'd been elected president of the union.

"Brothers, sisters, students, fellow faculty members—tonight we stand as one, no matter what our color, or our role here at this great university!" roared Sportin' Life, his head covered by a tweed newsboy's cap.

"Say it, brother! You are with us!" cheered two middle-aged Latina women I recognized as servers from the Dunster House cafeteria.

"Harvard is the richest school in the richest country in the world, yet the people who serve its food, and clean its buildings, and file its papers—in other words, the folks who keep the show on the road—are making third-world wages!"

"Right on!" yelled Hal Wasserstein.

"It's time to get a raise, to a living wage!" thundered Butch Hubbard, as though his offering earlier in the day at Earl's funeral had been a mere oratorical warm-up.

"A raise, to a living wage!" the crowd began to chant as lines of demonstrators moved in near-choreographed unison from one quadrant of the Yard to the other, trailed by camera-wielding representatives of the local, and perhaps national, media. What was local to Harvard often became national in impact, especially with a personality such as Butch Hubbard in the mix. Footage of Sportin' Life would be front and center in all the coverage, much to the consternation, no doubt, of our new president.

It was when I looked over at Percy Walker that my creeping admiration for Butch Hubbard's willingness to buck Harvard officialdom became tangible respect, because I saw the expression on Percy's face. His large, watchful eyes were tearing up with emotion, and it stuck me that Hubbard really was giving voice to people who had none. No one would listen to what Percy had to say—but they'd listen to a tenured Harvard professor who happened to make for great television. Percy had seen opportunity come, then go—yet it was not in his nature to demonstrate, or to make demands. He needed someone like Hubbard. A lot of people did. Heck, maybe the university did, too—who else but a media-savvy agitator could keep the place honest on matters of race?

Suddenly I was tired, bone tired, the kind of tired that responds only to the hottest of baths and a strong cup of tea. I slung my backpack onto the opposite shoulder to shift the weight and slipped away as the crowd began to disperse into the cold but shining evening.

# 16

## Seven Leagues

**M**y neighborhood, which lies due north of the Law School, about halfway between Harvard Square and Somerville, could charitably be described as a bit down at the heels. But its mix of turn-of-the-century clapboard houses, families with children, and graduate students on a budget suits me to a tee. My attachment to Cambridge was primal—I was becoming one of those people who can't live anywhere else, which was absolutely foolhardy, given the odds that I would earn tenure at Harvard. But that was a worry for another time. That night, I rambled happily home through the crisp night air, soaking in the familiar sights as if I had been gone for weeks, not days. I hadn't noticed before, but there was a full moon that night, and it seemed a good omen.

To revive my spirits, I had stopped by my office and changed shoes. From flat loafers, I had switched to my favorite pair of high-heeled boots: the tall skinny black leather ones that make me appear to be slender and interesting. I call them my Seven-League Boots because I feel like a Colossus striding the planet when I walk in them. At that moment, it felt like those boots were solely responsible for getting me home from Princeton. The sky was filled with stars, and the cobwebs started to clear from my brain as the Square receded behind me.

Striding home on high heels with both a new backpack full of papers and a medium-sized suitcase would have been a chore, except for the fact that I had recently broken down and purchased what I call stewardess gear: one of those anonymous black boxes on wheels. Since I seem to be incapable of traveling light, I had no choice. Jess has vowed she'll never give up her Louis Vuitton satchel, but she's a cab girl from the get-go, anyway.

Of course, I was traveling lighter than I wanted to be, thanks to my missing backpack. I had checked in with Maureen Kelly before leaving Princeton, only to be told that it had not turned up at Ivy Club the day after the party. It was what we had expected, and strangely, it left me feeling hopeful. If someone had stolen my bag, it meant that the culprit was somewhere in Princeton, not here at Harvard. And it meant that my brother had nothing to do with it, since he wasn't at the party. But it did make me wonder who had seen me in Earl's office, or in his home. And what they thought I had that was worth stealing.

Why, I wondered, had I felt uneasy going into detail about the contents of my backpack in front of Marti Waterstone? Had I become suspicious of everyone who ever said two words to Earl Stokes? Despite her rebellious posture, Marti was and always would be a Waterstone, and at a certain point her allegiances could shift accordingly—whatever that meant.

In the back of my head I could hear my mother's voice as I walked: "Nikki, what are you thinking, dragging that heavy load down those dark streets alone in high heels?" Though we had lived in a middle-class neighborhood in Detroit when I was growing up, my family was all too aware of the deterioration in the city around us. My mother in particular was a stickler for security, and if she knew half of the things I had done that fall, she would have moved into my apartment in Cambridge and kept me under lock and key. But she was blissfully unaware, and I kind of liked fancying myself as an intrepid girl detective. I was walking home alone that night to prove that I could do it.

Within minutes I turned onto Shepard Street, and noted that our neighbors had finally finished putting on their new roof—just in time for the snow, I thought. I rent a room from Magnolia, aka Maggie, Dailey in a three-story house whose ground level she occupies as not just the landlady but the presiding spirit. Once brilliantly blue, the building is now a weather-beaten shade of bluish gray. Maggie purchased it in the early 1970s and has been slowly but surely renovating an interior battered by decades of big-family living. The bottom two levels now boast freshly painted walls and hardwood floors polished to a fierce sheen. In contrast, my third-floor aerie is in its original condition, and though it's cramped, it's cozy, too. I have a bedroom, a kitchen, a living room, and a bath. The decor can only be described as eclectic—the typical grad student mix of Goodwill, street finds, and a few solid pieces from home.

As I pulled my wheeled bag up over the wooden front steps and onto the porch, I inhaled delightedly. I could smell wood smoke from the fireplace and cake in the oven, which meant that Maggie was home.

The pile of mail for me on the foyer table was formidable, so I passed it by. It would still be there in the morning. Wheeling past a pile of outdated magazines and two bags of recyclables waiting to be hauled curbside, I tripped and fell noisily against the kitchen door.

"Lord Almighty, who's this marauder in our midst?" Maggie Dailey called out.

"It's just me," I replied as I stepped into the kitchen, ditching my bag in the hall outside. "No one exciting, like a sexy burglar all in black." Maggie's black Labrador retriever, Horace, looked up sleepily from his usual spot on the kitchen floor.

"Sister Professor, you are a picture!" Maggie exclaimed. "Home is the sailor, home from the sea, and the hunter home from the hill." She engulfed me in a warm embrace.

"Leave it to you to have a quote for everything," I said, hugging her back.

Maggie could not resist a long, throaty laugh. With her towering Afro, long sari-style skirt, and V-necked sweater embroidered at the sleeves with Asian-looking symbols of indeterminate origin, she would have fit in easily at the demonstration I'd just left in Harvard Yard. In fact, I was a bit surprised that she had missed it. Maggie Dailey was a Cambridge classic, a true throwback to the days of revolutionary poetry spouted in coffeehouses, and girls in black turtlenecks and matching berets both angling for the poets and trying to compose their own free verse.

Maggie held me at arm's length while she conducted a visual inspection. "Sit right down," she concluded, "'cause I have rarely seen a person so in need of a cup of tea and a piece of my homemade pound cake."

Maggie knew me like a book, as my father would put it. Her flowered ceramic pot was already bubbling with a fragrant mix of orange spice and Lemon Zinger. The aroma filled her kitchen, which was as cluttered with books and papers as the other rooms in her domain.

"I was just about to have a cup myself," she said, gesturing for me to sit in a chair across the table from her. She poured my tea into a mug emblazoned with the crimson Harvard seal, a touch of sarcasm, no doubt, from a woman who had refused to step into the Coop since she'd been denied tenure in the Harvard English Department thirty years earlier.

"All right, let's hear it," she commanded.

So out it poured, the tale of Earl Stokes's death and the burning of the Center for African-American Studies at Princeton; the approach by Hayden Fleming; Marti Waterstone, and the theft of my backpack; Butch Hubbard's grandstanding at the funeral, and his subsequent leadership at the living wage rally. I left out details of Earl's troubled family life and his purported infidelities: there would be time for that discussion, if it turned out to be relevant, later.

Maggie paused, and then pronounced, "As usual, you've been in it deep." She shook her head. "Earl's death was in the papers here, but it was small. Piece made it sound like he wasn't absolutely coming to Harvard, anyway—you know they always take the local angle. 'It was rumored,' is as far as it went in the *Globe*."

She leaned back in her chair and shook her head again, so hard that her earrings jangled noisily. "I've known Butch Hubbard for almost twenty years. He's built that department into a real powerhouse. Believe me, the man wasn't always on TV and in the papers, like he is now. He started out shy, in his tweed coat with the suede patches on the elbows—Mr. Ph.D."

"That look is way over," I informed her. "Now it's Burberry for days."

Maggie snorted. "Tell me, why you gonna take a gypsy cab if you can drive in a Lincoln Town Car? Man's paid his dues—let him live large."

"That's the problem, as the president sees it," I said, pouring myself another cup of tea. "Lots of cost overruns, and showy expenses at Afro-Am. Butch Hubbard is a champagne socialist—champagne for everyone. It's possible Earl was to be a corrective to all that bling-bling."

Maggie laughed out loud, and reached for another slice of pound cake. "That school's been tryin' to court black folks who'll show the colors and balance the quota sheet, but shut up while they're at it, since Jesus was a baby." Even thirty years after her abortive tenure review, the pain and anger were still visible in Maggie's big brown eyes.

"Fact is, Sister Professor," she informed me, "Harvard needs Butch Hubbard more than he needs the school at this point. He could teach anywhere, or just retire and write books, not to mention keep up the PBS appearances and the morning shows." She leaned across the table. "In fact, I heard that he was one of the first people that Leland Townsend called when he took the presidency. That's the kind of juice Butch has. I don't see the man messing with someone like Earl Stokes and jeopardizing all that." Rapping her knuckles on the table to reinforce her point, she continued, "Butch is a showboater, but he's got a good heart—you saw that at the rally. And did I tell you that three years ago, he got Harvard to donate a whole slew of books to Cambridge Rindge and Latin School?—not to mention the three kids he helped get scholarships."

Clearly my suspicions were not shared by my landlady.

"If anybody had it in for Earl Stokes, could have been the cops down there," Maggie speculated. "Sounds like their investigation is movin' like molasses in January. Could be they have their own agenda."

Didn't everyone? It made my head spin: no matter how I reviewed the facts at hand, the list of potential suspects in Earl Stokes's death was beginning to resemble the cast of a medium-sized Broadway production.

As usual, Maggie sensed the shift in my mood immediately. "How's your brother? When will your momma be able to brag on two doctorates in the family?"

"By next spring," I told her. "He's got himself a new girlfriend. But I don't think Momma is going to be meeting her."

"White?" Maggie said instantly.

"No, Maggie, actually she is quite the black American princess. I'm just not convinced that she cares about him. I think she may be playing him." I told her about seeing Kayla with Yusef.

I said nothing about the cufflink. That's how scared I was for Eric.

"You may be right about that girl," Maggie mused. "But maybe she knows this Yusef from some class she took, or something. Don't be so suspicious of everybody. Just because you're caught up in these investigations of yours doesn't mean the whole world is guilty of something." She leaned toward me. "What I want to hear more about is this Yusef Jones. 'Cause I can see that he's got your attention, Sister Professor."

"You must have some kind of supernatural powers," I said, awestruck. "Either that, or I have the world's worst poker face. How did you know that?"

"Doesn't matter—I know I'm right. So what's he all about? It's not every day that a good black man comes along, you know."

I shook my head. "Don't be so sure that he's a good man, Maggie. I don't know that for a fact. Quite the contrary. And I haven't seen him for days, he seems to have skipped town without even saying goodbye. If there was any chemistry there, wouldn't you think the man would have come to say goodbye?" Yusef Jones had been on my mind, I had to admit it—mostly because of his absence at Earl's funeral. My kind of man would never miss his own father's burial.

There were hurried footsteps on the stairs, and suddenly Dante Rosario appeared in the doorway, in full black-tie regalia. In the two weeks since I'd seen him, his dark brown hair had grown longer, and now it brushed the edges of his starched, stand-at-attention collar.

"Thanks for helping with these studs, Maggie," he said, pausing in the doorway. "I never can get dressed for one of these events without an extra pair of hands."

"My pleasure," she purred.

I stared at her. Him I avoided looking at altogether. And yet somehow I was exceptionally aware of how fierce his tuxedo looked.

"You saved me. I didn't want to show up at Townsend's house looking like a kid from Southie."

"I think you pass inspection," Maggie declared.

"Then I'm gone." I felt his eyes on me and glanced up involuntarily. "Nice boots," he commented.

Then was gone.

"Oh. No. You. Didn't." I pronounced slowly. "You're helping him get *dressed* now? I thought you didn't approve of flirting with white boys."

"I don't, but someone's got to bring that boy to heel," she said, smiling evilly at me. "We can't have 'em out there thinking they can walk all over us. Those fancy boots of yours ain't working if they can't bring him to his knees, my sister."

"Oh, now that you have Rafe, you think you're all that, don't you?" I rose and refilled my mug. "I'm going to remind you of this episode if you ever break up with him."

"That isn't going to happen, Sister Professor," she replied assuredly.

The fact that Dante and I were barely speaking struck me at that moment as supremely juvenile; yet I wasn't going to be the one to break the silence. And I definitely wasn't going to permit myself even a fleeting thought as to who his companion for the evening might be. A black-tie affair on a clear moonlit night at the home of President Townsend—that was the kind of party I needed to be attending. How had he landed on the president's invitation list when I hadn't? It was high time for me to get back to work. My *real* work—not this futile detective sideline of mine.

Resolutely, I stood up and started for my room. Maggie got up from the table, too, and headed with me down the hallway. "I'll help you with that bag. You look like you need to crash—even all this tea hasn't done it for you."

She knew damn well that despite our joking, that Dante sighting had set me back; but like the wise woman she was, Maggie Dailey said not one more word about him as we hauled the suitcase up two flights of well-worn stairs. My plants looked green and well cared for, and my cat, Keynes, mewled happily at the sight of me. Now I was really home.

Turning to head back down, Maggie said, "We missed you, Sister Professor—all of us."

I didn't know exactly what that meant—and at the moment, I chose not to care.

After a quick shower to revive me, I put on my sweats and unpacked my suitcase, then sat down at my desk to boot up my computer. Keynes wound himself around my leg and purred contentedly. While unloading the contents of my suitcase, I dropped the folder that was supposed to contain the syllabus for Earl's class. I'd been so preoccupied with all the craziness at Princeton that I never had examined the spreadsheets inside it closely. The folder had been sitting in the zipper compartment of my roller bag since I'd brought it back to Eric's dorm room Friday afternoon. Despite my resolve to stop spending precious time playing sleuth, I find the papers irresistible. Impulsively, I picked up the folder and perused the dense columns of numbers on the first page. My inspection showed them to be the budget for the Center for African-American Studies at Princeton, with headings for Plumbing, Insulation, Materials, Permits, Legal Fees, Architectural Fees, Electrical, and General Furnishings. I skimmed the columns, curious to see what the totals for the various categories were. I paused when I got to the fees column. Doing the math in my head, it looked like almost a quarter of the budget was general contracting fees. I had no idea what the norm was, but whoever the general contractor was on this job stood to make almost $30 million.

Behind the spreadsheets in the folder were two pages of notes in what looked like Earl's handwriting, including a list of four candidates for the job of general contractor on the project. After "John A. Cohen Building," "D'Amato and Sons," and "Princeton Planning and Construction," I saw "Smalls Contracting."

Princeton is not a big city. How many Smalls could there be within its limits? It was at least a distinct possibility that the contractor in question was a relative of the Reverend Creflo Smalls, confidant to Eula Stokes and leader of the Beulah Baptist congregation. Which would make perfect sense, I thought, sitting back in my chair. A project like this would almost certainly be subject to a minority set-aside—a requirement that part of the work be done by woman- or minority-owned businesses. Creflo Smalls was the sort who would picket building sites that failed to comply with federal regulations on the hiring of minority contractors and workers. In other words, it might have paid Princeton to hire him just to eliminate the threat of high-profile trouble on a project of keen interest to the local African-American community. Who had actually received the commission to build? How far along had they been when the fire started? And most importantly, what would happen to their fees if the center never got built?

I was going to need to get some research and spadework done, and quickly. I had to find out more about Smalls Contracting and the permits filed on this project. There was no point in asking Eula Stokes anything about her beloved pastor, who would not have been likely to share business details with her, in any event. I had only one real option, and thankfully, it was only a flight of stairs away. Jess's erstwhile boyfriend, and Dante Rosario's roommate, Ted Adair, was a smart and resourceful public interest lawyer. And since I knew that Dante was out for the evening, it was safe for me to venture downstairs and enlist his help.

I knocked softly on the door, and seconds later it flew open.

"Teddy!" I exclaimed. "Do you have a minute?"

"For you, of course. Come on in."

I followed him down a dark narrow hallway and into a spacious living room lined floor to ceiling on two walls with bookshelves. A fire crackled in the fireplace, and the floor was littered with newspapers, magazines, and half-filled cups of coffee. I looked for evidence of female occupation, but found none. The scent of the fire and the memory of a couple of noteworthy encounters with Dante on this very floor filled me with completely unproductive desires. I shook myself and turned my attention to the matter at hand.

"I'm sorry to bother you, Teddy, but I need some help." I filled him in on the situation with the building project, and explained what I needed.

He made some notes, and then nodded slowly. "Yes, we can do this. It'll take a couple of days, but I've got someone who I can trust to handle this."

I rose from the oversize armchair and hugged him. "Thank you. You're the best."

"So when are you and my roommate getting back together?" he said innocently as we walked toward the door.

"Given that we aren't even speaking, I wouldn't hold my breath on that one. More importantly, though, when are *you* and my best friend getting back together?"

Ted smiled broadly. "It could be soon." He glanced down at his watch. "She's helping with a delivery, and I'm picking her up afterward."

"Godspeed, Teddy. You'll call me, right?"

"I always call, remember?"

When I returned to my apartment, I knew from the moment the door clicked shut behind me that I was done for the day. Although I could see that there were no fewer than fifty new e-mails in my in-box, six from my boss Carl Irvin alone, I decided they would have to keep. Despite the fact that it was only eleven, I felt an overpowering urge to crawl under the blankets and take a temporary leave of this world, with Keynes snuggled at my feet. I put Earl's spreadsheets on a shelf above my bed, next to a sepia portrait of my grandmother in her youth, and turned out the lights. The moonlight was so bright that it cast shadows on the floor of my room. That had to be a promise of some kind of benign magic to come.

# 17
# Back to the Future

I know quite well that I was appointed to the Crimson Future Committee not for my wit, charm, or way with words, but because I know my way around a spreadsheet. Ostensibly, I am one of two representatives from the Graduate School of Arts and Sciences; in reality, I'm the chief number cruncher.

Created by the disgraced former president of Harvard, Leo Barrett, the Future Committee is intended to analyze how Harvard College and the university's ten graduate schools can coordinate their fund-raising efforts, given the vast disparities in the endowments of the respective divisions. Quagmire would be another way of describing it. Harvard's fund-raising and governance philosophy, which was that every school was highly autonomous—"each tub on its own bottom"—had worked splendidly for the professional schools—Medical, Law, and Business, but horribly for the Ed School, the Div School, and others. This committee was supposed to overcome generations of separation and devise ways of advancing the common good. Don Quixote would have found it dismayingly difficult.

Asif Zakaria, a tenured Medical School professor and the most contentious member of the group, was the first to join me in a second-floor conference room at the Harvard Faculty Club. That day we were in what I referred to as the birdcage room—a sun-filled space with bamboo-motif wallpaper and white and gold furnishings. It was an oddly eccentric space in a building where most of the rooms had recessed bookshelves of aged, dark wood lining the walls from floor to ceiling, and chandeliers that would be elegant in the finest New England house museum.

I had strategically chosen a seat in the middle of a row of chairs on one side of the table, an arm's length from the carafes of water, tea, and coffee set out on a silver tray. I was confident that I'd need several infusions of java to get through this gathering, our first since former chairman Ian McAllister had been convicted of embezzlement. Bob Raines, a tenured professor at the Kennedy School, had been appointed our leader in his stead.

Asif Zakaria looked around the nearly empty room and sniffed. "Aren't we due to commence in five minutes?" He poured himself a cup of coffee and smiled in my direction, almost as an afterthought. "How are you, Professor Chase?" he asked.

I looked down at the spreadsheets neatly lined up in front of me, the result of seven hours of Amtrak-induced leisure time. Today I had the confidence of the well prepared, a stance I planned to cultivate in spades. I was wearing a good-little-professor brown wool suit with gold jewelry and sensible heels. Looking up, I gave Asif what I hoped was a dazzling smile. He was off and running before I could even acknowledge his greeting.

"With Bob Raines at the helm," he said, "I thought we might become a bit more punctual as a group."

As if on cue, Raines hurried in, accompanied by Rena Seidman from the Business School. Rena was impeccable in a dove gray Chanel suit and killer black Prada heels. I am a huge fan of Professor Seidman. I'd learned a lot about style just watching her wardrobe for the past few months, and she could match me decimal point for decimal point when analyzing a spreadsheet, given that she was among the first women ever to get tenure at the Business School. She winked at me as she settled into a chair across the table.

"Most impressive, Nikki," said Bob, observing my best-girl-at-school presentation on his way to the head of the table. Before sitting down, he announced, "I intend to start on time, no matter who's here or isn't."

"I applaud you, Bob," said Rena, whipping out a snakeskin portfolio with the initials "RS" monogrammed onto the lower left-hand corner. "I have a graduate seminar at noon, then tea with the bursar, and my therapist at three."

"Why don't you just send us your schedule for the day in advance on e-mail as an attachment, Rena?" Asif sniped. "Then I can make sure none of the surgeries I'm due to perform will conflict with your hairdressing appointment."

Any rejoinder Rena Seidman could have delivered was cut off by the noisy arrivals of Dante Rosario, Michael Treger from the English Department, whose last novel had been a finalist for the National Book Critics Circle Award, and Jennifer Blum, a lanky brunette undergraduate who specializes in conservative cultural politics and radically short skirts. As always, she settled in next to Dante.

Tony Walters from the School of Public Health, one of the most alarmingly underfunded of the graduate divisions, wandered in gripping a paper cup from Starbuck's. Malcolm Bird, the assistant dean for student affairs, had been unexpectedly called to McLean Hospital because an Asian exchange student from Taiwan had taken an overdose of Valium the previous evening, Bob Raines informed us. Every year at this point in the semester, at least a few students cracked, and cracked badly. Often they were women, and from a foreign culture. The pressures they faced, combined with a sometimes overwhelming sense of isolation and homesickness, had been poignantly depicted by Michael Treger in a recent article in *Harper's* about a microbiology whiz from Cambodia who slit her wrists in her dorm room after receiving a C on a final.

Bob dispensed with the expected holiday wishes and got straight to the point: annual giving was down badly, and it was our job to recommend ways to further reduce operating expenses, or face the consequences of additional increases to what is already one of the highest tuition levels in the country. The matter was so urgent that President Townsend would join us shortly for further elucidation.

"The point is," said Rena Seidman crisply, "what is being done to implement our previous recommendations? We've already spent countless hours on this project, and to what end?"

In last month's New Century report, we had advocated consolidating support staff for several of the graduate divisions, a sensitive topic not only with the unions, who had enlisted considerable support from students, but also with administrators who'd spent years building up the assets of their respective fiefdoms.

"An excellent point," chimed in Jennifer Blum. "Whether it's the federal government or the administration here, bureaucracy moves like quicksand."

"President Townsend needs time to get his arms around this," Dante pointed out. "He's got a new development director, and he's digesting our recommendations. We should give him a chance." I marveled at his ability to render me utterly invisible. He hadn't looked at me once since he'd arrived.

"I'm not saying we should mount a palace coup," Rena was saying testily.

"We have our brief, and we will follow it," said Bob Raines, struggling to regain control of the conversation. When he motioned to me to pass out the latest spreadsheets, I took the opportunity to get up and pour myself another cup of coffee.

Through the still-open door to the room, the voice of President Leland Townsend reverberated up and down the hallway. "Saw the piece in the *Globe* this morning, Butch," we heard him say. "Once you have your travel and entertainment budget under control, you can lecture me on the minimum wage here at Harvard."

Butch Hubbard's reply was muffled, but clearly did not go down well with Townsend. A few months back, it had been widely rumored on campus not only that Butch Hubbard and Janice Borden were having an affair, but also that Butch had charged dinner at Nobu in Tribeca and two nights at the Four Seasons to his departmental account, when in fact he and Janice were nominally guests of the *New Yorker*'s literary festival in Bryant Park. There was also talk of an excursion to a cultural celebration in Havana, where Butch and his Afro-Am colleague Dawson Childers rubbed shoulders with the likes of Gabriel Garcia Marquez, not to mention Fidel Castro himself. In an interview in the *Crimson*, Sportin' Life had defended the junket, arguing that the cultural fruits of the African diaspora were nowhere more evident than in pan-racial Cuba.

When Leland Townsend entered the room a few minutes later, his face was set in a tight-lipped smile. The sleeves of his shirt and jacket were a quarter inch too short, exposing his wrists. With his loose-limbed stride and shock of bristly, snow-white hair, he suggested that Ichabod Crane had been reincarnated as a well-connected New England aristocrat, a descendent of abolitionists, missionaries, and even a great-aunt who wrote brilliant poetry while barely leaving her garret in Newtown for three decades. Sitting down to the right of Bob Raines, he apologized for being late.

"We were just getting started," said Rena Seidman, smiling widely.

After going around the table to introduce the members of the committee, Bob Raines handed Townsend a copy of my spreadsheets and laid his hands out on the table in front of him. "We have a formidable task ahead of us. Today's *New York Times* reports that in Atlanta, Emory University is even looking into ways to buy toilet paper more economically. Projections we made in the New Century report only months ago will have to be significantly revised."

"I've reviewed Nikki's new analysis," said Dante Rosario, "and she has highlighted some important implications. You can clearly see that the rate of return on the investments for the endowment is down. You've got an issue in the investment office." We all knew that part of the problem was the scandal that I had uncovered in this very same investment office, which had left them a bit short-staffed, to say the least.

"As much as I sympathize personally with the union members, we have to think about layoffs, not raises," chimed in Tony Walter of Public

Health. "We've already let go about ten percent of our clerical staff, and that may be just the beginning."

"What about a temporary freeze on faculty raises?" suggested Michael Treger, to stony silence. Unspoken was the general knowledge that his latest novel, a historical piece set in Salem at the time of the witchcraft trials, had been sold to producer Scott Rudin, with Nicole Kidman to star: there would be no need for freezes on toilet paper or anything else in the near future in the Treger household.

"Our ultimate goal," said Leland Townsend, "is an equitable balance of resources." He looked around the room at each of us. "Your prior numbers planned on ten percent growth a year in the endowment, and given the thirty and forty percent increases in the previous three years, that looked conservative at the time."

"In a way, we're victims of our own success," Rena Seidman suggested. "We've been caught short by our optimism."

"I did a historical review, and this is the first time in nine years that the return rate has been in single digits," I interjected. "Plenty of people on Wall Street didn't see that one coming."

"Do we really need that new student center that may look like an oversize doughnut, by that overpraised, overpriced Dutch architect?" asked Asif Zakaria.

"All new building projects are temporarily on hold," said Leland Townsend, adjusting the small black reading glasses perched on the tip of his nose.

Had Princeton's endowment suffered comparably? I wondered as I watched Jennifer Blum lean over to whisper something in Dante Rosario's ear. How could it not have? If so, could the fire at the new Center for African-American Studies have been set by someone not necessarily of conservative political leanings, but with connections to a fund-raising effort now cut off at the knees?

"Tuition increases are also on hold," Townsend continued. "They've already been rising at twice the rate of inflation—we've got to draw a line in the sand somewhere."

"So we're facing real budget cuts," I said bluntly.

"Unavoidable," Leland Townsend said crisply. "As of next Monday, I'm issuing a directive to each and every department head, asking him or her to cut five to ten percent of the annual budget."

You could have heard a pin drop in the room. These were measures already being adopted by lesser schools: what would budget cuts mean at one of the country's most prestigious institutions of higher learning?

"We're talking potential layoffs of junior faculty, not just clerical workers," observed Rena Seidman.

"It's not yet come to that," Townsend assured her, "but let me make this clear: I am not here to win a popularity contest, but to maintain the excellence that Harvard personifies, while cutting waste and unnecessary extravagance."

No wonder Townsend had been courting Earl Stokes, with his saggy-sleeved jackets, modest home, and national best seller: he would have been the personification of Harvard's New Scholar, providing excellence without pretense or superfluous flourishes. The more I thought about it, the more I marveled that Earl had stayed so long at Princeton, given that he was a made-to-order Yankee in all the ways that really mattered.

"Travel to conferences, and budgets to hire speakers to come here, will be the first items to be trimmed," Leland Townsend continued.

"We have a plethora of homegrown talent in any event," Bob Raines added.

"In a way, this is an exciting time," said Jennifer Blum, tossing her brunette mane back behind her shoulder.

Townsend ignored her flagrant brownnosing and proceeded to outline in excruciating detail for the next forty-five minutes each aspect of the budget to be pared, from faculty merit increases to retirement parties to the size of orientation booklets for arriving freshmen, now rendered obsolete in any event by the possibilities of the Internet. The point, our new president stressed over and over, was to see the forest for the trees, and balance responsible allocation of the considerable resources we had with a relentless scrutiny of all that fell to one side of our core educational mission.

Had Townsend viewed Earl as a potential hatchet man at Afro-Am, and not just a spy? It is much easier, after all, to clean house with no hires in your debit column. Would our new president risk alienating Butch Hubbard so profoundly that he would leave of his own accord?

There was only one way to find out. When the meeting broke up, I had to corner Townsend somehow, and ascertain whether Earl had been tapped to *lead* Harvard's Afro-Am Department, rather than just join it. Because if that had been the case, Butch Hubbard's life would have turned decidedly less sportin', no matter how you shuffled the proverbial cards.

# 18
## The First Rule of Holes

Leland Townsend was a man on a mission, and he walked like one. I was hard-pressed to keep up with his long-legged strides as he loped down the hallway of the Faculty Club in the wake of Jennifer Blum, Bob Raines, and Dante Rosario. Jennifer had her arm tucked securely under Dante's, and they were laughing about a movie that they'd both seen. Possibly together.

Screw 'em, I thought. If she was his type, then let him have her and live with the consequences. I had more important things to do.

Turning a sharp left, Townsend was clearly headed for the faculty dining room. I caught up with him one step past the coatroom, before he'd reached the desk of the maître d', who would no doubt escort the president to a table reserved exclusively for him.

He spotted me from the corner of his eye. "Professor Chase, your numbers were compelling today."

"Depressing would be a more precise description, don't you think?" I said.

"Through no fault of yours," replied Leland Townsend. "It's a very good analysis."

Though he wore a fashionably narrow rep tie, a sky-blue shirt, and a well-cut gray wool suit, Townsend still managed to convey the sense that he'd be more at home in khakis and a barn jacket at the duck pond on his property in the Berkshires. Despite his reputation as a no-nonsense administrator and a fiscal conservative, there was something permanently rumpled about him that made all kinds of people comfort-able in his presence—with the notable exception of Butch Hubbard, so it seemed.

He glanced down the hall toward the dining room. "It looks as though my lunch date has yet to arrive. What can I help you with, Pro-fessor?"

"Please call me Nikki," I said, sidestepping Bob Raines and Michael Treger, who were obviously lunching together. "I need just a word with you, and it has nothing to do with the Future Committee."

"Come with me," he said, walking toward a bank of pay phones that were rarely in use these days, given the number of cell phones now on campus. The end of the corridor was as quiet as a library. Glancing at his watch, he continued: "I don't have long."

"Earl Stokes was my mentor," I said quickly.

At the mention of his name, an expression flickered across Town-send's face. Not so much sadness as . . . disappointment. And frustra-tion. It was quickly replaced by a composed, sorrowful gaze. "What happened is terrible—a real loss for all of us."

He'd given me the opening, so I took it. "I know you approached Earl about coming to Harvard," I started, but Townsend instantly cut me off.

"Our talks were preliminary," he said hastily.

"Yes, I've read as much in the papers. I just have a question," I said. "Would he have been placed in the Economics Department, or in Afro-Am?"

It was a crazy, impulsive thought, a question intended to provoke him into telling me *something*. But not entirely crazy, I thought, as I voiced the query—after all, Earl was an economics professor, too, and my department had an opening for a new chair.

The amount of time that it took our president to compose his answer sent my pulse rate up a notch. I seemed to have genuinely startled him. "There's really no point in my addressing that," he finally responded, "because it was not clear at all that Earl wanted to leave Princeton. He seemed truly conflicted, on a number of levels."

Several of which had to involve his wife, I thought to myself.

"You said that he was your mentor. Did he ever discuss it with you?" Townsend's eyes were locked on me now.

"Yes, he did," I replied. "When I last saw him, I had the feeling that he was planning to leave Princeton. In fact, I was certain of it. But who knows what he was really thinking?"

Townsend seemed to relax a bit at this answer. "Yes, well, it's a loss for all of us. No matter where he might have been headed. Will you call my office and give my secretary Mrs. Stokes's address? I'd like to send my condolences."

"Certainly." I nodded.

"Professor Chase—Nikki," he corrected himself. "Would you do one other thing for me?"

"Of course, President Townsend," I replied.

"Make an appointment to come by my office sometime soon. I'd like to speak with you about your thoughts on how we might do a better job attracting black faculty members. Not for Afro-Am. For the entire university."

I nodded, unable to hide my surprise. "I'd be happy to do that."

"You needn't look quite so shocked," he said lightly. "I may have an issue with the choices Hubbard has made. But that doesn't mean that I don't care about this issue. I had quite enjoyed hearing Professor Stokes's views on this through the years. His death is a real pity."

As I watched his image recede into the dining room, I ruminated on the brief conversation. It didn't take a genius to figure out what he was really asking me. Townsend needed some black allies in what was shaping up to be an ongoing and epic struggle between him and Butch Hubbard. He was offering me the chance to be a pawn in their chess game—which could be a useful education for me in university politics and the exercise of power. I wasn't sure whether to feel flattered or appalled.

I walked slowly back to the entrance to the Faculty Club and retrieved my coat; by the time I'd walked the five minutes to the broad stone steps of Littauer, which houses the Economics Department, I was in a down-and-dirty funk.

Hadn't my careful preparation been appreciated by the committee? Hadn't the president of the university given me a few moments of his highly valued time? Then why did I feel so useless? The real problem was that Townsend was at the pinnacle of a highly variegated human food chain, whose intermediate members were in a position to make my life miserable. Janice Borden's warnings about my growing reputation as a minder of other people's troubled business echoed in my head as I entered my office for the first time in nearly a week. I was reminded of another of Rafe Griffin's admonitions: *You know the first rule of holes? When you're in one, stop digging.*

Gwen, my secretary, was a picture of Kelly Girl perfection at her desk, dressed in a form-fitting but tasteful cowl-necked sweater and plaid pants that looked like Burberry knockoffs. A habitué of T. J. Maxx, Marshall's, and Filene's Basement, Gwen could write a cogent article for a woman's magazine on dressing for the office on the type of budget she shares with her husband, a Cambridge firefighter. As an assistant professor I was lucky to have a secretary, period. No doubt I'd have to scramble to keep her if impending budget cuts hit junior faculty first, a strong likelihood.

"Irvin called," she announced before even saying hello. "Twice so far this morning."

"Merry, merry, to you, too," I said, sighing.

"Welcome back, boss," she said while sipping from a cup of takeout coffee from Dunkin' Donuts. "I just thought I'd get the bad news out of the way."

In another life, Gwen might have been one of those smart, wise-cracking secretaries in a 1930s screwball comedy. Now that it was a different century, she was going to night school to get a degree in education. Pictures of her husband and two-year-old daughter adorned her spotless desk, along with a two-foot-high stuffed Christmas tree made of printed green-and-white cotton and decorated with tiny homemade ornaments. Sometimes I wondered if I could be Gwen when I grew up, but I knew that wasn't likely.

Though she had placed my mail in neat piles—divided into memoranda, printouts of daily phone logs, student term papers, and general university circulars—the rest of the place did nothing to improve my mood. Between the Future Committee, my second career as a Nancy Drew wannabe, and the grunt work I was still performing for Carl Irvin, I'd been neglecting my own course preparations and end-of-semester paperwork. Student essays from my International Economics class covered the bottom shelf of a small bookcase next to my desk; I was staring at hours of work that needed to be commenced immediately.

"How was Princeton?" asked Gwen from the doorway.

"Peachy," I retorted.

"Coffee?"

"*Please*. And make sure it's boiling hot."

"Coming up," she murmured, and retreated to her own, more orderly neck of the woods.

I couldn't attack the piles of paper awaiting my attention without a quick jolt of positive energy. And I wanted it to be from something other than caffeine. At this hour, I figured Jess would be about to break for lunch after her morning rounds had been completed; she answered her cell on the second ring.

"Where've you been, girl?" she wanted to know. "I left two messages at your place yesterday with Maggie."

"She must have forgotten to mention it to me," I speculated. "We were dishing about Earl's death and Butch Hubbard's speech at the living wage rally."

"I read about it in the paper," Jess said. "You were there?"

"Ran into it in the Yard, purely by accident."

"I want to hear all about it, tonight at Maggie's party," she continued.

"What party?" I asked as I discarded mail into the wastebasket beneath my desk.

"You know Maggie's holiday potluck special is tonight at seven P.M. sharp," Jess reminded me. "I'm bringing apple and walnut pie."

"Baby Watson's?"

"You best believe it! But if I take it out of the bakery box and cover it with foil, no one will know that I didn't spend the better part of last night making it."

I doubted that anyone would fail to see through the charade; Jess and I have both been deemed domestically challenged by mutual friends. "The crust will be too perfect," I predicted.

Maggie had indeed mentioned the party before I left town, I now recalled, but in the ensuing commotion surrounding Earl's death I had forgotten about it completely. Maybe a holiday gathering was just what I needed to get into the swing of things for the season, given that I had not mailed one card, nor purchased a single present, and it was already December 12. Not to mention that the only holiday party I'd attended so far, at Ivy at Princeton, had culminated in petty theft.

"I think I'm free to attend," I told Jess balefully, "since there isn't a man interested in me anywhere on the eastern seaboard."

My litany of woe was interrupted by Gwen's appearance once more in my doorway. "Irvin," she mouthed.

After signing off hurriedly with Jess, I pushed down the blinking light on the other phone extension.

"May I see you in my office in half an hour, Professor Chase?" he said in his usual overbearing manner. "We have quite a bit to discuss, including your upcoming presentation at the AEA."

"I'll be there," I assured him before hanging up and asking Gwen to grab me a takeout tuna sandwich to eat at my desk. A week's worth of mail had to disappear in the next twenty minutes. It never ceases to amaze me, the amount of paper generated by an academic institution. Maybe Jennifer Blum is right in thinking that all bureaucracies are inherently inefficient by definition. In the time it took Gwen to return with my sandwich, I had disposed of enough extraneous paper to fill my basket three times over. Auxiliary units from Gwen's area had to be pulled in to meet the demand for waste receptacles.

"When you think of the number of trees—," she began.

"Don't get me started, Gwen," I warned her, "not when I have to face Irvin in ten minutes."

I applied a light coat of war paint in the ladies' room and then ascended the stairs to the second floor, where Carl Irvin was installed in a corner office with a wide view of the Science Quad and the Law School. His secretary, Stephanie, greeted me with barely concealed dislike: since the day we'd met and she'd been openly incredulous that I was not the professor's secretary, but rather the professor herself, we'd been on frosty terms.

"Happy holidays, Professor Chase," she said with the faux warmth of a midday talk-show host.

"Same to you, Stephanie," I said, in an equally insincere tone of voice. "I believe that Professor Irvin is expecting me."

"I believe he is."

I followed her down the hall, wincing involuntarily at her exaggerated, swivel-hipped walk.

Carl Irvin did not get up from his desk when I entered the room. A large man with snow-white hair and blue eyes, he had lost both a colleague and his best friend when our previous chairman, Ian McAllister, had been imprisoned for embezzling. Since I had been instrumental in exposing the scheme that put McAllister behind bars, my very presence in the department was an ongoing irritant to him, to say the least.

"Veronica," he said, with a snide smile. You'd never know that Carl Irvin was only acting chair of the Economics Department at Harvard; he carried himself like a man to the chairmanship born. "I've been tracking your movements by the e-mails you send—or fail to."

I chose to laugh that one off. "Like an electronic trail of bread crumbs."

With a furrowed brow, he continued, "You do have a way, Veronica, of wandering off the beaten track." He paused. "I suppose it's one of your charms."

I peered at him closely for the first time and realized that he wasn't himself. The cocksure veneer was scratched, and he looked . . . troubled.

I sat up straighter in the red leather chair across from his desk. Acting purely on instinct, I leaned forward. "It was pretty rough being down in Princeton this week. It was quite a shock to people to have Earl Stokes suddenly gone."

"I can imagine that it was disturbing," said Carl Irvin as he took a pile of papers from the left-hand side of his desk and moved them to the right. "I remember what it was like here after Rosezella Fisher died."

*You mean after she was murdered,* I wanted to say. How quickly people revert to euphemisms. It had only been three months.

"So—let's go through your paper," he suggested. We spent the next twenty minutes immersed in my AEA presentation. We were arguing about whether I should include the full output of a supporting series of regressions I had conducted when Stephanie interrupted us.

"Sir? President Townsend is downstairs. He wants you to come down and say hello to the Treasury Secretary. They're in the lobby."

"Should I step out to the hallway?" I asked.

"No—wait here. This won't take long."

I wandered idly around his office, pausing to look at the neatly ordered files on his desk. He had a wire holder with seven or eight manila folders labeled "Urgent," "Students," "Investment Corp," and the like. I saw the edge of a piece of paper protruding from one of them. The headline read "For Immediate Release—Draft." It was an announcement of some sort. Without thinking at all, I edged the paper out of the manila folder.

It was a press release announcing Earl Stokes as the new head of the Harvard Economics Department. The draft was dated Thursday, December 6. The day before he died.

Take it? Put it back? The sheet of paper seemed to be glued to my hand. As footsteps approached, I slipped it back into the file folder and turned toward the door. I'd made it almost to my chair before Irvin entered his office.

"Now where were we, Veronica?" he asked.

Apparently, we were on the brink.

# On Holiday

"**Yeah, yeah,** that's it. That's good."

Emboldened, I slid my hand farther down, feeling a strangely familiar knobby bone covered by soft flesh.

"Keep coming, that's right. Don't be gentle, baby."

A primal scent emerged as I plunged deeper. It had been a long time since I'd done this. I had to admit—it felt kinda good.

"I told you, Sister Professor—you know how to handle a turkey," Maggie declared triumphantly.

I grinned at her as my hand disappeared farther into the twenty-pound bird. I had been tasked with sliding herb butter under the skin to keep the breast meat moist while roasting. I hadn't been this intimate with any object, human or otherwise, in quite some time.

"I haven't felt this way since high school biology class. But I think this turkey and I are going to have to get married now."

Late Thursday afternoon found me surrounded by pine boughs, red ribbons, and Christmas kitsch. Maggie Dailey was having a party, and no matter how much I wanted time alone to assess what it meant that Earl had been slated to be the head of Harvard's Economics Department, I had to table it for the evening. Like it or not, I was on holiday for the night.

I'd come home early, too stunned by what I had learned in Carl Irvin's office to concentrate on further cleaning out my in box and answering the plethora of phone and e-mail messages that had built up during my absence at Princeton. Gwen had scooted out early as well, to attend to the head cold her daughter had contracted from the other kids at day care.

As I'd followed in Maggie's wake that afternoon in the kitchen and the dining room, vacuuming, holding up strands of evergreens to twist and ribbons to tie, and listening to her hum "The Christmas Song" along with Nat King Cole, I'd entertained a vision in my mind that would remain just that, a vision: Earl Stokes as my boss, my department chairman. I saw us eating at the Faculty Club, catching up on shop talk; Earl and me meeting in his office to go over my course list for the upcoming semester while NPR or jazz played companionably in the background, the sound track to our stimulating, intellectually challenging jobs and lives. After experiencing Carl Irvin as a dissertation adviser, and Ian McAllister as a department chairman, I realized now that I had unconsciously resigned myself to working with people whose styles and life experiences were worlds away from mine, to being the permanent outsider—nose pressed to the window while the members of the club chatted cozily inside. This was how the world worked, whether on Wall Street or at Harvard—wasn't it? Even a fleeting glance at an alternate scenario was positively tantalizing, and now as remote as ever.

Earl had hinted at this when I visited him in his office, and I'd missed it completely. He'd said that Townsend had found a new department head who would be beneficial to my career. How could I possibly have known that he was talking about himself?

On the way home, I'd turned it over and over in my mind. At first I had been puzzled about how on earth Townsend had come to select Earl as the next Economics Department chair. It wasn't the field of study in which Earl was best known, and there was an embarrassment of qualified economists, on our campus and around the world, who would have killed for that job. Some had Nobel Prizes, and plenty more were headed in that direction. But on reflection, I realized that naming Earl the new department head in Economics would have been a master-stroke for President Townsend—a clear signal of his commitment to diversity, but done his way. Not Butch Hubbard's. And the beauty of it would have been that it was not directly confrontational with Butch—how could Hubbard activate his followers and the media, if all the president was doing was elevating another black man? It might have been enough of a power play to get Hubbard to leave Harvard. It certainly would have been sufficient to render Hubbard a lot less relevant. No wonder the president had been so dismayed over Earl's death. And no wonder Hubbard had been so cocky in the days that followed. I wondered how much of this Butch had seen coming—and how much it would have been worth it to him to blunt Townsend. How far would a man like Hubbard go?

Rafe Griffin was the first to arrive at Maggie's fete that evening, dressed in his Sunday best, sporting a festive plaid flannel blazer, a neatly pressed white shirt, navy wool slacks, and highly polished black loafers. Despite Maggie's best efforts to update his look, Rafe clung stubbornly to his conservative style. He had a political philosophy to go with it, and that should have been a knockout factor for Maggie, but instead it seemed to be part of his charm. They were truly a case of opposites attracting.

I greeted Rafe at the door wearing my brightest smile and The Dress. My spirits lifted as I saw an appreciative expression flicker across his face as he approached me. The Dress is sleeveless, snug, and black, with a flirty flared skirt. Made of a slimming fabric that is light enough to move with the wearer but heavy enough to stay put when dancing, it stops just above my knees, and looks best paired with pearls and high-heeled sling-backs, both of which I was wearing. I don't wear it often, because I don't want to exhaust its powerful magic. But tonight seemed worthy of taking it out for a spin.

"Welcome home, child," Rafe said, handing me the pecan pie that was his signature dish, and tonight's potluck contribution. "I hope you took my advice and left all that doom and gloom back at Princeton." He kissed me lightly on the cheek. "You look beautiful."

Observing my wistful facial expression, Rafe took the arm I wasn't using to balance his pie and led me through the maze of Maggie's hallway to the kitchen, which was, as usual, action central.

The hostess was wearing a red apron emblazoned with the saying, "A Woman's Place Is in the House—and Senate."

I laughed. "There *are* women in the House and Senate now, Maggie—that apron's way outdated."

"Twenty years old, and still in use," she declared proudly as she pulled the turkey from the oven and wiped her hands on the apron's faded fabric. "Without our generation, Sister Professor, you wouldn't be sittin' in that office of yours, lookin' so high and mighty."

"She'd find a way," said Rafe from behind me. "Nikki was born to be tellin' people what's what, just like another beautiful woman that I know."

Much to her obvious consternation, Maggie blushed. Though she and Rafe had been dating for almost three months, she still acted like a giddy teenager in his presence.

She looked over at him. "Pecan pie, again?" she said in mock disgust.

"You got a good thing, you stick with it, like a good woman you keep warm and close," said Rafe with a smile.

Maggie rolled her eyes and ordered me into the dining room to set the table, which was already overlaid with a white lace tablecloth, a recent find from a vintage store in Somerville. Rafe took napkins embroidered with Guatemalan Indian motifs out of a drawer in the sideboard as I pulled the silverware out of another: it was only the best for tonight's celebration. Christmas came but once a year, and Maggie Dailey wasn't going to let her friends forget it.

"It's serve yourself," said Rafe, putting the napkins in a neat pile to one side.

"You don't have any sons hidden away in a garage somewhere?" I teased him. "I need a man secure enough in his masculinity to help set a lovely table."

"You called?" said Ted Adair from the doorway, laughing. He placed a large brown earthenware dish on the table atop a ceramic trivet painted with plump, fluffy-haired angels. Maggie had dragged out every holiday tchotchke she owned.

"Long time, no see, Nikki." As he leaned over, he whispered, "Tomorrow I'll have it for you—the four-one-one on that construction company in Princeton."

There was no way that Ted Adair would have known that phrase before he met Jessica Leiberman. Though he ran a legal clinic in Roxbury that serviced clients from several housing projects, Ted was hopelessly square in all the right ways, a perfect balance to Jess's occasional flakiness and high spirits. When she entered the room directly behind him, I knew there'd be plenty to catch up on once he was out of earshot.

"Ted made something with marshmallows in it," she announced in lieu of a greeting. Jess's long, dark, curly hair was pulled up in a cascading knot that vaguely resembled the top of a pineapple. She was dressed in black leather pants and a dark green sweater with Santa hats knitted into the design.

"Girlfriend, you're not even Christian," I teased, looking at the sweater's pattern.

"In December, everyone is a goy. Besides, Christian Lacroix's not doing menorahs this season," she informed me, giggling. "Just kidding—on sale, Macy's, last week." Jess's mother ran a small but very successful boutique in Hewlett Harbor, Long Island, where her daughter grew up to develop killer shopping instincts.

I watched Maggie and Rafe talking with Ted and Jess for a moment and felt my spirits lift. The candlelight and the music were working their magic, and everyone was falling into holiday flirtatiousness and good spirits.

"Don't just stand there, Sister Professor, make yourself useful," barked Maggie, hustling by with a large cut-glass punch bowl filled with a coral-colored concoction, her famous—or infamous—holiday punch, made from a secret family recipe that combined fruit juices with more varieties of liquor than anyone dared to count. "Set this down on the table, pour some into the cups on the sideboard, and get this party roarin'."

Without a word Rafe stepped over and assumed the bartender duties. By the end of my first cup of punch, I had nearly forgotten Carl Irvin's name. By the second, I was hallucinating that a very handsome black man almost ten years my junior was calling my name from the doorway.

"Nikki Chase, you're a sight for my sore eyes," said Justin Simms. It was no hallucination, just a dear friend whose large, lively brown eyes were smiling at me. He was dressed, as usual, like a model from *GQ*, in a cashmere turtleneck and a pair of elegantly draped wool trousers. Justin was the president of the Harvard Law School Council and an all-around flirt. Just what the doctor ordered.

"You look fantastic!" I exclaimed.

"He sure does," said a tall, shapely woman with a slight southern inflection in her voice. Draped in a long, cream-colored fringed shawl, Alix Coyle towered over us in high-heeled cowboy boots.

A warm glow flowed over me at the sight of my friends. "Have you two met?" I asked excitedly. "Justin Simms, Alix Coyle. You may have seen Alix onstage at the ART." Alix and I had met earlier that fall—she had been Rosezella Fisher's best friend. And was now becoming one of mine.

"I haven't had the pleasure," said Justin, grinning.

"I know a Harvard man when I see one," Alix countered. "There's somethin' about the way he carries himself—it's what my momma down in Texas would call the pep in his step."

"I've got plenty of that, in my step and elsewhere," said Justin shamelessly.

Alix was at least fifteen years older than Justin Simms, but by the time Maggie had circled the room with a trayful of appetizers, they had made a date to go dancing when the Tennessee Williams revival at the ART shut down shortly for a holiday break. It was that kind of party.

I wondered where he was. But I wasn't planning to ask. If Dante was coming to this party, I'd know it soon enough. My reverie was cut short by the arrivals of Butch Hubbard and Janice Borden. I had to steel myself to avoid looking too surprised to see them: Maggie hadn't said word one about inviting Sportin' Life, not to mention Janice.

"Nikki!" said Butch, clearly in his party mode already. "You know Janice, I assume?"

"We were chatting in her office just yesterday, as a matter of fact." With annoyance I noted that Janice was wearing a form-fitting jumpsuit of tie-dyed velveteen that I'd just seen in *Essence* on a rap star at the MTV Awards: this girl was show biz for days. No wonder she and Sportin' Life were so, well, close.

"You saw her piece in the *New Yorker*?" Butch asked proudly.

"That was months ago, Butch," Janice noted coyly.

I couldn't remember the last time I'd called my department chairman "Carl." I said quickly, "Of course I saw it. It was very interesting. I'm jealous—I'm sure it was read by a hell of a lot more people than my latest effort for the *Journal of Modern Economics*." I laughed, as though making light of the mad scramble to publish among junior faculty.

"Actually, I read your piece," said Butch Hubbard.

Whether or not it was due to the effects of two cups of punch, you could have knocked me over with a feather.

"It was beautifully written, Nikki, as well as tightly argued," he continued. "You know, you could be Earl Stokes's heir. Your material is intellectually sophisticated, but you write in language the lay reader can understand, too. It's a real talent, all too rare among academics." He raised his glass of punch and clicked it against mine.

I was just beginning to see Sportin' Life in a whole new light when he cut to the chase: "Janice's got it, too, in her own field. In a few years, you ladies will be doing Harvard even prouder." Raising his glass again, he said: "To the next generation." Janice Borden practically glowed at his side: these two looked to be far more than a rumor.

I raised my cup again: "To our mentors—for paving the way."

Leland Townsend has a real problem on his hands, I thought as I sipped my punch. This man could be utterly charming—perhaps lethally so—certainly enough to give the president a serious fight for the hearts and minds of the students, the alumni, and the press.

"Hear, hear," Maggie Dailey interjected, carrying a groaning platter of turkey to the dining room table.

"Hear, hear," echoed Janice. Then her tone changed. "*Hello.* Who's that?" She gestured toward Dante Rosario, who had just entered the room.

"He's one of my housemates," I replied casually. "He lives downstairs from me."

"Well, girl, I hope you're paid up through the month, because that's a real nice amenity to have. The only thing that comes with my apartment is access to the gym on the top floor. Introduce me."

"Why don't you just go on over and say hi," I suggested. "He's very friendly."

She proceeded to do so, and in short order the two were laughing and deep in conversation.

Suddenly overwhelmed by the desire for a cigarette, I dug one out of my purse and lit it hastily.

"You are *totally* hooked, girlfriend," Alix Coyle whispered in my ear as she placed a large pan of homemade cornbread on the table next to Maggie's victuals.

I exhaled a plume of smoke and shook my head adamantly. "I can quit any time I want to."

Alix laughed. "Uh-huh. Right. And I ain't talking about those cigarettes, darlin.' "

"That cornbread smells just like the kind my mother makes," Justin Simms interjected.

Talk about laying it on thick: Justin's mother, whom I'd met, wears Hermes scarves and looks as though she'd as soon bake cornbread as go out and hoe the back forty. Much more Diahann Carroll than Esther Rolle.

"I may be approachin' your momma in the age department, sugar," Alix told him, "but that's as far as the resemblance goes, I hope."

Though Justin and I had never been more than friends-in-flirtation, and I knew that Alix was just messing around, I had no desire to eavesdrop further on this badinage. Out of the corner of my eye, I could see Janice and Dante talking and laughing with Maggie. Accordingly, I made for the opposite corner of the room, where Butch Hubbard was engrossed in conversation with Rafe Griffin. It was either that, or take a swing at somebody, and that just didn't seem productive.

You had to give it to the man: Sportin' Life could engage with an incredibly wide range of people. Though utterly at ease with power brokers, he was equally comfortable interacting with nomadic sheepherders in the sub-Sahara, as I'd seen him do on a PBS special called *The Unknown Continent*. With his Harvard T-shirt and Red Sox baseball cap, he looked like the mayor of Boston's emissary on the African continent.

Now he and Rafe were on to the need for more black cops on the Harvard police force.

"There are two of us on a force of eighty," Rafe told Sportin' Life. "The young people, they're off to the rent-a-cop companies, thinkin' that's as good as they can do. The more confident ones, they go to the city, lookin' for the pension and the chance to strut the streets in that uniform, roarin' around in those cars like they see on the cop shows on TV."

"The very name of Harvard intimidates," added Butch Hubbard sympathetically. "We need to see recruitment at the high schools and the junior colleges—we need to represent in the neighborhoods."

Wincing involuntarily at Sportin' Life's use of hip-hop slang, I waded in nonetheless. "From what Earl Stokes told me, the Jersey police are the worst anywhere for arrests for driving-while-black—and this includes black cops doing the harassing."

"You put on the uniform, you join the brotherhood in blue," Butch Hubbard said. "I was stopped twice on the Jersey turnpike driving back up here in my SL 500."

Rafe nodded solemnly, as though we were discussing the state of the nation's nuclear readiness. "That's a fine, fine car—in a vehicle like that, the police are seein' you as a gangsta with a gun in the trunk."

Sportin' Life, dressed for the party in a black turtleneck and a tweed jacket, laughed heartily. "If only I'd been wearing my bow tie when they pulled up in the patrol car!"

When Rafe joined Butch Hubbard in a deep guffaw, I decided I could take no more of car and cop talk. Pointedly I said to Sportin' Life, "I wonder if Eula and Earl Stokes would have been happy here in Cambridge. They had such deep roots in the Princeton community."

"Eula could have used a change," replied Butch Hubbard, "especially if it involved some distance from Pastor Smalls. Earl? Despite what I said on television after he died, I have no idea whether he planned to come to Harvard or not. I filled his ear with reasons why, but he held his cards close to the chest. That was Earl—proper, intensely aware of appearances."

*As if you're not,* I thought.

"Tragically," Butch Hubbard continued in the Sportin' Life style we knew so well, "we'll never know what Earl was thinking, or writing—will we?"

Maggie appeared suddenly at Rafe's side bearing plates of turkey with stuffing, green beans with almonds, candied yams, and pieces of Alix's cornbread. My own contribution was a special cranberry sauce infused with chutney, a recipe I'd learned from an old boyfriend. With satisfaction I saw it next to each portion of turkey on the respective plates.

"Eat, drink, and be merry," said Maggie, looking at the three of us. "I can tell by these faces y'all weren't talkin' about the Celts score just now."

"They beat the Knicks last night," said Ted Adair over her shoulder.

"This sure beats matzoh ball soup," said Jess, a forkful of turkey in her hand. "Thank God the Jews weren't the first ones to hit these shores."

"Praise the Lord and pass the bacon," laughed Alix Coyle.

Two hours later, the party was winding down. Alix and Justin had departed for a dance club in Central Square, Butch Hubbard had gone off to another party, and Ted and Jess were laughing in the kitchen with Maggie and Rafe as they washed dishes and talked. Dante and Janice were nowhere in view, which was a matter of no real importance, but nonetheless all I could think about. I found myself alone in the dining room among the dessert remnants, feeling a bit like one of the stray animals left behind as Noah's Ark was pulling out of the dock. It was just me, the pumpkin pie, and a bowl of whipped cream. I was seriously contemplating diving in headfirst when a familiar voice from behind me interrupted my reverie.

"You're not playing fair, Nik."

With what I hoped was an imperceptible tremor of delight, I turned to find Dante Rosario regarding me from the dining room doorway.

"I have no idea what you are talking about," I replied as he walked toward me.

"You can't expect a man to give you space when you bring out this dress. I consider that a strict violation of the cease-fire rules."

"What happened to your new friend Janice?" I asked, backing gingerly around the table.

"Who?" he asked, laughing. The distance between us was closing alarmingly quickly.

"We're not speaking, remember?" I backed into the foyer and decided to make my stand at the foot of the stairs.

"Not a problem. I didn't actually have conversation in mind, anyway."

I laughed and shook my head adamantly. "You actually believe that I am this susceptible to your charms, Rosario?"

"Ah, but I'm not relying solely on charm, Juliet." Somehow now we were standing quite close. "I've got mistletoe," he murmured. "And I'm not afraid to use it."

# 20
## Potentially Harmful Attachments

"**S**o, tell me. Everything. Tell me everything."

"Jessie, I told you. You won your fifty bucks, now leave me alone!"

It was the morning after Maggie's holiday party, and Jess and I were on the phone recapping the night's events. The crisp winter sunlight streamed through the slanted windows of my third-floor garret, and I stretched contentedly from the warm confines of my bed.

"All I want to know is how on earth that man learned to kiss that way," I declared. "It's completely unfair. There's no defense against it! I mean, I am still really angry at him, and look at what happened. I turned into a marshmallow. This is completely unacceptable behavior."

Jess laughed happily. "So are you two back together?"

"Who knows?" I shrugged. "I definitely can't think about it right now. What does Maggie put in that punch, anyway? Love Potion Number Nine?"

"I've seen her adding bourbon and Cointreau. Can't speak for the rest." Jess sighed dramatically. "I think I may really *love* him, Nikki. You remember the *Nutcracker?* My mother would take me to Lincoln Center every year, and it occurred to me this morning that Teddy is like . . . he really is like the Cavalier. He's so strong and so true, and so—"

I bolted upright in response to a sharp knock at the door.

"Nikki, it's Ted!" a voice called out with more cheer than seemed possible at this early hour.

"Where are you, anyway?" I muttered into the phone. "Because your Cavalier is banging on my door right now." Groaning audibly, I called in the general direction of the door, "Wait one second!"

"Don't bestir yourself on my account, sleepyhead," I heard Ted say with a laugh. "I have to get to work, so I'll slide this information under the door."

"Gotta go, Jess. Yes, I will definitely call you later, sweetie. Bye."

I staggered out of bed and picked up a two-page memo Ted had clipped together. Even in my groggy state, I could see that his findings were conclusive: Pastor Creflo Smalls was at the helm of the construction company building the Center for African-American Studies at Princeton, now a pile of charred ruins. Officially owned by Beulah Baptist Church, Smalls Construction was also under investigation for irregular building practices, including fire code violations at several of their sites. If Maureen Kelly of the Princeton Police was so sure the fire was set deliberately—even if not by pros—could contractor carelessness or malfeasance also have contributed to the blaze? One way or the other, it looked as though Eula Stokes's confidant and confessor was directly implicated in her husband's death.

Collapsing into the overstuffed easy chair across from my bed, I sighed deeply. My busman's holiday was definitely over. I had to get back to work understanding what had happened to Earl. And what my brother's cufflink was doing at the scene of the crime. I set my computer to booting up while I dialed Eric's number. I was hoping that for once, maybe he and Kayla were bunking at his place.

To my great relief, he answered the phone.

"Hey, it's me," I said. "Just calling to see how you are."

"I'm fine," he said. His tone of voice belied the statement. To my ear, he sounded distracted. And worried.

"You sound a little out of sorts," I coaxed.

"Do I?" He paused. "It's nothing important. It's just that a book's got a hold of me."

Despite myself, I laughed at the old reference. All of us kids loved to read when we were growing up, and there were times when we were so transfixed by something we were reading that we essentially couldn't deal with life until we finished the book. My parents loved the fact that we were reading, and it became a plausible excuse for not engaging in family activities. Once a book had a hold on you, you had to finish it before you could get back to real life.

"A novel?" I probed, skeptical that he actually had time to read when finals were underway on campus. This could just be his way of getting rid of me.

"Nonfiction," he replied. "Look, Nikki-I've-got-to-go," he said, suddenly in a rush. "I'll call you."

I looked at the phone receiver as the dial tone buzzed insistently at me. Now, why did that conversation make me feel more worried than I was before? My little brother was involved in something. Maybe it had absolutely nothing to do with Earl Stokes. But I was willing to bet that it had something to do with Kayla. And by association, with Yusef Jones, too.

My e-mails were up on my laptop screen by the time I got out of the shower, and I clicked on the first one as I sipped a steaming cup of coffee. It was from a student, and when I tried to open it, an ominous error message erupted on my screen:

*This e-mail contains potentially harmful attachments.*

I recoiled from the computer, shaken. *Lord,* I thought. Don't let that be an omen of the aftermath of my recent nocturnal activities. Nor Eric's.

• • •

**Two cups of coffee** and one hour later, I was ready to head out the door. I had artfully arranged my teaching schedule so that I had no classes to teach on Fridays that semester. So I was free to spend the day digging out from under the avalanche of e-mail and snail mail in my office. And to try to piece together a few more facts about Earl, and Butch, and the Harvard Economics Department.

As I headed out, I noticed a phone message Maggie had slipped underneath the door: it was the second from my mother in as many days. Each day that passed without my securing a reservation on a plane to Detroit made it less likely that I was going to make it home for Christmas. Yet I didn't have the nerve to pick up the telephone and discuss this directly with my mother. Much as I disliked passive-aggressive behavior in others, now I seemed to be backsliding into it myself. *Note to self,* I thought, as I pulled my apartment door shut. Stop at travel agency and get tickets home. Then buy witty holiday cards, sufficiently ecumenical to offend no one on mailing list. Buy memorable but affordable gifts and photogenic wrapping paper and bows. Plan dinner menu that includes every old family favorite, plus one new exciting and delicious dish to join the permanent holiday rotation. And gain no weight during the entire month of December.

The holidays used to be effortless fun, but they were becoming increasingly stressful. More and more it fell to me, as the only daughter in the family, to create the Kodak moments for my parents and brothers, while still meeting every professional obligation, and then some. Men had no idea how lucky they were. No one in life would expect a similarly situated male to produce a perfect prime rib and a flawless AEA paper, both in the same week. And to look good doing it.

Compared to the holiday fuss, this investigation was almost a relief. I mused over the state of play as I strode down Mass Ave in the brisk morning air. I realized that the first priority was to pin down as cleanly as I could Earl Stokes's professional intentions right before his death: was he indeed to have become the head of the Harvard Economics Department? Press release or no, it was too vital a fact to accept as true without a second source. The whole issue of who benefited if Earl died might come down to that one issue. According to Butch Hubbard and Janice Borden, Harvard's Afro-Am Department was not on Earl's agenda, period. But a lingering mistrust of both of them, and their respective agendas, motivated me to seek out another source of information, one unclouded by personal ambition or vendetta.

By the time I reached the Harvard campus and Littauer, most of the office personnel were in place and hard at work; the halls were buzzing with activity. The light was on in Dante Rosario's office on the first floor, just off the lobby, but I hurried past it, not ready for a close encounter with him. The only man I wanted to see that morning worked on another floor of the building. I descended the stairs to the basement, looking for Percy Walker, the building's chief custodian.

Though I hadn't seen him since our chance encounter at the living wage rally two nights before, our friendship dates back to my freshman year in college, and I knew that I could trust him implicitly. Originally from South Carolina, Percy Walker is one of the most hardworking, dig- nified men I know. He was wheeling an industrial vacuum cleaner down the hall when I caught up with him.

"Hey," he said, looking up when he saw me. "Now there's a sight for sore eyes."

I smiled sheepishly. "Bless you. I know I look like something the cat dragged in. I'm still recovering from a Christmas party last night."

Percy grinned. "Must have been a good one."

I groaned theatrically and rubbed my temples. "Why didn't some- one warn me about the punch you folks from the South make for the holidays?"

"My papa was a moonshiner," Percy confided. "Made a corn liquor that'd knock you flat after half a mason jar full—that's how they drank it back in the day." He wound the hose of the cleaner around the base of the machine, wheeled it into a long, dark supply closet, and shut the door. Then he ambled over to the soft drink machine. "Coke? Sprite?" he asked me. "I don't have anything stronger than that, or I'd offer it. Hair of the dog that bit you, you know."

I accepted a Diet Coke and sat next to him on a discarded bench from one of the lecture rooms upstairs. "Percy, I'm jammed up," I began.

"Oh?" He swigged his soda.

Last year when I'd been investigating the death of my friend Rosezella Fisher, Percy had provided me with an invaluable clue: he saw and heard everything that went on in the building. At age seventy, he was highly observant and had an excellent memory to boot. If there was going to be a new department chair, by osmosis that news would have seeped through the walls. And Percy would have heard it. I was positive of that.

"Have you heard the name Earl Stokes mentioned in the last two or three months?" I asked him.

He thrust his hands into the pockets of his overalls. After a long silence, during which I focused mainly on the pleasures of a truly icy cold soda, he said: "I believe I have. Just last week I was fixing the banister leading to the second floor—you know, the one that's been broken for a few months now, ever since that visiting scholar from Finland slipped on a waxed floor and knocked a big chunk of it to kingdom come."

Patience, I told myself: Percy was a southern-style storyteller. The train would not arrive in the station until it had traversed two streams, a field, and several bridges, at the very least. "So you fixed it," I prompted him.

He nodded slowly. "I had just finished, so there was a pretty little stretch o' quiet. And then I got a call that the thermostat was busted in the office of that new boss of yours."

"Carl Irvin," I interjected.

Percy nodded again. "That's the one. He was in a meeting with the new president—now, *that* man has manners. Always gives me the time of day. Anyway, they asked me to check it, even though they were in a meeting. Now you know, this building is on steam heat, and I've told them they need to replace those old thermostats. Those things don't work, never have, that's why people are always opening the windows in this building."

*Dry cleaners, post office, make a hair appointment,* I thought idly. Lots to do before the holiday recess.

"So the president told Irvin that this man Stokes had just turned down the offer to come up this way. Happened at the last minute, and the president seemed real angry. Said Stokes had decided that he was happy where he was—had no urge to travel just then. Mentioned unfinished business there, things he had to do."

*Ding, ding, ding, we have a winner.* "When did this happen?" I interrupted.

"Well, let's see. It was snowing that day, because I remember all day I had on those heavy snow boots, the ones that really keep your feet dry but make you hot when you have to wear 'em all day. Friday—that's right. Friday evening, it was."

I had seen him Friday—that very day—in the early afternoon. Something had happened right after I saw him that had changed his mind—some unfinished business. Unexpected unfinished business, apparently.

The Center for African American Studies? Maybe the book, the mysterious, potentially scandal-filled tome that seemed to have spooked half the populace of Princeton? Or maybe something that I had missed entirely. Whatever it was, neither Butch Hubbard, nor Janice Borden, nor anyone else at Harvard had a need to keep Earl out. Earl Stokes had been asked to replace Carl Irvin as the head of the Economics Department—but Earl had turned down the job, and Irvin knew it.

"I've got some unfinished business myself," I told Percy.

He looked over at me with wide, brown eyes. "Take care what dust you're stirrin' up, Professor. Don't forget what happened to Sister Rosezella when she started lookin' into other people's business."

When I reminded him of Ian McAllister's fate, he regarded me even more intently. "Where he's gone, he can't come out on no probation—can he?"

I gave a short, bitter laugh. "I hate to tell you, Percy. But my money is that McAllister will be out before the next academic year begins, if I know anything about how things work in the justice system. So don't be surprised if you see him sooner rather than later."

"Well, I've been around a few years, child, and plan on bein' around a few more," Percy Walker told me. "I guess by the end, I really will have seen it all."

I nodded, thanked Percy for the soda and the information, and headed toward the stairs. One door closes and another one opens. I had been certain that Butch Hubbard had something to do with Earl's death. But if Earl had turned down the offer to come to Harvard, then the only folks who had any interest in harming him all lived in Princeton. Of course, it was possible that Hubbard didn't know that Earl had turned the offer down at the last minute. But if I knew anything about Butch, it was that he was sufficiently plugged in to know down to the nanosecond if he was in professional jeopardy.

"Watch your step, Juliet."

I stopped abruptly and found myself inches away from Dante Rosario. His office was just at the top of the stairs to the basement at Littauer, and I hadn't even seen him coming.

"Little light-headed this morning?"

"*Don't* flatter yourself, Rosario. I'm just trying to sort some things out."

"I've got office hours right now. You want to talk?" He accurately read my expression and laughed. "I really do mean *talk*. My secretary's here. So your virtue is safe."

The truth of the matter was that I did need to talk some things out.

"Come on," he cajoled. "I've got some time right now. Fresh pot of coffee, too."

I considered it for a moment, and then sighed resignedly and followed him into his office. I didn't have much time, and I needed to get my thoughts straight.

We sat in chairs on opposite sides of his desk and I rapidly filled him in on the events of the past week. "It's a little complicated. But there are basically only three reasons that someone would have wanted Earl dead."

"Let me guess," he interrupted. "Money, sex, and revenge."

In spite of myself, I smiled. "That's actually not a bad list."

"You see, despite that skirt you're wearing, I was listening to every word you said. So take the money angle first. You think this Reverend Smalls may come into some real money now that this building has gone up in smoke."

"It's possible. He was the contractor on the building, and presumably there is an insurance policy that is going to pay out now that the structure has been destroyed. He's been involved in incidents like this before—Teddy told me that Smalls is being investigated by the town of Princeton and the New Jersey State Attorney General's Office. He's received numerous state and federal grants to build low-income housing in the black community, and defaulted on the deals. But I don't know for a fact that he stands to gain monetarily from this. What I do know is that he seems to have Eula Stokes in his sway."

"We're on to the sex angle now."

"Yes, such as it is. I mean, it's possible that this is an old-fashioned love triangle. Smalls and Eula are in love, so Smalls decides to take out her husband and clear the field."

"Very thirties way of doing business, don't you think?" Dante leaned back in his chair.

"I know—you'd think a divorce would serve the purpose just as well. Unless there's a big life insurance policy involved."

"Well, you knew Stokes pretty well. What was the state of their marriage?"

I shook my head ruefully. "That's the whole problem. I knew him well in some ways, and not at all in others. I had never met his wife until the night he died, and I just found out that he had a son that same night."

He leaned forward slightly. "Yes, the professor's son. I want to hear more about that one."

There was no way that I was going to tip my hand on that. It was serving my purposes just fine to have Dante thinking that Yusef Jones was interested in me. So I'd deleted the sighting of Kayla and Yusef from my narrative earlier. And now I just smiled a Cheshire cat smile.

"The point is that Earl's life was compartmentalized. And there was very little interaction between his personal contacts and his professional ones."

"I think you just answered your own question about the state of his marriage, Juliet."

"You mean, if it was a good one, she'd be more prominent in his life," I stated flatly. "Yeah. I'm sure you're right." I paused and sighed. "There are rumors about his private life involving multiple women."

"One of *your* heroes was a cheater?"

I bristled instantly. "We don't know that for a fact. I said that they were rumors."

"Rumors that his wife might have heard about?"

"She definitely knew about them. I first heard about them from her and her pastor, as a matter of fact."

"She the jealous type?"

"You mean, did Eula kill him because he was cheating on her?" I leaned back and considered that for a moment. "I just can't see her doing that. Especially not this way. If someone like her was going to kill her husband, she'd have a lot easier ways to get it done than burning down an entire building." *Like pills,* I thought.

"But what if her boyfriend was going to benefit from the building going down? Two birds with one stone?"

"You're good." I grinned. "Very noir. That's not inconceivable. I've got to find out what the economics of the insurance coverage on this building are. Who benefits now that it's off the table. And what life insurance Eula is going to collect." I crossed my legs and leaned toward him. "I just can't help thinking, though, that there could be a whole different angle to this. If Earl was offered a department chair at Harvard, why did he turn it down? Don't you think Princeton would have had to offer him something pretty big to keep him there?"

"Like Fleming's job, you mean. Head of the Princeton Economics Department."

"You got it. I was positive that Butch Hubbard had something to do with his death, because I was sure that he'd been offered Butch's job. But he hadn't been. This is like musical chairs—literally. What if some department chairmanship was going to be, or already had been, offered to Earl to keep him at Princeton? The current occupant just couldn't be happy about that. And Zanda Fleming is utterly devastated by Earl's death. I know it's more than the loss of her party walker. She's lost something more, but I can't figure out what it is."

"Maybe she really wanted that book he's writing to be published."

"The book, the book. That one is driving me nuts. I keep hearing about it, but no one has a manuscript, and Earl never said anything to me about it. If Zanda wants it published, why doesn't she write whatever the story is herself?" I stood up resolutely. "I've gotta go." The weight of the conversation was propelling me to take some sort of action—I had no idea what, but I couldn't sit still any longer.

"Not yet, Juliet."

I read the expression in his eyes and slowly backed away as Dante came from behind his desk toward me. "You promised, Rosario. Talking only."

"So sue me."

"Sorry. Got a date." I glanced at my watch and winced visibly. "I'm already late."

He looked at me skeptically. "Where did you say this professor's son lives?"

"I didn't say, actually," I replied, smiling as I pulled the door closed behind me. As I headed for my office on the second floor of the building to keep my aforementioned date, which was with a tuna sandwich on my desk, my cell phone rang insistently. It was Gwen.

"Finally! I've been looking all over for you. You've got to call the Princeton police station right away," she said. "You want me to put you through?"

Thirty seconds later, I was on the line with Detective Maureen Kelly. "I wanted you to hear this from me first, Professor Chase," she said soberly. I fought a tide of nausea at the sound of her voice. "I just sent two detectives to Holder Hall. We're arresting your brother for the murder of Earl Stokes."

# 21

## The Family Liar

It was snowing, yet again. We hadn't had snowfall like this on the East Coast in several winters. Whether or not it was due to the so-called greenhouse effect, or some other man-made environmental disaster, in the past few years winter in Cambridge had become a shadow of itself, a gray, gloomy interlude between fall and spring rather than a full-fledged season with blizzards and hailstorms and other natural wonders serving to disabuse human beings of the notion that we are running the show. Now winter was back with a vengeance, and it was clear that the humans weren't in charge.

Some days we can't even get the trains to run on time. It had taken forty-five minutes to get out of New Haven alone. There was ice on the tracks, a sick passenger in the last car, and technical problems with a door that wouldn't close. I hadn't felt this helpless since my days at the investment bank in New York, when I was forced to ride the East Side IRT each day to Wall Street with carloads of other ill-tempered commuters.

I was on my way to Princeton on the fastest mode of transportation that I could afford. My rickety car had been on the fritz for weeks, and plane fare was out of the question, so it was back to my old friend

Amtrak. I had brought along a stack of term papers from my International Economics class to distract me from the sickening worry that I felt for Eric. The first phone call I'd made after getting the news of his arrest from Detective Kelly was to Rafe. He'd told me to find the best lawyer I could and then get down to Princeton, so I'd called a black Law School professor at Harvard who happened to be one of the best criminal attorneys in the country. We'd become friends through the informal network of black Harvard faculty, and I knew that he'd be the best counsel by far in an emergency. He'd promised to make some calls, and to fly down the next morning. But the most important thing, he told me, was this: *Don't let your brother say a word until I get there.*

I hadn't called my parents, though. I knew that I would have to, eventually, but I held out the vain hope that I could make this go away before they even knew about it. This was clearly some kind of mistake, and it would be much better to call, laughingly recounting Eric's minor hiatus in jail, once the episode was over. I refused to consider the alternative, which was that my brother was in serious trouble. It would be cruel to drag them through this unless it was really necessary.

It was past nightfall by the time I disembarked from the "dinky train," wheeling my stewardess bag over a walkway crunchy with ice and freshly fallen snow. The silence was eerie, and ominous. The only other passenger on the train had been a middle-aged man in a baggy ski jacket: given the time of year, most of the traffic was obviously headed in the opposite direction, as students and faculty fled the campus for points west, north, and south.

I didn't have a key to Eric's dorm room, so I was going to have to take a cab to the police station, suitcase in tow, and figure out the rest of the night from there. I found my brother in a conference room at the station. At least they hadn't been dumb enough to actually put him in a holding cell. As I entered the room, he looked at me with an expression of pure anguish: his eyes were red, and his clothes disheveled. His khaki pants looked as though he'd slept in them, and his dark green polo shirt was adorned with a blob of what appeared to be dried ketchup. I had never seen my little brother like this: As a kid he'd cultivated creases in the front of his jeans, and insisted that my mother iron not just his casual cotton button-downs but even his T-shirts.

"Nikki!" he cried. "Have you told Mom and Dad?"

"Of course not," I said, trying to maintain a jocular tone. I wanted to hug him, but then we would both start crying, and that would get us nowhere. "This is a crazy, stupid mistake, and you're going to be out of here in no time. My friend Professor Jackson from the Law School is making some calls right now, and he'll come down if we need him tomorrow morning." I sat down across the table from him. "Eric, what is going on?"

He smiled tightly and shook his head. "It's like you said, Nikki. It's just a stupid mix-up, and I'm sure they'll let me go very soon. I haven't done anything wrong, so there's nothing to worry about."

I saw the expression on his face, and my heart sank lower. It was a joke among us kids that Eric was the least capable liar by far in our family. He was constitutionally unable to deceive anyone, because when he did, the guilt was writ so large on his face that you could read it from across the room. Our brother Jason, on the other hand, was sinfully good at it. Eric and I called him the family liar and always turned to him if he was in the car when we got caught speeding so that he could talk us out of a ticket.

"Eric," I said, this time injecting a note of urgency into my voice. "You're clearly involved in this in some way. Tell me what is going on here."

He looked down at the table, and then out the clear glass walls of the conference room, without speaking.

So now it was going to be the silent treatment: as the baby in the family, Eric used this technique from time to time with other members of our voluble crew. We come from a clan of chatterboxes and attention-grabbers, and nothing is more effective than pure silence for stating your case.

"I'm glad that you understand that you should not be talking to anyone around here," I said sharply. "But, honey, you've got to talk to me."

He shrugged sheepishly and shook his head. "There's nothing to say, Nikki."

Almost angry now, I stood abruptly and slung my backpack over my shoulder. "I'm going to get a coffee and try to find the detective who called me about you. I hope you're really thinking about this. I can't help if you clam up on me."

As I strode down the hall, I resisted the urge to turn around, go back into the conference room, and shake him. *Calm down,* I thought. He's embarrassed and scared, and he needs some space. I forget sometimes that even though my brothers and I are very close, there are still issues between us. I guess all siblings have rivalries. Mine with Eric was always over who was the true intellectual—me, the former Wall Street sellout who still didn't really have street cred with the intelligentsia because my field was something as crass as economics and industrial organization, or him, the purist, who only ever wanted to research and teach and write, and for whom money and power had no allure. I was sure that it was killing him to have to have his big sister ride into town to rescue him. I had to cool it, or I'd never be able to get him to talk to me, so I could figure out what we should do.

I turned the corner and found Maureen Kelly's office. She was there, alone, reading a piece of paper, when I entered her office like a fury.

"What the hell are you doing?" I hissed. "You know that my brother had nothing to do with Earl Stokes's death."

She looked up, impassive, and gestured for me to sit down.

"Professor Chase, it's time you faced up to something. Your brother definitely has some connection to what happened to Professor Stokes."

"What are you basing that on?" I demanded, hoping that my powers of deception were better than my brother's. I knew that I had Eric's matching cufflink from the soil at the site of the new Center for African-American Studies. So what did she have?

"I've got a witness that places him at the site of the murder that night. Says that he was tailing the professor to the scene and that he followed him into the structure. Few minutes later, your brother comes out, and ten minutes after that, the building's up in flames."

"Who is this witness?"

"A Princeton student."

"Does this person have a name?"

Maureen Kelly shook her head. "Not for public attribution."

"So you hauled my brother into a police station based on an anonymous tip?" I flared.

"*We* know who the informant is," she barked back at me. "And the person claims to have the shirt that your brother was wearing that night, and says that it has some stains on it that appear to be blood, and maybe gasoline."

"Does this witness have a freaking photo of him lighting the match, too?" I snapped. "This is bull! My brother loved Earl Stokes, and his family. He would never do something like this."

"I agree, from what I know, it isn't at all clear what the motive would be. Still, there's the physical evidence, and the statement of this witness. So we had to bring your brother in."

"Who knows about this?" I asked sharply. "Are you announcing this arrest?"

"Absolutely not. That doesn't mean that it won't get out, but it won't be coming from us."

I shook my head again. "You can't believe this story. You must know that it doesn't make any sense," I said insistently. "My brother has absolutely no reason to have harmed Earl Stokes. That's just crazy."

Abruptly, Detective Kelly got up and closed the door to her office. "Let me tell you something, Professor Chase. Sometimes we make an arrest because we're sure we have the right person. And every now and then, we have to do it just to see what happens next."

I nodded wordlessly. "When can I take my brother home?"

"We've got to do an arraignment, and then the judge can set bail. We'll try to get that done in the next couple of hours so that he doesn't have to spend the night here." She smiled wryly. "You've got a hell of a lawyer. He practically ripped me a new you-know-what, right through the phone wires."

"You're not putting my brother in a cell, are you?"

She shook her head. "I'll be sure of that, Professor Chase. There's no need for that right now."

Despite myself, I almost felt grateful to her. This was as bad a jam as my family had ever been in, and she was making it better for my brother than any other cop would have.

The sound of running feet gained steady force outside Detective Kelly's door, and then a thunderous knock sounded on the door.

It was Lieutenant Bellock, wearing a grim expression. "We've got a situation," he said.

"What is it?" Detective Kelly asked, rising quickly from her chair.

"One of the janitors over at Little Hall just found a corpse, Detective. They don't have a positive ID yet, but it fits the description of the occupant of the dorm room."

I was amazed that they'd say the name in my presence. But they did. Bo Merriweather had just been found dead.


Midnight found Eric and I back in his dorm room. The long arm of my Law School professor friend had been sufficient to get Eric released for the night, with a promise not to leave Princeton. Once inside his room, I'd found more evidence of my brother's emotional state: shirts, pairs of pants, and socks of several colors were arrayed on every available surface, and day-old food encrusted the dishes in the sink of the kitchenette. This was the room of someone preparing to move, or in the throes of an emotional upheaval.

It occurred to me with a mounting sense of alarm that my brother Eric, the prepped-out, conservative member of the family, might be taking drugs of some sort: uppers, maybe, to get through exams? Sleeping pills? After all, it was not unknown on college campuses for students to seek out chemical help with the pressures of finals, the holidays, and maybe romantic difficulties.

Which brought me round to Kayla French. There was no question in my mind that she had something to do with my brother's current troubles. Her very absence tonight told me that they'd had some kind of falling-out. Perhaps she bailed out on him when she learned he was arrested? Or perhaps she had something to do with him having been arrested to begin with. It didn't take a genius to figure out that an anonymous source claiming to have the shirt Eric was wearing that night could only be her, or someone close to her. But that would mean that she had some tie to Earl, other than her midnight meeting with his son.

"So where's Kayla tonight?" I asked innocently. "You haven't mentioned her all night."

"Exams," he said tersely. Then he went back to washing the pile of dishes in the sink.

"Are you hungry? Did they give you anything to eat at the station?" I asked. Suddenly I was ravenous. Perhaps just with the relief that he wasn't spending the night in a cell.

"I've got a couple of frozen dinners in here," he replied, turning to the refrigerator he kept tucked under his desk. "You want one?"

I nodded and watched silently as he started opening the paper boxes and tearing off the plastic covers.

To break the awkward silence, I turned on the television set. On the local NBC affiliate, a talking head with the requisite blond hair and expensive dental work announced in solemn tones that Bo Merriweather, leader of the conservative student group at Princeton and organizer of the recent rally to protest Professor Yusef Jones's lecture on the endangered black man, had been found dead in his dorm room, an apparent strangulation victim. Merriweather had been a controversial, even polarizing figure, the talking head went on to say, as if to leave no doubt in the mind of a single viewer that Bo's political beliefs had led directly to his death.

"Maybe they did, and maybe they didn't," I mumbled under my breath.

My brother heard me. "Are you talking to yourself, Nikki?"

"They're trying to make it sound likely that some crazed black person went after Bo Merriweather because of his politics."

After a pause Eric replied, "We don't know that they didn't."

"And how would a dark-skinned perpetrator get into Bo Merriweather's dorm room, undetected?" I continued.

233

Eric shrugged. "You're the detective, Nikki—I make no claims in that department. Maybe someone dressed up as a cleaning person, or a repairman. You see that on the news all the time. Fake gas man—black or white, it doesn't matter—enters residence under false pretenses, then robs the place, terrorizing the residents."

"Not on this campus," I speculated.

"How many white people do you think there are on the cleaning crew Larnell is part of?" my brother asked me.

I ventured a guess: "Zero."

"You win the free trip to Hawaii, madam," said Eric. "The Caucasian content in Buildings and Grounds is a big fat goose egg. There may be a few guys from El Salvador in the gardening end of things—that's it."

"So we've concluded—what?" I asked him as the TV broadcast segued to the local weather report, where the news of more snow to come in the next few days was delivered by a young black woman with straightened hair and a luminous smile. *Why were the full-ancestry black broadcasters all in sports or weather?* I had asked myself more than once. The people of color who were anchors seemed to inevitably be a hybrid of several ethnicities, of which black was only one, so as not to upset the status quo too quickly.

"We've concluded absolutely nothing," my brother said. "What I'm speculating—and it's pure conjecture—is that no one on the buildings crew here was involved—too risky. Bo Merriweather was so vocal that he alienated other conservatives, too, people who thought he shone too bright a light on the cause, and invited undue scrutiny."

"So the range of possible suspects encompasses the left, black activists, the right, and everyone else who falls in the middle of the spectrum?"

My brother nodded.

"That leaves us with a lot of ground to cover," I told him.

"Us?" he said, sitting up straighter on the couch.

"You're holding out on me, little brother, and I'm tired of it," I said bluntly. "You know a lot more than you're saying about how you ended up in jail tonight." He looked down at his lap. "And from the way you keep twisting little knots in your hair at the back of your neck, I can tell that something is really bothering you. Not to mention the fact that your room looks like it belongs to a deranged psycho on a bender. So talk."

At the mention of his childhood nervous tic, he smiled slightly. Then he sat forward on the sofa and really looked at me.

"I do know something. But I—I don't want you running off to the police with it."

"You know you can trust me, Bun. Come on."

"Well, you remember I told you that a book had a hold on me, and I couldn't stop reading it?"

I nodded silently.

"I found a copy of the manuscript that Earl was writing. The book that everyone had been talking about."

"How did you find that?" I asked sharply. "I've been looking all over for that thing!"

"You remember that passkey to Earl's office that Larnell gave you that night? Well, I decided I needed one, too."

"You were there in his office before I was that morning, weren't you?" I remembered the fresh pick marks on one of the locks, and my sense that someone had gotten there before me. It had never crossed my mind that it was my little brother. But of course, he knew when I planned to go. So he beat me to it.

"Why?" I asked simply.

He shook his head. "I wanted to know what was in that book. For my own reasons."

*Dammit.* That girl has such a hold on him, I thought. What's her game? I had to keep calm, or I'd never learn what he discovered in that manuscript.

"Earl was writing an exposé," Eric continued. "But it wasn't of the Princeton police or anything. It was actually a rebuttal of many of his conservative critics. He takes on some of the Princeton faculty. Which is I guess why Jeb Wolf was so concerned about it. And there's a special chapter in there about Bo Merriweather."

"Really?" I replied. "A whole chapter?"

"Well, he was using Bo to illustrate a point. About self-hating blacks."

It took at least ten seconds for his point to sink in. "Merriweather was black?"

Eric nodded. "Apparently so. He got up under Earl's skin so badly that Earl had him investigated by a private detective. And it turns out that he was passing! Can you believe it? So Earl was going to 'out' him, along with a few other folks. He writes in the manuscript that it was your exposing the former Harvard president as passing for black that made him determined to write that particular chapter. Bo was just the perfect lead example of how far some folks go to distance themselves from their heritage. Even so far as becoming rabid conservatives."

"Did Bo know about this manuscript?"

Eric shrugged. "Don't know. And now he's dead. So we'll never know."

"You know, he could have killed Earl to keep this from coming out."

"Yeah. Although that seems pretty extreme."

"That's an understatement, little brother. But whether Bo knew about this manuscript or not, who killed him?" I looked at my brother for a long moment.

He shrugged and said nothing.

"Where is this manuscript right now?"

"I have it in a safe place."

"Eric, you've got to give it to the cops. They need to know about all of this. For not the least reason that it will get them off your tail. This kid had every reason to want Earl dead—why aren't you giving them a reason to let you go?"

"Because I got this manuscript by breaking into Earl's office, and they may think that I invented the whole thing myself, anyway, just to clear my own name. I don't have any real proof that he's the author of this thing. It's just a printout of a manuscript—there's no evidence that he wrote it."

"Geez, Eric—you have a hundred excuses here! Who are you trying to protect?"

Eric looked over at me defiantly. "I'm not a pawn in your scheme, Nikki. Not yours and not anyone else's."

We were at a standoff, and I could tell that the best course would be to step back. He had to figure this out for himself—I just had to keep him from ending up in jail in the meantime.

"Hey, those microwave dinners have to be done by now," I said lightly.

"So you really think that Bo might have had something to do with Earl's death?" he asked more calmly, as he withdrew two meals from the microwave.

"Princeton is a small, mostly quiet town," I reminded him. "Two murders in a month constitute a virtual crime wave. I just wouldn't be surprised if somewhere down the line, we find out that the two overlap somehow."

My brother put two dinners of meat loaf and gravy-covered potatoes accompanied by string beans down on the table. "But what could the connection be?"

"When I figure that out," I told him, "I win not only the free trip to Hawaii, but also a new set of Louis Vuitton luggage. That stewardess number is distinctly lacking in the stylin' department."

When my brother Eric burst out laughing, I decided that I hadn't heard a sweeter sound in years.

# What Matters

"**S**o it's true?" I murmured into the phone.

"Absolutely," the mellifluous male voice responded languidly. "Size definitely matters. If the guy's laptop screen is really big and thick, you can be *sure* he's not wealthy. Rich guys always buy the newest models, which are getting smaller and thinner all the time."

"So the rule is, rich men like thin women and thin electronic devices?"

"Pretty much," Matthew chuckled. I could listen to his voice for hours: low-pitched and soothing, it was a beguiling mix of authority and empathy.

"Are we getting anywhere?" I asked.

"Patience, Nikki," he replied. "There's a firewall that I have to get through." It was six o'clock Saturday morning and I was sitting at the desk in Eric's dorm room, trying with the assistance of Matthew—the help desk man at Harvard—to hack into Earl Stokes's computer. It was uncharted territory for us; normally our conversations consisted of power flirting interrupted periodically by a discussion of mistakenly deleted e-mails, the need to clean one's hard drive periodically, advice on disk fragmentation and virus removal, and mutual dismay over why

Bill Gates loaded his operating systems with more superfluous features than a foreign sports car. But Matthew seemed more than game to take on the challenge.

"Are you sure that this is going to work without my being in Earl's office on his computer? Because I can get myself back in there if I have to."

"I told you, there's no need for breaking and entering. That is completely passé in this day and age." Matthew paused for a moment, and I could hear him tapping furiously on his keyboard. "University IT systems are notoriously bad with security, because the philosophy behind their design is an open and easy flow of information. They *want* people to be able to get access. Unlike corporate systems, where the whole idea is to keep anyone from knowing anything."

"I guess that makes sense. You read in the papers all the time that computer security systems are so tight, but I guess that only applies to the business world."

"Well, I can tell you, those corporate systems are getting viruses and worms every day, so don't believe the hype."

"I know that I won't understand it, but just for the heck of it, tell me what you're doing, Matthew."

"Okay, in basic terms, I'm downloading a sniffer program through your machine that can detect passwords and other keystrokes. I had you log on through your brother's computer because he's on the Princeton Dormnet system. Which is great for us, because once you're in the Princeton network, you can basically give free access to that system to other people who are not on the system. So now I can get in and go anywhere your brother could go. And the sniffer is going to get me Professor Stokes's password."

"So this would be a lot harder if I didn't have Eric's password."

"Yeah. But I'd still get it done," he said assuredly.

"But now, how does the information get back to you in Cambridge?"

"A packet will transfer the information from your brother's computer to mine, via the Harvard server."

He might as well have said, "I wave my magic wand, and the information instantly appears in a poof of white smoke." I comprehended basically nothing from this so-called simple explanation. But I was only interested in one thing, anyway. "So once you get the password, will I be able to see Earl's documents? And his calendar?"

"You'll be able to look at his Word files. And as long as his calendar is in Outlook, yes, you'll be able to see it. Hold on. I'm going in for the password now. Princeton uses a password system called P-Synch, and once I have his password, I'll be able to access everything."

I waited, not breathing, until I heard Matthew sigh. "Got it. Now, let me see." There was more tapping of the keyboard, and then he announced triumphantly, "I've got his employee ID."

"How did you get that?" I breathed.

"There's a directory on the network that has it." He snorted softly. "This is almost too easy. What else is it that you needed?"

"Calendar," I reminded him. "And e-mail in box."

"Okay, let's open up Outlook."

"What's his password, by the way?"

He laughed. "You would never have guessed it. Thelonius66." He paused for a moment. "Bingo. We're in. You're driving now."

I took control of the cursor again, and found myself about to navigate through Earl's e-mail system as if it were my own, right from Eric's dorm room.

"Matthew, promise me that you will only use your powers for the forces of good," I said. "You are incredible!"

"My pleasure," he replied modestly. "Nothing that any good computer geek wouldn't have been able to do."

"I don't believe that. One more promise: if this professor gig doesn't work out, and I open my own detective agency, will you be my partner?"

"Just say the word, Nikki," he laughed as he rang off. "Let me know how it works out."

My first task was to try to find the manuscript that my brother told me about the night before. I know I could have waited for Detective Kelly and her crew to find it. But I needed to know, right then, if my brother was lying to me. He had taken off after our late dinner for parts unknown, and I was starting to feel that I was running out of time with him. I knew, better than he, what might happen to him if he kept the wrong kind of secrets.

I scanned Earl's Word folders, looking for the right heading. There were folders on evaluations, lectures, outside speeches, and the like. And one that just said "Color, Part 2." That turned out to be the one that I was looking for. I didn't have time to read every chapter. But I quickly found the one that Eric had told me about. I was dizzy with relief as I read it—my little brother had been telling the truth. Earl had been planning to "out" Bo Merriweather as a black man turning on his own race with vituperative anger. Now I just needed to know whether Bo had known of Earl's plan—and if so, why someone else had wanted Bo dead.

I didn't want to log out of the system without poking around in a few other areas first. Earl's calendar seemed like a sensible place to go, since I'd lost possession of his Palm Pilot. As before, initially it yielded few surprises. There were classes to be taught, and deadlines for handing in exams and finals. There was a drinks date with Earl's publisher in Manhattan, and a party for a retiring Economics colleague at Hayden Fleming's house.

But I did spot something new. Earl had jotted an electronic note to himself to give his secretary a bonus in her Christmas card, and to get in touch with "C.S." more frequently in the New Year. I leaned back in my chair, flummoxed by this new information. Who was C.S., and why did Earl Stokes require additional contact with him or her? Could it have been Creflo Smalls? If so, why on earth would he and Earl need to get together more often?

I had not given the minister two seconds of thought lately, but now I was forced to think about what role he might have played in Earl's and possibly Bo's death. Was Earl helping Creflo Smalls behind the scenes? I could not imagine how, or why, unless Eula had convinced her husband that the congregation would require more support of some kind from Princeton sources. Did Smalls have something on Earl, after all? If Eula knew about Earl's cheating, perhaps the reverend did, too; it certainly wouldn't have been beyond Smalls's ken to use this knowledge as leverage, but for what—to get additional contacts on the Princeton campus?

If Smalls Contracting had wangled their way into the deal to build the Center for African-American Studies, maybe the reverend was pressuring—or even blackmailing—Earl to use his influence with the school administration on behalf of the building company. And maybe, just maybe, Earl had gotten tired of Smalls's tactics, and threatened to expose him, thereby making himself an obstacle the reverend had to remove in order to keep his scam afloat. Of all the theories I'd conjured up to date, this one struck me as the most plausible. I'd have to run that one past Rafe.

The sound of the phone ringing startled me so that I nearly jumped out of my skin. I half expected it to be the Princeton cops, calling to bust me for illegal computer hacking. But to my surprise, it was Dante Rosario.

"I've got something for you," he announced without preamble. "It's about the professor's son."

"What?" I asked, genuinely confused. "*You've* got something about Yusef?"

"Did you check this guy out before you started dating him, Nik?"

I bit my tongue. I obviously wasn't dating him, I hadn't talked to him for almost a week now, but Dante didn't need to know that. "Yes, as a matter of fact, I did check him out. I did an Internet search on him."

"So then you know about the lawsuit."

"Lawsuit?" I had read at least twenty articles on Yusef Jones, and hadn't seen one referencing a lawsuit.

"*Yusef Stokes v. the Estate of Sloane Waterstone*. You've never heard of that suit?"

"Yusef doesn't use the last name Stokes," I said slowly. "He goes by Yusef Jones." And that was the name I had done the Internet search on. Not Yusef Stokes. *Dammit, what an amateur mistake,* I thought, furious with myself.

"Tell me about this lawsuit," I demanded. "Are you sure it involves

Earl Stokes's son and not some other man who happens to have that same name?"

As it turned out, it was the same man, all right. And quite a story to boot. Six months ago, Yusef Jones—aka Yusef Stokes—had filed a lawsuit against the estate of one of the matriarchs of the Waterstone family, Sloane Waterstone, who had died of breast cancer at the age of fifty-six the prior year. The suit alleged that she was his biological mother, and that he had a claim on her estate. Which was worth millions of dollars.

"Did the document you found talk about how Sloane Waterstone is related to the rest of the family?"

"Yes. It says that the executor and sole beneficiary of the estate is her brother, Cameron."

"So this Cameron Waterstone stood to inherit anything that she was entitled to?"

"Until Stokes filed this suit, yes."

"So what happened to the case?"

"The paper trail runs out pretty fast. I asked Ted to check it out, but he thinks it must still be pending."

I sat back in my chair, digesting this information. So Yusef Jones was a Waterstone. What did that mean for Earl?

"Does it say anything about Yusef's father?"

"The papers state that Earl Stokes is the biological father."

I felt like I was struggling around in a dark room. Yusef was Earl's son—but not Eula's. How long had he known that? I wondered. The lawsuit had been filed six months ago—so it wasn't as if either of them had received some sudden shock days before Earl was killed. But maybe it did explain the estrangement between father and son. If Yusef discovered his parentage under the wrong circumstances, it would certainly explain his derision at the party the night Earl died. And Eula's hectoring insistence that Earl had female friends that she didn't know about. Six months wasn't long enough to heal a hurt that deep.

I wondered how the truth of his parentage had come out. And why it was still such a secret, if a lawsuit had been filed. That made it public information. Princeton was a small town, and the Waterstones a prominent family. Yet no one seemed aware of the connection between the two families. Yet.

I could think of only one person who could shed light on this.

"I've gotta go," I said urgently. I paused for a moment. "Thank you, Dante." I said, meaning it. "I owe you one."

"I look forward to collecting, Juliet."

**Forty-five minutes later** I was facing Marti Waterstone across a table in Buxton's Deli. She was as beautiful as ever in a severe black hat that brought out the porcelain texture of her skin and the elegant lines of her cheekbones, as well-angled as those of Katharine Hepburn.

"Thanks for coming out on such short notice," I said to her as we sipped our respective cups of coffee.

"I needed a break anyway," she confided. "My last term paper is due Monday, and I've been up all night. If I have to review the failure of our national welfare policy one more time, I think I'll scream."

"Doesn't exactly sound like ideal pre-Christmas reading," I sympathized.

"It's not," she admitted. "But I hate the holidays anyway. I'm known as the family Scrooge. All that phony togetherness—as if anyone in my family can stand each other. Why is it any different for one day out of the year?"

"It can't be easy being part of such an illustrious family," I said carefully before biting into my cheese omelet.

Marti nibbled on a toasted corn muffin. "Some days I wish I'd been born on a farm in the middle of Kansas, like Dorothy in *The Wizard of Oz*, she told me wistfully.

"Farm life is no picnic," I assured her. "By now you'd be married to a beefy hometown boy, with two or three kids in tow."

Marti smiled. "I kind of doubt it," she said assuredly.

I cradled my coffee mug in my hands. "Look, Marti, I need to ask you about something that's been nagging at me."

She looked up with a sanguine expression. "Yeah, I figured you must be back down here so soon from Cambridge again for a reason."

"The night my backpack was stolen, after leaving the party at Ivy —"

She shook her head. "I've never heard word one from that lady cop. Figures—it's not high priority, especially now that they've got Bo Merriweather's murder on their hands."

"Do you see any possible links with Earl's death?" I asked her.

After a pause, Marti said: "Bo Merriweather had more enemies than John Gotti. The list of people who hated him would stretch from here to midtown Manhattan. Earl Stokes, on the other hand, was one of the finest men I've ever met."

"Even the most highly regarded people have their secrets," I said casually.

She laughed. "The old skeleton-in-the-closet syndrome—we've got plenty of those in the Waterstone clan. My great-aunt Bernice tried to join a Catholic convent, and my cousin Alfie was arrested for statutory rape after he got one of his students at the Fieldston Day School pregnant. Ten years after the fact, my uncle is still paying off the child support."

I looked over at her. "I guess it's pretty common to feel that you can have your way with people if you come from enough money. Look at all the trouble the Kennedys have gotten into—"

She blanched visibly, but retained her composure. "That's why I hate being a Waterstone sometimes. It's more of a curse than a blessing," she said bluntly. "You have no idea, Nikki."

"Maybe I do," I said in a low tone so that the students at the surrounding tables couldn't make out my words. "I just read about the lawsuit."

"What lawsuit?" she asked coyly.

"The one that Yusef brought against your father," I said flatly. I was bluffing, of course. I had no idea whether Cameron Waterstone was her father. But I knew the accusation would get her talking, whether I was right or not.

"Did Yusef tell you?" she demanded.

"Actually, no. You want to fill me in?"

She sighed audibly. "I keep telling my father that he can't buy people's silence. He thinks that if he throws enough money at Yusef, he'll keep quiet about this. But it can't be kept quiet. I don't know why he doesn't just settle this lawsuit. But of course, he blames me for the whole thing."

"You? Why?"

"Because I found out about it when I was researching a paper on my family for the Princeton Historical Society. I stumbled across it because I went to the town hall to look at the birth certificates for some of my other family members, and somehow Yusef's came with the rest. I guess when Earl and Eula officially adopted him, they never made the original birth certificate a closed file. Because there was my aunt's name listed as his mother. My dad begged me not to tell Yusef—but I felt that he had a right to know. So I called him up and went to see him." She shook her head. "I asked Professor Stokes to tell him, but he refused. He really thought that it would be too much for Yusef, that he couldn't handle the truth. But people have a right to know what their histories are," she said, defiantly.

No wonder Marti's family had almost disowned her: it had nothing to do with waitressing at P.J.'s, or cavorting across Europe and Asia on a student jaunt. She was a true muckraker. One who was going to cost them potentially millions of dollars.

"Why didn't you include all of this in your paper for the Historical Society?" I asked.

"I said that *Yusef* had a right to know. Not the rest of the world."

"Marti, you may not even know what you unleashed when you told him that."

She shrugged. "I know, I didn't expect the lawsuit."

"That's not what I'm talking about, Marti."

It took her a moment, then comprehension dawned. "You mean Earl?"

"He may have been murdered. And this may have been the reason."

"I can't believe this!" She seemed to be genuinely aghast. I felt the same sense of disbelief. It was a topsy-turvy world in which Marti Waterstone turned out to be first cousin to one of the most radical professors of African-American Studies in the country.

Maybe that emotional upheaval was the reason that Yusef had not attended Earl's funeral; there had been a clear strain between the two of them right before Earl died. I felt sure that Earl would not have approved of Yusef's suit—too divisive, too upsetting for both families. For Earl Stokes's generation, certain things were better left unsaid, whereas for Yusef Jones, unrelenting confrontation was apparently not only the only path to truth but also a way of being in the world.

"Had you heard that Earl Stokes was writing some kind of book?" I asked casually.

"Yeah, there was a rumor going around that he was writing a memoir."

"Would this have been in it?"

She shrugged. "Maybe. He had a lot on his conscience; maybe that was his way of lightening the load a bit. Catharsis, you know." She frowned. "I'm still reeling from what you said about his death. Who could have killed him?"

"Why not Yusef?" I said boldly. "Fratricide. Crazed with anger over finding out that his mother wasn't who he thought she was."

"No way." She shook her head adamantly. "I was there when he found out about it, remember? He took it the way you would expect—he absolutely did not believe me at first. But he didn't get a crazed look in his eyes, or anything like that. Besides, it was six months ago—he wouldn't have waited this long if he was out of his mind with anger, would he?"

I agreed that it didn't seem likely. And I looked at her with real respect. By all rights, she should have hated Yusef, and been quite happy to see him accused of murder. After all, wouldn't she personally stand to gain—financially and otherwise—if his suit failed? Instead, here she was defending him. Those were real family ties, and I admired her for that.

"So do you know of anyone who would have wanted to hurt Earl?"

A look crossed her face, and I zeroed in on it.

"What?" I demanded.

"It's nothing. Just something minor that Yusef said when I talked to him after his lecture earlier this week. I asked him how he was, and he said that he was good. That he'd found a kindred spirit. At first I thought he was dating someone new."

"But now?"

"But now I wonder if he wasn't trying to say something else." She leaned closer to me and dropped her voice. "Is it possible that Earl could have other kids that we don't know about?"

If Marti Waterstone was Yusef Jones's cousin, then clearly anything was possible.

## 23
## Unfaithful

A brilliant shaft of blue-white winter sunlight flooded the vestibule of the Beulah Baptist Church as I opened the door of the church an hour after my breakfast with Marti Waterstone on Saturday morning. The more I had thought about our conversation, the more certain I was that she was guilty of nothing more than raging idealism. Marti would have had no reason to kill Earl, when she was the one who had told Yusef about his true heritage to begin with. And her family would have to know that Earl's demise would only put more of a spotlight on his son—which was the last thing they would want.

The morning's developments made me want to talk to the various members of the Stokes family. Starting with Eula. I had walked to their house on Witherspoon, but found it deserted. My hunch was that she would have found her way to Beulah Baptist—with Christmas so close, I was certain that the church would be a beehive of activity, and like any good church lady, she'd be right in the middle of it. Even in a time of grief.

The snow crunching under my feet was almost the only sound I heard on my walk to the church. All that morning, from the sidewalks of Nassau Street to the snow-encrusted walkways of the campus, a lovely hush had enveloped the landscape. Apparently, the students, faculty, and other staff were packing up and heading for parts unknown, leaving Princeton a stately Potemkin Village. The university's well-tended grounds exuded serenity born of confidence in the rightness of its history and its proper place in the national scheme of things. It was this same confidence that had enabled Marti Waterstone to reach out to Yusef Jones, yet underestimate, perhaps, the consequences of her actions. I hoped that I was wrong—but I had a terrible feeling that she had set a series of events in motion that had led to Earl's death.

On the streets surrounding Beulah Baptist, tidy brick houses alternated with row homes covered in aluminum siding of the sort seen more often in working-class neighborhoods in Baltimore and Philadelphia. The people who lived here—taxi drivers, pizza makers, home health care attendants—would tithe a portion of their hard-earned wages to a charismatic preacher offering a moment of exaltation once a week, a chance to forget ornery customers and overbearing bosses and demanding children—in other words, a bit of transcendence not found in the bottom of a bottle, or in a pipe. I had a bad feeling that this particular preacher was an unworthy vessel for their hopes and their earnings.

Exuberantly bushy wreaths tied with red velvet ribbon adorned the front doors of Beulah Baptist. Inside, fashionable icicle lights hung at ceiling level illuminated the front hallway. A rhythm-and-blues inflected version of "Hark, the Herald Angels Sing," with electric piano and tambourine accents, reverberated through every inch of the church's interior. I assumed that this might be a Saturday-morning rehearsal for the Christmas pageant advertised on the bulletin board in the vestibule.

I walked to the back of the sanctuary and listened as the choir finished the number. As I watched a woman in the front row of the singers raise her head to the rafters, I thought of my Aunt Dahlia back in Detroit, the most enthusiastic member of her local choir, and of how much her life in the church defined her. I thought back to what I had learned about Smalls Contracting and the financial interest that Creflo Smalls had in the Center for African-American studies. If he were indeed a shyster, his betrayal of these people's trust would not be the least of his crimes.

As if on cue, the reverend himself appeared near the altar as the harmonies of the choir drew to a close.

"Beautiful, my people, beautiful," he pronounced. "Now, y'all take a break. There's some food down in church hall, so help yourselves."

Laughing and talking, the choir dispersed. I noticed how many of the women in the group stopped to talk with the minister on their way down the aisle. Creflo Smalls greeted them, as a king would address the ladies in waiting in his court. He didn't seem to notice me, standing in the background; but playing it safe, I stepped back a few paces to observe his interactions.

"Reverend!" said a very thin woman who bore a striking resemblance to the late congresswoman Shirley Chisholm. "Let me help you take the toys to the children in Trenton next week! They enjoy so few of the advantages that we do here in Princeton."

"A charitable thought, Sister Adelaide," said Creflo Smalls, smiling widely. He had a new, more closely cropped haircut, and bristled with self-importance and the adulation of his faithful. "Sister Stokes will be leading the drive—I'm sure she'll give you a call to make the necessary arrangements."

"Oh," said the woman, deflating visibly. "You won't be doing it yourself?"

"The holidays make unusual demands on my time and attention, sister," he told her. "So many lost souls in need at this time of year."

"Of course, I understand," she said morosely, and trailed the others down the aisle.

Following an intuition, I remained in the sanctuary after they left. And sure enough, Eula Stokes emerged from a door behind the pulpit. She wore a well-tailored plaid blazer and an ankle-length wool skirt. She was clearly determined to present an organized facade to the world, despite trying circumstances in her life that I could only guess at.

"Creflo," she said sharply. "Sister Andrea says that the two of you had dinner last evening. Is that so?"

He laughed with what could only be described as disdain.

"And if I did?" he said. "A man has a right to a decent meal with a parishioner, doesn't he?"

Eula's facade cracked slightly as she regarded him with a disappointed frown. "She told me more than dinner was involved. But I told her that had to be a lie."

"Now, Sister Stokes, surely you understand that a man in my position has to be able to enjoy the company of many members of the flock. I thought I made that perfectly clear some time ago."

She nodded mutely and watched as he disappeared down the aisle. I quickly stepped into a shadowed corner, hoping that somehow he wouldn't see me. If he did, he chose not to acknowledge me as he swept from the sanctuary.

I turned back toward Eula in time to see her crumple into a pew. Her head in her hands, I heard the sound of muffled sobs begin. She rocked slowly back and forth, as the intensity of her grief seemed to build. It was almost too much to bear to see her like this.

"Mrs. Stokes," I said softly, approaching her quietly. "Please, is there something I can do for you?" I knelt in the aisle next to her as she raised her head. "Please. I know that this must be the hardest possible time for you. Professor Stokes would hate to see you in so much pain."

She sighed heavily and took a ragged breath. "Child, I thought you went back up north. Don't you have school to teach?" A sob escaped her as she exhaled. "You can't be Earl's substitute forever, now, can you? No one can stand in for Earl Stokes for long."

"Certainly not Creflo Smalls," I said gently. I put my hand on her arm in solidarity as she looked at me. This woman needed a friend, and at that moment, that was all I intended to be for her. Earl Stokes was almost a tangible presence in this sanctuary, and I knew instinctively that he would have wanted me to comfort her, not interrogate her.

"I guess there's no fool like an old fool, is there?" she said soberly. "For me to think that the reverend would be faithful to any one woman. Especially someone like me."

"Mrs. Stokes, I know it sounds presumptuous, but I think Reverend

Smalls is a bad man. I think he may have been damaging the university in some way with his business dealings. And I think he may have been trying to hurt Professor Stokes in some way, too."

"Why do you think that?" she said, sounding startled.

"Well, I know that his contracting firm was involved with the construction of the new Center for African-American Studies. And I've seen the financials, and it looks to me like he was padding expenses to defraud the university. Possibly even violating the fire and safety codes at the site."

"I know," she said quietly.

"You know?" Now it was my turn to sound startled.

"Yes, child, I know. I've been lookin' into the goings-on in that building ever since Earl passed, and I've found plenty." She turned to fully face me. "I asked Earl to help Reverend Smalls get the job at the center, you know. So some of it's my doin'."

"No, it's not your doing—"

She interrupted me by holding up her hand. "Oh, yes, it was. I was so mad at Earl that I would have set the devil himself loose on him. Instead, I set Reverend Smalls on him. To make him know that I could have a man after me, too, the way he had those women. And now see where we are."

"You really have proof that the reverend was stealing money from the university as part of this project?"

She nodded. "I'm the church bookkeeper, child. I have papers, invoices, all of it." She sighed heavily. "I suppose it's time to be turning all of that over to the police."

"Let me ask you something—what does Smalls get, now that the building has been destroyed?"

She smiled a small smile. "Nothing much. Man was behind on his insurance premiums, I know that for a fact. You should have seen his face when he heard that. I don't know if they're gonna pay him anything."

"Did Earl know what the reverend was doing? I mean, with the finances."

"No, I don't think so. Earl wasn't one to question those kinds of details. Besides, I told him to work with the reverend. So he did it. Didn't ask any questions." Which meant that whatever else he might be, Creflo Smalls was probably no murderer. If Earl didn't even know about the finances, then there was no reason for Smalls to want him dead. Come to think of it, he had every reason to want him alive—if there was no insurance payout, then Smalls's best bet was to have the Center built. With the pressure from Eula, Earl was much more useful to Smalls alive than dead.

"Why were you so angry with Professor Stokes before he died? Was it the news about Yusef?" I asked.

She looked at me, surprised again. "How do you know about Yusef?"

I shook my head. "Long story. But basically, you can thank the Internet."

"I begged Earl to tell that boy years and years ago about his momma. It's not as if he wouldn't have been able to handle it. Now Yusef's got himself so worked up that he's gone off and tried to sue those folks. And that's just wrong. That woman didn't want him. But I sure did."

A look of pain crossed her face, and I realized how it must feel from her perspective. The son she raised as her own, and clearly adored, was publicly suing for recognition from a dead woman who was his mother in only the least important sense.

"He'll come to his senses, don't you think? He just needs some time."

"Maybe. Lord, I just pray that he hasn't done anything stupid."

The unspoken thought hung in the air between us.

"Do you think he was capable of hurting Earl?"

"Not on his own, no, never," she said adamantly. "But that girl is another matter."

I knew before she said the name who she was speaking of. But there was something that I didn't know.

"It was bad enough when he found out about his own momma," she continued. "But when he found out that Earl had another child, too, it was just too much. And the two of them together, only the Lord knows what they might have done. I just pray that my baby has better sense than that."

I prayed that my baby brother did, too. But I was beginning to sense that Kayla French might be pretty persuasive when she put her mind to it.

Eric was out when I got back to his dorm room an hour later. But I got him on his cell phone and asked him to meet me for lunch at The Annex. Maybe it was crazy, but I'd had so little luck getting him to talk in private, I figured it couldn't be any harder to get him to tell me the truth in public. Besides, I was suddenly starving, and I had a feeling it was going to be a long day.

When he entered the restaurant, he looked more composed than he had the night before. He wore a black and orange knit cap, and I marveled at the sight of my little brother, so studious, so erudite, yet so credulous in terms of social position and entrenched traditions, sporting Princeton paraphernalia. Though I was proud of my affiliation with that college in Cambridge, I would no more wear a Harvard-emblazoned article of clothing than do the Electric Slide in the middle of the Square.

No wonder my brother had been attracted to Kayla: with her dancer's posture, her impeccable grooming, and her ease in uptight Princeton social circles, she was a model of the well-adjusted young African-American woman, socially mobile and intellectually razor-sharp. She was bound for a bright future—or so it seemed.

I watched his demeanor as he settled into the booth. Given that he'd been arrested just the day before for murder, he was remarkably sanguine. As if he had settled on a course of action and was determined to follow it to the end, come what may.

We ordered—a Western omelet and fries for him and a chicken Caesar salad for me—and then confronted each other across the table.

"How are you holding up? You look pretty good."

"Yeah, I'm okay. I was helping Kayla study for one of her exams."

"Really?" I sipped my Diet Coke to hide my surprise. He was actually still spending time with her? "She seems so cool and collected, I can't imagine that she would need any help preparing for a test."

"I know it seems that way—but she's actually very stressed, and she needed me this morning."

I winced at the expression on his face when he spoke about her. "I guess I shouldn't be surprised to hear that," I said casually. "People are often living far different lives than they appear to be—look at Earl."

"What about him?" Eric asked.

"There were women, Eric, lots of them—he was on Nassau Street with a blonde a few nights before he was killed. A counterman at one of the stores saw them, talking in an intimate way."

"Maybe this woman was involved in his death," my brother posited. "Maybe it was a crime of passion."

"It's funny you say that. I have a friend up in Cambridge who believes that murder is almost always about love or money."

"Then we have to find this blonde," said Eric with resolve, sitting up straighter in his chair at the suggestion that there might be a plausible suspect out there who would exonerate him.

"Are you serious about that?"

"Why are you asking me that? Of course I am. Do you think I want to go to jail?"

"Eric, you've got the keys to the cell in your own hands. We both know that." His eyes dropped to the table. "I'm not asking you to do this for me. I'm asking you to do it for our parents. I haven't told them about this yet, because it could literally kill them. But I'll have to if it goes on any longer. Please, Eric. It's not a game anymore." He twisted his napkin in his lap, and I pressed my momentary advantage. "Do you remember the petite blond woman we saw exiting Earl's funeral?" I asked. "She was weeping at the casket; she really seemed to care. Who is she, Eric? I think you know."

When I saw the look on my brother's face, I knew that if I could just get him to break now, we'd be home free soon.

After a seemingly endless pause, he said: "Her name is Cheryl Sutherland."

"C.S." Of course. I'd seen in the notes on Earl's Palm Pilot—the person he'd vowed to see more of in the New Year. I'd assumed it was Creflo Smalls.

"She's Earl's secretary," my brother continued.

"She's also Kayla's mother—isn't she?"

Eric nodded slowly.

"How long have you known this?" I asked him, struggling to contain my frustration and annoyance. If he had shared this information with me days ago, it would have saved everyone a lot of grief. "When did she tell you that Earl was her father?"

"She didn't," he replied soberly. "It's true," he added defensively, accurately reading the disbelief on my face. "I know you think that I'm infatuated with her. But I've had some concerns. Especially since she turned me in to the cops yesterday." He shook his head. "I still can't believe she did that."

"So what are you saying, then? That you snooped around and found this out on your own?"

He smiled wryly. "You may not be the only detective in the family, after all. But I wouldn't call it snooping. We've been sending a lot of time together, you know. I overheard her talking on the phone a few days ago. She thought I was asleep, but I heard most of the conversation. She was talking to someone named Cheryl, and Earl's name came up, and I put two and two together. She was talking to Earl's secretary, and I couldn't figure out why she would be doing that."

"So?"

"So I talked to a couple of the other secretaries who worked with Cheryl and Earl. And it turns out there were rumors about the two of them from years back. You know this is a small town. Lots of second and third generation families here. A lot of those secretaries have had their jobs for years and years, and no one forgets anything. The rumor was that Earl was the father of Cheryl's daughter. It wasn't very hard to track down the birth records at the hospital here. I got the final confirmation earlier this morning."

"Do you know any more about how it all happened? Did Cheryl and Earl marry at any point?"

Eric shook his head. "I don't think so. One of the secretaries told me that Mrs. Sutherland's family has been in Princeton for years, just like the Stokes's. Her dad was the town butcher. She married too young—he was a state trooper, and he abused her. She was just as glad when he left. When she started working for Earl, she thought she'd died and gone to heaven, because he was the kindest man she'd ever met."

I regarded my brother quizzically. "Here's the part of the story I can't fill in—how did she keep Kayla in the dark for so long about her father? And her own family—how did she explain this child with caramel-colored skin?"

"The person I talked to said that Cheryl told them she'd gone to the Village to a jazz concert soon after her divorce, and hooked up with one of the musicians after the show," Eric told me. "She told them it was the one-night stand that changed her life. She is so proud of Kayla, Nikki."

I suppressed a snort of derision. Proud of her, indeed. This girl had tried to destroy my brother's life. "Why do you suppose that she sent the cops in your direction?" I asked innocently.

Eric shrugged. "I assume that the police learned that Earl was Kayla's father before I did, because they called her into the station yesterday morning for questioning." He paused. "I know it doesn't look great that Kayla was at that African-American Studies party the night that Earl died. They probably came at her pretty hard, and she must have panicked and given them my name."

Apparently, my sweet brother didn't know that Kayla French had given the police far more than his name. She'd given them an article of his clothing with incriminating evidence on it. She'd clearly been planning to kill Earl for a while, and my brother had been a key part of her plan. He was her fall guy.

"So what happened that night, Eric?" I demanded. "The night Earl died. Where were you, where was she, and by the way, why the hell am I having to drag this out of you?"

"Listen," he snapped, "if I thought that she was guilty of something,

I would have gone to the cops with it. Remember, I was with her that night, we were together almost the whole evening."

"*Almost* the whole evening?" I repeated pointedly.

"We left Earl's party and we were walking to an after-party at one of the clubs. I swear, we were apart for no more than twenty minutes the whole night—I left her to run back to my room because I lost a cufflink and I needed to replace it. So she met me at the party, and we were together the rest of the night. Just because she's his daughter doesn't mean that she did anything wrong, Nikki," he said defiantly. "I know her. I've spent a lot of time with her these past few weeks. She's a good person."

It was clear he was trying to convince himself of that.

"She must have felt that Earl left her with a hole in her soul, once she found out the truth," I commented.

"Apparently, Earl always paid for everything," my brother stated, "but that's different from having a real relationship with your child. Imagine living in the same town as your real father, so close by, yet so remote. The gossip is that Cheryl told Kayla that she had to go along with the secrecy even after Kayla had met Earl, because of his position in the community, and at the school."

"No wonder Kayla became such a devoted student of his: she wanted both to be near him and to impress him. She wanted to win his love and acknowledgment in some way," I speculated.

"No doubt," my brother said.

"So when she met up with her father at that building site, her anger must have gotten the better of her," I continued, as if having reached an inescapable conclusion.

My brother looked over at me with an expression of pure anguish. "Aren't you taking this Nancy Drew thing too far, Nikki? How could a person of Kayla's stature overpower a man like Earl?"

"We'll never know what happened that night, Eric—with the pills he was taking, Earl might have stumbled, or passed out, and given Kayla an opportunity. Maybe it was an accident. But no one had the motive Kayla did. Certainly not Yusef—he may have disliked Earl for all kinds of reasons, but he knew who his father was, thanks to Marti Water-stone."

"What about Eula Stokes?" my brother insisted, his voice rising, his composure on the verge of deserting him once again. "Maybe she knew about all the other women, and just lost it."

"She knew about the women," I told him, "but she didn't want Earl dead. She loved him, just like she imagined that she loved Creflo Smalls until he betrayed her, too. Women like Eula find ways to get their revenge, but they don't kill. Her sense of self-preservation is too strong."

Eric's eyes started to well with tears. "Kayla never had a chance, Nikki—with Earl it was all too little, too late."

I put my hand over his on the table in front of us. "We're going down to the station now, Bun. We have to get your name cleared. It's not going to be much longer before all of this hits the press, and I'm not letting your future be hurt any further by this girl."

At the mention of the media Eric seemed to lose his resolve momentarily. But he regained his balance once we had paid the check and wandered out in the streets of Princeton, where the shop windows glowed with brilliantly illuminated displays of toys, fine candies and other foodstuffs, kitchen utensils, books, and other accoutrements of the good, solid lives enjoyed by its citizens.

"What was the title of Earl's book, anyway?" my brother asked, raising his chin a bit.

"*In Plain Sight*," I told him as I tucked his arm in mine.

# 24

## Orange Crushed

Nightfall on Saturday evening found me once again on my way to Earl Stokes's subterranean office in Dickinson Hall. I suppose it was a sentimental journey, but I found myself drawn to it, perhaps as a way of getting straight in my own head who he really was and what had happened to him. It had been exactly one week since I had learned of his death. Somehow, I felt years older.

The rest of that afternoon had been a frenzied blur of calls to Professor Jackson, the Harvard Law professor who ultimately helped us ensure that my brother's record would be expunged of any notation about his arrest on Friday. Detective Kelly was still behind closed doors with Kayla French. I imagined that it would take a while before she would discuss what really happened the night Earl died. But somehow, I was confident that Detective Kelly and her team would get it out of her.

Earl Stokes, my hero and father figure, had feet of clay. He'd had a secret life involving a daughter whom he had failed to claim as his own. I had to accept that much. But I also had to remind myself of the good that he had done in the world—the courage he had shown, and the intelligence. And the resilience in the face of incredible challenges.

With the passkey I'd gotten days earlier from Eric's janitor friend

Larnell, I opened the door to Earl's office and stood there quietly. I could still smell the lingering scent of his aftershave. I wished that I had something more tangible to remind me of him and what he had meant to my life. I sat in his chair and faced the door, and noticed his computer screen. I smiled, thinking of what he would have made of my Matthew-assisted hacking spree.

Then I stopped cold as the thought formed for the first time that day. I was certain that Kayla French had killed Earl Stokes out of some misguided hatred over his role as her father. But why had she wanted to kill Bo Merriweather?

Had Bo discovered Kayla's paternity, and been holding it over her in some way?

I swiveled pensively in Earl's desk chair as I thought about the last time that I had seen Merriweather. He was leading the protest march outside Yusef's speech. He'd been particularly full of hubris that day. I remembered him saying that the *National Prospect* was about to expand, that the university was fully supportive of him. I remembered how he had been shadowing Earl the night he died. I'd mistaken him for a reporter, the way he had hovered so closely. I wondered if somehow he had seen what happened that night. And paid for that knowledge with his life.

Something was nagging at me. It was the same feeling I'd had when I was in this office the last time, during that dawn search I'd conducted. I looked at the corner that held Earl's file cabinets, remembering how something had pricked at me when I was looking through them. I'd thought it was that the pile of architectural drawings that had been heaped in the corner when I visited Earl on my first afternoon in Princeton was missing, but that wasn't it. Because I knew that Lloyd Eastman had moved them to his office.

I closed my eyes and exhaled. Something in Earl's files hadn't been right.

It came to me in a flash, and I groaned aloud and made a dive for Earl's computer. If I was right, then I still had quite a lot of work to do. It seemed to take hours, but it probably only took seconds for his computer to boot up, and I quickly logged on as him, using the password that Matthew had told me. Thelonius66—perhaps the jazz musician Thelonius Monk cut a great album in 1966, I thought—whatever it meant, it was the key that I needed. I went into Earl's old files, this time looking for his personnel records. And without much effort, I found what I needed: Lloyd Eastman's file. There was a letter dated Friday, December 7, stating that as Earl was likely to leave Princeton, he wanted it clear that Lloyd Eastman should not succeed him as the head of the Program in African-American Studies—that Earl had serious concerns about Eastman's personal conduct that needed to be discussed in private.

"*That's it,*" I muttered to myself. What had been nagging at me was the letter I had seen regarding Lloyd succeeding him as department chair in Earl's files—the paper copy had included a glowing reference for Lloyd. But the signature hadn't been Earl's. I certainly knew what his handwriting looked like—some part of my brain had registered that, but not clearly enough. The letter was a fake, and the signature was forged. Left by Eastman as a red herring for the inevitable police review of Earl's files.

So if Lloyd Eastman was a liar, did that mean there were more important things he was lying about?

"I have been looking all *over* for you." The male voice startled me badly. I turned to find Yusef Jones, Earl's son, in the doorway.

"Yusef?" I asked, quickly getting to my feet. "What—what are you doing here? And where have you been? I didn't see you at the funeral service."

"Yeah, I sent some jazz musicians in my place. I've been busy. Finding out who killed my father," he replied soberly.

I shook my head wryly. "You've been beaten to the punch on that one," I began. "They just arrested Kayla French. She's at the police station right now."

He nodded. "I know. But they've got the wrong person. She wasn't the one who actually killed him. She was just the bait."

I looked him over carefully, all six feet four inches of him. I had no idea what was coming. But I was fairly sure that if my recent conclusion about who had killed Earl was wrong, and I had to take this guy on in a fistfight, I was screwed. "How do you know that?" I asked, feigning calm.

"Because her husband was the one who killed Earl." He advanced farther into the office.

"Her *husband*?" I repeated, my stomach starting to churn. Kayla French, married? *Please, Lord, not to my brother. Lord, don't let him have been that stupid.* About ten seconds later, a more immediate worry surfaced. Yusef Jones could certainly be the spouse in question. Which would make him the murderer. Which would mean that I was in an exceptionally vulnerable spot as of that moment.

He must have read my expression, because a bitter smile crossed his face. "Don't worry. I'm not her husband." Yusef pulled the office guest chair toward himself and sat down across Earl's desk from me. "It's taken me a few days and a lot of Benjamins, but I finally figured out what that girl was up to, thanks to you."

I shook my head helplessly. "I have no idea what you're talking about."

The strained smile crossed his face again. "Why don't you tell me what you know, Nikki Chase, and then I'll fill you in."

"I know that Earl is Kayla's father. And that his secretary, Cheryl Sutherland, is her mother. My brother told me that." I leaned toward Yusef. "I'm assuming that Earl was the source of all Kayla's great clothes and jewelry, by the way, right? He was sending her money to keep her from letting the world know that he was her father." It was hard for me to swallow that he would have paid his daughter to keep her quiet, rather than acknowledging her. But maybe he was trying to protect Eula and Yusef. Not just himself.

"Yeah, some of that money came from Earl. But most of it came from someone else." Yusef settled more deeply into his chair. "Kayla French came after me when I came to town on Friday. That was one of the reasons that I agreed to come to town in the first place. She had called me months before, claiming to be my half sister. Disparaging Earl and looking for money, basically. She had heard that I filed a lawsuit against a wealthy family, and she thought I might be a source of cash for her. The girl has expensive tastes, you know."

I nodded. "Did you have any hint that Earl had another child before she called you?"

He shook his head. "My mother was always suspicious of him. Always worried that he was cheating on her. I never could figure out why. Until I learned about my own parentage. So now nothing can shock me. But I didn't quite trust Kayla."

"Why not?" She sure had gotten Eric to believe in her—but he was probably an easy mark compared to Yusef Jones.

"Something about her didn't seem right. She was too interested in money and too little interested in family ties. So I decided to spend some quality time with Cheryl Sutherland. I ended up throwing a few bucks her way to loosen her tongue."

"And?" I prompted.

"And it turns out that Kayla was determined to hurt Earl. Determined, maybe, to even kill him."

"But why?" I exclaimed. "Anger over all the secrecy?"

Yusef nodded. "Anger. Bitterness. Over the fact that he never publicly claimed her. And maybe greed, too. Earl came into a lot of money when *Color Counts* hit the best-seller list. As I said, the girl has expensive tastes."

"But when you came in here just now, you said that you didn't think she killed him."

"That's right. As agitated as she was, she didn't have the stomach to hurt him herself. Maybe she was squeamish. Or maybe she just didn't want to run the risk of getting caught. So she set out to find someone to do it for her. And don't you know, she found him."

"Who?" I could barely breathe.

"I missed my own father's funeral so that I could fly to Vegas to confirm it. She married him, and then she got him to do what she didn't have the balls to do."

Yusef paused for a moment and then made his pronouncement. "I think her husband, Lloyd Eastman, was the one who killed Earl."

At that moment, several seemingly impossible things happened all at once. Out of the darkness, I saw a silver object moving swiftly toward Yusef's head. Before I could speak, Yusef crumpled to the floor. And the very same Lloyd Eastman stood before me at the entrance to Earl's office.

"Y'all have made this too easy," he declared. "Both being here, so I can deal with you at the same time."

I stared at him for a moment, then at Yusef's form, crumpled on the floor. Eastman had hit him in the head with the butt of what I now saw to be a small revolver.

"You got his password, huh?" he said, nodding toward the computer. "Lucky for me, I was in my office, and got an electronic notification that Earl Stokes was active on the network. That's the second time it's happened. I figured unless it was his ghost, it had to be someone making trouble. And I was right."

"So it's true," I stated flatly.

Eastman nodded, almost sheepishly. "Yeah. It's true."

He started toward me, and instinctively I kept talking. "But why did you agree to marry Kayla? And then kill her father? I mean, what was in this for you?"

Eastman snorted dismissively. "*Agree* to marry her? Girl, I *insisted* that she marry me. I want what's coming to me, and that was the only way to be sure that I'll get it. There's money at stake here. Real money. Earl had a lot more than me. Always has. You know his family has been in this town for three generations. What you may not know is that there is real money there. The grandfather ran a funeral home, and Earl was set for life a long time ago."

Eastman was still on the other side of the desk from me. I needed to keep him talking so that it would stay that way.

"So you and Kayla were positive that even though Earl had never claimed her publicly, she'd inherit his money? I mean, he has a wife and another child, how much dough were you really expecting?"

Eastman shook his head impatiently. "You really don't know Earl, do you? He made a lot of money off that book, *Color Counts*. And then he decided to get his affairs in order. He made a will for the first time. And he showed Kayla exactly what she'd be getting. Guilt was kicking his butt, he felt badly that he had never publicly acknowledged her. So he was going to make it up to her, he said. Oh, yeah—there was some real money at stake."

"But I don't understand what the rush was on her part. She could have waited years for his death. So could you. He would have kept paying her bills for the rest of his life, wouldn't he?"

Something I said must have pressed one of his hot buttons. Because all of a sudden, Lloyd Eastman was really angry.

"It had to happen because I was *tired* of waiting!" he snapped. "I was tired of waiting for all of it. *I* built this department, you know." His voice was getting louder, and he gesticulated with the revolver. "I was his second in command for my entire life—*I* was the one making it all happen while he was out getting all the awards and making all the money. I was the one who worked with the architects, who had the vision for this new Center for African-American Studies. But don't you know, there he was, taking all the credit. They were practically going to name it after him, when it was *me* who built this entire enterprise."

Eastman huffed indignantly, and then continued. "If Kayla hadn't gone and rubbed his face in it, I would have had him out of here, and everything would have been fine."

"What?"

"That silly child," he laughed bitterly. "The very day of the party, Earl had told Harvard he was going up there. Accepted their offer to be the head of the Economies Department. But then Kayla told him we were married. Told him that afternoon, right before the party. I was *this* close to getting him out of here! And then she told him that, and he changed his mind. Just about tore my head off, insisted that he'd have me fired, and the marriage annulled. And then he makes this speech to me about why he really shouldn't leave Princeton, anyway. For the good of the department, he told me. For all the black students to come who would need this department, need the new building. Like we'd just collapse without him. I'd have convinced them to build the damn thing! We don't need him!"

It occurred to me then that Kayla had very little to do with this in the end. She was the catalyst for Earl's death—but this wasn't about her at all. Or even about Earl's money. Eastman hadn't wanted Earl dead for any other reason than that he was crazy with jealousy. Kayla was just a convenient excuse. It wasn't about love or even about his money. It was about power. I thought about all the academic rivalries that I had been a part of—who knew that two decades of internecine squabbling could drive someone to an act like this? It seemed unimaginable. But Earl must have seen it coming, somehow—he had known to write that letter for his files about Lloyd. Unfortunately, he must not have understood just how truly mad Lloyd had become.

Making sense of all this was well and good, but I had to buy some time to figure out how I was going to get out of Earl's office alive. "How did you get Earl alone that night, anyway?" I asked, glancing around the space to see what could be turned into a weapon of defense.

Eastman seemed to think we had all the time in the world, because his tone became more expansive. "It was the easiest thing in the world to get him to the construction site that evening. I simply told him that I would meet him there after the party—to discuss what we should do about this marriage. I was worried at first that he'd bring Zanda Fleming along with him, but in the end they parted and he came on alone."

"But he couldn't have been alone. Kayla was there, wasn't she?"

"Oh, yes, she was. That was part of the plan. She was to distract him. While I did what needed to be done."

"And that worked?"

"Absolutely. The only wrinkle in the whole plan was your brother." He smiled coldly. "He's crazy about her, you know. She kept trying to ditch him, but he was hanging around like a love-struck puppy. Finally, she deliberately snagged her coat on his cufflink, and sent him home to find another one before they could go on to their next party that night. Then she came in, we met, and we waited for him. And then I took a rock, and . . . well, you know how it ends."

I felt a terrible chill, despite the heat from the boiler. Poor Earl never had a chance—and he died knowing that his own daughter was crazed with anger at him. What a selfish, hateful act. A tight knot of anger uncurled in my chest—there was no way this SOB was going to do the same thing to me.

"I assume that you were the one who killed Merriweather. Why did you have to do it?"

"Because he saw us coming out of the building that night, that's why." Eastman laughed languidly. "Hell, for all I know, he wanted to kill Earl himself. He was following him around that party all night, looking daggers at him. There was no love lost there. But when he saw us come out, and the building going up in flames, he put it together. Tried to blackmail us. Got greedy. So I let myself into his dorm room, and . . ."

I nodded mutely. His delicacy in not sharing the details was absolutely touching.

"This has all worked out very well up to this point," Eastman continued in a self-satisfied voice.

"You shouldn't have come after my brother," I said, sounding bolder by far than I felt. "Letting Kayla try to make him take the fall for what you two did. If you think I would let that happen, you're crazy."

Of course, the problem was that he really was crazy. He was on a drunken control binge, and I think he really did feel invincible.

"Your poor little brother. Quite gullible."

"Yeah, he's got terrible taste in women. Maybe this will cure him of it."

"Your brother, simple as he is, doesn't know what really happened. He's besotted with Kayla, and he has no idea about this marriage. And my wife surely will not be testifying against me. They have no physical evidence on either one of us." The hand that held the gun was slowly starting to move upward. "You and he"—he kicked at Yusef's motionless body—"are the only two who really know anything. And you'll be taken care of shortly."

"How the hell do you plan to explain two people dead of gunshot wounds in Earl's office?" I asked, trying to sound exasperated and not alarmed.

"I don't know, murder-suicide?" he shrugged. "I'll think of something."

I'd been scanning Earl's desk as we talked, and I'd found my weapon of choice. Earl's pearl-handled letter opener was sitting in a cup on his desk. I just had to get to it. And get that gun away from Lloyd Eastman.

Grandma always said it was better to be lucky than smart. Never could argue with that, but that night, it was indisputable. Because just as I went for the letter-opener, Yusef Jones went for Lloyd Eastman.

Apparently, the blow to his head had stunned him, but not seriously hurt him. Maybe he had been playing possum all along. Whatever the case, his hand shot out and grabbed Eastman by the ankle. He yanked him off balance, and that gave me just enough time to get around the desk. The gun went off as the three of us tumbled in a heap to the floor. I jabbed the letter opener into what I hoped was Eastman's arm and not Yusef's and was rewarded with a howl of pain. I saw the gun fall from his grasp, but Yusef got to it first.

He rose to his full height, towering over Eastman, and pointed the barrel right at his temple.

"I should pull this trigger, man," he hissed.

"Yusef," I said firmly.

"Don't worry," he said. "He's not worth it."

I reached for the telephone as Yusef laughed bitterly under his breath. "Just another American black man headed to jail. Ain't that something."

# Epilogue
## The Last Word

"Another kir royale, Sister Professor?" Maggie called out from the kitchen.

"Yes, definitely," I shouted back. "Another round for everyone!"

Maggie, Jess, Alix, and I had decided to have a girls-only New Year's Eve party at Maggie's house in Cambridge, and we were all officially sloshed, even though we still had ten minutes to go until the new year.

"You know what they say," Jess said as she squinted at an image of Dick Clark reciting the history of the ball drop from Times Square on Maggie's thirteen-inch television. "Whoever you're with on New Year's Eve is who you'll be with all year."

"That is *absolutely* not true," I declared. "Otherwise, Prince Roger would be here, pontificating about how expensive it is to repair a BMW, the way he was last year."

"Lord, I remember that one," Maggie said, as she returned with a blush pink cocktail in each hand. "He was as good-lookin' as Denzel, but that boy had an attitude problem. I couldn't *wait* for you to kick him to the curb!"

"Well, point of fact, I was the party rolling to the curb, not him. Remember?" I called after her as she returned to the kitchen for more drinks.

"Hey, nobody's keepin' score," Alix drawled. "All I can say is, here's to high heeled boots, the better to kick some serious male butt!"

Jess laughed and took a deep sip of her drink. "This is *exactly* what the boys think we're doing right now!"

I spied my old backpack out of the corner of my eye and silently drank a toast to Zanda Fleming. She had tracked me down in Princeton the morning after my encounter with Lloyd Eastman to return it, and to let me know that it had been Hayden Fleming who had stolen it that night at Ivy Club.

He'd been trying to reconcile with Zanda for months, and was certain that Earl Stokes was a romantic rival of his. Thus the early-morning search of Earl's office—he was looking for clues as to the status of Earl and Zanda. He'd decided to rifle through my backpack at the party on the off chance that I might have found something in Earl's office that would be of interest to him. Even after Earl died, I guess his insecurity was such that he had to know what had gone on between them.

"He's a control freak, what can I say," Zanda had told me. "There was never anything between Earl and me except friendship and respect. Hayden sees a rival almost everywhere. That's what drives him."

She wasn't sure about starting up with him again. But I heard in her voice that they weren't quite done with each other yet. There was a lot of that going around. Yusef Jones and I had a couple of interesting dinner dates and three long-distance phone calls before Christmas. But he'd finally told me to call him once I got that other man out of my system.

At least it was going to be easier than I'd thought to keep in touch with Yusef. Zanda had told me that given the notice his scholarly work had received, it was almost certain that Earl's chairmanship of Princeton's Program in African-American Studies would be offered to his charismatic, erudite son, Yusef. I really liked the idea of him a mere train ride away. And Eula would be over the moon. But I didn't envy Detective Maureen Kelly if one of her people ever stopped him for speeding.

"Nikki, telephone," Maggie called from the kitchen. I hadn't even heard it ring—that's how pleasantly buzzed I was. As I swung through the kitchen door, she gave me a mischievous smile. "It's five minutes to midnight, Sister Professor, so don't get too carried away."

I knew what that meant.

I'd made it to Detroit for Christmas, with my brother safely in tow. It had turned out to be a holiday for the memory books, despite the fact that I never did get around to wrapping a single gift, or baking even one batch of cookies. My father declared that we would eat out at a swanky new restaurant downtown on Christmas Day, so there was no cooking, no cleaning, and no angst. Just my family, together and safe. Needless to say, Kayla French did not get brought home for dinner.

On the plane home I'd remembered, finally, the last thing that Earl Stokes had said to me, the night that he died. We'd been enveloped in a crowd at the party, surrounded by chattering people and the swell of the music. Silently, he'd beckoned me to join him. As I moved toward him, I saw that he was about to introduce me to the president of Princeton. I'd shot him a look of excitement and nervousness as I approached. He'd smiled and leaned forward, whispering to cut through the din of the crowd. "Don't worry, Nikki," he'd said. "Just look 'em right in the eye."

I'd never forget him, I knew that. And if I could take that one lesson, to see people and things as they really were, not as I wanted them to be, and to face them head-on, then I would be one step closer to being the person I wanted to be.

I picked up the phone and heard Dante Rosario's greeting, muffled a bit by the raucous sound of male voices in the background. "How's the boys' party going?" I asked.

"The usual. Rafe and Teddy are fighting over whether the Knicks can recover in the second half of the season. Nothing new. You'll be up late tonight, Juliet?"

I smiled as I leaned against the wall. "Could be. But I figured I wouldn't be seeing you again for a while, now that the excitement is over. You have this habit of disappearing once the drama ends."

"Even if that were true, you'd still be seeing a lot of me." He laughed softly as shouting erupted in Maggie's living room. The New Year's Eve countdown had begun. "I have the feeling that with you, Nik, there'll always be another adventure."

# About the Author

Pamela Thomas-Graham is a Phi Beta Kappa graduate of Harvard College, where she was awarded the Captain Jonathan Fay Prize—the highest annual award bestowed by Radcliffe. Also a graduate of Harvard Business School and Harvard Law School, Pamela was an editor of the *Harvard Law Review*.

She is currently the President and Chief Executive Officer of CNBC, the global leader in television business news. She is responsible for the network's operations, which provide business news programming and financial market coverage to more than 201 million homes worldwide. Prior to joining NBC, she was a Partner at McKinsey & Company, the world's largest management consulting firm. One of the leaders of its Media and Entertainment practice, Pamela became McKinsey's first black woman partner. The subject of a Harvard Business School case study, she has lectured widely on finance, ethics, and management issues.

Pamela serves on the boards of the New York City Opera and American Red Cross of Greater New York, and is a member of the Visiting Committee for Harvard College, Jack & Jill of America, and the Economic Club of New York. She has been profiled by *Fortune, The New York Times, Ebony,* and *The Wall Street Journal* and has been named "Woman of the Year" by *Ms. Magazine, Glamour,* and the Financial Women's Association.

Originally from Detroit, Pamela divides her time between Manhattan and Westchester County with her husband, writer and attorney Lawrence Otis Graham, and their three children. Pamela's prior books have been translated into German and Japanese. *Orange Crushed* is the third entry in her Ivy League mystery series.